SIN STREET

———————————

Paperback Trade Inn
145 East Fourteen Mile Rd
Clawson, MI 48017
(248) 307-0226

SIN STREET

Three couples, in three small towns. Three sets of lies and secrets. Three questions... Can they get together? Can they stay together? Can they stay alive? The answers lie somewhere in the shadows on Sin Street.

Previously available only in electronic format, these sinfully delicious stories of erotic romance have now been combined for a paperback collection. Included are the tales...

Skin Deep

Erin's an ex-cop. Noah's the much-younger potential criminal who's dating her sister. Could she make a worse choice for the love of her life?

Lie To Me

MaryJane has been alone with her guilt a long time, drowning in a cold sea of secrets. She thinks the truth is her worst nightmare...until a Federal Agent with an agenda shows up to prove her wrong.

Dirty Shame

TV heartthrob Dare Daniels has it all: money, fame, and a few kinks in common with his pretty new assistant, Josephine "Joey" Fiorello. Too bad he's also got a target on his back...

Welcome to Sin Street, where dark secrets and steamy sex meet for drinks after work!

Paperback Trade Inn
145 East Fourteen Mile Rd
Clawson, MI 48017
(248) 307-0226

PRAISE FOR SELAH MARCH

LIE TO ME

"5 Kisses!...Selah March tells a riveting story of what happens to someone who falls into a trap of her own making by living life as a lie, and why making a new life isn't the best course of action if one plans to fall for an undercover cop who can ruin everything she's worked so hard to keep secret. You'll be left clutching the edge of your seat and anxious to find out how it all unfolds and whether or not the hero and heroine have a chance at making a life together. 'Sensational' is the only word to describe this tale of espionage, suspense and last, but not least, two lost souls searching for a love they never thought possible!"

—Joni
Two Lips Reviews

"4 Stars!...With its fast start, good suspense elements and strong erotic tone, March's story will keep readers well entertained...Drew Donnelly and MJ Peters are about to get up close and personal. The question is, does Drew know MJ's secrets before he seduces her? Also, what will she do when she discovers the truth about Drew? This smart-mouthed, sarcastic woman has good reason for the secrets in her life. Before Drew showed up in her small town, she was doing pretty well. With him in her bed and now in her head, all that is about to be shaken up."

—Leigh Rowling
Romantic Times Book Reviews

ALSO BY SELAH MARCH

Her Black Little Heart

SIN STREET

BY

SELAH MARCH

AMBER QUILL PRESS, LLC
http://www.amberquill.com

SIN STREET
AN AMBER HEAT BOOK

This book is a work of fiction. All names, characters, locations, and incidents are products of the author's imagination, or have been used fictitiously. Any resemblance to actual persons living or dead, locales, or events is entirely coincidental.

Amber Quill Press, LLC
http://www.amberquill.com
http://www.amberheat.com

All rights reserved.
No portion of this book may be transmitted or reproduced in any form, or by any means, without permission in writing from the publisher, with the exception of brief excerpts used for the purposes of review.

Copyright © 2007 by Selah March
ISBN 978-1-60272-991-9
Cover Art © 2007 Trace Edward Zaber

Layout and Formatting provided by: ElementalAlchemy.com

PUBLISHED IN THE UNITED STATES OF AMERICA

To my crit partners,
Barb, Don and Eva, who save my life
on a regular basis.

To my children,
who make that life worth living.

To my husband,
without whom I'd have no life at all.

TABLE OF CONTENTS

Skin Deep 1

Lie To Me 71

Dirty Shame 157

ң
SKIN DEEP

SIN STREET

SIN STREET

CHAPTER 1

October

Later, when everything settled down, and Erin looked back on how the year played out, she had to laugh. If she'd known in October what she knew in January, she might've slammed the door in Noah's face. And what a tragic end to the story that would've been…

She met him on a Saturday evening. He came to the door and asked for her sister. Her younger sister.

Her much younger sister.

"I'm Noah. Is Suzie around?" He was in costume for the Halloween party they'd be attending that evening—faded jeans, a ten-gallon Stetson, and a black shirt that matched his longish hair. Erin found herself staring. Not often you came across a cowboy in eastern Wisconsin.

"Uh…yeah. I think she's almost ready."

He leaned against the doorframe and smiled at her, and if she'd been staring before, now she gaped. Young—very young, maybe twenty-two. Which was her sister's age, so that made sense. His hair was so dark and glossy it looked almost reflective, and his strong jaw was clean-shaven, unlike many of the guys who orbited inside Suzie's zone. Guys who seemed to think "patchy stubble" or "unkempt goatee" were code for "über-cool manly man." His voice rang deep but smooth, and so soft she had to strain to catch his words. And his eyes? Carolina blue—that shade of summer-in-the-Southland sky so intense it took your breath away.

"Can I come in?"

"What?"

"Can I come into the house to wait for Suzie?" He was still smiling, wide and unconcerned.

"Yes, of course. Sorry." Leaning heavily on her cane, she moved aside to allow him through the door. He towered over her—at least five inches above her five-eleven-and-three-quarters—and his shoulders were broad enough to block her view of the staircase for a second or two.

She cleared her throat and said, "My name is—"

"Erin. Suzie told me."

"Good memory." So Suzie had talked about her older sister who'd moved back into the family home. *What else had she mentioned? Maybe how much she didn't welcome the inconvenience?*

He leaned against the closed front door, stretching his endless legs before him. Only then did she see the boots—definitely not the get-along-little-doggies kind. More like the steel-toed-shit-kicking variety. *Interesting.*

"So," he said, "are you joining us tonight?" He took off the hat and swept a long-fingered hand through his hair, which instantly transformed him from a cowboy into a good-looking guy standing in her foyer.

She shrugged. "I haven't made up my—"

"Erin needs to stay home and rest. Right, sis?" Suzie said from the doorway that led to the hall. She smiled, but her dark eyes narrowed as she looked at them standing there together. A sign of bad weather on the horizon. The tail of the black cat costume she wore dragged on the floor behind her as she crossed the room to grab Noah's wrist.

Noah glanced at Erin. "She doesn't look tired to me."

Suzie's chin came up in that defiant way Erin knew too well. "She's recovering from a gunshot wound."

Erin flinched. "Really, Suzie's right. I should stay in and—"

"And what? Dole out candy to the kiddies? Sounds like a crappy way to spend the night." Noah slid an arm around Suzie's shoulders. "We'll watch out for her, won't we? Make sure your sister has a good time."

During the long pause that followed, Erin watched the play of emotions over her sister's lovely face. She opened her mouth to decline the invitation, but Suzie's next comment made her voice dry up in her throat.

"Half."

"Huh?" Noah's brow creased into a frown.

"She's just a half-sister," Suzie said, her mouth tight around the words.

Ouch. But okay, not unreasonable. Nobody looking at them would ever mistake them for full-blooded siblings. Not with Suzie being so small and dark and…well, "slinky" was the word that always popped into Erin's mind when she thought about her younger sister. Nary a freckle marred Suzie's flawless olive complexion, while Erin clearly had inherited more than her fair share, plus the unruly auburn hair that went with them. Not to mention the Mulally height and solid, well-built frame. There'd been kids back in school who'd refused to believe they were siblings at all.

Noah coughed into his fist and said, "Well, all right. We'd better get a move on."

He made a polite, ladies first gesture, and waited while they got their coats and bags. Under cover of slipping on her leather jacket, Erin whispered, "Suzie, I'm sorry. I don't mean to—"

"Oh, don't be silly, Erin. Of course you're not too old for Halloween parties." Suzie laughed, high and sweet, like the words she'd just put in Erin's mouth were the funniest she'd ever heard. Her training as a theatre major was paying off big time.

"Too old?" Noah stepped up and slid a hand under Erin's elbow to steady her as she wobbled a bit in reaction to Suzie's sneak attack. He took a second to look her up and down. "You can't be more than twenty-six."

Suzie's laughter took on a shrill note. "Flattery will get you nowhere, Noah. She's thirty-two, and proud of it." As if that were the most amazing thing she'd ever heard of.

"Wow. We'd better hurry and get to that party before she slips into senility, huh?" The sarcasm in Noah's comment was nearly lost in his deadpan delivery.

Erin snorted.

Suzie sulked.

They left the house.

* * *

"D'you mind if I ask how you got shot?" Noah had to lean in close to make himself heard over the roar of the frat-house crowd.

Erin sighed and sipped her beer. A fair question, and politely posed. Just not anything she wanted to talk about, especially under these circumstances. "It was an accident."

"What kind of accident?"

She sighed again. *Nice guy, this Noah, and cute—no doubt about that.* But why was he here, standing next to her in a corner of the dark and smoky room, when Suzie was on the dance floor?

"The kind of accident that involves a twelve-year-old car thief and a gun that turned out to be not a toy after all."

He looked at her, his eyes widening with comprehension. *Damn.* She'd meant to be cryptic, but this one caught on fast.

"You're a cop?"

She shook her head. "Not any more."

He started to say something else—another question, no doubt—but was jostled by a girl dressed as Cleopatra who apparently needed to squeeze past him in a hurry. One of his large, boot-clad feet bumped Erin's cane, knocking it sideways, and she fell against him.

"Sorry—God, I'm sorry. I didn't—"

"Not your fault," she said and righted herself.

"Do you want to sit down? There must be someplace we can find."

And as much as she hated admitting she couldn't stay vertical much longer, she let her pride take the fall on this one. "That would be great."

He ducked his head and whispered, "Stay right here. I'll be back."

She watched the way he moved through the crowd, seemingly oblivious to how all the girls stopped and looked up at him, and how the guys stepped back to give him room. It wasn't just his height and breadth, although they were part of it. It was the confidence in his stride. She'd seen it before in longtime; highly ranked members of the force. The casual air of commanding the space around them. Some people found it arrogant or irritating or intimidating. She found it hot as hell.

The scent of too-liberally-applied aftershave caught her attention, and she turned to find another man standing in Noah's vacated place next to her.

"Hi there. Come here often?"

Hoyt Carrington Carlisle III, otherwise known as "Trip," and one of Suzie's closest associates. Tan—even in late autumn—blond, and built like a linebacker under his expensive, faux-distressed jeans and leather jacket. The three times he'd stopped by the house in the week Erin had been in residence were enough to cement her dislike for him, based on both his behavior and the sick feeling he prompted in her gut. But when she'd tried to talk to her sister about the guy, Suzie had told her to mind her own business.

Tonight, he was dressed as an asshole frat-boy. Which is to say he'd declined to wear a costume.

"Trip," she said, "what's new?"

He ran his hand over his blond crew-cut and grinned. "Nothing I'd tell a cop." He laughed, and the sound was brittle. His eyes had a glassy look to them, and he seemed hyper and a little twitchy.

She forced a smile. "Suzie's here somewhere."

"Yeah, I've seen her. Nice little pussy action she's got going on, huh?"

Okay, now he was just trying to provoke her. She looked away and gripped her cane, fighting the urge to slam it so hard into his balls he wouldn't be thinking about Suzie's or anyone else's pussy for days to come.

She caught a flash of a cowboy hat above the crowd. Noah was making his way back to her.

But Trip was talking again. "So what's the deal with you anyway?"

"What do you mean?"

"Well, are you gay or what? I mean, you know—female cops? Playing with guns because you don't have dicks."

The comment caught her off guard in its casual bigotry. Who should she defend first—cops or lesbians? She squeezed the grip on her cane and counted to ten. Assault with a deadly weapon was not on her agenda tonight.

Then Noah was there, his wide grin in place and two fresh beers clutched in his giant hands. She watched his face compress into hard lines when he saw Trip.

"Noah," Trip said and nodded a greeting. "Dude, where's your apron? Diner closed tonight?"

"It's a restaurant, and I've got the night off." Noah's tone was easy and light, but his face remained a mask of tension. He plainly didn't like Trip. Which only proved he had the sense God gave cabbage. If only she could say the same of Suzie.

Trip smiled, and Erin thought of a feral dog. "Your date was going to tell me if the rumor about female cops is true." He nudged her again, making her lean hard on her cane to keep her balance. "Spill it, Erin. You all a bunch of bull dykes or what?"

Noah drew a hard, quick breath. Before he could speak, Erin shook her head and winked at him. Then she waited until Trip lifted his beer to his lips and said, "Why? You got a sister in mind for me? God knows if I had to grow up with you, it would put me off men forever." He choked, then spit the beer, spraying Erin and Noah along with himself. The outraged look on his face was worth the warm shower.

She glanced up at Noah. "Let's get out of here."

Laughing, he took her arm. Before ushering her away, he leaned into Trip and murmured something. Whatever it was made the asshole stare after them, his sloppy mouth gaping like a landed trout.

Noah led her toward a closed door. "Down here. There's a common room nobody's using."

Her knee throbbed as she made her way down the stairs, one step at a time. God, she hated this. Hating being a cripple, having to rely on other people. It made her want to bite somebody.

The room was empty, just as he'd promised. Surprising, given the pool and foosball tables in the corners, and the large-screen TV decorating the far wall. Erin settled herself on one of the sofas and thanked Noah when he passed her a beer.

"You don't need to stay. Just come get me when you and Suzie are ready to go."

"Don't be stupid. I'm not leaving you down here all alone."

"Noah, really, you—"

"Suzie will have a better time without me hanging around. I don't dance."

Ah. Her sister did love to show off on the dance floor, so not dancing was a drawback. He dropped down on the sofa next to her.

"All right, so...what are you studying?" she asked him. A variation on "what's your major" and totally lame, but the best she could come up with on short notice.

"I...uh..." He glanced away. "I'm not in school right now. I work construction in the warmer months, and I work in the kitchen at Carradine's in the winter."

"You're a cook?"

He grimaced. "I chop vegetables and peel fruit and wash dishes when I have to."

"Oh."

"Not very inspiring, I know. But I'm saving up to go back to school."

"You don't have to justify anything to me. Nothing wrong with honest work. I did a lot of it before I finally went to college."

He turned so his entire body faced her. "Why did you become a cop?"

Wow. No punches pulled there. "I was in law school. Got all the way through my second year and decided I was sick of it. Wanted to help people on a more...I don't know...tangible level. I suck at science, so medicine was out, and I haven't got the patience to be a teacher. So..." She shrugged. "Understanding the law can help make you a good cop."

"And you were a good cop." He nodded, sounding sure.

"I never got the chance to find out. I was shot my first month on the job."

He digested that in silence. After a few seconds, he said, "A twelve-year-old kid, huh?"

"Yeah. He stole a car and drove it into a ditch. Then he jumped out and pulled a .45. I saw how young he was—he looked about eight or nine, real short and skinny, not even sure how he reached the gas pedal—and I thought it had to be a toy. Stupid."

"You wanted it to be a toy."

She looked at him, feeling her face flush. "What?"

"You wanted it to be a toy. So you wouldn't have to shoot him. Isn't that what happened?"

"Let me guess. You were a psych major before you quit school."

His turn to blush. "Busted. But am I right?"

"You're not wrong."

He reached out, picked a strand of her hair off her shoulder and played with it. "You got lucky. He could've killed you."

"He didn't." She found herself staring again—at his mouth this time. Not as flashy as those blue eyes, yet just as pretty. Not particularly full, but wide and flexible, and when he licked his lower lip in preparation to speak, she stared harder.

"Erin?"

"Yeah?"

"I...uh..." His voice faded, and she looked away from his lips to meet his gaze. He blinked and said, "I don't usually do this. I want you to know that up front."

"Do what?" But she knew what was coming. She'd have to be senseless—that is, completely bereft of all five senses—to miss the signals he was giving out. She would bet he was reading the same from her. Hard to miss the heat between them. She waited to see what his pick-up line would be, fully expecting to be impressed. Empathy and a sense of humor got her every time. His looks didn't hurt either.

He exhaled, long and slow. "I don't want you to think I'm trying to step out on Suzie. Your sister and I, we've never...we don't—"

"I get it. But you are dating her, right?"

He shrugged. "We're just friends. She's says she's not into me like that. And anyway..." He shrugged again and looked away, frowning.

"Anyway what?"

"She's not the most riveting person when it comes to conversation."

He had balls, too. Who said that to someone's sister? Even if it was obvious she and Suzie weren't exactly close? "Then why do you hang around?"

"It's complicated."

Not as far as Erin could see. Suzie was a beautiful girl. Even if she wasn't putting out, that didn't mean guys wouldn't seek her company. The question was, what did this guy want from Erin, when he could be upstairs with her sister and a crowd of younger, prettier women—even if he didn't dance?

She waited, watching his face. Finally, he said, "I like you. I'd like to see you again."

"To what purpose?" Amazing how the formal lawyer-speak reared its ugly head when she felt defensive. Or suspicious. And now she was both.

"To spend time with you, naturally." He sounded a little annoyed, but she wasn't buying this shit. Not even on sale.

"To spend time with me, doing what exactly? Come on, Noah. You might be used to courting little girls, but if you hadn't noticed—"

"I noticed." His gaze swept over her body, and she fought the urge to cross her arms over her chest.

"Then let's cut to the chase. Is there somewhere we can go?"

His eyes widened. "You mean...now?"

She looked at him hard, taking his measure. "You say you and Suzie are just friends, right? You're not lying about that?"

He shook his head. "Never even kissed her."

Good God, my sister is an idiot. "Then can you think of a good reason why we shouldn't just go for it?" She laughed when his eyes got wider still. "I'm not looking for love in all the wrong places, Noah. I promise—no strings attached."

A tiny voice that seemed to emanate from her gut and her head at the same time asked why she wanted to trade herself so cheaply. She told it to shut up. Clearly, the voice had no idea what it was like to go without sex—the kind that happened between two people and not just one lonely woman and her vibrator—for more than a year.

"All right," he said. "Do you care? It's a big house. I'm sure we could find an empty room with a bed or a sofa—"

"And a lock on the door. I'm not into exhibitionism."

"Right." He stood and saluted, softening it with that pretty white grin, and bounded up the stairs in search of a place where they could play a round of trick-or-treat.

* * *

They kept the room dark. She couldn't stand an overhead light glaring into her eyes, though she wished she could see Noah's face. The pounding of the music two floors down all but drowned out every little creak of the ancient box-spring and sheet-less mattress as they sat on its edge.

Erin looked toward the windows, where the moon shone in and made patterns on the bare wooden floor. She shivered. "Kind of creepy in here. Why is this room empty?"

"Don't know. Guess they didn't have enough pledges this year." He touched her shoulder. "We don't have to do this. We can go downstairs and talk some more."

She nearly agreed. This had all the markings of a major mistake, and what had she been thinking anyway? Going all Mrs. Robinson on a guy young enough to be her little brother. Seducing her sister's friend. Not like her—not at all. Maybe it was the effect of the full moon.

But she could feel the heat rising from his body, and the tension in even his fingers where they rested on her shoulder. He wanted this—wanted her—and it made her feel…alluring? Was that the word? Plus, she had this suspicion that maybe she was in for a surprise. Noah came off as reserved and almost painfully polite, but something else lurked beneath the surface. She'd seen a flash of it when Trip had tried to insult her. Something determined, almost unyielding. Hard as flint, but maybe just as useful in striking a flame?

No time like the present to find out what he was hiding under that nice-boy façade. "You said you liked me. Show me."

First kisses could be so awkward. The unfamiliar scent and taste of another person—the inevitable bumping of noses, and where did you put your hands?

Not this time. He met her halfway, turning to curl his long body around her, and took instant control. He tasted like beer and spice and young, healthy male, and his mouth was just as flexible and talented as she'd predicted.

"How old are you?" she whispered against his neck when he pressed his face into her shoulder and reached beneath the back of her sweater to unhook her bra.

"Twenty-three." His mission accomplished, he slid his hands under the front of her sweater and cupped her breasts as if he'd been doing it for years. Then he kissed her again, his tongue tracing over the swell of her upper lip before pushing inside. The boy knew what he was doing.

Her sweater and bra were gone, but when he pulled away to work at the fly of her jeans, she stopped him. "Let me." Another reason to be glad about the lack of light in the room—he couldn't see her blush over her own clumsy struggles to get undressed without hurting her leg. Nor could he see the surgery scars.

He stripped to his shorts and watched as she folded her jeans and set them on the floor.

"You always so tidy?"

She cleared her throat. "I'm nervous. It's been a while for me, and with the weakness in my leg, I can't move like..." She wanted to say "like I used to," but that made her sound like she'd once done this professionally or something.

"It's okay. I've got you." And all at once, he did.

Warm skin over long, lean muscles settled against her, pushing her into the mattress. His hands stroked her shoulders and down over her chest. Soft touches that grew more possessive. His fingertips against her nipple, fleeting at first and then a pinch and the drag of a nail. He licked a long stripe between her breasts and over her collarbone, then blew a stream of cool air, raising shivers over the surface of her skin.

He pulled back to look at her, as if asking permission to continue. The moonlight lay over his face, highlighting the sharp angles of his jaw and making his eyes glow like blue beach glass.

"Blue beach glass?"

Crap, did she say that out loud? She turned her face into his shoulder and gritted her teeth against a wave a shame. His laughter ghosted over her with a low, humming tickle. He slid his fingers along her jaw, finding the point of her chin and using it to pivot her head. She squeezed her eyes closed. Maybe it was time to call a halt to the whole thing.

"Hey," he whispered and dropped a quick kiss on her nose.
"What?"
"Open your eyes."
"Why?"
"I want to thank you for the very poetic compliment." He sounded amused.
"Go to hell."
There was a pause as he shifted against her. His erection nudged her thigh. He stroked the underside of her jaw with the pad of his thumb, warm and steady. "Come on, Erin. Open your eyes."

She compromised by squinting at him. "Are we doing this, or what?"

"Yeah. I think we're doing this."

He moved, using his whole body to light a fire between them. Had it ever been this good? The slide of skin on skin? The twist and pull of muscles and tendons as they found their groove? She couldn't remember. Didn't want to.

She felt herself swell and grow wet beneath the press of his leg between hers. He moaned when she trailed her nails down his back and under the waistband of his boxers. Then he rolled away, and she closed her eyes when she heard the tear of a foil wrapper.

Tight at first. Stretching that was painful and satisfying at the same time. His hand brushed the place just above her knee where the scar tissue lay, ugly and sensitive. She flinched. What did he feel there? The rough pucker where they'd fished out the bullet and gone in to fix the damage it had left behind? Did it distract him? Make him wish he was with someone else?

"Hey, you still with me?"

She pressed her shoulders back into the mattress to better see his face. His brow was creased, his mouth pulled into a flat line. Such concentration in his gaze as he stared down at her. Like she was riddle he was determined to solve. Why did that make her so hot?

She nodded, and he pushed into her, slow and hard, all his weight behind each stroke. Steady thrusts, deep and deeper, making her remember why she liked fucking. Why it felt good, even when all she felt was self-conscious. Tiny pinpricks of sensation—not pleasure, exactly, but something close—rushed outward from the place where his cock did a slick shove and drag. Again, again, and then again, and yes. Right there. Spring-loaded tension twisted in her belly and all her limbs, hot and tight and forcing her—yes, forcing her, with some primordial command from her reptile brain—to tilt her hips against him, seeking friction against her clit.

She slid her hands to his hips and pulled him tight, rocking and rubbing and clenching around him. He made a quiet, hurt moan in the back of his throat. When he came, it was sudden. He shook all over, muscles hard under her hands. No sound at all, unless you counted his ragged breathing.

She held still under him. Waited for the last of his shuddering to fade. Wished she hadn't distracted herself with thoughts of her scar or what he looked like while he fucked her, because now it was over and she hadn't—

"You didn't finish?" His voice was filthy-low and grainy, like he'd been gargling with sand.

"It doesn't matter." Surprising how casual she sounded about it, even as her nerves hummed with frustration.

"The hell it doesn't." He slid down her body, then lifted his face to look at her. His hair had fallen in his face, making him look so impossibly young. But his voice was a man's when he said, "Gonna take care of you. Gonna make you come."

Something in the way he said it—like he was going to inflict an orgasm on her whether she wanted one or not—made all that building tension in her limbs and belly dump straight into her cunt. And that was just wrong. She hated bullies. That was another reason she'd become a cop. To help even the score against the bully-boys who took what they wanted and always got their way.

"Gonna make you feel so good, Erin."

He was already hard at work, with his fingers inside her, deep and twisting and God, she couldn't...couldn't...not quite... Then he moved, changed the angle, and thumbed her clit in quick circles.

"Come on, let me see it. Wanna see you come."

Her wounded leg flopped hard against the bed, but she didn't feel the pain. Just his hot breath on her belly and the amazing things he did with those equally amazing fingers. She felt sweat bead along her hairline. Her vision grew blurry and whited out around the edges. She could feel her body bracing itself, as if for an expected assault.

He pressed once on her clit, hard, and held it down. Trapped it. Made it pulse under his thumb. And then he laid his mouth on the juncture of her thigh and torso and bit, dragging his teeth in the crease. She had just enough time and control to press her fist to her mouth to stifle what was born to be a scream, then she was gone. Working her hips in fast circles against his hand, digging her heels into the mattress. Fighting for breath against the unceasing rock and roll of her release.

"Yeah," he said when he disengaged his hand and crawled up to press his face against hers. "That's what I wanted to see. Just like that."

All right, so maybe there was something to be said for bullies. She hadn't come like that in forever. Quite possibly ever.

They lay there a while. She watched the branches from the tree outside the window make spooky patterns in the moonlight on the ceiling. He dozed, but that was okay. He'd earned his rest. After about twenty minutes, she moved out from under him because her leg had begun to throb. She needed to find her bag with the prescription bottle in the side pocket. She was an hour overdue for her pills.

"Hmm?" He sounded sleepy, but happy, as he sat up and brushed the hair out of his eyes. "Time to go?"

She pulled on her jeans and sat on the edge of the bed to slide into her sneakers. "Suzie's probably looking for us."

"Right."

In another ten minutes, they were downstairs once more. The crowd, as a general kind of thing, seemed drunker. They found Suzie in a corner, half-leaning on Trip.

She looked at them blearily. "Hey, you guys. Was a good time had by all?"

Erin felt Noah's hand tighten on her arm and forced herself not to make eye contact. She opened her mouth to give some non-committal response, and Trip said, "Looks like somebody got fucked, huh?"

Out of the corner of her eyes, she saw Noah's head snap up, and felt him... *My God, he's vibrating with rage.*

Suzie laughed. "Well, you know Jeff and Carlene. They never make it through a party without christening somebody's bed." Her sister was looking past them, into the crowd. Erin turned and spied a couple stumbling through the middle of the room. The girl's hair was a ratty mess, and whatever her costume was meant to be, it was torn beyond recognition. The guy wore a shit-eating grin.

She felt Noah's grip on her arm relax, but when she looked at him, he was still staring at Trip with a cold kind of fury, totally out of proportion to the situation. There was a story there, somewhere...

"I'm driving Erin home." Noah's voice was as cool and flat as his eyes.

Suzie shrugged. "Might as well take both of us. Trip's gotta help clean up." She pouted, and even drunk and petulant, she was beautiful.

Trip smirked. "One of the drawbacks of being Delta Sig's Vice President In Charge of Entertainment."

"I'm sure you take your responsibilities very seriously," Erin said, injecting just enough sarcasm to make Trip squint at her.

Noah grunted, as if something had struck him as funny. But when she looked, Erin saw nothing but a set jaw and a grim smile.

She reached for Suzie's hand and tugged her away. "Let's go, Suzie-Q."

As it turned out, her sister needed far more support to make it to Noah's car. Erin walked in front of them, leaning hard on her cane and counting the steps. Telling herself the pills would kick in any time.

The drive home was quiet, with Suzie passed out in the back seat. Noah didn't look at Erin. Possibly regretting their little tryst already? Well, that was fine. She hadn't lied when she said, "No strings attached." And, aside from the pain in her leg, she felt pretty damn good. Thoroughly satisfied.

That was what she was thinking as she watched him half-carry Suzie up the walk and set her on the doorstep. Erin tossed him her keys. He unlocked the door and helped Suzie into the house. Erin stood on the sidewalk and looked at the moon, big and orange and halfway down in the west. *Pretty night. Not too cool for Wisconsin in nearly-November.*

"I'd like to see you again."

She jumped, twisting her leg and grimacing.

"Sorry, didn't mean to—"

"It's okay." She looked at him, craning her neck a little to see his face because he stood too close. "Um…are you sure? It's not necessary, Noah. You don't have to."

"I have to because I want to." And then he kissed her, his mouth taking hers with a kind of authority she shouldn't have liked, but did.

She reached up and brushed the hair out of his eyes. "You know where to find me."

CHAPTER 2

November

Yeah, he knew where to find her. And he wanted to. He wanted nothing more than to drive up to the house and bang on the front door, and when Erin answered? He'd grab her and run.

Okay, maybe that was bullshit. Erin was no skinny little nothing he could drag around like a doll. He remembered lean muscles under all that soft, freckled skin. He'd be on his back in two seconds flat if he let loose with the me-Tarzan-you-Jane shit. But if she went with him willingly...

Yeah? Then what? The last thing his life had room for was a serious relationship. With a cop, no less. Jesus, what was he thinking?

His dick was more than happy to tell him in the cold hours between one and six when he couldn't sleep, and could only think about the moment she finally came around his hand, making a noise that sounded like a big cat's purr. *And what the fuck was all that about? Seriously, dude—* When was the last time he'd shot off like that, no warning and no control? Not cool, but just another indication of how far gone he was on this girl. *Woman? Whatever.*

Just as good a reason as any to steer clear. No matter how bad he felt about it. So he didn't call, and he didn't go to see her. He sublimated his guilt by cleaning his nine-millimeter and checking the ammo twice a day, whether they needed it or not.

Which was why, when he met her on the sidewalk the day before

Thanksgiving, he was surprised. Although in a town the size of Kelston—barely two thousand souls, even with the Kelston College student body added into the population count—it was common to meet half the people you knew on any given day. So maybe it was the way she stopped and smiled and laid her hand on his arm that amazed him.

"Noah?" She was dressed all in black—black wool coat, black jeans, black ski cap and gloves. Somehow, it made her face glow.

"Erin. How are you?" His voice sounded way too high and a little breathy. *Shit.* "I mean—it's good to see you."

"Right. That's why you made such an effort to call or come out to the house." She was still smiling, but he could hear the lurking edge of sarcasm. The wind picked up and blew her hair into her face.

"Yeah, about that—"

"Don't sweat it. I didn't really think you—"

"Hey. No. I meant it when I said it. I just—"

"Thought better of it later?" She slipped off the ski cap, twisted her hair to the top of her head, and pulled the hat on again. He could see her eyes now. *Smoky hazel.* And her cheeks were pinking in the sharp air.

He shoved his hands in his pockets because they wanted to reach out and touch. "It's complicated."

"You said that before."

He shrugged. "It seems a lot simpler at the moment." *Stupid, stupid shit.* He should walk away. He should run away, for both their sakes.

"What does that mean?" The cold air turned her breath into steam. He wanted to taste it.

"It means I'm a jerk. When can we—"

She held up a leather-gloved hand. "Hang on. You expect me to make a date with you now? After three weeks of nothing?"

A woman carrying a load of packages bumped into him and dropped a bag. After he'd helped her by reorganizing her load, he turned to face Erin again. She looked skeptical, but maybe not completely beyond his reach.

"Erin, I'm sorry. I have no excuse or explanation, other than stupidity." The first lie he'd ever told her because he had an excellent excuse: he couldn't afford to get involved with a cop. Not with his plan finally coming together. Which begged the question...why was he still standing here?

She looked at him a long moment. Then she said, "What're you doing for Thanksgiving?"

"Nothing. Got the day off. Probably watch a little football."

"You can do that at our house."

"Is that an invitation?"

"What do you think?"

He laughed. "I know Suzie. I think you'd better check with her."

She stiffened. "It's my house, too. And besides, Suzie's going out."

"With Trip?" Damn, why did he say that? And in such a snarky tone of voice? Because he clearly had some fucked-up need to make her suspicious.

"Yes, with Trip," she said and narrowed her eyes.

Yep. There it was.

"Why do you care, Noah?"

He sighed. "I don't. I shouldn't, but that guy is—"

"Bad news. I know. But I think Suzie will have to find out the hard way."

Not if he could help it. Shit, he'd almost said that out loud, too. Another good reason to steer clear of this woman—she made his tongue run loose and stupid.

"So are you coming or what?"

He pulled his hands out of his pockets and crossed his arms over his chest. "What are we having?"

"Pizza and beer. You bring the beer."

He pretended shock. "So much for tradition."

"Don't push your luck. I'll see you around two." It sounded like a statement of fact, but there was something like hesitation in the way she tilted her head.

"Sounds good." He leaned down and kissed her cheek. She started, pulling away from him. The color in her cheeks deepened. She turned and headed down the street without looking back.

He watched her go, knowing he was making a mistake.

* * *

He showed up on the front porch at a quarter to two, a six-pack of good beer in one hand and a rented movie in the other. For later. Just in case they needed something to pass the time. He rang the bell and waited, but no one came. He could hear a raised voice from within the house. Someone sounded angry. He listened, and after a minute, he identified the voice by its cadence as Suzie's.

He tried the door. It swung open when he turned the knob. Another feature of small-town life he'd never get used to—front doors that didn't lock automatically upon closing. But lucky for him because whatever Suzie was shrieking about might have some bearing on his plans. So long as she insisted on dating Trip Carlisle, everything about Suzie Mulally was of interest to him.

He stepped into the foyer, slipped off his jacket and hung it on the coat stand. Suzie's every shrill word—coming from the kitchen, he thought—became instantly audible.

"I can't believe you'd do this to me. After I took you in."

But now he could hear Erin as well.

"It's my house, too, Suzie."

"Yeah, you would bring that up. Rub salt in the wound."

He heard Erin sigh. "I don't get it. You said yourself you weren't serious about him. What difference does it make—"

"What difference does it make? What *difference* does it make?"

"Calm down." Erin's voice softened. He had to strain to hear it. "You're going to make yourself sick."

"Shut up and quit trying to mother me. You suck at it."

"Suzie—"

"You suck at being a sister, too. Just like your mother before you." Now Suzie sounded almost savage.

Noah wondered whether he should go ahead and make his presence known. Or maybe leave, since it was obvious he was the cause of the problem.

"You're just like her, Erin. Invading my life, taking what's mine—"

"Then you're serious about Noah? Is that what you're saying?"

"It doesn't matter whether I'm serious or not." The sound of high-heeled shoes on tile seemed to echo off the cathedral ceiling. "Get a life, Erin, and quit trying to steal mine." A door slammed. A few seconds later, he heard the sound of a car starting up in the attached garage. Which meant Erin was alone in the kitchen.

Should he stay? Go? Return to the front porch and ring the bell? The choice was taken out of his hands when Erin stepped into the foyer from the dining room and stopped cold at the sight of him.

"I rang the bell, but nobody..." He let his voice trail off when he saw the look on her face. "You want me to go?"

She shrugged and eyed the six-pack in his hand. "You're here now. Is that cold?"

He slid a bottle out of the cardboard carrier and held it out over the parquet-tiled floor. She stepped forward to claim it and he noticed.

SIN STREET

"Hey! No cane?"

Her crooked smile looked self-conscious. "I'm trying not to use it around the house for a few hours at a time. Cut way back on my pain meds, too. The rehab is working."

He grinned back at her. "You like pepperoni or what?"

* * *

Five hours later—stuffed with pizza and most of the six-pack, and burnt out on the NFL—he turned to her and said, "What's the deal with you and Suzie?"

Erin let her head fall back against the arm of the sofa and shifted against the cushions as if the very subject made her want to run away. Noah countered by tightening his grip on her ankle where it lay in his lap. When she didn't answer, he said, "I guess I imagined all that yelling, huh?"

That made her look at him. "I wasn't yelling. She was. And you shouldn't sneak into people's houses and eavesdrop on their private conversations. It's rude." He could tell by the way she enunciated each word that she was feeling the effects of the beer. Not drunk, but maybe a little buzzed. And it's wrong to take advantage of women under the influence, sexually or otherwise. He asked the next question anyway.

"What was Suzie fighting about?"

She flung her arm up to cover her face, giving him an excellent view of the way her white T-shirt hugged her breasts. Made it hard to concentrate on what she was saying, muffled as it was. "I don't want to talk about this."

"But you're going to anyway, right?" He pressed his thumb into the soft place just below her ankle and felt her bare foot twitch on his lap.

She moved her arm and looked at him. "Why do you want to know? What difference does it make?"

Reasonable question. But he wasn't nearly drunk enough to be put off by questions, reasonable or otherwise. "Tell me." He slid his fingers under the hem of her jeans and tickled her calf. This time, her entire leg jerked. Good thing it was the uninjured one.

She sighed. "Okay, short version: Suzie and I aren't just half-sisters. We're also first cousins. Our mothers were sisters, too."

He took a second to process this. "Okay, that's unusual, but not unheard-of. Doesn't explain all the hostility."

Erin rubbed her eye with one freckled hand, smearing her mascara.

SIN STREET

"My mother left me and my dad when I was two. Dad married Suzie's mother, Melinda, six months later, but he never got over his first wife. My mother, I mean."

"Sad, but not your fault."

"It gets better," she said with a wry kind of smile. "Suzie came along when I was ten—a surprise pregnancy. Shortly after that…"

"Shortly after that, what?"

"My mother made her triumphant return. She and my father ran off together, leaving Melinda with me and Suzie and a mountain of debt."

"Ouch."

"Yeah. Sounds like a script for a soap opera, doesn't it?"

"And then what?" he asked. Because there had to be more. There always was.

Erin scrubbed her hand over her face and grimaced. "My parents were killed in a boating accident off the shores of Aruba. All Dad left for us was this white elephant of a house and his collection of hunting rifles."

Noah thought about offering condolences. Somehow, it didn't seem like Erin would appreciate the sympathy. "And what about Melinda?"

"She…didn't handle it well. Got depressed. She died a about ten years ago." Erin looked away, first at the ceiling and then into the middle distance. "You're taking an awfully big interest in the details of my life."

"Yeah. I am."

There was quiet while he continued to massage her leg. After a few minutes, she said, "So what's your story? Aside from the college-education-put-on-hold, I mean?"

A fair request for information, given what she'd just shared with him. Too bad he couldn't be as forthcoming. "No story. Just a guy trying to make his way."

She struggled to sit and leaned back on her elbows. "Bullshit. Everybody's got a story. Where did you grow up?"

"Minneapolis."

"Family?"

"Mother, father, two older sisters."

"Hmm." Her smile was smug.

"What, hmm?"

"The baby of the family with two older sisters? That explains your smooth way with women."

He laughed. "I have a smooth way with women?"

"Please. You know it." The way her smile widened and her eyelids fell to half-mast looked distinctly like an invitation.

"Erin?"

"Yeah?"

"How drunk are you?"

"Why?"

He lifted her legs and set them aside to move up the sofa in the direction of her mouth, which he fully intended to kiss, drunk or not.

"Why do you think?" He leaned over her, watching as her expression turned calculating.

"First you have to give me one more piece of personal information. Something...real."

He knew what she meant. And he wanted to give her something, damn it. He wanted to be real with this woman, even just a little bit. He closed his eyes and swallowed. When he opened them, she was looking at him intently. "Okay, well, I had a girlfriend. She died."

Erin's eyes widened. "Yikes. I'm sorry, Noah, I didn't mean to—"

"It's okay. I don't talk about her much is all." He leaned in closer. "Now? Now can I?"

She snaked her arms around his neck and pulled him down on top of her. And he'd only meant to kiss her, because...drunk, remember? Or a little buzzed, but still. Not cool. But it wasn't a kiss so much as a slide of lips, wet and hot, then clash of tongues and teeth and moist, beer-scented breath shared between them.

Erin buried her hand in his hair and held on as she ran her mouth over his jaw and down his neck. "You have a condom with you?"

"Yeah."

They didn't speak again 'til their jeans were kicked off into a pile on the floor next to the sofa. He was pinching her nipple through her T-shirt and bra, rolling it between his fingertips and liking the way it made her bite her lip. "You ready? Tell me you're ready, Erin, because if you keep humping my leg like that, I'm gonna—"

"Ready, ready, I'm ready."

He heard himself growl and wondered what it was about this woman that brought out a beast he didn't know he possessed.

He slid home. Filled her on the first stroke. Hot-slick-oh-God-so-tight. In his head, he held onto the vague hope he'd be able to last longer this time. Not embarrass himself. But she wasn't making it easy, moving under him like that, all twisty, and rocking like all she wanted was to get him deep and keep him there. Quicksilver shivers shot through him when she moaned and worked her hand between them to touch herself.

He slowed his pumping. "I can do that. Let me—"

"No. You just...fuck me, Noah. Do it."

Pleasure rode his spine like a down-bound train, rolling his hips without conscious control. He could feel it under his skin—the twitchy, tense heat. Scratching in his veins, ready to burst out. Ready to send him flying.

Not without her. Not this time. He gathered her close and pulled her up to sit in his lap, impaled on his dick and with her legs wrapped around him. Her face crumpled up in what looked like agony, and for a second he panicked. *The leg?* Christ, had he—

Then she lifted herself, using his shoulders for leverage, and dropped again. The sound of their bodies striking was like a slap in a quiet room. He grabbed her hips and brought them forward, changing the angle, and she tightened around him 'til he could barely move.

She tilted her head away, baring her neck and collarbone. Another invitation and he went for it, licking and biting and sucking her flesh in time with the short, sharp pulses of their hips. She came, silent and sweet, moving just the bare minimum against him. But it was enough to push him past the point of no return. It swept over him like a wall of flame, scorching him with pleasure. He felt his arms shake around her. Heard her make a little humming sound with each exhalation. Wondered if he'd be able to move from the sofa without falling on his ass.

By the time he'd taken care of the clean-up and returned from the bathroom, she'd slipped back into her jeans and was nearly asleep.

"Should I go?"

She shook her head and smiled. "Get down here."

He curled around her, clinging with one hand to the back of the sofa in order not to fall off. The last thing he remembered was laughing at himself for renting a movie to pass the time.

* * *

"Wow. Cozy."

He jerked at the sound of Suzie's voice, sharp and hurting the insides of his sore head. *Shouldn't have fallen asleep.* Now he'd feel like shit the rest of the night. *Except...damn.* That was the light of day pouring in through those windows, wasn't it?

SIN STREET

He twisted his head around to see Suzie standing in the center of the living room, her purse and heels in one hand, and the other on her hip.

"Uh. Hi?"

Her face, which was beautiful when she smiled, but somehow even more lovely when she glared—like now, for instance—didn't change.

"What's going on here?"

Noah looked down at Erin, who continued to sleep peacefully. He slid his arm out from beneath her, and she grumbled. Then she turned into the back of the sofa and lay still. He sat and then stood, slipping on his boots and cursing the kinks in his back.

"Let's go talk in the other room." He took Suzie by the elbow and escorted her into the foyer. "Did you have a good time?"

"More to the point, Noah, did you?"

He sighed and ran his hand over the stubble on his jaw. "It's not what it looks like, Suze."

"No? Then what is it, precisely? Because it looks like you're cheating on me with my sister."

Okay, that's just stupid. "I can't cheat on you, Suzie. We aren't involved that way. And given that you just spent the night with some other guy, I guess maybe you don't have the right to…aw, crap. Don't cry."

"It's my house. I'll cry if I want to."

And he almost laughed, because…funny, right? Like the song? But Suzie never did have much of a sense of humor, especially about herself.

"Be fair, Suze. You've been telling me for months that we're just friends."

She pulled a tissue from her purse and dabbed at her eyes. "Friends don't have sex with other friends' sisters."

He thought fast. Could he afford the truth? If it meant losing Suzie's trust, could he tell her how felt about Erin?

And how did he feel anyway?

"Nothing happened. We were drinking beer and watching TV, and we fell asleep. That's all."

She blinked at him. "Really?"

"Really. I wouldn't lie to you about something like that. You know how I feel about you, Suze."

He would have liked to call her smile anything other than triumphant, but there it was. Victory over Erin, written all over her pretty face. And so much more like seventeen than twenty-two, standing in the foyer in her bare feet, with her makeup smudged. "Well, all right, if you say so."

"I do. Now go on upstairs and get a nice, hot shower and some rest, why don't you?"

She slid him a sideways glance, and he felt his stomach do a quick roll. "You want to join me?"

Damn. There was a word for girls like Suzie, and it wasn't a nice one. "No, I need to get to work before they fire my ass."

She fluttered her lashes at him, stretched up and planted a kiss on his mouth. Champagne and cigarettes and lies were what he tasted. "Don't forget about me, Noah. We could have a good time together."

A little late in the day for that. He recalled how hard he'd worked for her attention in the months before her sister had moved in with her. And all she'd needed was a little competition from the right person. *Yep—much more like seventeen than twenty-two.*

He shook his head and bent to tie his bootlaces. When he straightened, Erin was standing in front of him, her arms crossed over her chest.

"Nothing happened, huh? Nothing? Really?"

He looked away, his tongue thick and his throat closed with guilt. Or was that shame? So hard to tell the difference sometimes.

"That's good, Noah. I'm glad it was nothing because it won't be happening again."

"But—"

"But what?"

"She doesn't have to know."

The look Erin gave him might've razed another man. As it was, he felt withered and small. "Bad enough we're interested in the same guy. You think I'd sneak around behind her back on top of it? She's my sister. And, apparently, I just screwed her boyfriend. Again."

"No. I told you, it's not like that."

"Then why did you lie to her just now?"

He had no answer. Or—any he could give her without spilling more than would be good for either of them.

He grabbed his jacket from the coat stand by the door. When he looked at her again, he could see the hurt beneath the anger in the way she hunched her shoulders and cradled herself.

Yeah, this had been a mistake. But he'd known that going in, hadn't he?

He left without saying goodbye.

CHAPTER 3

December

It wasn't her first Christmas alone, but it was the first Christmas she'd ever spent alone in this old house. With Suzie barely speaking to her and no one in town she felt comfortable calling after all these years away, she didn't have much choice. And so Erin spent the twenty-third through the twenty-eighth of December surfing the Internet, watching TV, eating frozen dinners and nasty Chinese takeout, and wishing she hadn't put all her books and her Playstation™ into storage.

And thinking about Noah. But not good thoughts. Because he was an asshole who didn't deserve any positive energy directed his way. None. So she squashed those memories down—the ones of how his hands felt on her skin, how his lips felt on her mouth, and the way his eyes crinkled when he smiled.

Her dreams were another matter, though, because a girl apparently couldn't trust her unconscious not to throw up dirty pictures on the movie screen in her brain while she's trying to sleep away Christmas day in peace. *Damn it.*

Suzie returned from her skiing trip looking refreshed, and that was nice. Erin loved her sister—she did. And it used to be that Suzie loved her back. Adored her, in fact. She could recall long nights in a double bed, while the wind banged that same shutter that always came loose every winter, no matter how carefully Melinda tried to secure it. Suzie at seven and she at seventeen, listening to the radio and making up stories. Suzie had loved her. Trusted her. Wanted nothing more than to be with her always.

And then Erin had graduated high school and left home because things with Melinda were too hard. She reminded her stepmother-slash-aunt too much of her father and what he'd done to them. So she'd gone, leaving Suzie to deal with Melinda's moods and unhappiness. Not the kindest thing she could've done, but hell—how was she to know how bad things would get?

"I hope you didn't run the furnace too much. The gas bill—"

"Don't worry, Suzie. I kept the thermostat set at sixty-eight during the day and sixty-five at night. And I told you I'd pay the utilities this month. I have a disability check coming."

Suzie sniffed. "Nice for you, getting paid for sitting around."

Erin said nothing. She just raised her eyes to Suzie's face and stared. After a moment, her sister looked away with a mumbled, "I'm sorry."

Erin let it go because…really? How did you respond to something like that? Every once in a while, she wondered what had happened to the little girl Suzie had been, with her black curls, big, brown eyes and her sweet disposition. Now and again she caught flashes of the Suzie she'd known—like when she'd first been shot and there was some serious debate regarding whether she'd keep her leg below the knee. Then Suzie had cried and clutched at her in her hospital bed. She thought she remembered a promise, too—something about Suzie always being there for her. But that might've been the morphine talking.

"What're we doing for New Year's Eve?" Erin wanted to call back the words as soon as they were out of her mouth. The look Suzie sent in her direction could've stripped the blue-striped paper off the kitchen walls.

"I don't know what we're doing," Suzie shot back. "I know what I'm doing, which is going to a party with Trip." She turned away and peeled her sweater over her head. "It's hot in here. I'm turning the heat down."

"Well," Erin said to the dregs of her coffee, "I guess she told me."

* * *

Three evenings later—at eight o'clock sharp, and you had to give the jerk props for punctuality—the doorbell rang. Erin could hear

Suzie's blow-dryer running in the upstairs bathroom. She was going to have to get up and answer that door. Going to have to let Trip into the house. Make small talk with him. Wish him a Happy New Year. What if she pretended to be dead from boredom—lying right here on the sofa—instead? That would be bad, wouldn't it? Rude, at the very least. And one mustn't be rude to the little sister's boyfriend. Up to and, but not including, fucking him, of course. Twice. She should try to remember that.

Okay, this was the two glasses of Chardonnay on an empty stomach talking. And there went the doorbell again. She sighed and hauled herself up and out of the cocoon she'd built of sofa pillows and afghans. Just as well. She needed to pee anyway.

"Hi, Trip."

"Hey there, Officer Erin. What's shakin'?" Trip sort of oozed his way into the house, looking spectacular in a classic tux and shiny shoes that must've somehow floated above the mess of slush and salt on the sidewalk.

"Not too much. Suzie will be right down. I hope." That last part she kept to a mumble as she headed for the downstairs bathroom. When she emerged, she found Trip sitting on the sofa. As she limped across the room, he slid something square and shiny into the pocket of his black wool coat. Something suspiciously like a mirror.

But he wouldn't be so stupid as to do a line or two of coke with her in the next room, would he? *Or would he?*

She got her answer when he looked up at her, grinned, and wiped his nose on the back of his hand. *Asshole.*

"Here I am!" Suzie swept into the room on a cloud of perfume and hairspray, a vision in crimson silk and pearls. Erin sneezed.

Trip stood and held out his hand. "Gorgeous, babe, as always." As he leaned down to kiss her sister, he winked at Erin over the top of her head.

Arrogant bastard. He thought she wouldn't say anything about the illicit drug use with Suzie in the room. *And he's right.*

"Have a great time, kids," she said as she followed them to the door, suddenly feeling eighty years old and vaguely crotchety.

"You watching the ball drop all by yourself tonight, sis?" Trip couldn't seem to keep the smarmy grin off his face. Nor could he seem to keep still, jingling his keys in his pocket and tapping his shiny shoe on the foyer floor. All at once, Erin developed a sick feeling in her gut.

"Trip? You're not driving, are you?"

"Ah, hell, no. Got a limo for the night. Only the best for my girl."

Nothing to do but let them go, unless she wanted to make a scene and generate even more bad will between herself and Suzie. What could she do, after all? Accuse him of being a coke-head? What if he denied it? Would she ask him to assume the position against the foyer wall and pat him down? And if he refused to comply?

She was no longer a cop. Unfit for active duty, and she'd refused the desk job the department had offered, so now she was just another civilian. Time to get used to that fact. Besides, Suzie was a big girl—or she wanted to be. Maybe it was also time to start treating her like one.

No...that wasn't going to fly. No squelching that protective instinct—not tonight. While Suzie was arranging her black velvet wrap around her shoulders and fiddling with the contents of the tiny bag dangling from her fingertips, Erin took a moment to turn on the cop-mojo and threaten Trip's life. Subtly, of course.

"You take care of my sister. She's very precious to me. Do we understand each other?"

His green eyes widened at her tone of voice—flat, no-nonsense, and as final as the grave she'd see him in if anything happened to Suzie on his watch.

"Yeah. Sure." He swallowed visibly. Then he seemed to rally, the grin sliding back into place. "Whatever you say, Officer Erin."

"What are you two whispering about?" No missing the suspicion in Suzie's voice. Clearly, it was going to take her some time to get over the whole you-tried-to-steal-the-boyfriend-I-didn't-want-in-the-first-place thing.

"Your big sis was just telling me to mind my manners and keep you safe from all the big, bad wolves." Trip held out his arm, and Suzie tucked her hand into its crook. When she looked at Erin, something in her eyes softened for an instant. Erin could see a smile hovering at the corners of her lips.

"Oh. Well...have a good night." Suzie bit her lip, as if she wanted to say something more. Then Trip was tugging her out the door, and they were gone.

Watching through the window, Erin saw Trip help Suzie down the front walk, letting her lean on him so the combination of ice and four-inch heels didn't topple her. Only when the limo pulled away from the curb did she move into the kitchen and set about making herself a roast beef sandwich, heavy on the hot mustard.

Twenty minutes later, the roast beef soaking up the excess alcohol in her system and making her feel a little less wobbly, she returned to the living room and switched on the TV. She'd just managed to find that perfectly comfortable spot inside her cocoon once more, when the doorbell rang again.

"Christ on a cracker." She hauled herself up again and made for the door. She looked through the peephole, and... *Oh, God. Noah.*

She opened the door. "What do you want?"

He hunched against the doorway, his head down. "Suzie. Need to speak with her."

"She's not here. Come back day after tomorrow. Or better yet—"

She'd been about to say, "Don't come back at all." But then he lifted his head, and the expression of misery on his face stopped her dead. "What's wrong with you?"

"Where did she go? Is she with that bastard?"

"If you mean Trip Carlisle, then yes. But what—"

"Fuck." His eyes narrowed, and his lips thinned. She could practically taste his rage. "How do you let her keep seeing that guy? Do you even know anything about him? If you were anything like a good sister—"

"Hey." And maybe it was because he was putting a voice to the guilty thoughts that had plagued her ever since she'd stepped into the living room and seen Trip hiding the evidence of his cocaine habit, but all at once Noah wasn't the only enraged person standing in the doorway. "Who the fuck are you to say that to me, buddy? Get off my doorstep and don't come back."

He didn't move. She tightened her hand on the doorknob, wanting to slam it in his face—and not wanting to at the same time. Because he was clearly upset about something, and she wasn't reading jealousy in his attitude. Did he know something about Trip she didn't?

"Get in here." She opened the door farther and moved out of the way. He remained motionless for a second or two more, then stepped inside. She braced herself for the apology she was sure he was about to offer.

Instead, he said, "This sucks. I can't believe you just let her go."

She blinked at him. "Okay, look. You." She felt the furious words bubble up in her throat like bile. But again...that misery under his anger. It didn't make her want to touch him or anything. Not unless a right hook to his jaw counted.

"Yeah, go on, bitch me out. Not like I don't deserve it." He pivoted and stalked toward the kitchen like he owned the joint. "You got anything to eat?"

Oh, that's just... He doesn't really expect...

But apparently it wasn't roast beef on rye he was after because, as soon as she turned the corner, he grabbed her and pressed her into the corner made by the refrigerator and the wall. He used his whole body to keep her there, all six-foot-something of long, hard muscle.

"What the hell, Noah? Are you drunk?" But she already knew the answer to that. He didn't smell of beer or wine or whiskey. The scent rising from him was muted, but she couldn't mistake it from this proximity. She'd experienced it before, rising from the bodies of men thrown down over the hoods of police cruisers, their hands cuffed behind their backs. He smelled like desperation.

He tangled his hands in her hair, pulled her head back and went for her throat, fastening his lips and teeth on her collarbone. The same spot on which he'd left a mark just a month before. There were traces of it still, purple and brown, but she'd quit covering it with makeup, thinking it was faded enough to escape notice. Now it would be dark again. Part of her...the stubborn part that wouldn't listen to reason...the part that had gotten her shot by a seventh grader...was nothing but glad.

She struggled at first. Because that's what a woman's supposed to do in a situation like this. Fight off her attacker, or at least make a good show of it. Except he was coiling like a snake around her, his endless leg hooking behind both of hers to pull her tight against him, and his arms wrapping around her like he meant to crack her ribs. No space to breathe or move. No space for anything but giving in. Why did that feel so good when it shouldn't? When she should hate him for overpowering her?

The first kiss felt like a bare-knuckled brawl in her mouth. She let him have her anger then, and all her frustration. Bit his lip, hard. Tasted copper and liked it. So did he, if the way he snarled was any indication.

Then they were on the cold tile floor. The only sign he wasn't completely out of his mind was the way he lowered her. Not gently, but carefully. Mindfully, politely. Like the bank robber who wishes the teller a nice day.

He humped her good leg as he tore off her T-shirt, ripping it at the neck. Her sweats were gone next, leaving her in nothing but a pair of wool socks. Jesus, those tiles were like ice against her bare ass. Then his tongue was back in her mouth, tasting sour with whatever emotion fired him. Distracting her from whatever he was doing...which was opening and pushing down his jeans because there he was, hot and heavy against her thigh. His fingers fumbled at her nipple, too rough for pleasure, though he was clearly trying to make her want this. And God help her, she did.

"Slow down, Noah." It came out breathy and begging, but he seemed to hear it because he softened his touch on her breast.

"Need this," he said, his voice cracking. "Need you."

"I'm right here." He moved against her, restless, and she ran her hand in circles on his lower back. "Easy, okay?"

"Okay. Easy. Yeah."

But he grabbed at her hips like he couldn't help himself, with dragging fingers that would leave more marks. Like whatever dug this black pit of rage in him was yelling in his ear to hurt her, to make her pay. The first thrust took her by surprise, deeper and harder than it had to be, and she whimpered against his shoulder.

He froze. "Tell me to stop, Erin."

She bit her lip and held still.

"Goddamn it, tell me you want me to stop."

She didn't, because it would've been a lie, and this was no place for lies. So he took her, relentless, like the whole world owed him this fuck on her cold kitchen floor. Like he wanted to break her, and it ached. Deep inside it ached, but she loved it, and she didn't care if that made her sick or bad. Pain-pleasure-pain shot through her, like barbed threads of silk, and she urged him on.

"Go, baby. I'm right here. Do it." She scratched along his spine, knowing she was leaving raised red trails on his skin.

He rubbed his face in her hair and made a sound that could only be a sob. He twisted his hips and lifted her good leg high, so her sock-covered ankle rested on his shoulder. His face dripped with cold sweat, and it splashed her as he drove forward. The wet, thick sound of fucking filled the kitchen. Pounding into her and receding, no time to breathe in between, and the pressure built and built until her vision grayed out and white static filled her head. She was coming, sharp and hot, each spasm wringing her out like an old washcloth.

He thrust into her hard and held. She waited to feel him shudder and release, her own body still pulsing. Soon, she'd hurt. The friction alone would leave her swollen and sore.

She waited...but he only held fast another second. His muscles still tense, his breathing still high and tight. Then he dropped her leg and pulled out of her. *He didn't come, and why is that? Is he thinking of*

Suzie? Was that what this had been—all of it? Was she just a poor substitute for her sister?

She dug her nails into his back and said, "Noah, what—"

"I can't. Want to, but I can't." He crawled off her and propped his back against the cabinets under the center island, his legs sprawled out in front. His cock was hard and red and furious. It looked uncomfortable.

She sat and reached for him. Because maybe he didn't want her like he wanted Suzie, but she still wanted him. If that made her pathetic, then she'd deal with that later. "Let me—"

"No." He closed his eyes. When he spoke again, his voice was a low babble. She had to strain to catch his words. "Remember that girlfriend I told you about? Her name was Katie. We were together all through high school, then she left Minneapolis and came to college here. Got mixed up with some bad people. Got hooked on drugs. Cocaine, crystal meth."

His face twisted with the last words. He took a breath and said, "Her sophomore year, she didn't come home at Christmas. Stayed here, with her new friends. Overdosed on New Year's Eve, was in a coma for Valentine's Day. They took her off the machines just before the first of spring."

"My God, Noah, I'm sorry." *Lame. So utterly lame.* But what else could she say?

Now his face was a blank. He continued as if he hadn't even heard her. "I was in school in Minneapolis—a year ahead of her. I dropped out and just..." He ran his hand through his hair. "I dunno. Fell apart. Got drunk a lot."

"And then?"

"And then, last year, I came to Kelston. I thought maybe I could make sense of it here. Thought if I walked the streets where she'd walked, maybe met some of the people she knew..."

"And did you? Find some people she knew?"

His gaze sharpened on Erin's face. "Yeah. I did." He yanked up his underwear and jeans, covering himself as if he'd just realized he was sitting there half-naked. "Oh Christ, what did I do here?"

"It's okay."

"No. God, no, it's really not. Did I hurt you?"

Now would come the apology. And she'd have to reject it because she'd wanted this as much as he did. Maybe more. She didn't make those marks on his back in self-defense.

"I shouldn't have come here."

"Noah—"

"I won't bother you again."

"Wait." She followed him into the foyer. "Who is it you met?" She had that sick feeling in her gut—it had returned pretty much the second he'd said the word "cocaine."

"It doesn't matter."

She grabbed his arm. "It matters. Was it Trip?" She read the answer in the way his face closed up and even the sudden, sharp line of his posture shut her out. "What are you planning, Noah?"

"I don't know what you mean."

"Don't stand in my house and lie to me. Are you...you are, aren't you? You're going to hurt him. Kill him, even?"

He huffed in a way she guessed was supposed to be a laugh. "Crazy. That's just plain—"

She reached up and grabbed his jaw, cradling his chin in her palm and pushing her nails into his cheek. "Listen. You ever been to prison? You know what that's like?"

He stared at her for a long second. "Doesn't matter. I'll get out eventually. Katie's dead. She never gets to come back from that." He disengaged his face from her grip and stepped back out of range. And then he was gone. So very gone, like he'd never been there at all.

The slam of the door bounced around in her head. She looked down at herself, standing naked in her foyer, except for her wool socks. Christ, they hadn't even used a condom. Not that she was worried—she'd been on the pill forever and a day, and Noah hadn't come anyway. And she felt fairly certain he didn't harbor any dread diseases. *Still—stupid. Very.*

The clock in the living room chimed nine times. *Three hours to the new year.* Somehow, it felt like she'd lived a whole month in the past forty-five minutes. She gathered her clothes from the kitchen, turned off the lights—all but the one in the foyer, so Suzie could see if, by chance, she made it home before dawn—and climbed the stairs to bed.

* * *

The phone rang, echoing in the relative emptiness of her dark room. Erin fumbled to answer it, adrenaline surging through her body. *Eleven-fifteen.* Couldn't be good news, unless her baby sister had finally wised up and dumped Trip's druggie ass.

"Hello?"

"Erin." Not a question. He sounded sure.

"Noah?"

"I'm sorry, Erin. I'm really, really sorry." His voice had a soft quality. Almost sleepy. "I didn't mean it."

"Which part? The part where you fucked me on the kitchen floor because that was—"

"No. The stuff I said about you and Suzie." He sighed. "You're a good sister. Better than she deserves."

"Careful."

"Sorry."

Erin reached up and clicked on the lamp next to her bed. "So, now what?"

His breathing deepened. "What d'you mean?"

"I think we should talk about you and Trip. You can't go through with—"

"I don't want to talk about that. If you make me, I'll hang up."

Jesus, he sounded about four years old. Maybe he and Suzie were a good match after all. "Why did you call? What do you want to talk about?"

"Hmm...how about that sound you made tonight? That sort of whimpery noise when I—"

"God, Noah, is this your idea of a joke? Dirty talk in the middle of the night?" She heard fabric shift against fabric. Just a whisper, barely discernible. But when she closed her eyes, she got a clear vision of him sprawled on his bed, half-dressed. Which was insane because had no idea where he lived. She'd certainly never been inside his bedroom. But she could see him just the same, and maybe she had the color of the sheets wrong, but she knew what he looked like—cheeks flushed, lips parted, eyes lazy.

"Not joking. And it's not even midnight."

She sighed and leaned back against her pillow. "Are you drunk?"

"Nope."

"You sure? Because you sound—"

"Tired is all. They're short-handed at the restaurant. I worked two double shifts in the last two days."

Well, that explained some of what happened earlier in the evening. Exhaustion did funny things to people. Stripped away inhibitions. Of course, she was perfectly well-rested and couldn't rely on that excuse.

"So anyway, I was remembering that sound you made.

Remembering a lotta stuff really." His voice was thick and somehow blurry, like he was having trouble forcing out the words. Then he groaned, low and quiet, and Erin flushed from her face downward.

"Noah, are you...uh...you aren't...are you?" She couldn't bring herself to say it out loud.

His answer was non-responsive. "Remembered how much I love the way you feel and sound and smell. But what I really wanna know is how you taste. All over."

She closed her eyes. "Noah. Please." She gripped the blankets at either side of her and held on.

"And I was thinking," he continued, ignoring her completely, "that if I was any kind of lover, I'd already know. So I guess I owe you, Erin."

"No. That's all right."

He was silent for a second. "You don't want me to? Maybe you don't like that?"

"No, of course I...I mean, yes, I like it, but—"

"Hmm."

God, that guttural humming thing he was doing was going to be the death of her. "Noah, we should hang up now."

"Touch yourself for me."

Like she hadn't even spoken.

"Oh, God. No, I will not do that. We're done here." But she clutched the phone like it was keeping her alive and listened to him breathe in her ear. Jesus. Her own, private obscene phone caller. Christmas come late.

"Okay then, don't touch yourself. Just listen."

She clenched her jaws together, so utterly torn between what she knew she should do and what she wanted. She could feel her nails digging into her palm right through the wool blanket. When he groaned again, her heart tripped double-time and a steady pulse took up residence in the lower portions of her body. Specifically, the portions she wasn't going to touch.

"You're so hot and sweet and soft," he said, his voice dropping into a gritty register that made her toes curl. "I know you might not want to hear that—the soft part—but it's true. Every time I touch you, that's what makes me lose control. Never had such trouble with control before you, not even when I was fifteen and me and Katie were..." His voice faded. She heard him shift again. Heard the movement of bedsprings, old and squeaky. Heard something that sounded an awful

lot like a sob, rough and painful.
"Shh, Noah, it's okay. You'll be fine."
"I don't think so. I think I'm screwed, Erin. Think I'm losing it."
"No. I've got you. I'm right here." The same thing she'd said earlier, but he'd been way too far gone in his own head to hear it then.
"Forget that stuff. Tell me more—tell me why you like to…uh…"
"Fuck you?"
She tried to say, "Yeah." It left her mouth as a moan.
"Touch yourself first. Tell me what you'd ask me to do, if I was there right now."
She shuddered so hard the bed shook. "Noah, I can't. I—"
"Please. I know it's wrong to ask, but I'm lying here and all I can do is think about you, and I can't…I can't…"
She couldn't deny him. Couldn't even lie to him—pretend she was doing what he asked and then not…do it. Mostly because she wanted to, and that was a new little kink she didn't even know she had.
She slid her hand under the covers and then inside the ratty pair of boxers she'd worn to bed. "Yes. Okay. I'm…doing it."
He sighed. She could practically hear him relaxing. Closed her eyes and saw him sinking into his bed. "Does it feel good?"
"Yeah, it's—I'm a little sore. From before. But it's good."
He cursed. Something she didn't quite catch, muffled and terse, but it had to be profane, whatever it was. And then, "You're incredible, Erin. I want you so much."
She moved her fingers against her clit, swirling in circles, and listened to him breathe. "More than Suzie?"
He grunted. "Never wanted Suzie. Not like that. Only had to be near her so I could get close to—"
"Don't." *Talk about a buzz kill.*
"Now I just wanna be near you. All the time. God—wanna lock you in my room, tie you to the bed so you can't get away from me."
And that should've been way too creepy—way too psycho-stalker-with-a-collection-of-random-body-parts-in-his-basement, but instead it turned her on. Because, yeah, she knew he was on the edge of something bad. But she also knew what was inside him, in addition to all that rage and lust for revenge. Good stuff, like loyalty and tenderness and humor.
Or at least she thought she knew. And maybe that made her stupid. Blind and reckless. And maybe it would make her—eventually—an accessory to murder for not calling the cops. But what would say to that

uniformed officer who showed up at her door? "I know this guy, and he may or may not be planning to kill this other guy over something that happened a couple years ago." She had no proof. She didn't want proof. She wanted to pretend he'd never told her. It was getting easier to do just that by the second as she imagined his mouth on her, his tongue, his teeth...

She moved her fingers faster, stopping to dip them into herself and collect moisture. Letting them slide, slippery-wet against her clit, then pressing hard. He'd bite her there. Make her jump, then lave away the sting with the flat of his tongue until she couldn't stand the sweet, achy bliss.

His breathing sounded ragged in her ear, like he was barely holding on.

"Are you close?" She whispered it, almost hoping he wouldn't hear, because dirty talk had never been her thing. She wasn't good at it.

He grunted again, and for the second time, she pictured how he must look, lying on his bed. "God, yes. You?"

She didn't answer, concentrating instead on the heat coursing through her and the fantasy of his mouth on her, slick and relentless.

"You are, aren't you?" he murmured. "Come for me, Erin. Let me hear you."

She felt that first tug low in her belly—that tightening that signaled the start. "Is that what you want? To hear me lose it?"

His breath hitched. "You sound like an angel when you come, Erin. Dirty angel, moaning and whimpering for me."

"Noah..." Her voice broke with the hot burst of pleasure, and she was lost to it. Far away and right up close at the same time, she heard him groan, sharp and deep. Then he repeated her name, again and again, in disintegrating string of sound that faded fast into gasps and pants and silence.

Finally he cleared his throat. "I'm sorry." Honest contrition there, but for which part? The earlier, angry sex? The obscene call in the middle of the night? Or dragging her into the dark side of his life?

"You said that before." She softened her tone and whispered, "And I said it was okay. But we really need to talk about Trip and—"

"No." The finality in his tone was like the slam of a door. But when he spoke again, he sounded almost amused. "We can't keep having sex every time we see each other."

"Why not?"

"Because."

"That's not a reason."

"I want to get to know you."

She frowned, feeling the last of the afterglow slip away. "But you won't talk to me about the most important thing—"

"Drop it, Erin." Again with the cold, hard finality. "Is that all you want from me? Just sex?"

"You know better than that."

"All right then. We should try…dating."

She sighed and scrubbed her fist over her face. "I can't."

"Because of Suzie? You think it's better if we just bang each other every time we meet? Because your sister would be totally cool with that, right?"

He had a point. And Erin had the obvious solution. "Maybe we shouldn't see each other at all. She'd be very cool with that."

There was a pause. Her stomach twisted in the silence, knowing he was about to take her up on it. Call her bluff, and she'd never see him again. Instead, he said, "Is that what you want?"

Was there a good reason to lie? Absolutely. A thousand of them, starting with Suzie and ending with Noah's apparent intent to kill Suzie's boyfriend. But Erin told the truth. She'd always been a sucker for the truth. "No.

"Me neither." He yawned. The sound was muffled. She imagined him covering his face with one his big, square hands. He said, "You know where Carradine's is? On the corner of—"

"I know it."

"Good. Stop by there Friday night around closing. We'll go out."

"But—"

"I know you don't want to sneak around. I know you're a better person than that." His voice was warm and deep. The sound of it send a buzz through her body. "But don't you want a shot at figuring this out before you decide it isn't worth hurting Suzie over?"

She opened her mouth to answer and discovered she had nothing to say.

"Erin? I'll see you Friday."

The click in her ear bounced around in her head for a few seconds before fading. She glanced at the clock. Two minutes to midnight.

She lay awake and listened for the chimes that would herald the new year. But even as doubt and fear tangled her thoughts, weariness pulled at her. And satisfaction. Nothing like two good orgasms in one night to sink a girl into the dreamless black. She heard the clock in the living room sing out once…twice…five times…

CHAPTER 4

January

Noah leaned against the north wall of Carradine's, watching the traffic flow over the bridge from the other side of town. The cold trapped in the bricks seeped through his down jacket. *Not many people on the sidewalk, especially for a Friday night. Weather too bad— freezing rain in the forecast. A nice complement to the bitter wind.*

He'd been there half an hour, waiting for Erin. With every passing minute, it became more obvious she wasn't going to show. He wished he could be surprised, or even disappointed. But after the way he'd behaved? Like a lunatic, all but raping her on her kitchen floor, then calling her after like some horny, lovesick school kid with a hard-on he could've used to pound nails. Not to mention practically admitting he planned to kill her sister's boyfriend first good chance he got. Standing him up was the sane thing to do. He was lucky she hadn't asked for a restraining order.

He was about to walk away when his cell rang. He pulled it from his pocket with numb fingers and flipped it open. The number that flashed was the landline at the Mulally house.

"Erin?"

"Noah, it's Suzie."

Crap. Tactical error. "Sorry, Suzie, I—"

"Listen, can you come over? I...I need to see you." Her voice hitched, and she sniffled.

"Are you all right? Is Erin—"

"I'm fine. Just come, okay?"

"I'll be there in twenty minutes." He flipped the phone shut and headed down the block to where he'd parked his car. Worry twisted his gut. Suzie came off as clingy sometimes, but he'd gotten to know her well enough to see the strength lurking under that needy-little-girl exterior. She was more like Erin than she'd ever admit. And not given to making SOS calls for no good reason.

By the time he was within sight of his car, he was sprinting.

* * *

Suzie met him at the door and flung herself into his arms as if she hadn't seen him in months. Which…okay, he hadn't been around since Thanksgiving, but he had kept in touch, calling her at least once a week. Because she was still his friend, even if he did have a thing for her sister. And wanted to shoot her boyfriend in both kneecaps before putting a third bullet between his eyes. Other than that…yeah, best buddies for life.

"Noah, I don't know what to do." She hung limp from his shoulders as he half-carried her into the living room. "Tell me what to do?"

"About what? Where's Erin?"

She pulled away and looked at him. Her eyes were rimmed in pink instead of the usual goopy black stuff. "I thought you came to see me." Her chin quivered.

"I did. I just wondered—"

"I'm right here." Erin appeared in the doorway, a tall glass of water in one hand and two pills in the other. "Take these. You'll feel better." She held the pills and water out to her sister, and didn't look at Noah.

"What's going on?" He didn't mean to sound so sharp, but they were making him nervous. The pair of them, with their tense mouths and their meaningful eye contact.

While Suzie downed the aspirin, Erin said, "Trip was caught with half a kilo of coke in his trunk. He's being booked for possession with intent to distribute." Her voice was flat, but she finally lifted her eyes to meet Noah's.

He had to struggle to keep from laughing out loud. Trip Carlisle in prison, after all this time—wouldn't that be a kick in the head?

Suzie finished the water. "Try to find a little compassion, Erin. You know this is a mistake. Trip would never"—she hiccupped and wiped her mouth with the back of her hand "—sell drugs. For God's sake, his family is loaded."

Erin shrugged. "We'll see."

"It's a mistake. Somebody's trying to frame him." Suzie turned again to Noah. "It was awful. They stopped us for speeding and then there was something about the registration on the Jaguar, and the next thing I knew, Trip was in handcuffs. They bent him over the police car and searched him like a common criminal."

Noah pictured the scene as Suzie described it, then coughed into his fist to hide the grin that threatened to take over his face.

The phone on the table in the foyer rang. Erin left to answer it. She reappeared a few seconds later and handed the cordless receiver to Suzie without a word. Then she leaned in the doorway. Noah watched as she reached down and rubbed at her wounded leg. She stared off into space as she did it, as if unconscious of her action. He closed his eyes and remembered the pink, puckered scar just above her knee. What it felt like under his fingers. How it made him feel weirdly protective, like he hadn't felt since…Katie. Yeah, he'd done a real good job protecting her, hadn't he? He shook his head. *Time to get a grip.*

"Oh, Trip, that's amazing. That's so wonderful! Do you need a ride home from the— No, I understand. Call me later, okay?"

Suzie turned off the phone and beamed at Noah. "Trip's been released."

Erin moved out of the doorway. "On bail? But there wasn't even time to arraign him."

In the time it took to look at her sister, Suzie's smile turned smug. "I told you it was a mistake. His father's lawyer got him released. Something about illegal search and seizure, and the governor's office calling."

Noah shoved his hands in his pockets to keep from reaching out and shaking Suzie. Pain stabbed at his temple like an ice pick. Of course Trip had managed to get himself released. *Just like last time.* Why had he even let himself hope? He cleared his throat. "That's great. I'm happy for you. I need to go."

Suzie barely glanced at him on her way out of the room. "That's fine. Thanks for coming over. Hope I didn't interrupt anything important."

Rage flooded him, black and poisonous. He opened his mouth to tell Suzie what she could do with her thanks, but she was gone. And there was a touch on his arm, firm and warm. He looked down and saw

Erin at his side.

"Noah, listen to me."

He shook off her hand and made for the front door. She followed him. "Please, Noah."

"What? What could you possibly say?" He glared at her, knowing he was taking his anger out on the wrong person. "Better luck next time? There's not going to be a next time. I'm not letting him get away with it. Not again."

"You can't—"

"Don't tell me I can't. He killed Katie, Erin. He got her hooked on cocaine and speed, and God knows what else, and he killed her."

"And she had no responsibility? Seriously—doesn't Katie have a piece of this at all?"

He felt his hand curl into a fist. "Don't."

"Why not? You're not strong enough to take the truth? I don't believe that for a second."

He was going to punch something. It couldn't be Erin—he wouldn't hit a woman, ex-cop or not. *But if she kept talking like this...like any of this was Katie's fault...* He was definitely going to slam his fist somewhere.

Erin stepped closer. The expression on her face was a challenge all by itself. "I'm not saying Trip isn't a bad guy who deserves to go away for a long time. I'm just saying that you can't make Katie a victim here. Not completely."

"Shut up."

"No. You're in my house, and I'll say whatever I want to."

"Fine. I was leaving anyway."

"You can do that. But running away won't change it." She touched his arm again. He felt the muscles beneath her hand bunch and twist, as if trying to repel her. "I saw your face when you thought Trip was in jail, Noah. You were relieved. I know you're angry, but you don't really want to—"

He yanked his arm away. "Don't tell me what I want."

Erin reached out to him again, but before she could make contact, Suzie reappeared in the doorway of the living room. "She's good at that, isn't she, Noah? Big sister Erin, always right there with all the answers, telling you how you should feel."

Shit. How much had she heard? "Suzie—"

"No, it's okay. I understand. You two have some big secret between you—like you think I don't know you've been fucking. Like you think

I'm stupid."

Erin turned toward Suzie. "It's not like that."

"No? What's it like then? How is this different from what your mother did to my mother, Erin?"

Oh, Christ, look what he'd started. He moved toward Suzie. "That's enough. You don't know what you're talking about."

She laughed. It sounded bitter and ragged and old. "Right. And I'm supposed to believe you? The one who dumped me for my sister?"

"I didn't dump you. We never—"

But Suzie was off and running. "You're no different from my father—weak and stupid. He let Erin's mother lead him around by the dick. Erin will do the same thing to you. She really is just like her mother—a slutty bitch with a cruel streak." She stared straight at her sister as she spat the words.

Noah felt his blood chill at the look on Suzie's face. "Stop. Just…stop."

Erin's voice was flat and quiet when she finally spoke. "Time for you to go, Noah."

He looked at them as they gazed at each other in the dim light of the foyer. He sighed and ran a hand through his hair. "Fine. Give me a call when you work out the drama, okay?"

Erin's tone never changed, nor did she glance at him when she said, "Don't hold your breath."

Damn. Cold as ice. He shouldn't have come here—that much was plain. He'd done himself no favors, and just fucked everything up worse than ever. He let himself out into the freezing rain.

* * *

He spent the next hour sipping from a brand new bottle of Jack Daniel's and cleaning the nine-millimeter. Because that's the kind of combination that always led to good things. His mouth twisted into something like a grin at the thought of him accidentally shooting himself while courting the perfect state of drunkenness. And all over a woman he never would've met if somebody hadn't taught a twelve-year-old how to hot-wire a Chevy.

"She'd be keeping the peace on the mean streets of Milwaukee, and I'd be…" Where would he be? Right where he was? Still trying to grow big enough balls to take down his target? Or already in jail and awaiting trial for murder one?

SIN STREET

A voice in his head—the voice that tended to show up when he'd been drinking—began asking questions. Who was he kidding, playing a poor man's Clint Eastwood? Hadn't there been enough death? Enough grief? Was this really what Katie would've wanted?

He lifted the bottle to his mouth again, and his cell rang. He contemplated letting it lie there on the bed, unanswered. Then he reached for it, flipped it open and saw that the call came, once more, from the Mulally residence.

"What?"

"Noah?" Suzie again.

"Yeah."

There was a pause. Clearly, little Suze wasn't used to being spoken to so gruffly.

"Listen, I'm sorry about before, but—"

"Don't sweat it. I'm kinda busy right now, kid. I'll talk to you later."

"Wait. Don't hang up. I need your help."

He laughed. "Your boyfriend get arrested again? Tell him to call his daddy's lawyer. That always seems to work out real well for him."

"Noah, listen to me. It's Erin. We...there was a fight."

"Yeah, I remember."

"No, listen." Suzie's voice shook. She sounded as if she'd been crying yet again. "After you left, I...I said some stuff. Erin didn't even fight back. She just stood there and took it, and I..." Her voice faded. She sobbed into his ear.

"What do you expect me to do about it?"

"Find her! You have to find her. It's so cold outside, and she didn't even take a coat, and it's sleeting hard and—"

"Erin left the house? On foot? In this weather?"

"That's what I'm trying to tell you, Noah. She's gone, and she didn't take the car." Suzie sucked in a long, hitching breath. "I'm scared. Noah, what if she..." Her voice hitched and faded.

Things must've gotten pretty damn bad between the sisters for Erin to take off like that. Erin didn't run. If he knew nothing else, he knew that.

"Stay by the phone, Suzie. I'll find her."

He left the gun on the bed and the bottle on the floor.

* * *

SIN STREET

He found her outside Carradine's, huddled in a ball on the sidewalk, her face pressed into her knees. The freezing rain had soaked through her jeans and sweater and sneakers. When he pulled her to her feet, she fell against him as if she didn't have the strength to stand. He picked her up, carried her to his car, and settled her into the front seat. Then he got in and cranked up the heat.

"Jesus Christ, what were you thinking, Erin?"

She didn't answer, letting her head fall against the window with a thud. He tried to ignore the anger and fear churning his gut and concentrated on navigating the slick streets. God forbid he get stopped for reckless driving—not with a half-frozen woman in his car and whiskey on his breath.

When they pulled into the parking lot of the motel, she roused. "Where are we?"

"My place."

"You live here?" She spoke in a whisper, but he could hear the confusion in her voice.

"It's cheap. Trying to save money for school, remember?" He got out and moved around to the passenger's side.

When he opened the door and looked down at her, she said, "School. Right. Will that be before or after prison?"

He reached in, pulled her out of the car and hoisted her into his arms. "Can we talk about this later?"

She nodded and buried her face in his neck. "I didn't know where else to find you. I don't have your cell number, and under the circumstances, I thought asking Suzie would be"—she coughed and shivered—"awkward."

He had to laugh, even as he splashed through a half-frozen puddle and felt the icy water seep through the seams of his boots. He set her down to unlock his door, then tried to lift her again. She fought him, muttering something about being neither an invalid nor a baby, and he ended up dropping both hands to her shoulders and pushing her into the room. He flicked on the overhead light and kicked the door shut behind him.

He watched her face as she looked around the shabby room. Pistol laid out on the bed, whiskey bottle sitting on the floor a few feet away. Dusty blinds on the window, stained wallpaper, threadbare carpet, cheap bedspread. He hadn't noticed his surroundings in a long time— the room was just a place to sleep and keep his stuff. Now he noticed. His face went hot with shame.

"Sorry for the mess. You can dry off here. I'll call Suzie and let her know you're not dead. Then I'll take you home."

"No." She turned to face him. Her eyes were dull, her face empty. "Don't make me go back there yet. Unless"—she looked from him to the gun and back again—"I mean, I could get my own room. But I can't go home. Not yet."

"Don't be an idiot. You can stay here as long as you want. I just thought you'd be more comfortable in your own house." He grabbed the automatic and snagged the bottle of J.D. off the floor, crossed the room to the closet, and set them on the top shelf, alongside the box of clips. He heard the creak of old springs behind him. When he turned, she was sitting on the edge of the bed, her face in her hands. For the first time ever, he saw her as fragile.

"Oh...hey, Erin, it's gonna be okay. Really." He went to her and knelt next to her, wanting to lay his hand on her head or her knee or her shoulder. Wanting to give her comfort. But he didn't know how. The blind leading the blind. The broken trying to mend the shattered. He'd be a hypocrite to make the attempt.

She started to talk. He could barely hear her at first. The words became more distinct when she pulled her hands away from her face and just stared at the dirty carpet.

"...don't even know who I am anymore. Suzie's wrong—I'm not like her. I was never her child, never hers at all. But who am I? Not my mother's daughter, not a cop. Can't even be a good big sister. Guess I'm just some skanky slut who screws my sister's boyfriends. Has nothing to do with my mother, though. She shouldn't have to take the rap for that, too." She took a breath, and he tried to slip a comment or two in there between all that self-loathing, but then she was clutching his arm and looking panicked.

"Oh God, I'm gonna—" She pressed her fist against her mouth and gagged.

Without a word, he dragged her to her feet and into the bathroom. He held her hair off her face as she lost it into the toilet. Crooned quiet, sympathetic noises in her ear, and laid a single kiss on the back of her damp neck.

While she rested on the floor, he turned on the shower.

"Can you undress yourself?"

"Still not a baby, Noah."

"Just asking."

He stripped. When they were both naked, he took her elbow and guided her into the shower, stepping in behind her. She turned her back to him and let the water strike her face and soak her hair. He grabbed the miniature soap the maid always left and picked at the paper wrapper. Damn, but his hands were shaking.

He let his sudsy fingers hover over her shoulders, not knowing whether to touch or just…let her alone. She hadn't moved or made a sound. Maybe he should step out, give her some space. Maybe he was a disgusting, insensitive jerk for letting his dick get hard under these circumstances.

He almost dropped the soap when she shifted backward and pressed against him. "Is that an extra shower attachment, or are you really glad to see me?"

The tension melted with their laughter. He guided her to lean forward once more. She braced her forearms on the shower wall. The hot water ran in rivulets down her back. He slid his hands, slippery with soapsuds, over her shoulders, her neck, and into her hair. Then down over her shoulders again, tracing the constellations of pale freckles.

"God, that's good." Her voice was rough and sultry, and his dick twitched in reply. When she turned to face him, her eyes were no longer empty and flat. She smiled at him and stretched up to lay a kiss on his chin. "Mind if I finish up by myself?"

He nodded, pulled back the plastic curtain and stepped out of the tub. He used one of the two available towels to dry himself and wrapped it around his waist. *What next?* Her clothes lay in a sodden heap on the bathroom floor. She couldn't wear those—he'd have to let her borrow something of his. Good thing she was tall.

She opened the shower curtain and stuck her head out into the steamy air. Shampoo ran down the side of her face. "Can I sleep here tonight?"

"Sure." Because it wouldn't be torture to have her in his bed and be unable to touch her out of some twisted sense of chivalry he'd only just discovered in himself. All right then. He'd bunk on the floor.

He picked up their clothes and moved into the other room, where he tidied up as best he could and switched off the overhead light. A streetlamp cast long, slanted shadows across the room through the lopsided blinds. A few seconds later, he heard the water turn off. Then the door opened and she appeared, her hair dripping on her shoulders and water running down the length of her naked body.

"Uh…there's a towel on the rack in there. I'll get it for you." He tried to pass her in the tight space between the end of the bed and the bathroom door. She blocked him with a hand on his hip. The towel he'd used to cover his fading hard-on dropped to the floor.

"Noah?"

"Yeah?" He stared over her head at the cheap paneling on the wall. Afraid to look at her. Afraid he might lose control.

"Remember what you said on the phone the other night? About how you owed me?"

Oh, Christ. He'd been half out of his mind with exhaustion and rage. Not fair to expect him to remember what he'd said. But he did remember—of course he did. The dirty fantasy he'd conjured was seared into his brain, probably forever.

"Yeah?" His throat made a weird clicking sound when he swallowed.

She ran her hand up his side, over his ribs, then to the center of his chest. "It's time to pay up." She shoved him. As big and solid as he was, he stumbled back, tripping over his own two feet.

He sat down hard on the edge of the bed, making the mattress bounce. "Are you sure? Maybe you should rest. You've been through a lot tonight."

She laughed, short and harsh. "A fight with Suzie doesn't count as 'a lot.' Just another pleasant evening at Casa de Mulally."

"And I was the cause of this one."

"Not your fault, Noah. If it hadn't been you, it would've been something else." She reached up and skimmed her wet hair off her face. "I can't live there anymore."

He shook his head. "It's your home."

"Just a house. I can find an apartment somewhere. Things will be tight for a while, but I'll figure something out."

He crossed his arms over his chest, consciously attempting to look intimidating. "Tell me the deal with you and Suzie. The whole thing this time."

"What makes you think I didn't tell you the whole thing the first time you asked, back at Thanksgiving?" Oddly, she didn't look intimidated in the least.

"Call it a hunch."

She sighed. "Remember when I said Melinda didn't handle my father's abandonment well? That was an understatement. She pretty much lost her mind over it, except it took years. Years of screaming and locking herself in her bedroom for days on end. Years of her telling me she hated me because I was the worst of my mother and father combined. By the time I was seventeen, I'd had enough of the drama."

"So you left?"

"Yeah. Saved up my money from whatever jobs I could get and took off the day after graduation."

"And then what?"

She shrugged. "I guess with me gone, Melinda turned on Suzie—who just happens to look exactly like my mother."

"Ouch."

"No kidding."

"What happened, Erin?"

"Melinda overdosed on sleeping pills when Suzie was twelve, but not before spending a lot of time in and out of hospitals. And I was completely out of touch. No one knew where to reach me, so…"

"Suzie went into foster care?"

"Yeah."

He nodded. "That explains the abandonment issues. She can't stand to have anyone walk away from her, even if she doesn't want them in the first place."

"Right. That's why I can't really blame her for—you know. How she feels about us."

"I get it."

"I should've been there for her. I swore I would be." She swallowed visibly. "And now all she wants is for me to be gone, so that's what I'm going to be."

He couldn't offer her a place to live or even to stay for more than a day. And she deserved better than a crappy motel room anyway. Still, the desire to offer shelter and comfort was strong.

She smiled crookedly at him and crossed her arms over her chest as if she were suddenly self-conscious. "You have something I could wear overnight, 'til my clothes are dry?"

"I thought you wanted…I mean, you said—"

"Yeah, well, I only ask once." She glanced in the direction of his faded erection. "And you don't seem very interested."

He pushed himself up off the mattress and moved to stand in front of her again. "Looks can be deceiving."

"I'm not a mercy fuck, Noah."

"No, you're not. Definitely"—he curled his hand behind her neck and drew her face up 'til their lips grazed together when he spoke—"not a mercy fuck."

Her skin was damp and cool against him, except where her breasts rubbed against his chest. He pressed his thigh between her legs and felt her tense. Felt his dick wake up and take interest again. When she didn't respond, he pulled her closer and whispered, "It's okay if you changed your mind, but don't make this about me. I want you. Every time I see you, I want you."

"What about when you don't see me? Out of sight, out of mind?"

"You're not going to make this easy, are you?"

"Answer the question, Noah."

He sighed and tasted frustration in the back of his throat. She wanted an answer? Okay, fine, but it might scare her shitless. He took hold of her shoulders and bent her backward, so he could look down into her face.

"You're never out of my mind. Not since the first time I saw you at the house. I walked in and there you were, looking so damned..."

"Tall?"

He laughed. "Tall. And strong and beautiful and way, way outta my league. And then, at the party—"

"When I came onto you."

"Yeah. Couldn't believe my luck. Thought I'd died and gone to a heaven where all the angels were freckle-faced redheads."

Her turn to laugh. "Poetic."

"No. Just the truth." His throat had grown tight. He swallowed against the thickness. "I think about you all the time, Erin. Can't stop thinking about you—"

"Except when you're thinking about killing Trip Carlisle."

He looked away. "The only reason he's still alive is that I couldn't...couldn't stand the idea of never seeing you again."

"Oh, Noah." She leaned into him, forcing him to wrap his arms around her.

"Tell me what you want, Erin."

"Make love to me." She whispered it into his shoulder. "And don't kill Trip. Don't make me be in love with a murderer."

Something hot swelled in his chest. Without speaking, he moved until the backs of his knees brushed the bed once more. Then he sat, bringing her down against him. She straddled his lap, and he nuzzled her breasts. "How's your leg? Can you kneel on it?" He closed his lips around her nipple.

"I...ah...I think so. For a few minutes, at least."

He lay back on the bed and gripped her hips. "Come on up here."

She looked down at him. The corner of her lip curled into a smirk.

"What did you have in mind?"

"Thought I'd settle that debt." He tugged on her hips and guided her 'til she kneeled over his face, straddling his head as she'd done his lap. Her body felt tense under his hands. "Is this okay?"

"I've never, um...done it like this before."

"Lean forward and grab the headboard. Take a little weight off that leg."

There was a pause as he waited to see if she'd do it. He might be the one on the bottom at the moment, but this position left her vulnerable, and he knew it.

After a few seconds, her weight shifted forward. "All right," she said, sounding unsure.

He moved his hands inward 'til he could spread her apart with his thumbs. "Going to touch you now."

He pressed the flat of his tongue on her clit and held it there, feeling her quiver. Then he slid it down, using the tip to flick at her entrance and then work itself inside. The taste of her...what he'd been wanting for weeks. He felt her swell and grow wet against his mouth. Her pelvis trembled within the span of his hands.

"Noah, please." And if his cock hadn't been hard enough to break bricks before, the choked little sob in her voice...Jesus, what he wouldn't do to be with her all the time. Come home to her every night—or have her come home to him. He wasn't picky about how it might work.

He repositioned his hands so he could hold her open and exposed to his mouth, while sliding his fingers inside her. So slick and hot on his hand...he tried not to remember how she'd felt on his cock. Tried not to want it again. Because this was for her.

He slid his tongue into her, alongside the fingers still buried deep, then out again to lick a slow line up to her clit. Her breathing came harsh and fast, and he heard the headboard creak under her hands as she rocked against his mouth. He sucked at her, feeling her swell and pulse, and when she spoke, it sounded like she'd gargled with ground glass.

"Noah, I can't...I need..."

He moved his hands to her hips once more. She released the headboard and shimmied backward 'til she was poised over him. She grabbed his cock to steady it, lifted herself high on her knees and sank down, encasing him.

He groaned, and the sound vibrated in the tension between them. The look on her face—eyes half-closed and mouth half-open—made him want to flip her onto her back and pound into her, like he'd done on her kitchen floor. She braced her hands on his chest and moved her body in an undulating roll that started at her hips and worked its way up her spine. And then she did it again.

Pleasure shot through him like a misfired flare, lighting him up and burning every nerve ending on its way back down his spine. She kept moving, faster now, with her head thrown back and the long line of her throat striped with shadows. Her fingertips bit into his chest, and her arms began to shake. He twisted his hands in the bedspread, clenched every muscle below his waist to keep from letting go too soon, and held on.

"Erin...tell me you're close." He barely recognized the guttural growl of his voice.

She opened her eyes and looked down at him. "Need to feel you on me. All over me."

Thank God he'd rented a room with a king-sized bed. He grabbed her around the waist and rolled them, feeling her ankles hook behind his hips. He caught her hands in his and pushed them above her head, and with his toes digging into the carpet past the foot of the bed, he gave her all he had.

He felt her hands spasm where their fingers were entwined. Then came the heat and the way her inner muscles closed around him, pulling him in and holding him tight. She spoke his name, and that was it for him. Bliss crackled and popped and melted his mind. His primordial, reptilian brain took over, and it was all yes-more-now-fuck...'til it was just black and warm and heavy drawing of breath into starved lungs.

"You all right?" she whispered, and shifted under him.

He moved off her with a mumbled apology. Because he didn't weigh two-twenty and couldn't possibly be crushing her or anything. Jesus, what a selfish son of a bitch he was. He'd meant to offer her comfort. That's what this had been about—giving her something after all the taking he'd done. But her touch found every wound and raw place, and soothed them somehow.

They lay together for a while. He nuzzled her shoulder. "Love your skin. So smooth."

She scrunched her nose. "Freckles.

"Mmm. Freckles good. Freckles pretty."

"You're crazy."

"Nope. Freckles are a sign of profound beauty. Bet yours aren't even skin deep. Bet they go all the way down to your soul."

She laughed and kissed him, letting her lips linger against his. "Noah, we really need to talk about—"

"No, we really don't."

Her soft smile dissolved. She looked away.

"We don't need to talk about it," he said, "because you're already so good at talking people out of doing stupid, self-destructive things."

She turned to stare at him again. "What're you saying?"

"I'm saying you're right. I'm not a murderer, and I don't want to become one."

She sat up and pulled the sheet to cover her breasts. "When did you decide this?"

"Does it matter? And I was serious about talking people out of bad shit. You ever consider becoming a probation officer? Maybe a social worker?"

She scrubbed a hand over her face and ran it through her damp hair in an obvious gesture of frustration. "One thing at a time. I want to know—"

"All you need to know is that, when you leave tomorrow morning, you can take the gun. Throw it in the river. The clips, too."

"But what about Trip? You've been planning this so long, how can you just...let it go?"

He tucked his hands behind his head and grinned at her. "I'm pretty sure my girlfriend won't marry a convicted killer. And anyway, I hear conjugal visits suck."

Her eyes got big. "Marry? First you're picking out my next career, now you're planning a wedding?"

He waggled his eyebrows at her. "We can get Carradine's to cater."

"You're insane. Just please...admit it. You've lost your mind."

"That's what happens when you fuck a guy's brains out. They tend to get misplaced." He pulled her down against him and held her close. "Don't worry. We'll look for 'em in the morning. Now it's time to sleep."

CHAPTER 5

February

Erin watched Noah doze. The slow rise and fall of his chest beneath her hand was a sharp contrast to her own panicked panting. She curled against him in the half-light and waited for the lingering effects of the nightmare to pass.

The glowing alarm clock on the bedside table said it was five in the morning on the thirtieth day of what Noah kept calling their "engagement"—a full month after the first time they'd made love in this motel room. Twenty-nine days past the big confrontation with Suzie, when they informed her—as gently as possible—of their status as a couple. Also the twenty-ninth day since Suzie called Erin a selfish cunt just like her mother, and stopped speaking to her, looking at her, and acknowledging her presence in the house they continued to share.

But a month of hateful silence from her sister had also been a month of Noah's almost-constant company. Of long strolls down slushy sidewalks by the river, and dinners made out of leftovers from Carradine's kitchen. Of hours in bed spent talking and laughing and making fireworks rocket up and down each other's spines. Sometimes she thought she'd singe her fingertips on the heat between them. Other times she wondered if she'd gotten lost in a fantasy and was even now drooling away her days on a psych ward somewhere.

It took ten days for that sensation of unreality to fade. After the second full week, she stopped looking over her shoulder and waiting for the other shoe to drop. At the end of the third week, she quit telling Noah to shut up when he mentioned a wedding.

And today? Today, when the sun finally rose, they'd be looking at studio apartments. Because as fond as she'd become of this ratty little room, it was time to trade up to something with a kitchenette and maybe two whole closets.

Which was why the bad dream took her by surprise. In it, she'd been alone on the bridge that spanned the river on the south side of town. She'd been holding Noah's automatic and the box of clips wrapped in a motel sheet, just as she had in the pre-dawn hours after he proposed marriage...the first time. Standing just out of the glow cast by the streetlight, waiting until there were no cars on the bridge to drop the weapon and its ammo. A symbolic gesture—totally unnecessary. They might have sold the gun. God knew they could've used the cash.

But Noah wanted it gone. Wanted no part of it—even the money it might bring—and she could get behind that sentiment. A new start. One that didn't include revenge fantasies or morbid obsessions with the past.

Except in the dream, she wasn't alone as she'd been on that morning a month ago. Someone was with her, standing just out of sight, where the shadows were thickest. And when Erin held the bundle over the railing and let it fall, that someone threw herself off the bridge. Screamed Erin's name as she fell.

"Hm? Erin? You okay?"

She turned and found Noah staring at her with dazed and dilated eyes. He ran a hand through his tousled hair. "What's wrong?"

"Nothing. Go back to sleep."

He blinked at her. "You sure?"

"Yes." She lifted her hand and pressed her palm to his face.

"Christ, you're freezing. Come here." He sat up and pulled the blankets more snugly around her. "Better?"

"Yeah. Thanks." The dream was already fading. Suzie's cry no longer echoed in her head. The two splashes—first a small one, then another, larger one as her sister's body hit the rushing water—were nothing but memories.

But even in sleep, the sense of impending disaster circled like a bird of prey, ever closer.

* * *

SIN STREET

They were leaving the third prospective apartment, debating the need for air conditioning and a garbage disposal versus off-street parking, when Erin's cell rang.

"Hey. It's me." Suzie sounded subdued, but that might've been her imagination. "Can we talk?"

"Right now? I'm kind of in the middle of—"

"Come to the house." A little louder now. A little edge in her tone. "I need to see you."

"Why? You think of some more nasty names to call me? Because you can do that over the phone."

"Please." Despite the polite language, it didn't sound so much like a request.

Erin sighed. "Fine. I have to pick up a few more boxes of my stuff anyway. I'll be there in an hour."

"Make it thirty minutes, and come alone."

"Don't push your luck, Suzie." She closed the phone and pinched the bridge of her nose.

"What does she want?"

She glanced up at Noah's frown. "She didn't say. You're going to be late for work."

"You shouldn't go alone."

She shrugged. "I have to face her again sometime. Besides, I want the rest of my stuff before she decides to give it to the Salvation Army or something."

"I don't understand why you put up with…" He let whatever he'd been about to say trail off into a testy grumble. "Whatever. I'll see you after work."

They parted with a kiss, and Noah took off down the street in the direction of Carradine's, leaving Erin with the car.

She found the front door standing ajar, which was a little odd, but not completely outside the realm of "normal" for her sister, who could be an airhead when she wasn't being a spoiled brat. Sometimes she managed to pull off both at once. Always a treat.

"Suzie?" The foyer was dark, as was the living room. "Suzie, where are you?"

Silence. But an unsettling buzz of tension in the air made her head for the second floor. Something was wrong here. Maybe Suzie was sick, or maybe what Erin was feeling was all the leftover familial dysfunction that had built up in the corners and crevices over the long years. If anything could haunt a house, it would be the kind of bullshit that had gone down within these walls.

Erin sighed and started up the stairs. What she really wanted to do was go back to the motel and take a nice, long nap, so she'd be fresh when Noah got home from work. Not likely if Suzie wanted another pound of flesh. Being called a thieving whore tended to disrupt her sleep cycles for days.

She reached the top of the stairs and made her way down the dim hall. What was with the lack of light anyway? Did Suzie forget to pay the electric bill again?

"Stop right there." Not Suzie's voice. Deeper, male, familiar... *Trip Carlisle.*

Erin started, her hand instinctively going for the gun that would never again be holstered on her hip. "Trip? What's going on? Where's—"

"Don't turn around. Stand there, and keep your hands where I can see them."

Okay, this had to be a joke. "Trip, what—"

"I said, don't turn around, bitch!"

The blow caught her just behind her left ear and knocked her into the wall. She bounced off the plaster and dropped to one knee, more out of habit than anything else. Basic training: when under fire or attack, get down. The ringing pain in her head didn't register as strongly as the thought that Suzie wasn't in the house—or if she was, she was being far too quiet for comfort.

"Suze?" Her voice echoed throughout the relatively empty second floor. So many rooms devoid of furniture that had been sold to pay the Melinda's doctor and hospital bills...

A hand gripped her hair and hauled her back to her feet. "Man, you really don't know when to shut up, do you?" He twisted his fist, pulling her around to face him. Even in the barely-there glow provided by the streetlight outside the window at the end of the hall, she could see the high color in Trip's cheeks, and the glassy, almost feverish gleam in his eyes.

Stoned off his ass. Of course...because there's no better party than a coke-head with a gun.

"Trip—"

"Shut. Up." He pressed the muzzle of the pistol—smaller than the one she'd tossed over the bridge, but no less deadly—into her cheek. "This is what we're gonna do. We're gonna go into Suzie's bedroom and you're gonna call that asshole Noah and tell him to get over here."

"He can't. He's working."

"Then I guess you'll have to be persuasive, won't you?" He pushed her, and she stumbled toward the bedroom. "I know you can do it. You managed to get him to quit sniffing around Suzie. I should probably thank you for that, huh? You must give great head. A real demon in the sack. Right, big sister?" He shoved her through the doorway of the bedroom and onto the flower-printed quilt that covered Suzie's bed.

"Where's Suzie? Have you got her tied up somewhere?" Warm, wet blood had begun to run down her neck from where he'd hit her. He must've used the butt of the gun to do it, the nasty son of a bitch.

"Don't you worry about Suzie." He laughed, and the muzzle jiggled against her cheek. "You think if she was here, she'd lift a finger to help you? Man, she hates you, Erin. Goes on and on about it. What did you do to her anyway?"

Suzie's voice, high and sweet and dripping with poison, answered from the doorway of the bedroom. "She left me all alone with a crazy person. And she never came back until it was way, way too late."

Trip started. The pistol's muzzle slid from Erin's cheek to settle against the spot just beneath her jaw. When he spoke, his voice shook. "I thought I told you to stay away for a few hours."

"I know what you said. Nobody tells me to stay away from my own house."

That's my girl. Sassy, stubborn...and stupid. "You should go, Suzie. Trip and I have some stuff to work out."

"Right." Her sister moved into the room. "Because leaving you alone with my boyfriend worked out so well for me last time."

Erin ground her teeth together and tried to fight back the deeply ingrained urge to defend herself. It was a losing battle. "Noah was never your boyfriend, Suze. You didn't want him. Let it go already."

"Yeah, you'd like that, wouldn't you?" Suzie's eyes were cold and hard with dislike, like frozen pebbles at the bottom of the river.

"Cut the shit, you two," Trip said, his voice back under control. He pointed at Erin. "You. Call Noah. Do it now."

"What if I refuse? You'll shoot me? Blow my brains all over the bed?"

Trip's eyelid twitched. "Maybe."

"You don't have the balls."

The second blow from the butt of the pistol caught her over her left eye. She didn't see stars—she saw planets. Big, rotating suckers, with their own moons and satellites. Her breath exploded outward. Copper flooded her mouth from the spot where her teeth had sunk deep into her tongue. She fought to keep her head above a wave of dizzy darkness.

Trip pulled her upright from where she'd fallen against the mattress. "You believe me now, cop? Do you?"

Suzie's voice drifted over her. "Don't knock her out, Trip. We need her conscious."

"Right. Sorry."

Erin opened her eyes and watched her sister move toward the big, walk-in closet on the other side of the room. "I'm going to pack a bag now. For later. When we leave."

Forcing the words over a swelling tongue, Erin said, "Oh, you guys are going somewhere? A little vacation, just you and Trip?"

Trip lifted the gun and used the muzzle to tap the sore spot just above her eye. The pain made her flinch.

"That's enough with the smart talk, cop. Pick up the phone and dial."

"Why? What are you going to do when Noah gets here?"

Trip didn't so much smile as bare his teeth at her. "We're going to have a little chat about his dearly departed girlfriend. And if your boy can't be reasonable and forget all about his little vendetta, he's going to find himself in a world of hurt. I know people who can make him disappear." The blond man's face twisted, making him look years older and decades more sinister. "Or maybe I'll just do the job myself."

She turned her head to look at Suzie. "You told him about Noah's girlfriend? Why would you do that?"

Her sister shrugged. "What's the point of eavesdropping if I can't use the information?"

This was all getting way out of hand. "Trip, I can tell you for a fact that Noah has no intention of giving you any trouble over what happened with Katie."

"You can tell me that for a fact, huh? Pardon me for being a skeptic, but I'd prefer to hear it from him. Make the call."

Shit, shit...and shit again. There was no way this was turning out well. What she wouldn't give to have her service revolver at hand—or even that automatic of Noah's she'd pitched over the side of the bridge.

"And then what?" She tried to make her voice soothing, but it came out with an obvious edge of frustration. "If he says he'll keep his mouth shut, then what, Trip? You'll believe him? Or you'll kill him anyway?"

Trip shrugged. "I guess we'll see."

"Right. Well, you'll have to kill me too, won't you? And Suzie?

What makes you think you'll get away with that?"

Suzie came up behind Trip and laid a hand on his shoulder. "He won't have to kill me. I know the meaning of loyalty. Unlike some people."

Without taking his eyes off Erin's face, Trip reached up and patted Suzie's hand. "I'll get away with it. I always get away with it, don't I?"

"But—"

"No more, Erin. Make the call, or I'll blow you away now and get Suzie to do it. Which would make her an accessory, and you don't want that, do you?"

Suzie was already up to her neck in it, but what was the point of saying that out loud? Erin reached for the phone. It felt cold and hard in her hand.

Noah's cell rang and rang, finally dumping into voicemail. She left a message asking him to come to the house right away. Telling him it was an emergency. He'd check his messages on his next break. She knew that—he always did, and he always returned her calls. Which gave her less than an hour to turn this situation around so no blood was shed tonight. Unless it was Carlisle blood, in which case...no great loss.

She took a deep breath, preparing to try once more to talk reason and sense into Trip's thick, drug-addled brain. But even as she started to speak, there came the sound of the front door bursting open and Noah's voice shouting her name.

"Answer him," Trip said and pulled her off the bed by her hair.

"Why? So you can kill him? I don't think so, asshole."

Trip's face contorted with rage. He didn't waste time striking her face or head, but went straight for her injured leg, kicking it viciously, twice and then once again. Agony shot through her, and she crumpled to the bedroom floor, gagging. Suzie made a soft sound, but Erin couldn't tell if it came from pain or satisfaction.

"Answer him, or I swear to God I'll go downstairs and take him out where he stands."

She looked up into Trip's face and saw that he was just as insane as he sounded. Gritting her teeth against the pain, she dragged herself across the carpet to the bedroom doorway. When she reached it, she leaned against the doorframe and called, "I'm here, Noah. Upstairs."

Then she pressed her face into the wood and prayed.

After that, things happened fast. Faster than the seconds between the twelve-year-old putting the stolen sedan into the ditch and jumping out of the driver's seat to face her. Faster than her shouted warning to the kid, identifying herself as a cop and telling him to put down his weapon. Faster than her instantaneous choice between go-on-shoot-him-that's-a-gun-in-his-hand and stop-wait-that's-gotta-be-a-toy-and-you-don't-want-to-hurt-a-little-kid-do-you?

And over it all was the shrieking agony in her leg, making her stomach roll and her vision gray out. It told her Trip had done some real damage, but what did it matter since she was about to watch Noah die?

Footsteps pounded on the stairs. Trip shouted at Noah to freeze. Noah yelled back, calling Erin's name. The room spun as she fought to stay conscious. The next thing she heard was the gunshot...

Loud, making her ears pop and crackle. The scent of burnt cordite in the air assaulted her, which...not Trip's pistol then, because...

Erin opened her eyes and tried to focus. In the hall lay Trip, facedown. The back of his head was...gone.

She closed her eyes, leaned over, and let the nausea have its way. The movement made her leg sing with pain, but she endured it long enough to rid herself of everything in her stomach. Slowly, ever so slowly, the sickly mist cleared from her mind and the world righted itself. Even the throbbing in her leg receded a bit. When she pulled herself upright again, Noah was crouched next to her, his hand on her back, rubbing gentle circles. He crooned nonsense into her ear, his voice broken. When she looked at him, she saw his face was streaked with tears.

He reached up and touched the bloodied mark above her eye. "We need to get you to the hospital."

She blinked at him. "What...how did..." She looked past him, to where Suzie was sitting on the floor with her back against the closet door. Next to her was her own puddle of vomit. On her very pale, very still face was a look of profound shock.

Across her lap lay a rifle. The last one—the very last from their father's collection. The only one they hadn't sold. The one Melinda had insisted they keep loaded and ready at all times. For protection, she'd said. At the time, Erin had thought her aunt-slash-stepmother was beyond paranoid.

"What're you smiling about?" Noah asked.

She shook her head. "Nothing. Suzie?"

"Yeah." Her sister's voice sounded flat. Dead. Scary in its utter lack of emotion. And she didn't meet Erin's eyes. Just kept staring straight ahead, at nothing.

"You called Noah, didn't you? Before you came back to the house?"

"What if I did?" Okay, that was better. Not so lifeless. More of the bratty little sister she knew and loved.

"And that whole thing about packing to leave town with Trip? That was an act?"

Suzie shrugged. "I needed a good reason to be messing around in the closet."

"You're a genius. And a hell of an actress."

"Nice of you to notice."

"And the bit about the eavesdropping? More Academy-award-winning performance?"

"No. I fucked up." Suzie looked at her then. "I was so pissed off at you. I wanted to punish you—both of you. But I didn't expect Trip to turn into a homicidal maniac."

Noah's frown was awesome to behold. "Can we do this later? After we call the cops and get you both checked out by doctors, maybe?"

Erin looked up at him and smiled. "I love you, Noah."

He started as if she'd slapped him. His frown softened. "I love you, too."

Across the room, Suzie snorted. "Oh, for Christ's sake. Somebody dial 911 already."

Erin laughed, then winced as the tiny vibrations woke up the pain in her leg. "Speaking of which, why didn't you do that earlier? When you called Noah?"

Suzie shrugged again. "Trip was insane, but he was right about one thing—he always managed to get away with it. I thought it was time someone took him out of the equation permanently."

Noah turned his head and looked at Suzie over his shoulder. "Then why call me at all, if you planned to use the rifle on him?"

"I figured you had a right to see him die, after what he did to your girlfriend." Suzie set the rifle aside, hauled herself off the floor, and moved toward the beside table.

As her sister was reaching for the phone, Erin said, "Wait. This could be construed as premeditated murder. We need to get our story straight. You especially, Suzie."

Suzie smiled then. It was the first genuine expression Erin could remember seeing on her sister's face in a long time. "Don't worry. If there's one thing I know, it's how to play defenseless and dumb."

"I'm sorry I doubted you. I mean, I really believed..." Erin felt her throat tighten.

Suzie's smile faded. "You really believed I'd let that jackass kill you? Or the guy you love?" She ran a hand through her black hair and sighed. "I don't hate you that much, Erin."

Noah leaned down and pressed a kiss to the top of Erin's head. "I guess that's a start."

CHAPTER 6

August

They lay together on the lawn in back of the house, long after twilight. The damp air, full of the chirp of crickets and the buzz of fat mosquitoes, made everything slow and achy. Like a bad hangover.

Noah curled himself around Erin's body and tucked his face into the curve of her neck, where the scents of clean sweat and cut grass mingled and mixed. When he leaned up and kissed her, he tasted the beer they'd shared after dinner. He managed to open the top button of her faded denim shorts and work one hand halfway inside, wondering if they could get away with a quickie in the gathering dusk...

A door slammed, breaking his concentration. He looked up to see Suzie on the back porch swing.

"Don't mind me. I promise not to watch. Or sell tickets."

Erin's laughter vibrated his palm where it was pressed against the curve of her belly. He pulled his hand free and flipped over to hide the obvious bulge in his shorts. He tried not to sigh. Or frown. It was an effort.

God love her, but Suzie could be a pain in the ass. Living with her through the past six months, in the same house, sharing kitchen privileges and two tiny bathrooms? It hadn't been easy. Especially at first, when the investigation into Trip's death had nearly overwhelmed her already wobbly emotional health. Nearly overwhelmed all three of them, to be fair. The weeks it had taken for the district attorney to come to the conclusion of "justifiable homicide" had been some of the longest of his life, if only because watching Erin suffer right alongside her sister had nearly killed him.

Erin yanked up her shorts and pulled down her T-shirt. Then she leaned back on her elbows and said, "You're going out tonight?"

Suzie rocked the swing. The chains that fixed it to the roof creaked, and Noah thought about getting a ladder. Getting up there with an oilcan and taking care of that rusty squeak.

Maybe tomorrow.

"Thinking about it," Suzie answered. "There's a party at Delta Sig."

He felt Erin stiffen next to him. She sat up fully, stretching her bad leg in its hard, black brace out in front of her. "You think that's a good idea? A lot of people there knew Trip."

Suzie shrugged. "It's a good way to figure out who's my friend and who isn't. And I can't avoid them forever. Classes start next week." She brought the swing to a halt and stood. "Speaking of which—"

"Yeah, yeah, I know. I'm going to see the registrar tomorrow."

Noah could barely make out Suzie's face in the darkness, but when she spoke, he could hear the smirk in her voice. "My sister, the social worker wannabe. Gonna save the world, Erin?"

"Go play in traffic, brat."

Suzie's laughter echoed through the yard even after the back door slammed behind her. Erin settled down next to him again. He reached up and traced her profile with his index finger, stopping to count the freckles that dotted her nose. She turned and smiled at him.

"Let's go to bed."

He pressed himself against her. "You sleepy?"

"No." The devil in her eyes grinned at him and made him dizzy from the way all the blood in his body suddenly rushed southward.

The next thing he knew with any clarity was Erin's hands at his hips, pulling him down onto the bed. He couldn't have said where their clothes had landed. Down the hall, the shower turned on with a thud and a bang in the old pipes. He knew Suzie was good for twenty minutes under the spray, which meant they could afford to be loud if they moved fast.

Erin's skin was damp and cool under his hands. Sweat from his too-long hair dripped onto the pillow next to her head as he parted her legs around his hips and eased himself inside. The current that arced between them—wherever they were, whatever they were doing—flared hot and bright. The heat, the anticipation, the thick pleasure of knowing it didn't have to end. That he didn't have to leave when they were done. That they could fuck or make love or whatever she wanted, however she wanted it, for as long as he could stay conscious.

She urged him on, her nails scrabbling at the skin stretched taut over his shoulder blades.

"No," he whispered. "Slow. Like this." He pulled back, easy and smooth, and pushed inside again. And again, and one more time. She moaned his name.

He slid his hands beneath her and lifted 'til they sat intertwined. "Shh. I've got you."

She worked the muscles in her thighs, strengthened from months of physical therapy. Rising and falling. Levering up and down, and he let her go. Let her find her own pace and ride it out. Whatever she wanted, whatever she needed, forever and ever amen. All he could think—all he knew, from the top of his brain to the bottom of his soul was Christ-almighty-hot-tight-good. And home. So much home, inside of her.

The space between them was all heat and salty sweat, making it hard to slide his hand against her and touch...press...drag his fingertips in a slow circle and touch...

She gasped and closed down tight around him. He made some random sound, raw and choked off, and she laughed. She came that way, laughing and shivering and laughing some more. He followed her in hot-slick bursts and with more incoherent noises he'd deny later, if she'd let him.

They fell back onto the mattress. "Now," she whispered against his chest, "now, I'm sleepy."

He waited 'til she'd drifted off to slide off the bed and into his clothes. As he left the room, he looked down and saw the faint outline of the bloodstain on the hall floor—entirely imaginary, since Suzie had replaced that carpet months ago. But he could make it out, as clear as it ever was, because he all-too-often relived the moment he'd reached the top of the stairs and saw Erin slumped in the doorway, her face contorted with fear and pain. Trip standing over her, his gun in his hand. Suzie behind him, the rifle aimed at his head. The bitter panic of those ten endless seconds would abide forever somewhere in the back of his throat.

He found Suzie in the kitchen, switching her wallet and cell phone from one tiny black purse to another. He opened the fridge and pulled out a beer. "Be careful tonight, okay? You need a ride?"

She rolled her eyes at him. "What I don't need is another over-protective older sibling. Speaking of which..." She opened her compact and checked her makeup, then closed it and dropped it into the bag. "When are you going to make an honest woman of my sister?"

He froze, the bottle halfway to his mouth. "I...uh."

"I'm thinking October for the wedding. Something small and tasteful." She shut the purse with a snap and slung it over her shoulder. "And I hope you have at least one decent-looking friend I can hook up with. I'm not getting any younger, after all."

He set the bottle on the counter. "Erin and I haven't talked about it in a long time. Not since...well. You know."

Suzie stepped into the pair of black heels that sat next to her on the tile floor and reached for the jacket draped over a nearby stool. "Ask her again. I think she'll say yes."

"Why d'you say that?"

Suzie shrugged. "Sisters know these things. Plus, I found this in the trash upstairs." From beneath the jacket, she pulled a blue and white box. She held it up so he could read the words printed across the front: EARLY PREGNANCY TEST. "You'd think a pair of smart, mature grown-ups like you two would be able to read the directions on a box of condoms, but apparently not."

"Holy shit." A grin split his face so wide it made his cheeks cramp.

Suzie laughed. "I take it this means you're up for being a daddy." He advanced on her, and a look of uncertainty crossed her pretty face. "Noah, what..."

He enveloped her in a hug that swung her off her feet. His laughter boomed off the walls, no doubt echoing throughout the house. He'd wake Erin if he wasn't careful.

Suzie squeaked in his arms. "Noah, Goddamn it, put me down!"

He looked at her, sudden worry twisting his gut. This might be the best news he'd ever heard—and he was pretty damn sure he'd find Erin felt the same way—but maybe Suzie had a different opinion. The last thing they needed was another wedge between the sisters. "You're okay with this, Suze? You're not gonna go all freaky-bad-seed again, are you?"

She wrinkled her nose at him. "Thanks for the vote of confidence. I'll have you know I intend to be a very cool aunt."

He set her on her feet and tried to restrain the urge to offer up a high five that would've knocked her on her little ass. "Erin's gonna kill you for telling me. You know that, right?"

Suzie made a grab for her jacket. "Only if you squeal, big brother."

SIN STREET

With a flip of her hair over her shoulder, she sauntered away from him.

"And when you get around to talking weddings, mention how beautiful she'd look in a simple ivory gown. I could wear a green maid of honor's dress. I look hot in green."

He listened for the slam of the front door that signaled Suzie's departure. Then he picked up the box she'd left on the counter and headed for the stairs. It might be hours before Erin woke—she might even sleep until morning.

That was fine. He'd keep watch, lying beside her in the moonlight, thinking up names for fat babies with red hair and hazel eyes, and counting the freckles that were like beauty marks on her soul.

SIN STREET

LIE TO ME

CHAPTER 1

The worst three days of my life began with a death threat meant for somebody else, and ended in a hail of gunfire. In between, I managed to squeeze some of the hottest, dirtiest sex I've ever had. Of course, I'm only twenty-nine—not even close to my sexual prime—so there's really nowhere to go but up.

And as an extra, added bonus? Like the set of dishes you get for opening a savings account during the month of June? I sort of fell in love. I probably shouldn't skip that part.

It was forty-five minutes past closing time on a Friday. I was flipping through a pile of mail, half-listening to the bank's trio of tellers—Kristy, Gail and Tonia—chatter and giggle through the process of counting the cash and checks in their respective drawers.

"I'm totally serious, you guys. You have to go down to the market and check him out. He's totally like a movie star." Kristy's voice sounded breathless. Her red hair was in its usual disarray, sticking out in several directions at once. On her, it managed to look adorable.

"Ayuh. Brad Pitt or George Clooney?" That was Gail. I knew without looking. Hard to mistake that accent—flat as a board and no-nonsense, like everything else about her. Still, Gail had her charms.

Kristy laughed, and it was like Tinkerbell had dropped in to visit the lobby of the First National Bank of Port Jonah, Maine. "Neither. Darker, more dangerous. Brooding...like...I dunno...like Joaquin Phoenix."

"Who?" Tonia asked.

SIN STREET

I wasn't surprised she didn't recognize the name. Tonia didn't get out much, and when she did, she usually had at least two of her five kids with her. Kind, quiet Tonia—still waters ran deep there, I always thought.

I smiled to myself at the thought of Joaquin Phoenix working at the local Pick 'N' Save market, and went back to sorting mail. An envelope the size and shape of a greeting card caught my eye. Without turning it over to check the address, I ripped it open. A small, rectangular sheet of white paper slid out onto my blotter. In the center were printed these words:

OUR FRIENDS LIVE TO PROSPER
OUR ENEMIES LIVE NOT AT ALL
BE SMART
BE OUR FRIEND

Beneath the words had been pressed a single thumb-print, in dark, rust-colored blood.

I dropped the paper as if it were on fire and covered my mouth with both hands. I must've made a noise, because the girls up front quit their chatter.

"Everything okay?" Tonia asked.

She looked like she was thinking about coming over, so I rearranged my face and said, "Yeah, sure. You guys almost done? I want to lock up and get out of here." I guess my tone was a little sharper than I meant it to be because Tonia frowned and backed away. *Damn.*

I tucked the blood-stained note back into its envelope and flipped it over. It was addressed to the bank's branch manager, Regina James—a fact that made me feel only marginally less nauseated. I stood there and thought about my next move...and decided there was no point in getting upset over what was probably just a sick joke. I stuck the whole nasty mess under my blotter, resolving to deal with it the following morning, when Regina was due to return from her brief vacation.

I pasted my best assistant manager smile into place and approached the tellers. "Did everything add up?"

"Here you go." Kristy passed me her tape, which proved that her daily receipts matched the cash and checks in her drawer. Tonia and Gail did the same, without comment. They eyed me as if at any moment I might do something totally inappropriate—like curse them

SIN STREET

out or start throwing things.

For the thousandth time I wished I could start over from scratch with these women. But I'd blown my chance to make friends back when I was hired as a teller. They'd learned to avoid me then, writing me off as a cold, snotty bitch, and only warming to me by degrees in the intervening two-and-a-half years. I still had a long way to go.

I sighed. "Thanks, ladies. Gail, I think you have company."

A face was pressed against the bank's big glass storefront. It was attached to the huge, hulking body that belonged to the local lobsterman known as Davy Moran. Gail laughed, rolled her eyes and waved at the big man. "Ayuh. What can I say? He gets impatient."

A grin split Davy's sweet, bland features, and he returned the wave. Kristy handed Gail her coat and bag, and gave her a playful shove in the direction of the door. "Don't keep the man waiting."

Gail let herself out, and we watched through the window as Davy swept her into a hug that nearly obliterated her from view.

"Doesn't look like he even bothered to change out of his gear." Tonia turned and smiled at me and Kristy. "She's gonna smell like a lobster all weekend."

Kristy shrugged. "Gail won't care. She's Davy's girl, no two ways about it."

They gathered up their things and prepared to leave the bank. I waited around to lock up behind them, looking out the window at the gathering spring twilight and thinking about what Kristy had said. *Gail was Davy's girl.* Tonia had her husband and kids—she, too, was somebody's girl. And Kristy herself, so pretty and sweet and never at a loss for dates, would soon enough hook up on a permanent basis.

I, on the other hand, was nobody's girl. And I never would be, not ever again.

I was fine with that, mostly. That's the way things had turned out— the way it had to be. Nobody's fault but my own. It sucked, but I could take it. Life is hard, buy a helmet, right?

"See you tomorrow, MJ," Kristy said. There was a pause as she waited for me to respond.

I turned from the window and smiled at her and Tonia...sort of. I'm pretty sure whatever moisture may or may not have collected in the corners of my eyes was not visible from the other side of the room. "Have a good night, ladies."

Kristy looked at me. I looked at her. She nodded and let herself and Tonia out the front door of the bank.

SIN STREET

I locked the door behind them, double-checked the vault, turned off all the lights and equipment, and exited through the back door. Then I headed for the Pick 'N' Save to buy myself some dinner. On the way, I tried not to let stray thoughts of the note with the bloody thumb-print ruin my appetite.

* * *

The Pick 'N' Save lot was crowded—not unusual for late on a Friday. I parked my little black VW on the far side, under a row of pines, where the light from the early evening sun didn't make much of a dent in the shadows. Composing a quick shopping list in my head, I grabbed a cart and pushed it through the automatic doors.

Familiar faces, familiar voices, all of them friendly. A crowd of folks I'd called my neighbors for three years, but not a soul I could call more than a nodding acquaintance. And why was I all of a sudden feeling so sorry for myself anyway? I scooted past the deli and the bakery, turned a corner and nearly plowed into a group of five women arrayed in a semi-circle around a display of beefsteak tomatoes and seedless cucumbers. Trapped between the women and the veggies stood a dark-haired man in a full-length red apron over a white button-down shirt and jeans. He was a stranger to me—obviously, the new assistant manager of whom Kristy had spoken in such glowing terms. I checked him out as discreetly as I could while eavesdropping on the conversation in progress and pretending to peruse a nearby selection of strawberries.

"So what brings you to our neck of the woods, Mr. Donnelly?" That was Marie St. Clare, wife of Port Jonah's mayor and the local one-woman Welcome Wagon. Nice lady, don't get me wrong. Just comes on a little strong sometimes.

I watched out of the corner of my eye as the new meat—pardon me, the new assistant manager—kept right on unloading his box of cukes. After a moment of silence, he cleared his throat. "I came to Port Jonah for the wild nightlife." His voice was deep and his delivery slow, with the just the slightest edge of irony.

Candy Beecham, a plump matron of fifty, piped right up, hitting notes that could've shattered glass. "The wild nightlife! What wild nightlife? We're a quiet little town!"

The mystery man in the red apron shrugged and looked over the heads of the gathered women to meet my eyes. He smiled, and there was nothing slight about the irony this time. "I was misinformed."

I couldn't help it. I laughed right out loud, startling the collected matrons. They scattered like crows, in several directions at once, and I was left alone in the produce section with the only man I'd ever met who could quote *Casablanca* without falling back on the ever-popular "We'll always have Paris" or—God forbid—"Here's lookin' at you, kid."

"I'm Drew Donnelly." He wiped his hand on his apron and held it out for me to shake. I almost missed the gesture, so busy was I staring at his face. Even without the Irish name, you couldn't miss the Celtic coloring. All that unruly dark hair framing those rugged, melancholy features. But Kristy had been right—there was nothing pretty-boy-Pitt or suave-man-of-the-world-Clooney about this guy. "Brooding" and "dangerous" were excellent descriptions, but I would have added "edgy," and maybe "damaged" to the list. And his eyes…a subtle, shifting gray that made me think of troubled waters.

I closed my mouth, which had somehow fallen open without my noticing. Clearly, I was the one in trouble here, and the sooner I made a graceful exit, the better for everyone concerned.

I squeezed his hand once and dropped it like it was on fire. "MJ Peters. Nice to meet you," I mumbled. "Gotta go now."

He nodded, looking very grave. "Okay. 'Bye."

I turned my cart a hundred and eighty degrees and moved in the opposite direction as fast as dignity would allow. Call me conceited, but I swear I could feel him looking at my ass as I walked away.

All things considered, not an unpleasant sensation.

CHAPTER 2

Don't ask me what foodstuffs I threw into the cart. I spent the next twenty minutes keeping my eyes peeled for Mr. Red Apron and not paying much attention to whether I'd spend the weekend dining on tuna garnished with dog biscuits and drain cleaner. Much to my relief, he was nowhere in evidence. I made it all the way out to my car, and had one overstuffed paper sack tucked under my arm and the other wedged between my hip and fender while I dug in my purse for my keys. That's when I heard his voice.

"You shouldn't park way over here in the dark." He eased the sack from between me and the car, his face lost in the shadows. "It's not safe."

I unlocked the trunk, took the bag from him and set the groceries inside. "You are new in town, aren't you? There's nowhere in Port Jonah that isn't safe, any time of the day or night." I slammed the trunk and faced him. "If you're looking for danger, you came to the wrong place."

His teeth flashed in the dim light. "Mostly, I'm looking for something to eat, and somebody to eat it with."

"Sorry. I'm on my way home."

"Good. I get off work in an hour." He moved half a step closer. The skin on my arms prickled. "If you give me your address, I'll pick you up and buy you dinner. You name the place."

I started to shake my head, slowly and deliberately, so he couldn't miss the negative message. Then I stopped. He had me curious. If I

SIN STREET

knew Port Jonah—and I did—every unattached woman in a ten-mile radius had thrown herself into his path today. So why was he asking me to dinner? Because, while I don't need anybody to tell me I'm pretty, I'm still not what you'd call an obvious choice. Not compared to some of the local talent, at least. It made no kind of sense to my tired, Friday-night brain, so I went ahead and asked him. "Why me?"

There was a pause. His eyes narrowed as he considered the question, looking me up and down in my cream silk blouse, tan skirt and brown shoes. Then he shrugged. "Why not you? You got something against dinner?"

I had no answer for that. It had been a long time since I'd let a man feed me. And it didn't have to be a bad thing. Didn't have to be messy or painful or tragic or anything more than a simple meal shared by two strangers. *Did it?*

I saw Marie St. Clare exit the Pick 'N' Save. She made her way to her shiny blue SUV, pushing a cart full of groceries. I watched her watching us, not even pretending to be casual about it. "I'll meet you at Crawford's in an hour. Corner of Congress and State." When I looked at him, he had that grave, somber expression again, like all of this was very important business. "All right?"

"All right," he said. "I'll be there."

Feeling distinctly like I'd been played by a master of the game, I got into my car and drove home.

It took me five minutes to re-stock my cupboards and fridge with the few things I'd picked up. That left forty minutes to ready myself. I shucked my work clothes and took a quick shower—just enough hot water and soap to rid myself of the stink of other people's money.

As I was drying my hair, I checked its roots. *Almost time for a touch-up.* It always seemed to start growing faster when the warm weather threatened, and the quarter-inch of coffee brown showing through what my mother would've called "dishwater blonde" was just obvious enough to bug me. I'd have to spend the following Sunday bleaching it out, along with my eyebrows, for that perfect "natural" look. I checked my medicine cabinet for supplies and made a note to pick up a fresh bottle of 45-strength sunblock to keep my skin looking young and pale and tight. Then I shut the door and stared at my reflection for a few seconds...but what I saw was the note I'd opened and tucked beneath my desk blotter before leaving the bank. The one addressed to Regina. The one with the threatening message and the bloody thumb print. The memory of it was enough to make me want to crawl into bed and pull the covers over my head, and not come out until the sun was bright and shiny and everything felt safe again.

Not that anything had felt safe in a long, long time.

I slipped my blue contacts back into my eyes and applied mascara and a light coating of lipstick. A pair of jeans, a white cotton sweater and tennis shoes finished the ensemble, and I was out the door with ten minutes to spare.

The sun was down, and the air had developed a bite that made me wish I'd worn a jacket. Still, spring was on the rise, no doubt about it. You could smell it, like fruit left to ripen on a sunny window sill, competing with the brine from the sea and the scent of steaming lobster and crab that overpowered everything the closer you got to Crawford's.

The restaurant's lot was even more jammed than the Pick 'N' Save's, but the only vehicle I didn't recognize was the early-70s Triumph motorcycle parked in a corner space, under the eaves. It figured the new mystery man would have to be a biker—one of my very few true weaknesses. I took a moment to check out the machine. He kept it in nice shape. I ran my hand over the seat, imagining what it would be like to feel it purring between my legs.

"You're early."

I opened my eyes. He was standing in the doorway of the restaurant, watching my hand as it moved back and forth. I snatched it away and tucked it into the pocket of my jeans. "Yeah, well, so are you."

He smiled at me all lopsided, and all of a sudden I realized what a really bad idea this had been. This wasn't going to be any simple meal shared by strangers. This was going someplace messy, probably involving bodily fluids, and I was going to be more than a willing participant. If he smiled at me too many more times, I was going to initiate the mess.

"The place is packed, but I got us a table," he said, and turned to go back into the building.

That was my chance. I could've walked away, gone back to my car. Driven home. Eaten frozen pizza and watched a little Pay Per View. Gone to bed early like the virtuous woman I've never been. I thought about it in that split second, when everything teetered like the first domino in the row that's gonna knock them all down in a chain reaction.

I followed him into Crawford's, with my stomach growling and my palms sweating, and sin on my mind.

SIN STREET

* * *

"So what does MJ stand for?"

The lighting in Crawford's is not what you'd call "atmospheric." You could perform surgery by it, in other words. Generally, the glare bothers me, but on that particular evening I was hoping it would make it easier to meet my goal, which was to find fault with my companion.

Something. Anything. A flaw that would give me a reason to reject him.

Mostly, I found myself staring at his eyes. They were, in addition to being the "troubled waters" I'd mentioned before...unique. Unique is a good word. Handy. All-purpose. And Drew Donnelly's eyes, all smoky-greenish-gray with smudgy black rings around the irises, pretty much defined it. Unique, I mean.

And those unique eyes were squinting at me, clearly waiting for some kind of response to his simple query. I swallowed the bite of lobster I had squirreled away in my cheek and tried to do the same with the annoyance I felt rising in my throat. Not his fault I hated answering any kind of remotely personal question.

"MaryJane. And before you ask, I'm originally from Verona, Indiana, where I grew up the only child of Chet, an auto-parts dealer, and Janice, a homemaker. I have an accounting degree that isn't worth the paper it's printed on, and I'm twenty-four years old." There. That should hold him for a while. I took deep swallow of wine in a vain attempt to wash away the bitter flavor of deception. After three years of lying to everyone, all the time, I kept hoping it would get easier. It never did.

"What kind of music do you like?"

I sighed and rolled my shoulders. "Do we really have to do this?"

"What?"

"This...getting-to-know-you portion of our program." I shrugged. "It's not like you're committing the details to memory or anything."

He did that lopsided sort-of-smile, the right corner of his mouth curling up in a way that made my chest hitch in the middle of drawing a breath. "What kind of music do you like, MaryJane from Verona, Indiana, twenty-four-year-old only daughter of auto-parts dealer Chet and homemaker Janice, and holder of an accounting degree that isn't worth the paper it's printed on?"

I stared at him. He stared back. I blinked first. "Contemporary jazz. Light classical. Basically anything without lyrics."

His sort-of smile widened into a full-blown grin. My chest hitched twice more, and my nipples hardened to bullets under my sweater. He reached for his beer and lifted it halfway to his mouth. "Aren't you going to ask anything about me?"

"Huh?"

He took a swig and set the glass on the table. "You're a funny girl, MJ." I was pretty sure he didn't mean funny "ha-ha."

He was still on his first beer. I, on the other hand, was on my second glass of wine. I get stupid when I drink, which is why I so rarely do it.

"Umm...how old are you?" I pulled the question out of the air, just to have something to ask.

"I don't know if I should tell you," he said, and took another sip of beer. "You might decide I'm too old for you."

This? This is where living a life built entirely on lies gets you. Take notes—they could come in handy.

"I doubt that." I fiddled with my napkin. "So...how old?"

"Thirty-five."

I smiled at him. "That's not so bad. I have a brother who's the same age." *Shit.* See? Stupid when I drink. Can't keep my story straight to save my life. Luckily, right about that time, Jimmy Van Zandt ambled up to our booth.

"Hey there, MJ. What's up?" The red-haired, bearded fisherman bared his teeth at me in what I guess was supposed to be a smile, and totally ignored my dinner companion.

"Hello, Jimmy. Drew, this is—"

But Jimmy was already half in the bag and in no mood to meet new people. "So how come you don't return my calls, MJ? How come you hide when I come into the bank to see you?" He bent over me, backing me into the corner of the booth. The charming aromatic combo of dead fish and vodka rose from his canvas jacket. "You ashamed t'be seen with me?"

"Of course not, Jimmy. I just—"

He leaned in closer, as if to whisper in my ear, but his voice only got louder. "You maybe ashamed of how we fucked that time last fall in the back of my truck?"

Conversation around our booth quieted as people turned to stare. I caught Donnelly's eye. He was watching the scene closely, with a careful, guarded look. I shook my head ever so slightly, and he nodded in return. I was grateful he hadn't already gone all protective-caveman at the first sign of trouble. The last thing I needed was more attention.

I placed a hand on Jimmy's shoulder, applying steady, firm pressure, and said in a quiet voice, "Don't be silly, Jim. A girl would have to be an idiot to be ashamed of you."

He blinked at me, slow and woozy, and a shard of guilt lodged itself in my gut. Van Zandt wasn't a bad guy, not by a long stretch. I hadn't meant to hurt him. Who knew that a quick, semi-drunken roll in the back of a pickup would mean so much to him? I let my hair fall in a curtain that hid my face from Donnelly's gaze and stared deep into Van Zandt's bloodshot eyes, calling on that nifty version of the Jedi mind trick I'd learned from watching my mother deal with drunks every night of the week.

Softening my voice to a murmur only he could hear, I said, "I thought you were looking for a nice girl, Jim. We both know you deserve better than what I have to offer. I'm not the woman for you." I made sure to sound sorry about it—and, in a way, I guess I was.

It took a few seconds for the words to sink in. When they did, he backed off a few inches, then straightened and ran a hand over his beard. "Aw, you're not so bad, MJ. You're a nice girl. Sure you are." He grinned when he said it, a genuine smile this time that encompassed me and Donnelly both. He sounded sincere, as if he really believed I was a-okay, and deserved the attentions of a fine, hardworking man like him.

But I knew I'd have no more trouble with Jimmy Van Zandt.

He made some apologetic noises about interrupting our meal and melted back into the crowd. The folks around us resumed their dinner chat as if nothing had happened, though I knew better than to imagine the scene wouldn't be the topic of conversation for days to come.

I took a deep breath and turned to face Donnelly. "Sorry about that."

He shrugged. "Seemed like a nice enough guy."

"Yeah. This town is full of 'em."

A line appeared in the space between his eyebrows. "Not your type?"

"Is what not my type?" I downed the last of my wine and signaled the waitress for another glass. If I was going to be stupid, I figured I might as well go for totally moronic.

"Nice guys."

Whoa. Obviously, I'd unleashed my Sarcastic Voice earlier than I'd intended. "No, of course not. I like nice guys. I like all guys." Okay, now I sounded like a Class-A slut. Not that there was any doubt after the scene with Jimmy."

"That's good to know." He dug into his crab legs and let the matter drop. It was strange how he didn't appear put off by either my bad attitude or the revelation of my liking for casual sex. But maybe he had his own agenda, and it only included dinner and a quick bang.

Fine by me. The waitress brought more wine, and I tried not to guzzle it.

"So," he said when he was done with his crab, "you work at the bank?"

"How did you know that?" I sounded suspicious, but that's how I was feeling. Suspicious and paranoid and very, very punchy.

He looked at me without answering, and I felt stupid. *Of course. No secrets in Port Jonah, not even for the new guy in town.*

"Right," I said. "Assistant branch manager. A year-and-a-half now."

"That's great. You like it?"

I shrugged. "It's okay." No reason to tell him how my job was pretty much my reason for continuing to exist. That was just too pathetic to put into words. "How about you? You like working at the Pick 'N' Save?"

Crap, that came out snotty. Like maybe I thought overseeing the stock-boys and cashiers and making artful displays out of seedless cukes wasn't a worthy occupation.

But he just smiled and slugged back the rest of his beer. "It'll do for now."

This was the part where I was supposed to ask him what he wanted to do with the rest of his life, but frankly, I just wasn't up to making polite chit-chat. The combo of the wine and drone of conversation around us was making my head pound, and every time I closed my eyes, I got a 3-D, full-color peek of that damned note with the bloody thumb-print. Turning away, I reached into my bag to look for some aspirin. That's when another visitor chose to make his appearance at our booth.

"Hello there, Miss MaryJane. Going to introduce me to your friend?"

I flinched at the sound of the voice and looked at Donnelly. He was nodding in the direction of Chief Malcolm McDane of the Port Jonah Police Department. By the way he was setting his napkin aside and preparing to stand, I could tell he intended to shake the older man's hand.

I fixed my face in something approximating a smile and turned. "Chief McDane, this is Drew Donnelly. He's new in town."

McDane took Drew's hand and pumped it, giving him that shrewd once-over every cop masters before he's allowed out of the academy, I guess. With his other hand, he swiped at his own clean-shaven scalp. "Glad to meet you, son. Heard a lot about the handsome new fella in town from my two girls at home." He grinned, his meaty, sunburned cheeks bulging with fake good cheer...or maybe that was just me, being cynical.

"Good to meet you too, sir." Donnelly's voice was polite. Subdued, almost.

McDane settled his fists on his hips. "I guess that's your motorbike parked outside, huh?" As if he had to ask. As if he hadn't already run the plates. I clutched the bottle of aspirin and tried to resist the impulse to throw it at him.

Donnelly nodded. "Yes, sir, it is. I have a license for it, if you'd like to see—"

"Not necessary. I'll just remind you that this is a quiet town, and a machine like that can be a noisy bit of business in the early morning hours." McDane looked at me and squinted. "I'm sure MaryJane here will tell you how the citizens of Port Jonah like their peace and quiet."

I opened my mouth to answer, but nothing came out due to how my windpipe had squeezed shut. My eyes locked on McDane's badge where it winked at me from its place on the breast of his leather jacket. Like a bird mesmerized by a snake's eyes, I couldn't look away to save my life. *Cops.* Never could decide which emotion they inspired more of in me: gut-churning fear or just plain, hard hatred.

Donnelly cleared his throat. "I wouldn't want to disturb anyone, sir."

McDane pulled his gaze away from me and gave a grunt of open disbelief. "I'm sure you wouldn't. But just the same, I'll be keepin' a weather eye on you, if you know what I mean." He grinned again, no more sincere than the first time, and clapped Donnelly on the shoulder. At this rate, I was sure he was going to whip out his dick and start marking territory.

I waited for Donnelly to meet the challenge with a little testosterone-induced alpha male behavior of his own, like any other average, red-blooded, American moron. But when he spoke, his tone was even more polite than before. I had to listen hard to hear the slight, lethal edge beneath his words.

SIN STREET

"I'll be sure to stay out of trouble, sir."

McDane frowned, his big face snarling into a knot of perplexity and skepticism. After a few seconds, he shrugged. "Ayuh. See that you do." Then he was gone. I watched his back as he made his way through the crowd. The buzzing in my head made me want to swat at my ears. My hands felt heavy and numb where they lay in my lap, still curled around the aspirin bottle. All at once, I felt a tugging at my arm.

"Let's go." Donnelly was at my side, pulling me out of my seat. It was the first time he'd actually touched me, and I took a second to explore the sensation before reacting. His hand felt big and warm, and he held my arm like he was aware of exactly how much force he could use without causing discomfort.

"Wait," I said. "Did we pay the—" I looked and saw a roll of bills lying in the center of the table. Probably more than what the meal was worth, including tip. Donnelly was still tugging on me with one hand and waving to the waitress with the other. I tugged back, just on general principle.

"Come on, MJ. Don't make me make a scene."

He knew me well enough already to know I didn't want that. Points for being observant, if nothing else. I stood and discovered—to my surprise—I wasn't quite as loaded as I thought I was. My legs held me up just fine as I slid out of the booth. Donnelly guided me out of the restaurant with one hand on the small of my back, murmuring in my ear the entire time. Don't ask me what he said. Whatever it was, it kept me moving 'til we made the parking lot, and for that I was grateful.

I leaned against the corner of the building, in the dim glow of the streetlights, and sucked in a few lungs full of the cool air. The temperature had dropped, and my breath made clouds of steam. Donnelly stood with his feet planted apart and his arms crossed over his chest, shielding me from the front-door traffic. He said nothing, but his face asked a thousand questions. I figured I owed him at least one answer.

"Sometimes I freak out in crowds," I said, staring at the pavement. It was a lie and a fairly obvious one at that, but it was the best I could do at the moment. I glanced at him. His expression never changed.

"Yeah," he said. "I can understand that."

All at once, I was fighting-mad. It took all my self-control not to turn and kick him in the shins for being dim enough to just accept my bullshit. "No." I gritted my teeth and glared at him.

"No?"

"You don't understand. You don't know anything about me, so don't pretend you do just to get in my pants. It's not necessary."

There was a pause. He looked away, out over the parking lot. Then he nodded, as if accepting the premise he didn't have to work very hard to get me into bed. "Are you all right now?"

I took a deep breath and dragged my hand through my hair. "Yeah. I'm fine."

"Good. Can I take you home?"

The words themselves sounded harmless, but I didn't mistake what he was asking—my knight in shining armor wanted to know if his damsel in distress was putting out tonight. And if I'd had any brains at all—anything like the tough, streetwise kid I used to be—I would've said no.

But that kid was long gone, and in her place was a lonely, isolated woman in a small, out-of-the-way town. A woman who hadn't felt another human's touch on her skin in over six months, unless you counted a trip to the gynecologist in Bangor, and I didn't. Count it, that is.

Plus...three glasses of wine. And we've already discussed what drinking does to my IQ.

"Not my home," I said. "Yours."

SIN STREET

CHAPTER 3

I let him drive us both to Washington Court Place in my car. As trailer parks go, it's as classy a spot as you're likely to find in the state—clean and well-managed, full of faux picket fences and garden gnomes and JC Penney swing-sets. We coasted down the main drag, all the way to the back, to the smallest unit on the lot.

"Worried about your bike?"

"Should I be?" He turned off the engine and handed me the keys. It was so quiet I could hear both of us breathing.

I shrugged. "Half the town saw McDane shake your hand and give you the big welcome-to-Port-Jonah-I'm-watching-your-every-move-so-don't-fuck-up speech. Chances are good your property is safe for the night."

"Is that how it works?"

I shrugged again and finished it with a shiver. "Let's go inside. I'm cold."

"So you keep trying to prove." He leaned over the console that separated the seats and kissed me. If I'd been expecting something gentle or tentative, I'd have been disappointed. He pressed his mouth against mine, touching me nowhere else, but I felt it everywhere. Then he pulled away and got out of the car. He moved to lean against the front fender, with his hands stuffed in the front pockets of his jeans. I could see his breath making puffs of steam around his face.

I waited for the anger to jump up and take over my brain. When the temper tantrum missed its cue by thirty seconds, I pushed open the door, climbed out of the car and went to stand by the other fender.

He cleared his throat. "If you come inside, I'm going to...we're going to..." He paused. It was the first time I'd ever seen him at a loss for words, but I'd only known him four hours.

"Make sweet, sweet love?" I loaded the words with as much sarcasm as they could carry.

He turned his head and looked at me over the hood of the car. The expression in his eyes could be described as "piercing"—or maybe that's how he looked when somebody finally pissed him off. The muscles in my lower body did a little anticipatory ripple.

"Just so we're clear—I'm not inviting you in for coffee."

"Works for me. I don't drink coffee."

He nodded and pushed off the fender. I followed him, my heart pounding three beats for every step. He unlocked the door and held it open for me, but I shook my head. Walking first into dark buildings is a good way to get yourself hurt. Even nice girls from Indiana know that, so I sure as hell did.

He flicked on a lamp and the trailer's main room lit up. It was tiny, dominated by an unmade sofa-bed in the center. The kitchenette off to the right remained in shadow. To the left stood a closed door I knew must lead to one other small room and a bath. Really nothing more than a studio apartment on wheels.

He moved to straighten the disheveled quilt and sheets. "If I'd known you were coming—"

"You'd have baked a cake?"

"Made the bed anyway." He punched a pillow and let it drop. "Can I get you anything?"

The wine was wearing off, leaving me headachy and unsteady. "Water would be great."

He nodded and turned toward the kitchen. I wandered over to a low table that sat beneath a window on the other side of the room. On the table sat an ancient, battered portable stereo and a small collection of discs.

Tom Petty, early Springsteen, Chris Isaak and...oh, this had to be a joke.

I almost let the disc case slip through my fingers when Donnelly appeared at my side, holding an ice-cold bottle of water.

"Meat Loaf?" I took the bottle from him and held the disc up to eye level. "You're kidding, right?"

He had the good grace to look sheepish. "My sister says I'm a musical dinosaur with no taste. But I love that album. It's got a lot of heart." He gave me an appraising look. "You know it?"

I opened my mouth…and shut it again. *Know it?* I could sing every song on *Bat Out Of Hell*, with or without electric guitar accompaniment. The question was, could MaryJane Peters? I shrugged. "It's vaguely familiar."

He reached behind me and hit the play button on the stereo. An instant later, Joss Stone's throaty warble filled the room. When I raised my eyebrows, he grinned. "A gift from my sister. Her attempt to drag me, kicking and screaming, into the twenty-first century."

"She's younger than you?"

He nodded. "You should meet her sometime. I bet you two have a lot in common."

Or not.

Time to get down to the business at hand. I set my water bottle on the table and took a step closer, so that my nipples—hard again under my sweater, and why was that, just exactly?—brushed his chest. He tilted his head and gave me a look I couldn't read.

"You're in a rush."

"I'm opening the bank in the morning."

"So I shouldn't flatter myself that I'm irresistible?"

Instead of answering, I returned the kiss he'd laid on me in the car. I like to think I would've employed more finesse, but he didn't give me much of a chance. As soon as I made contact, he slid one hand into my hair and the other up the back of my sweater, pretty much taking control of the situation. He swung me around in the direction of the bed, knocking me off balance. I had a moment of panic…an instant of *Oh God, this is moving way too fast…*which I did my best to drown out by concentrating on the taste of him—sharp and dark, with a top-note of beer and a faraway memory of butter and salt. Tasty. His kisses were aggressive but not sloppy, and he knew how to use his tongue, which is more than I can say for every man.

Then the mattress hit the backs of my thighs and I was falling. I braced myself for the impact, expecting his weight to knock the wind out of me, and was pleasantly surprised when he rolled away at the last possible moment, bringing me with him so I lay sprawled on top. The neckline of my sweater gaped, showing the edge of my bra. I was glad I'd bothered with a pretty one.

"We should talk about protection," he said, and blew a piece of my hair out of his face.

Unbelievable. Not only the fact that I hadn't even thought about it—a true measure of how extraordinary everything about this evening was turning out to be—but that he had been the one to bring it up.

"Uhh…" My hair fell in his face again, and I reached up to tuck it behind my ear. "I really wasn't expecting this. I mean, I don't have…anything."

"Yeah. Me, too."

"You're serious?" A guy who didn't keep his own stash of condoms? "What, did you just bust out of a monastery or something?"

He laughed at that, and for the first time I noticed the hard bulge beneath my left thigh. I shifted, pressing and rolling my weight against it, and watched his face for a reaction. He rewarded me with the slight flutter of one eyelid and the tightening of his jaw.

"You'd make a lousy Boy Scout, Donnelly."

He gave me a long, even look that told me he wasn't buying the idea that it was all his fault. There was a pause between songs on the CD, and then Joss Stone began to lament the filthy nature of her lowdown, dirty man. I sighed and started to pull away. No sense in prolonging the torture.

He tightened his arms around my waist. "Going somewhere?"

"I thought…I mean, since we can't—"

"Can't what?"

I gritted my teeth. It's not nice to play games with the sexually frustrated. Maybe he needed a dose of crude and vulgar to snap him out of it. "I thought since we can't fuck our brains out, I'd hit the road. Better luck next time and all that stuff."

He worked his chin back and forth over my collarbone and the very tops of my breasts. What had been a five o'clock shadow when I met him was now a full bristle, and the prickling rub against my skin was making me bunch my fingers in the quilt at either side of his head. He stopped long enough to make eye contact again. "You lack imagination."

And we were rolling again. I landed on my back, with him poised over me, bracing himself on one elbow. "Yeah? What do you lack?"

"A conscience." He leaned in and ran his tongue up the side of my neck to my ear. "But only sometimes."

"Is this one of those times?" My voice came out all breathy. My hands were clutching at his waist.

"Looks like." He bit my earlobe, gently at first and then harder, 'til I made a sad noise you might call a whimper. I arched my back, pushing my breasts against his chest. They ached, heavy like leaden weights, my nipples twisted into painful knots. I wanted to grind them against him, desperate for friction. But first, I pressed my head back into the mattress and looked at him.

"Who are you?" I asked him. All of sudden I wasn't sure. I'd agreed to what I thought was a one-night-stand with a grocery store manager on a cool bike. At best, the new guy in town. At worst, a drifter. Just another short-lived encounter, with no prospects for any kind of real satisfaction—but no inherent danger either. "What are you?"

"I'm a dirty, dirty man," he whispered, mocking the words of the song as it played in the background. It sounded filthy, the way he said it. It made me wet. "You want me to show you how dirty?"

My voice caught in my throat, clicking when I swallowed. My bottle of water was too far away to help. I settled for blinking at him.

"I'll make you come before the next song is over."

I shook my head. *No. Not possible.*

"Yeah. Through your clothes."

"No," I croaked. It took some effort. His hand had found a nipple. He was skimming it in circles with his palm. I could barely feel it, which made it worse somehow.

"Yeah. You won't be able to help yourself." He caught the nipple between the first two fingers of his hand and squeezed, working it in a scissoring motion.

My breath hitched in my chest as I fought for control. "Please don't."

He froze. "You want me to stop?"

Did I? I was throbbing in places I'd forgotten existed, mostly because of what he said, and how he said it, although his touch was the perfect blend of tender and dominant...

"No," I said, hating the ragged surrender in my voice. "Don't stop."

He must have seen the humiliation in my face, because he pressed a kissed to my temple. "Shh. It's okay."

"Is it?"

"It will be." His fingers tightened on my breast again. "I'll make it good. You can hate me later."

I could feel my forehead creasing as I tried to puzzle that one out. Then the song ended and the next one began, and his manner changed again. He shot me a glance out of the corner of his eye as his head dropped over the tops of my breasts, and I suddenly felt like prey. Highly coveted and especially tasty, but prey nonetheless.

"Ready?" he said. Like a dare. Like a bet he knew he couldn't lose.

His thigh slipped between my legs, snugging up against my crotch like it knew the way home. I hissed between my teeth at the contact, fighting the urge to tighten around it. No reason to make it easy on the bastard.

He caught the peak of the other breast between his teeth, right through the sweater and bra, and held it there. It was my turn to freeze. He bit down, just a little...just enough to send a hard, electric throb shooting down my body. A split second later, he rocked upward, sliding his thigh against me as if to return the volley. The quick, complete circuit of sensation did something to my brain. I could feel higher functions shutting down like a skyscraper going dark for the night. I wish I could say I fought harder to maintain control, but I'd be lying.

He moved on me, slipping and grinding, bending his knee for leverage. The sound of denim-on-denim was almost loud enough to drown out the music. Then he was talking in my ear, and I couldn't hear anything but his raspy whisper, telling me what he'd do to me next time, asking me if I liked it when he did this, or was it better when he moved like that. He pinched and rolled a nipple—I couldn't even say which one—and I arched into him, making a noise I didn't recognize.

"Yeah, that's the way," he said, his voice like burnt sugar at the bottom of a hot pan. He kissed me, eating at my mouth like a starving man, and rocked that thigh of his just a little higher, pressing the inseam of my jeans into the sweet spot once...twice...and I was clenching hard, my legs squeezing his and my body jerking under him like I'd grabbed a badly-wired lamp.

I slid down the other side and landed dizzy and ashamed. He was dropping kisses on my cheek, his murmurs gone all soft and not so dirty anymore. I tried to squirm out from under him, but he wasn't having it.

"Lie still and be friendly for a minute." He smiled and winked like something was funny. "It won't kill you."

I shut my eyes rather than see him laugh at me and listened to the intro of the next song. My breathing came back to normal, slow but sure, and after a while I started to feel a little guilty. I shifted a bit to test the waters and sure enough—the bulge in his jeans hadn't gone anywhere.

"If you'll let me up, I'll return the favor." My voice came out half-strangled and sounding less-than-enthusiastic.

SIN STREET

He looked at me, his smile gone wry and a little cold. "Thanks. I'll pass."

"You think I can't do a good job?" Now I sounded indignant, and wasn't that sexy? "You think you're the only one with skills?"

"I think you feel obligated."

I tapped his arm, and he removed it so I could pull myself up to sit. "First of all, I don't feel obligated." A lie, but not a complete one. I enjoy the give-and-take of sex, and it had been a long time since I'd had the chance to indulge in the "give" part. My vibrator didn't seem to appreciate my efforts.

"And second of all?" he said, moving over on the bed, making the springs creak and complain.

"Second of all, lie back and shut up."

To my brief but extreme shock, he did just that. I slid to the floor between his heavy, black boots and tugged at him 'til his hips were in the proper position, then went for the button and zipper.

"Allow me." Again with the wry, chilly smile. Not sure what I'd done to deserve it, but I intended to melt it right off his mouth if I could.

Once his fly was open, I didn't waste time with the usual getting-to-know-you routine. In my experience, one guy's equipment is pretty much like another's, and even if there are differences, what are we talking about? An inch or three, here and there? A slight distinction in color or shape? You see the same variety in the produce section of any market, and it's all just as edible.

The irony of that thought made me smile.

He was hard and hot under my fingers, where I wrapped them around the base. When I licked the tip and tasted slick salt, he made a noise—not quite a gurgle, not quite a hiss—and the muscles in his thighs tightened. Yeah, he was a man, with the standard male response to stimuli. What else did I need to know?

"Comfortable?"

He lifted his head and shot me a look so cold you'd think I was auditing his latest tax return. Apparently, somebody could dish it out, but wasn't as fond of taking it.

I got down to business, working my mouth on him in the most efficient way I knew, employing lots of tongue where it did the most good. I listened to his breathing, gauging when to alternate tempo and pressure, judging when it was time to introduce a rougher touch and a few gentle bites. I kept an eye on his lower body, watching for the tell-tale muscle-clenching that meant he was about to peak...and backed off, blowing a stream of cool air and letting him suffer a little denial, just for the hell of it.

I was good. Given how out-of-practice I'd been, I impressed myself.

And except for that first little sound of surprise, he stayed quiet. I could feel him watching me—glowering, really—to the point where I was afraid to meet his eyes. The third time I left him hanging on the edge, he finally broke, grunting and curling up into a sitting position. Then his hand was on my head. I braced myself, waiting for the push, expecting him to force my head down and thrust himself into my throat 'til I gagged. My own fault really. There's no percentage in cock-teasing strangers. My father would've said I'd gotten what I deserved.

Instead, he pulled me up, one hand in my hair, the other on my arm, dragging me onto the bed and into his lap. Kissing me, biting at my lips like he meant to eat me up. It hurt, and it scared me, a little. I felt him shift, and something hot and sticky brushed my midriff, where my sweater parted from my jeans. He grunted again and quit using his teeth, though his hands on my arm and in my hair didn't soften.

It was then I noticed my own hands, hanging empty at either side. I'd gone ragdoll on him, acting purely on survival instinct, and it was no way to treat a man who'd provided a meal and an orgasm in one evening. I reached down between us and found the cause of his distress, watching his face for some sign of surrender. My thumb flicked over the tip, back and forth, and with each movement, the muscles in his jaws bulged.

"You're gonna crack a tooth there, tough guy." I kissed him, gently and slowly, because he deserved it. He dropped his face into my neck and muttered something, and kept muttering it as he thrust up into my hand. It might've been something dirty, but I think not. I think it was "MaryJane." I sat there, feeling him get hotter and harder, letting it pain me to hear that fake name on his lips in that moment when he was most vulnerable. It felt like a betrayal—maybe of both of us. But I pushed that thought away to someplace deep down where I kept all my hurts and concentrated on making him feel good.

Then every muscle in his body locked, and he sucked in air on a deep, achy sounding note. He shot in my hand, splashing it slippery wet and hot, breathing like he'd run the mile in a minute. I rocked him to the side and back, feeling the need to soothe him, feeling almost protective of this self-proclaimed dirty man. Whatever wounds he was hiding, thirty seconds' worth of afterglow affection wouldn't heal them. Nobody knew that better than me. But it couldn't hurt either.

He shuddered one last time and pulled himself together, sliding me off his lap in a way that let me know he was done with me. When he turned back, the wry, cold smile was gone. In its place was a grim line and a clenched jaw. His eyes were blank, as if he wasn't seeing me at all.

"You can use the bathroom to get cleaned up." He gestured toward the door. "Right through there."

He heaved himself off the bed, hit the stop button on the stereo and crossed the room to the opposite door, slamming it on his way outside. I didn't try to stop him, to ask him what was wrong. The silence he left behind pretty much said it all.

The bathroom was small, just like the rest of the trailer, but Donnelly kept it clean. I tidied myself as well as I could, wiped the mascara smudges from under my eyes, and stepped into the tiny hall. The door to the left led back to the front section of the trailer. If I knew anything about mobile homes—and, as it might be surmised, I did—the door to my right led to a bedroom. But that one was locked, with a padlock half the size of my fist, no less.

Weird. Gym equipment, maybe? But with a padlock that size...

I heard Donnelly moving around in the front room. I ran my hands through my hair, straightened my sweater and pushed open the door, ready to face him.

"Hey," he said, caught by surprise.

"Hey." What do you say to guy after you've humped his leg like a bitch in heat? Or after he's come all over your favorite spring sweater? At least the blank expression was gone from his eyes, and he looked like he might try to smile again...someday.

"I, uh, I'm sorry. About before." He scratched at his chin and stuck his hands in his pockets.

"Which part?"

His eyes widened a fraction, then narrowed down to skeptical slits. He could tell I was playing with him, which meant he was smarter than your average bear. But we already knew that, didn't we?

"The part where it got sloppy." He took a step closer, and then another. "And the part where I got surly, at the end."

"Ah," I said. "I wondered about that."

He was standing right in front of me, running his hands up and down my arms. "Not your problem." He pressed a kiss to my forehead.

SIN STREET

It felt like absolution—like he was forgiving both of us. For what, I didn't know, but I could always use a little extra mercy in my life. For about half a second, I felt almost peaceful.
Then I looked up into his eyes. *Troubled waters.* And unless I missed my guess, I was still the one in trouble.

CHAPTER 4

We didn't have much to say on the drive back to Crawford's. I kept waiting for him to suggest a second date so I could turn him down. I don't do second dates. They lead to complications—like third dates, for example. But he didn't ask, so I couldn't refuse. Didn't even try to kiss me. Just smiled, thanked me for the ride and got out of the car.

I watched him slide the helmet over his head, straddle the bike and start the engine. I swear I could feel the vibration travel through the asphalt, up into my tires and through the seat cushions into the lower half of my body. He put the bike into gear and accelerated out of the lot without looking back.

I sat there wondering if I would've said "no" to that second date after all. All the way home, I wondered.

When I hit the door, I threw my bag on the kitchen table, kicked off my sneakers and went straight for the shoebox I kept under my bed. It was covered in dust, and I sneezed as I pulled it out. I pawed through it 'til I found what I was looking for—an old, homemade cassette tape, given to me long ago by one of my brothers. Meat Loaf's *Bat Out of Hell*. I sat cross-legged on the carpet and held it in my hand for a long time. I couldn't have played it if I wanted to, since I didn't own a cassette player, but it felt good to hold it. Good, and scary. There were reasons I hadn't touched the box in three years or more. Life and death reasons.

When I finally tossed the tape back, it landed on top of the Springsteen and Bon Jovi CDs I kept hidden there. Reminders of my lost youth and abandoned identity—the Jersey girl I'd left behind. I reached for the box lid, then thought better of it.

"Who's to know if I listen to the old tunes, after all this time?" My voice sounded distant in my ears, like I was speaking from miles away. My insides felt a little hollow, too, but I put up a brave front for the dust bunnies. "Who's to know, and who's to care?"

I left the box lying on the floor next to the bed, uncovered. It gave me a little thrill to see it there while I got ready for bed, and that was enough.

* * *

The next day dawned cold and rainy, as early May mornings often do on the downeast coast of Maine. I overslept, waking too late to grab breakfast on the way out of the house. I parked the VW in the employees' section of the lot and ran for the back door of the bank, keys in hand. It was seven-thirty. I like to be early. I like to be first, if I can. It makes me feel as if I'm in control. I have some issues with that...maybe you've noticed?

This time I was disappointed. Regina was already behind her desk, sorting through the stack of mail that had accumulated in her absence. As I'd already weeded out and handled the urgent matters, I knew she'd find most of it to be nonessential.

Crap. The note. The one with the bloody thumbprint? My previous evening's debauchery with Donnelly had knocked it right out of my head. A pretty impressive trick, to be honest. Almost made me wish...but that would stupid, and I'd already been plenty stupid. Used up my quota for the season, in fact. And anyway, he'd made it plain he wasn't interested in a second helping of what I had to dish out. Time to put it behind me and keep moving.

"'Morning, Reggie," I called on my way to my desk, with every intention of snatching the note from under the blotter and presenting it to its rightful recipient, which would be the tall, leggy platinum blonde who appeared in the doorway of her office wearing a strained smile and dark smudges beneath her eyes. Apparently, her vacation hadn't done much for her in the way of rest and relaxation.

"Hey," she said, and sort of waved at me. I reached my desk and went for the note, recalling exactly where I'd left it.

It wasn't there.

I lifted the blotter and skimmed my hand underneath, thinking maybe it had gotten shoved further in. Nothing. I lifted the blotter, dislodging papers, spilling a container of paper clips, dumping my stapler onto the floor.

The note was gone.

Regina watched without comment, which I found a little odd. She was chewing her lower lip like she'd missed three meals and didn't know when to expect the next one. Finally, she met my eyes and asked, "Did you...lose something?"

No doubt in my mind she'd taken the note. Question was, did I confront her or let it go? The envelope had been addressed to her after all. I'd made a mistake in opening it. But the larger question—the one I felt deserved an answer—was why had she been snooping around my desk? The note had been hidden under the blotter. Covered entirely, if I remembered correctly, and I was sure I did. Which meant she'd gone searching for it—or searching for something else, and stumbled upon it.

I looked at her. She looked at me. Stalemate. I took a breath, fully prepared to ask...fully prepared to pin her to the wall, if I had to, with my questions. Because something funny was going on. I could feel it. And I'd had enough of "funny" to last my entire life. I'd run away and never looked back because of "funny." I was alone and miserable and halfway to clinically depressed because of "funny." And no, I most definitely did not mean funny "ha-ha."

But then something floated across the surface of my brain—a clear picture of the small, battered plaque my father kept on his desk in the back room of the bar. The room where he'd done his real business. Discretion is the better part of valor, it had said. I exhaled, shrugged and gave Reggie a fake smile. "No, I guess maybe I didn't. Lose anything, I mean."

She nodded, the relief so bright in her eyes it almost brought tears to my own. "I'm glad," she said. Then she turned and went back into her office and shut the door.

I stood there for a few seconds longer, wondering if maybe I'd made a mistake. Clearly, my boss was in trouble. I doubted I was doing her any favors in the long run by ignoring it. Then the buzzer at the back door went off, making me jump, and I had to run to let the first of the tellers inside.

All morning long, as I helped customers and fielded calls, thoughts of that damned note plagued me. How had Regina known to search for it in the first place? What kind of lunatic followed up a death threat with a memo—re: my bloodstained message of last week? How far could I to go to get answers? Was I willing to contact McDane? With what? I no longer had the note. When push came to shove, Regina could deny its existence. And, in the end, maybe the whole thing was just a sick prank. But my gut didn't think so. And my gut had saved my ass more than once.

I did my best to distract myself with mundane tasks, staying anchored to my desk and letting the tellers interact with the public as much as possible. At eleven-fifteen, I heard Kristy's unmistakable laugh, and looked up to see her talking to one of my least favorite patrons.

I had no good reason to dislike Aristotle Avramis, but dislike him I did. Maybe it was the way he lacquered his thinning, middle-aged hair low over his forehead, like some Donald Trump-wannabe. Maybe it was his ever-present tanning-bed glow, or the way his bulky shoulders filled out the expensive cut of his camel-hair coat, or the way his Italian loafers caught the glare of the fluorescent lights. Maybe it was the hard gleam in his eye, or the smile I recognized to be as insincere as my own. Whatever the reason, I hated to see him stroll through the doors of the bank, least of all on a day when I was already twitchy.

Avramis was a relative newcomer to Port Jonah, having beaten me into town by only six months or so. He'd been buying up waterfront property and investing in small businesses ever since. Certain folks—older ones, mostly—expressed mistrust, and they tended to couch it in terms of a dislike for new people in general, and foreigners in particular. But they warmed up to his money quick enough when he saved the marina from going under…and then Neery's Auto Parts Store…and the Video Shack after that. Some people said he'd taken controlling interest in Crawford's Seafood, too, but that was just a rumor—one that nobody in the Crawford clan seemed interested in confirming or denying.

"Kukla," he was saying to Kristy, all but pinching her cheek, "tell me, darling, would it be possible for me to see your manager for a moment?"

Avramis spoke with only the merest trace of a Greek accent—nothing like what I'd grown up hearing in the old neighborhood. Nothing like Mr. Papadakou, for instance, who owned the bakery just down the street from our bar, and always saved the sticky end-pieces of the Sunday baklava for me. His accent was damned near indecipherable…but his smile was genuine.

I shot a glance at Reggie's door. It was closed and the blind was drawn tight—her signal for "do not disturb." Keeping an eye on the counter, I went ahead and rapped on the window, then turned the knob and stuck my head in.

"Reggie, I'm sorry, but…" I let my voice trail off. My manager was huddled in the large chair behind her desk, her face turned into the leather. Her exposed cheek was splotchy and running with makeup. She glanced at me, and I saw stark, unmistakable terror from ten feet away. I backed out of the office and shut the door. Then I turned, stepped up to the counter and plastered on the brightest, phoniest grin I could muster.

"Our branch manager is unavailable this morning," I chirped, "but I'd be delighted to help you in any way I can."

I looked past Avramis to the hulking presence of his nephew, Georgie, who always seemed to shadow his left shoulder. Georgie's hands hung at his sides in black leather gloves that looked about two sizes too small, his round baby-face fixed in its usual slack, unfocused expression. I fought the urge to reach inside the container on the corner of the desk and hand him a lollipop.

Avramis's mouth turned down, but his brow stayed smooth, and I had a fleeting vision of someone injecting his forehead with botulism. I wondered if he got the treatments in Bangor, or if he had to fly all the way to Boston for the shots.

"You're sure she can't see me?" he asked, and his tone wasn't nearly so friendly anymore.

I smiled a little wider and offered my services again, which he brushed away with a well-manicured hand. "No. We'll come back." He leaned over the counter, 'til his nose was a mere two inches from mine. "Monday. Tell her, your manager. Tell her…Monday. You understand?"

I swallowed. "Yes, of course. If you'd like to make an appointment—"

"No. No appointment." Avramis's accent had grown more pronounced. This is how I knew he was angry. Furious, even. "You tell her. Monday."

He gestured toward Georgie and muttered something in Greek. Together, they moved through the lobby. People stepped out of the way to let them pass, which just plain pissed me off. I gritted my teeth, took a deep, cleansing breath and walked back to my desk. Where I sat and wondered what I was going to do about Reggie, who was clearly up to her eyebrows in some very bad shit.

I turned and stared at her door, with its pulled shade. *What's my next move? Confront her? Ask her what the hell was going on between her and Ari Avramis—if anything?* For all I knew, Reggie's little emotional breakdown was over a fight with her fiancé, and the threatening letter and Avramis's visit to the bank and pushy behavior were a total coincidence. I might've been overreacting. But you know? I really, really didn't think so.

Kristy's urgent whisper cut short the obsessive loop of my thoughts. "MaryJane? There's someone here to see you."

I looked away from Regina's door and straight into Donnelly's eyes. He stood in the lobby, wearing a brown leather jacket that had seen better days over a black t-shirt and jeans. He leaned on the counter as if it were a bar and Gail was about to serve him a frothy mug of whatever was on tap. I smiled at him reflexively, even as I told myself I wasn't happy to see him. Especially here. Especially now. And Kristy's giggle, growing louder by the second, was only one of the reasons why.

"Damn, girl. How did you hook him so fast?" She grinned at me, and I couldn't detect even a trace of bitchiness beneath it. I'd always liked Kristy. Under other circumstances, we might've been friends.

I stood and smoothed my skirt, feeling Donnelly's gaze cut across me like a pair of lasers as I approached. I was never so glad for the height and depth of the faux maple counter as when I put it between us.

"Good morning. What can I do for you today?" I kept my expression neutral and my voice at a professional pitch

"We need to talk," he said, clearly not buying my attempt at treating him like just another customer.

Gail leaned over and squeezed my arm. "Go on, take a break. I'll cover for you."

I murmured something that sounded like thank you and moved in the direction of the front doors. Donnelly followed me out. As soon as the wet wind bit through my blouse, I realized my error in forgoing my coat. Donnelly hooked a hand under my arm and half dragged me around the corner into the alley between the bank and the Video Shack next door, out of the weather. Then he pulled off his jacket and yanked it around my shoulders—a gesture that somehow fell short of good manners by virtue of the scowl on his face.

"We need to talk," he repeated.

"So you keep saying." I'd had about all I could stand of demanding, arrogant males of the species for one day, and it wasn't even noon. He could be nice, or he could go screw himself. I was just about to give voice to those sentiments when he stepped into me, backing me against the building. I forced my hands down, flat on the dirty, damp bricks, refusing to give him the satisfaction of touching him.

"What time do you get off?" He leaned in and pressed his lips against a spot on my neck, giving his words a double meaning that was hard to miss.

"I...one o'clock...but—"

"Good," he said down the back of my neck. "I'll meet you at your house at—let's say—three?"

He smelled like soap and motorcycle, with a side of old leather, and maybe a little spice and lime—like he'd used some aftershave or cologne several hours ago, but it had mostly worn off. I inhaled deeply, enjoying it while I could.

"Why?" I asked, pulling to the side a little bit so I could look at him. "What happens at three o'clock?"

"I told you. We need to talk."

"We're talking now."

He gave me that steady, even stare, and I let my gaze drop away. I'd never met anyone who could make me feel so thoroughly guilty so damned fast for my line of bullshit.

"Plus," he said, pulling me back into line against his body, "we have unfinished business."

I didn't bother with any coy protests. But this was stupid. Stupid as in "dangerous." Stupid as in what-the-fuck-are-you-doing-you-idiot? I knew better than this.

"I can't." I'd meant to say it with conviction, but it came out as a breathy whimper, making me cringe.

"Sure you can. Three o'clock. Your place." He reached up and tugged on a stray piece of my hair. All at once, it felt like my scalp was attached to other, more sensitive regions of my body. "I just need the address." His eyes were half-closed and sleepy. There was moisture beaded in his hair, and a fine mist of it on his brow and upper lip. I wanted to lick it off.

"No."

"Yes." The word sounded like the crunch of broken glass in my ear.

I found myself clutching the bricks, digging my nails into the crevices until pain shot up my arms. I shook my head.

"I won't hurt you," he said. "You know I won't hurt you."

I did know it. I don't know how I could be so sure of such a thing, but I was.

He kissed me then, and this time he was gentle, but still not tentative. When he was done, he traced my upper lip with his thumb. "Three o'clock?"

I nodded. "Twenty-two Crescent Drive. White house, blue shutters."

He smiled, just a little. I looked at him carefully, feeling my eyes get narrow and mean. If I'd seen any hint of triumph...just the slightest bit of smug...but no.

"Keep the jacket." He pulled it tighter around my shoulders and stepped away, leading me out of the alley. We parted on the sidewalk without another word. I watched him walk in the direction of the Pick 'N' Save, wondering what the hell I'd just done.

When I returned to the lobby, it was empty—not a customer in sight. The girls were clustered around the counter, waiting for me. They took one look at the jacket and broke out in grins a mile wide, nudging each other as if I wasn't standing right there. I had to laugh with them, which somehow made it a little more okay.

Then I noticed how Regina's office had gone dark in my absence. "She left?"

"Ayuh," answered Gail, sobering instantly. "Took off like a bat outta...umm...real sudden about ten minutes ago, through the back door. Didn't say nothin', at least not to me."

I looked at Tonia, who shrugged, and Kristy, who shook her head.

I sighed. "Okay, ladies. Almost time to lock the doors. Let's see if we can break some records in getting our drawers tallied today, whaddya say?"

I stared up at the clock on the wall. In a few hours, Drew Donnelly would be standing at my front door. If I decided to let him in—and that was a big if—he would be the first person to cross the threshold other than myself, the meter-reader and the odd plumber or repairman, in over three years.

The thought made me glad I'd missed breakfast.

CHAPTER 5

By two-thirty, I'd showered and dressed, then changed my clothes twice because I wasn't sure what one wore to a date that would probably consist of a quick roll in the sack, with maybe some conversation and a bite to eat afterwards. Emphasis on the "maybe."

I mean, I'd done the one-night-stand thing before—exhibit A: Jimmy Van Zandt—but those encounters had always been of the spontaneous variety. This seemed so...calculated. Sin with specific intent. Somewhere buried deep inside me, the seven-year-old who'd made her first communion with visions of becoming a nun was having a fit.

By two-forty-five, I'd begun having serious second thoughts. The stupidity factor of the entire endeavor suddenly seemed off the charts. Didn't I have enough to deal with—for Christ's sake, my boss was receiving death threats. The last thing I needed was to let someone into my life, after all this time of keeping to the plan, walking a straight line, and doing what I needed to do.

At two-fifty, I went around the house locking the doors and windows and pulling down the shades. My heart was pounding so hard, I swear it echoed off the walls. At some point, I remembered I still hadn't eaten anything.

At two-fifty-five, Donnelly knocked on the front door. I sat on the sofa in my darkened living room, hugging a pillow to my face, willing him to go away.

He didn't. He knocked and knocked, and knocked some more. He called my name. Or what he thought was my name. When that didn't work, he went around back to the door that opened into the kitchen and knocked there.

"Son of a bitch," I muttered. My neighbors were bound to start noticing. I got up off the sofa and went to speak to him through the thick, painted oak of the door. "What do you want?" Stupid. Like I wasn't the idiot who'd agreed to a little afternoon delight on my sacred home turf.

"Let me in, MaryJane."

"I'm sorry, Drew. This was a mistake." I leaned my head against the door and tried to swallow the lump in my throat. "My mistake, not yours."

Silence. I let myself hope he'd given up. At the same time, a bubble of regret began to swell somewhere under my breastbone. I knew when it burst, I'd be hurting like I hadn't let myself in years. Call me twisted, but I almost looked forward to it. It's nice to feel something now and again.

The door thudded hard, right under my head, making me jump. "Let me in." His voice wasn't any louder, but it scared me anyway.

"Go away, Drew. Don't make me call McDane."

Another pause. Then he said, "I don't think you're going to do that. Are you...Eva?"

And there it was. Three years of carefully constructed plans, lies and subterfuge. Three years of never letting anyone get close. Three years of knowing I'd likely die as I'd been living—alone and miserable.

Over.

It was like being thrown naked into a half-frozen lake. I dropped to the blue-and-gold speckled linoleum and just knelt there, trying to breathe, while he rattled the knob and called to me. After a minute or two, I dragged myself forward, reached up and unlocked the door. He swung it open, catching me on the shoulder because I didn't move out of the way fast enough. I saw him toss something on the counter—a folder from the look of it. Then he squatted and hauled me to my feet, squeezing the flesh of my upper arms a little harder than was absolutely necessary. I didn't look at his face.

He escorted me into the living room and deposited me none-too-gently on the sofa. Everything went a little blurry around the edges for a while after that. The next thing I recall is holding a tall, cold glass between my hands.

"Drink," he said.

I drank, and choked on what I'd thought was water and turned out to be vodka on ice. I drank some more, and it was...well, it wasn't okay, that was for damned sure. But it was better.

I looked at him then. His face was fixed in a calculating expression I'd learned to recognize while lying in a hospital bed some four-and-a-half years prior, and later in a few different interrogation rooms. That and the brown folder in his hand pretty much clinched it for me.

"You're a cop."

A muscle in his cheek twitched. "You say 'cop' like other people say 'child molester.'"

"What's your point?"

He sighed and ran a hand over his face. "You want to tell me why every word out of your mouth since I met you has been a lie?"

I knocked back a good-sized gulp of the vodka and tried not to shudder as it hit my empty stomach. "You have all the answers, Mr. Officer, sir." An eerie sensation of distance had descended upon me, as if I was watching everything unfold from the wrong end of a telescope. "Why don't you tell me?"

His eyes got all squinty in his stupid, handsome face. "Fine," he said. "Your name isn't MaryJane Peters. It's Eva Maria Pietras."

He looked at me like I was gonna deny it. I shrugged and nodded and took another swig of vodka.

"You're not from Verona, Indiana. You're from Bayonne, New Jersey. Your father, Chet, the auto-parts dealer? Is really Stanislaw, otherwise known as Stan, bar-owner and bookie. Your mother, Janice, homemaker extraordinaire?"

"Hey, now, wait just a second," I said, slurring just a little. "I never said she was anything extra...extra-anything."

"But her name's not Janice." He took a step toward me, and I tried not to cower. "It's Marjorie, and she tended bar for your father for thirty years, while raising you and your three older brothers out of the apartment upstairs. Isn't that right?"

I nodded, hiccupped and set the empty-but-for-melting-ice-cubes glass on the coffee table. "Stellar detective work," I said, enunciating carefully. "You should be very proud. Mind telling me how you pulled it off?"

His mouth turned down and he looked away, like maybe he was a tiny bit ashamed of whatever he was going to say next. "I lifted your prints off the water bottle in my trailer and scanned them into the system."

"You son of a bitch."

The look of shame evaporated, and he smiled that cold, wry smile I'd already learned to hate. "My mother is a really nice lady. You'd like her."

I came off the sofa with the intention of clawing his eyes out if I got the chance, but I'd forgotten about the full glass of vodka on an empty stomach. It hit me like a sledgehammer between the eyes, and I pitched forward, watching the floor fly up to meet my face. Donnelly caught me and hauled me back to my feet, holding my arms at my sides as if he knew the evil in my heart.

"So what now, officer?" I said, blowing fumes in his face. "You got me dead to rights—impersonating a nice, well-brought-up young woman without a permit. Whaddya gonna do about it?" I hiccupped again and wondered what would happen if I just went ahead and threw up all over his denim jacket. Bastard would probably arrest me for assault with a deadly weapon.

He looked down at me with his unhappy gray eyes and grimaced. "You're a sloppy drunk."

"The least of my problems." I disentangled myself from him and dropped down on the sofa. "And you're the one who poured the drink."

"I assumed you could hold your liquor."

"Based on what?" My stomach did a nasty roll and tumble. I thought about making a dive for the bathroom, but I wasn't sure if Officer Dickhead was armed. I didn't need a bullet in the back just because I'd rather puke in the toilet than on the nearest throw-rug. "Besides, I haven't eaten today."

"Christ."

I shot a glance at him. He looked irritated.

"You have food in the house?" He started to move toward the kitchen, glancing at me over his shoulder.

I shrugged. "Might be some peanut butter and jell—" And that was all she wrote. I was off the sofa like a shot, and this time my legs didn't fail me. I made it to the bathroom with a half a second to spare, and with Donnelly right behind me. The vodka burned twice as bad on the return trip, but I was beyond caring.

When I came back to something like full awareness, Donnelly was holding my hair off my face with one hand and cold washcloth to my forehead with the other.

"Such service. You always this nice to people whose lives you're about to ruin?"

His face was a hard blank and he didn't meet my eyes. "What makes you think I'm about to ruin your life?"

"Just a hunch." I pushed his hands away and pulled myself up off the floor. "I'm going to take a shower. It would be really great if you weren't here when I got out."

He looked up at me from where he squatted on the bathroom tiles. "Not a chance."

I stood under the hot spray, contemplating my next move. The bathroom window was too small to make it of any use as an escape route. The bedroom was too far away, as was the front door. And even if they weren't, where was I headed? My life—such as it was—existed solely in Port Jonah. Did I really want to start over from scratch? Find some other little hole-in-the-wall town where people didn't ask too many questions and just took it on faith that a pretty girl with a good work ethic was everything she said she was?

Of course, there was another option. I eyed my pink plastic razor with interest, wondering at exactly what angle I'd have to apply it to my wrist to get the most bang for my buck. Then I sighed and shook my head, imagining my father's face when the warden came to tell him how his only daughter had finally bought it. He'd be furious with me—letting the bastards get me down.

I hadn't come this far to pussy out now.

"You okay in there?" Donnelly's voice echoed off the tiles. He actually sounded concerned, which made that place in my chest—the one that had filled with regret earlier in the afternoon—constrict just a little bit.

"I'll be out in a minute."

I dried myself off, ran a comb through my hair, and pulled on my underwear beneath a navy-blue, terrycloth robe, feeling like I should be suiting up for battle. I didn't know what Donnelly wanted from me, but he was armed with the details of my previous life, and what did I have as a weapon? My charm and good looks? Something told me I was seriously outmatched.

Donnelly had set the table—lunch for one.

The sandwich was cut into triangular-shaped quarters, and arranged neatly on the plate. The napkin was folded precisely, and the milk was poured within a half-inch of the rim of the glass. I couldn't help but smile as I sat down and prepared to dig in.

"What?" He sounded defensive.

"I'm thinking they probably don't pay you enough, officer."

He scowled. "I haven't confirmed I'm a cop."

I quit smiling and just looked at him, 'til he glanced away and then back again. "Okay, fine. But stop calling me 'officer.'"

"Why?"

"Because it's 'agent.'"

Shit. "You're a Fed?" I threw the sandwich onto the plate and pushed back the chair with a loud scrape against the linoleum. "I've got a fucking Fed in my house?"

"Sit down and stop acting like a spoiled brat."

"Go to hell."

"Sit down, Eva."

"It's MaryJane, Agent Donnelly." I loaded my voice with as much sarcasm as it could hold. "Says so on my driver's license and social security card, too. Had it legally changed and everything. So you can go fuck yourself."

He stepped into me, so I could feel him from my shoulders to my knees. I had to crane my neck to look up at him. "Sit down," he said, softer this time. "Please."

I sat. But only because the scent of peanut butter was making me dizzy with hunger. He took a stroll around the kitchen, which was almost funny to see, since it's hardly the size for pacing. Finally, he came to rest leaning against the counter, arms folded over his chest. He watched me chew and swallow.

"So," I said between bites, "now what?"

He shrugged. "That's up to you."

"What does that mean exactly?" I sipped at the milk, then reached for the napkin.

"It means I'm wondering if you've got it in you to be honest."

My turn to shrug. "Try me and find out."

He didn't seem to like that answer. "Fine. Tell me what happened four-and-a-half years ago in Bayonne, in your own words. Tell me about the embezzlement." He unfolded his arms and his hand came to rest on the folder, which sat to his right on the counter. I was itching to see what was inside that bad boy—other than my mug shot, of course.

"Why, when you already know all the sordid details?" I dropped the last bit of crust on the plate, finished off the milk and wiped my mouth. Then I pushed the chair away from the table and stood. No reason to let him play "interrogation room" in my own damned kitchen. "Or does hearing me say it give you a cheap thrill?"

"Stop it."

I moved to face him, so there were maybe two feet between us. "I'm onto you, Agent Donnelly. You're a kinky bastard, wanting to hear me list my crimes with my own mouth, when you know damned well there's better things I could be doing with—"

He grabbed the back of my neck and jerked me right up close. "I said, stop it." His voice was all deep and tense, like he was barely holding onto his restraint. "Are you going to stop?"

I nodded, my lips an inch from his. He let go, and I stumbled backward. He ran a hand over his face and let it drop. I followed it with my gaze and couldn't miss the bulge in his jeans, which he took no pains to hide.

He cleared his throat "A half a million dollars is a lot of money, MaryJane. Do you expect me to just—"

"When did I say I expected anything from you?" I leaned against the fridge, mirroring his stance, and stared at him. "You started this. All of it. I was just living my life—"

"Lying to everyone—"

"Living...my...life." I said it with as much force as I could muster. "Not hurting anyone. Not so much as breaking the speed limit—which, for a kid from Jersey..." I let my words trail off. My eyes burned and I bit the inside of my cheek to keep from releasing the sob building in the back of my throat.

There was a flash of something in his eyes as he watched me struggle to hold it together and then the hard mask dropped back into place. "The bank never would've hired you if they'd known."

I gritted my teeth. "Which is why I chose a tiny branch, in a tiny town, in the back of beyond that doesn't bother with thorough background checks. They just looked for outstanding warrants and felony convictions for a MaryJane Peters—"

"And she has none. But neither does Eva Pietras." He looked genuinely puzzled. "You danced right out of that conviction, so why even bother with the new identity?"

"Danced out of the conviction?" It was all I could do to keep from reaching for the block that held the carving knives, there on the counter to his left. "You obviously don't have a clue what you're talking about, so let me educate you, Agent Donnelly."

"Please, do."

I hooked my still-damp hair behind my ears and took a breath to steady myself. My feet felt cold and numb on the linoleum floor, and I suddenly wished I'd taken the time to get fully dressed for this battle of wits. Too late now.

"For starters, I spent three months in lock-up following my arrest because no one in my family had the money to post bail after they raided my father's business and shut it down." I closed my eyes and let the single image of sunshine lined with the shadow of steel bars flash across the front of my mind. "That's after I got out of the hospital, of course, as a result of the beating I took from one of Bayonne's finest."

Donnelly tapped the folder. "It says here you resisted arrest."

I nodded. "I ran. I do that when somebody points a gun at me."

He squinted and shook his head. "You're saying the detective didn't identify himself?"

"It doesn't matter. I was in the wrong, and he was just doing his job. That's what you want me to say, isn't it?"

Donnelly stood there, staring at me like I was some alternate life-form.

"The truth is I don't remember anymore. I was scared and I ran. He caught me and he hit me...a lot. Did he say he was a cop at some point?" I shrugged. "Why should anyone care at this late date?"

The silence in the kitchen was making my head pound. All I wanted to do was crawl under the table and hide.

I sucked in a shaky breath. "Anyway. I made a deal to testify against Carl—"

"Your boyfriend, the vice-president of the bank." He didn't phrase it as a question.

"Yeah. And my father, who wasn't any more guilty than I was."

"Except that he was getting a cut of the money," Donnelly said. "A hundred grand, right? To pay off a loan from Big Eddy Benzini?" He pushed forward off the counter and stood up straight, hands on his hips. "Isn't that why you did it in the first place? To help out your dad? Isn't that what you said at the trial?" His voice got louder, bouncing off the kitchen walls.

"If you already know, then why are you asking?" Christ, I sounded pathetic.

"Because I need to hear it. All of it."

"Why?" I held out my hands, palms up. "Why are you here? What could the Feds possibly want with me now?"

He shook his head. Really slowly. Just once. "Nothing."

And then I understood. Talk about lousy, rotten luck... "Of all the gin joints, in all the towns, in all the world—"

"You had to walk into my produce section one week into an undercover operation I spent six months setting up." He glowered at me, looking utterly disgusted.

That's when I started to laugh.

CHAPTER 6

"You think this is funny?"

I should've listened closer to the edge in his voice, but I was too busy sliding down the fridge to land on my ass. I felt my robe ride up somewhere around the tops of my thighs and didn't care. Hysteria had me in its vice-like grip. The tears I'd earlier managed to stifle finally busted loose in a deluge, blinding me. I sat there on the linoleum and giggled and shrieked and whooped and choked. Not all of it was laughter.

I'm not sure at what point he lost his cool, but the next thing I knew, I was back on my feet and Donnelly was shaking me like a terrier with a squeaky toy. That lasted maybe five seconds before he apparently realized what he was doing and let go.

"Christ," he said, backing off and lifting his hands as if touching me had contaminated him. "Look what you do to me."

"Look what I do to you? Really?" I used the sleeve of my robe to dab at my face. "I mean...for real?"

"No." He visibly steeled himself with a deep breath, his hands curling into fists at his sides. "I'm sorry. I was out of line. But there's nothing funny about any of this."

"That's where we disagree. I think it's hilarious that you blame me for screwing up your investigation, when you're the one who wouldn't take 'no' for an answer in the Pick 'N' Save parking lot." I reached up and poked him in the chest with my forefinger. "Or do you remember it differently?"

Serious, scowly silence.

I shook my head. "But I'm the poisonous man-trap who ruined all your best-laid plans, right? Luring a righteous guy like you into sin, with my evil shopping cart and my nefarious grocery list. You and your inability to keep it in your pants had nothing to do with it."

"I don't...that's not—"

"That's not what you mean?"

"I don't know what I mean, all right?" He spun away from me, pacing a circle around the kitchen. This took maybe three seconds. When he got back to where I was standing, he pressed his fists against the door of the fridge at either side of my head and said, "You...you're making it hard for me to think."

Call me vain, but I find it tough to hold a grudge against a guy who's just admitted my mere presence interferes with his basic thought processes. "Can I ask a question?"

"You can ask. Can't promise I'll answer."

I rolled my eyes. Typical cop. "What was it that tipped you off to me? What made you run the prints? Was it my slip about the older brother?"

He nodded. "That, and the Jersey accent that popped up after the third glass of wine. The blue contacts didn't help either."

"Shit."

"Plus there was the way you reacted to McDane. Pretty extreme."

I sighed. "Anything else?"

He considered me for a second or two. "You want to know the big tip-off?"

"Yeah."

He looked away, as if trying to formulate his next statement. "Generally speaking, nice girls named MaryJane from Indiana can't...they don't..."

"Suck cock like I do?"

For a second, I thought I'd finally killed him with my filthy, unfeminine mouth. His eyes got huge in his face and his throat worked like he was choking on his tongue. Then he made a noise that sounded like a growl, which turned into a laugh, all rich and dark like a whiff of good coffee from a brand new bag. It made my mouth water—made me want to taste his laughter, to see if it felt as good on my tongue as it sounded in my ears.

I went with the impulse. His reaction was satisfying, if a little overwhelming. He slammed me against the fridge as if he meant to bust us both right through the door. I heard glass rattle around inside and had time to wonder if anything spilled before there was no more oxygen to feed my brain because he'd squeezed it all out of my lungs, pressing up against me so hard. If I hadn't known better, I'd have sworn there were secret messages encoded on the roof of my mouth, the way he used his tongue on me.

Fragments of thoughts, like I should try to breathe, and this would be a good time to maybe lift my arms, skittered across the surface of my brain, but my lungs weren't taking orders at the moment, and my limbs felt as if they were full of wet sand.

He eased off finally and I sucked in some air. He muttered what might've been an apology, then licked a trail up my neck and chased it with a bite to my earlobe.

"Bedroom," he said, more distinctly, but with a pained undertone. Like maybe it would cause him physical discomfort not to be kissing me for the thirty seconds it would take us to relocate.

I nodded, not interested in wasting perfectly good oxygen on words. He let me lead—if you could call it that—with his hands on my hips, propelling me along, out of the kitchen and down the hall. I stumbled through the doorway and he steadied me, wrapping his arm around my chest and pulling me back against him. I looked up and caught our reflections in the mirror. The room was dim and we looked like strangers—some other couple preparing to get busy in my bed. He nuzzled my hair, pulling my robe aside to get at my shoulder. I shut my eyes and turned in his arms, afraid to watch. Scared that if I let myself see, I'd freak out or freeze up. Ruin it somehow.

We moved toward the bed, and I heard his foot make contact with something—the box of tapes and CDs I'd left on the floor. He stopped and looked down. To distract him, I reached for his belt-buckle.

"You're in a rush again," he said. He didn't smile.

"I got cheated last night. I want my money's worth this time around."

His eyes narrowed. "Your money's worth?"

"Just an expression." I worked the belt open, then started with the buttons on his 501s. "Lose the shirt, Donnelly."

"I'm not sure I like your tone of voice."

"Somebody can dish out the bossy," I said, "but can somebody take it?"

His left eyelid flickered, and I knew I had him. Five seconds later, he was standing before me, completely nude. I took a step back and just…contemplated him. And wished real hard for a glass of water.

"Satisfied?" The edge in his voice was tough to miss.

"Not really." I untied my robe, slid it off my arms and tossed it onto the foot of the bed. Then I stepped out of the white cotton panties I'd slipped into after my shower and kicked them away. "Your move, Agent Donnelly."

He kept his gaze on my face. "Does this have to be a contest?"

"Doesn't it?"

"No." In move I'd seen before in a movie or two, he bent and lifted me, one arm beneath my knees, the other braced under my shoulders. "But so long as we're being competitive, it's Special Agent Donnelly."

"Special Agent?" I kicked my legs. "Put me down so I can genuflect, why don't you?"

"'Special Agent in Charge,' if you want to get technical."

"Christ, I thought the guns were supposed to be compensating for something with you law-and-order types."

He tossed me onto the bed and crawled in after me, looking distinctly predatory. I've made some dumb-bunny moves in my lifetime—up to and including getting involved with a Fed in the first place—but I knew when to lie back and shut up. The way he was looking at me? This was one of those moments.

He straddled my hips and sort of loomed over me. I got the feeling he was taking inventory. "What color are your eyes? The real color, I mean."

I looked away, feeling self-conscious. "Nothing special. Just…brown."

He appeared to think about that for a second or two. "Take out the contacts next time?"

I nodded, suddenly tongue-tied. Something about his assuming there'd be a next time made my heart skip three beats and then jump into overdrive. I reached up and brushed a curl off his forehead. He caught my hand and pressed his lips into the palm. Then he fell forward, catching himself on his forearms. I tasted his breath, felt his skin over every inch of my own. He leaned in and whispered, "Call me Drew when you come in my mouth."

It wasn't the statement so much as the tone of command in his voice that made my breath stop dead in my chest.

"Did you hear me?"

Hear him? My whole damn body had heard him, if the sudden rush of heat was any indication.

"I'll take that as a 'yes,'" he said, and I didn't even bother to roll my eyes.

Then it was all stinging nips in sensitive places as he worked his way down my body to his ultimate destination. Good thing I wasn't expecting any polite formalities, or even anything in the way of preparation, because what I got was the sudden swirling, dipping rasp of his tongue, over and over, slow and relentless. Not enough and way, way too much, all at the same time. Maybe he was waiting for me to ask for what I needed, but that was a little too close to begging for my taste. I twisted my hands in the sheets, bit my lip and hung on—an over-sensitized, shuddery mess.

Just when I thought I'd have to tell him to stop out of sheer self-defense, something changed. What had registered on the knife's edge of discomfort became compelling—a buzzing, almost peppery heat that built fast and made me grind against his face. I let go with a noise that could politely be described as a groan, and he answered with a low, feral-sounding grunt of his own that made my toes curl so hard I thought my calves would cramp.

"D-Drew—" My teeth chattered around the word as everything burst wide open.

He gentled his touch by the merest fraction, letting me ride it out, rather than pushing me through it. Time stretched like cinnamon taffy—the kind you could buy on the boardwalk in August—all sticky and hot and lazy and long. Seconds between the heartbeats, between the rocking waves and tingly shocks.

And then he was pulling away, climbing back up my body like he couldn't get to me fast enough. My hips kept rising off the bed, bumping my body against him, straining for contact. I heard the tear of a wrapper, felt his hands on my thighs, lifting. Then he was pressing inside me, shoving against me with very necessary roughness. I could feel the tension in him wherever we touched.

He stopped and heaved a huge breath. "You okay?"

"Yeah." I lifted one knee, shifting a bit under him. "You?"

He leaned over me again, bringing us into better alignment, and made a quick circle with his hips. "Yeah," he whispered. He leaned on one arm and rubbed his thumb back and forth over my bottom lip, his eyes slitted and hungry. When he kissed me, he finished it with two bites—the first one hard, the next one softer.

Then he began to move in a push-pull-pump rhythm that made my arms rise all by themselves and clutch at his back. I ran my hands up and down, feeling the muscles roll and twist. And then he began to talk, husky murmuring in my ear, full of lowdown, dirty intent. Words like "hot" and "tight" and "make you" and "beg me." His voice was barbed wire catching at me, dragging me down into someplace dark and thick with steam and slick, wet slapping sounds.

"Harder." I rocked under him, desperate again. Surprised I could be so desperate, so soon.

He lunged at me like he meant to screw me through the mattress, muttering a string of curses I could barely make out. I lifted my other leg and he grabbed it, hiking it to his shoulder. The change in angle caught me by surprise, made me sing out, and even the sound of my voice was startling. He clutched at my hips, using them to gain leverage to push deeper. I dug my nails into his back, and the noise he made sounded as if it was being wrung out of him against his will.

"Harder," I said again.

This time he hesitated, clearly torn. While I appreciated the sentiment, my patience was wearing thin. I leaned up and bit his shoulder. Hard.

"Fuck." He pushed me down onto the bed, grabbed both my wrists in one of his hands and held me there while he pounded into me at that perfect new angle I wanted to memorize for all time. "This what...you wanted?"

But I was too far gone to answer, coming around him, losing the rhythm as my body tried to shudder and pulse itself apart—more intense this time, though maybe not as sweet. Somewhere near the end, I opened my eyes in time to see him lose control. The muscles in his back quit rolling and started jerking, and his mouth twisted. Just before he shut his eyes, I caught a glimpse of something pained...troubled waters brimming over. His teeth made two deep, white marks in his lower lip and he swore a final time as he slammed us both into the mattress. Then it was just a matter of letting the spasms and jitters die out as our breathing settled into its normal patterns.

After a minute, he rolled off me and took care of practical matters. Then he pulled me close, anchoring me against him with one strong arm. I'm not a big cuddler, historically speaking, but this felt...not awful. We lay there a while. I was betting he'd be the first to speak. He didn't let me down.

"You ready to tell me the rest?"

I knew what he meant. If I'd been in my right mind, I might've resented his using my vulnerable, post-orgasmic state against me. But I wasn't. In my right mind, that is.

My throat felt sticky inside, like flypaper, and I wished for water, but not enough to actually crawl out of bed and all the way to the bathroom. I coughed and rasped and cleared out the debris as well as I could, and said, "Well, you know the DA dropped the charges in exchange for my testimony against Carl and my father."

"Right. But how did Carl and your father feel about it?"

"Carl threatened to have me maimed, which was only to be expected."

"And your dad?"

"He understood," I said and closed my mouth, unwilling to go any further in that direction.

Donnelly seemed to get it. "And then what?"

"And then I got the hell out and didn't look back."

"You've never been back to Bayonne?"

"My mother made it clear I wasn't welcome."

"Oh."

"Yeah."

Awkward silence. I lay there, staring at the ceiling. After a few minutes, I heard his breathing turn slow and even. For some reason, the padlock on the door in his trailer flashed into my mind, and I remembered all the bad shit I'd imagined.

"What're you smiling about?"

I hadn't realized he was watching me. *Sneaky bastard.* "I thought you were asleep."

"Resting my eyes." He shifted a bit and brought his hand down to stroke my arm. "Why the smile?"

I executed what amounted to a horizontal half-shrug. "I'm guessing you've got—what? State-of-the-art computer equipment in the back bedroom of your trailer?"

There was a pause—long enough that I wondered if he'd answer. Then, in a quiet, guarded-sounding tone, he said, "Among other things."

He meant guns. Of course he did. "I guess that's better than my first suspicion."

"Which was?" he asked, then lifted his head and pressed a kiss on my shoulder.

"A crystal-meth lab."

He snorted against my skin, which tickled like hell. I pushed him off and he fell back, laughing. "Another thing that sets you apart from the MaryJanes of the world—your naturally open and trusting nature."

For some reason, the sarcasm bothered me. I rolled away from him and pulled myself up to sit.

"Hey," he said. "I didn't mean—"

"It's okay. You're right—I'm cynical. A real tough broad." I perched on the edge of the bed, feeling more naked than I had at any point in the previous hour, and peeked at him over my shoulder. "You're allowed to tell the truth."

He pressed the heels of his hands against his eyes and let out a sigh. "I'm not usually such a pig. This investigation is kicking my ass."

I bit back a pointless comment about pigs and law enforcement and just looked at him, not knowing what to say. He wasn't really going to talk about his case, was he? I mean, I didn't know much about the rules of the Eff Bee Eye, but I figured that had to be a big one: No sharing details of an ongoing investigation with your brand new fuck-buddy. Especially if said fuck-buddy has a felony arrest record.

Plus, I really didn't want to hear it. The very thought of being privy to whatever nasty, sordid thing was going down in Port Jonah made my stomach want to surrender its contents for immediate inspection. And hadn't there been enough of that for one afternoon? Except...Christ, the clock on the bedside table read six-thirty, which made it afternoon no more. A bolt of restless energy shot up my spine, making me want to get up and get moving. To where, I didn't know.

Donnelly flopped over onto his stomach. He was so damned casual about his nakedness. It made me want to be contrary and grab the edge of the sheet and yank it back up over his perfect, Calvin Klein-model contours.

"You know a guy named Ari Avramis, by any chance?" he asked. "Early fifties, Greek immigrant, slick in an oily kind of way?"

I slid off the bed and walked to the dresser, hoping he'd take the hint and pick a different topic of conversation. I opened the top drawer, snagged a pair of underwear and a baby-blue t-shirt with a Crawford's smiling lobster logo, and pulled them on. He didn't seem to notice my change of mood.

Or if he did, he didn't care. "Anyway, this Avramis guy—he's a real player. Got his fingers in a lot of pies locally. We think he's been running drugs and guns out of the marina since he took ownership there."

I turned so I was watching his face in the mirror. His eyes were scanning the room, taking in every detail. It was on the tip of my tongue to say I didn't know Avramis. Had never met the man. My standard response to any situation: lie, and keep on lying. Of course, that particular prevarication would've been a stupid one. Easy enough to find out if Avramis had dealings with the bank. But the instinct was strong. Nearly irresistible.

I said nothing. Because the sick twist in my gut told me what was coming next.

Donnelly sat up in bed. I turned to face him. He said, "I know Avramis is into something at the bank—something with your manager, Regina James."

He swallowed. His mouth was a tight, crooked grimace. He didn't like having to do this. I could tell. I didn't give a rat's ass.

"And you want me to find out what it is." It wasn't a question.

He nodded.

I walked to the bedroom door and yanked it open so hard the knob bounced off the wall behind it, leaving a mark on the paint.

"Get out," I said. "Don't come back." I'd love swear my voice didn't wobble and break on the last few words, but I'd be lying.

CHAPTER 7

To his credit, he didn't bother acting surprised. He just hiked himself off the bed and reached for his jeans. He kept his eyes on my face as he dressed, and I watched him watching me, refusing to give him the satisfaction of looking away. You could've struck a match off the tension in the room by the time he pulled on his boots and stood up straight to face me.

"It doesn't have to be like this."

"Yeah," I said. "Actually, it does."

"I didn't come here to—"

"To what? Threaten to expose my past? Or fuck me into submission?" I tried to laugh, and it came out like a snarl through bared teeth.

"Stop it." His voice sounded raw. Apparently, I'd struck a nerve. "What did you expect? Did you think you could hide forever?"

"What did I expect?" I advanced on him. I don't know what he saw in my face, but he backed up a step. "What was I thinking? I was thinking that after I got my jaw and collarbone busted by an overzealous cop, and did the jail-time, and ratted out my boyfriend and my father—my fucking father, Donnelly, do you know that that means?"

"Eva—"

"Shut up. I'm talking now." I stopped maybe two feet in front of him, breathing hard and hating him. Not for what he'd done so much as for what he was making me feel. "I was thinking that after I gave up

SIN STREET

my family and my friends and my whole life and everything I ever knew, and came here and started over and was a good girl and a stand-up citizen for three solid years, that I'd earned myself some little sliver of peace. That's what I was thinking." I inhaled, tasting sex in the close air of the bedroom. "But I was wrong. Okay, fine, I can live with that. You need to punish me for my sins? You go right ahead. But you can't get me to turn on Regina—"

"She's in trouble, Eva—"

"It's Mary-Fucking-Jane." I pressed my lips together, suddenly terrified I'd bust out bawling if I kept going.

The muscles in his jaw worked, as if he wasn't having much luck hanging onto his own composure. "Fine. I'm telling you, your boss is in trouble. Avramis is serious business. He makes people go away forever. We don't find the bodies—they just disappear. You can help Regina if you just talk to me about what's going on."

"And I'm supposed to trust you because...?"

"Because I'm asking you to. Because I'm not threatening you, or forcing you, even though I could."

The brown folder, still sitting on the kitchen counter. Like a live grenade in the middle of my life, with Donnelly's finger on the pin. "Right. You didn't threaten. You thought you'd screw it out of me instead."

He lifted his hand, sudden and sharp. I flinched, but he was only going for his own face, as if he wanted to claw it off. "That's not how it was."

"Liar."

The word fell like a hundred-pound weight and lay on the floor between us. When Donnelly spoke again, his voice was subdued, defeated. "I'm sorry. I should never have touched you. That was a mistake."

"And?"

"And what? What do you want me to say?" I could hear his palm rasp across the stubble on his jaw as it drew it back and forth. "You want to believe some fairytale about how the good guys never fuck up and the bad guys always go down in the end, you go right ahead. But that's not my story."

"What's that supposed to mean?"

He shook his head and smiled. I hated to see it, all cold and calculating like that, but I was guessing I'd seen the last of anything warm or genuine. I didn't care. No, of course I didn't.

"Why the hell do you think I'm out here in this backwoods burg?" he said. "I've got ten years with the agency—what does that say to you? You want to talk about punishment, about guilt? Ask me what I did to pull this assignment sometime, MaryJane." He said the name like a curse, and suddenly I wished he'd go back to using Eva.

The phone on my bedside table rang, making us both jump.

"I should get that."

"I'm not stopping you." He didn't move.

The answering machine picked up after four rings. There was only silence on the other end.

"You should leave now." I put as much conviction into my voice as I could muster.

He nodded. "I'm going." He brushed past me on his way out of the bedroom. I followed him down the hall and through the early-evening dimness of the kitchen. He stopped with his hand on the doorknob and turned to look at me. "I know what you think. But what happened here today had nothing to do with the Avramis investigation."

"Yeah. Sure." I stared at a spot on the linoleum.

"Can I ask one question?"

Something in his tone made me look up. His expression was lost in the shadows.

I nodded. "Yes."

"If I hadn't…if we hadn't—"

"Fucked like weasels?"

He made a noise that might've been a laugh. It might've been a strangled, manly sort of sob, too, but I was betting on the laugh. "Yeah. If we hadn't done that, and if I hadn't gone poking around in your past…"

"Would I have helped you with Regina?"

"Yeah," he said, just above a whisper.

"Probably not." I took a single step toward him, but only because I just couldn't—could not—resist the weird, magnetic pull of our shared misery. "But at least I wouldn't hate myself so much right now. Or you either."

What little bit of light there was in the room bounced off his teeth when he smiled. "Sure you would. I'd still be a cop, right?"

He stood there a second or two longer. Then he turned and let himself out. I locked the door behind him.

* * *

I thought about tidying the bedroom and changing the sheets, but couldn't face the evidence of my own stupidity. On the other hand, I couldn't quite bring myself to jump into the shower and wash away Donnelly's scent. Mary, Mary, quite contrary—way to live up to my alias, huh?

And so I spent the night on the sofa, with the TV turned up loud and the rest of the bottle of vodka within easy reach, though I never went so far as to drink any. The phone rang again at eight and one more time around nine-thirty. Whoever called left no message.

Sometime after three in the morning, I slept, and found myself caught in the old dream—the one I thought I'd left behind when I said goodbye to Bayonne. The dream that wasn't a dream at all, but a memory warped into a nightmare.

I stand on the street outside the family business, the neon sign blinking and swirling over my head—Pietra's Bar and Grill. The block is deserted, which seems weird for a Friday night in July. I look down and see I'm wearing my work clothes—a skirt and heels.

Where's Carl? Why doesn't he come? We'll never make our flight if he doesn't hurry.

The sound of a ringing telephone drifts through the open window of the apartment over the bar. Someone's calling my name...*Dad?* I look up, but the window slams shut. Footsteps in the alley between the buildings and then a middle-aged man wearing a mustache and a dark suit appears in the mouth of the alley, holding a gun. Holding it on me.

"Don't move. Keep your hands where I can see 'em."

And I run, without stopping to wonder or think. Because he might be a cop, or he might be one of Big Eddy's boys come to settle up a day early. And when he takes me down with a right-cross and bounces me off the curb a few times for good measure, I tell myself I'm lucky he didn't blow my brains all over the sidewalk where I used to play hopscotch.

He's telling me I have the right to remain silent, and I'm trying not to pass out from the pain. I turn my head to look at him, once, square in the face. And he's not middle-aged anymore, and he doesn't have a mustache, and he's not wearing a suit.

He's Donnelly.

I woke up choking on what might've been a scream. The pre-dawn light was gray, pasty and cold. It reminded me of other light, in another place, where they never let you forget what a rotten excuse for a human being you are, living off the taxpayers' hard-earned cash because you couldn't manage to walk a straight line. The pain in my chest felt like an animal clawing its way out of a trap. I fought it because I knew if I gave in, I'd be worthless for hours. But there was no winning that war. In the end, I stuffed my head under the pillow to stifle the sobs that sounded a lot like they belonged to that trapped animal, and just let it all go.

It was seven o'clock and full daylight by the time I pulled it together enough to move off the sofa and into the kitchen in search of water. I flicked on the overhead light and was instantly mocked by the remnants of the snack Donnelly had made me. I thought about grabbing a garbage bag and dropping all of it—bread crusts, napkin, plate, milk-stained glass—into the trash. That way, every time I reached into the dishwasher, I wouldn't be wondering, *Is this the one he touched? Or was it this one?*

And then the brown folder caught my eye from its resting place on the counter where Donnelly had left it. On purpose? Was it a peace offering? Or would he be back to fetch it and maybe harass me some more? I closed my eyes and recalled a few choice moments from the previous evening, letting myself go a little boneless in the doorway.

"Oh, my God, will you get a freaking grip?" I made an about-face and headed for the bathroom. One scalding shower later, I felt sharp enough to wonder where the hell I was going to do my grocery shopping now that the Pick 'N' Save was no longer an option.

The phone rang while I was brushing my teeth. I waited to see if anyone would speak to my machine. Nothing. Which made four calls and four hang-ups in a row. If I hadn't been so deeply entrenched in my personal soap opera, I would've caught on to the weirdness sooner—or so I tried to tell myself. As it was, I went around the house checking the locks and scanning the street for unfamiliar cars...and every time I closed my eyes, I saw that missing note. You remember—the one with the bloody thumb-print?

Donnelly's voice seemed to seep out of the walls. "I'm telling you, your boss is in trouble. Avramis is serious business. He makes people go away forever. We don't find the bodies—they just disappear."

"Shut up," I said a little louder than was probably necessary, given that I was completely alone in the house.

That's when I got the bright idea to check my cell phone. I hardly ever used it, due to what could charitably be called spotty reception in pretty much all of Washington County. And what do you know? Five new voicemail messages, all of them dead air.

SIN STREET

The phone rang again while I was holding it, scaring me so much I dropped it and watched it bounce across the bedroom floor. I grabbed it just before it slid under the dresser.

"Hello?" I'm pretty sure I sounded breathless.

"MJ? Is that you?"

"Regina?" Of course it was Regina. Who else would be trying to reach me repeatedly on a weekend—or any other time, for that matter? I had no friends, and my family had disowned me.

"I've been trying to—"

"Yeah, there's something wrong with my phone. Sorry about that." Because lying was my thing—it's what I did. Even when I didn't have to.

"Listen, I won't be in tomorrow. Or the rest of the week, probably. I..." Her voice got a little funny. I couldn't tell if it was lousy phone reception or if she was crying.

"Reggie? Aristotle Avramis is coming in tomorrow to see you. What should I tell him?"

Silence.

"Regina?"

"I'm here. MJ, I need you to do me a favor. Two favors actually." Her voice had come back stronger, with an edge of resolve I'd heard once before, when she'd had to fire a teller who wasn't pulling his weight. "Are you listening?"

"Yeah," I said. "Shoot."

"I need you to tell Mr. Avramis for me that the arrangement is off. Do you understand?"

I swallowed. The air in the bedroom was suddenly very thick. "Regina—"

"Don't ask questions, MJ. The less you know, the better."

"But—"

"He's going to be angry, but he's not going to make a scene during business hours." Her voice softened. "I hate to do this to you, MJ. I'm sorry."

I took another breath. "What's the other favor?"

There was a pause. Then she said, "Force the lock on my bottom, left-hand desk drawer. In there, you'll find a file marked 'Avramis.'"

"Force the lock? Can't I just drive over to your house and get the key?"

She sighed. "I won't be here." There was another pause, then she said, "Take the file out of the bank. Do not read it, MaryJane. I'm not kidding." Her voice began to wobble again.

"All right, I won't. What—"

"Burn it. The whole thing. Every scrap."

"Regina? You're not coming back, are you?"

The pause this time lasted much longer. "I'm really sorry, MaryJane. I hope…" Her voice faded, and the line went dead.

Yeah. I hoped so, too.

SIN STREET

CHAPTER 8

I thought about calling Donnelly.

I thought about it while I tossed out the stale bread-crusts and put the plate and glass in the dishwasher. I thought about it while I changed the sheets and emptied the wastebasket in my bedroom. I thought about it while I paced up and down in front of the TV, an old Bogart movie playing on a station out of Bangor. (Not *Casablanca*. Because as weird as my life was, it hadn't yet attained that level of freakiness.)

I thought about it while I picked at a frozen pizza, and while I lay on the sofa and mostly didn't sleep, and while I got ready for work the next morning, and while I drove to the bank—a full hour ahead of my usual time, with a nail file, a hammer and two screwdrivers in my bag, and only a vague idea of how I was going to use them.

In the end, I told myself I didn't call because I didn't have his number. Like I said—lying was my thing. I'd gotten so good at it, I could even fool myself some of the time.

The lock on Reggie's drawer proved to be a lot easier than I'd anticipated. I guess if she hadn't indulged her love of antiques and gone instead with the standard-issue steel and aluminum, I'd have been screwed. As it was, I used the flat-head driver as a chisel, and the hundred-year-old oak surrounding the lock splintered under the fourth blow from the hammer. It took another ten minutes to destroy the drawer. But I was in, and that's what mattered.

The file lay all by itself on the bottom. In my heightened state of insanity, I'd have sworn it hissed at me when I reached for it. That

SIN STREET

sucker was thick, too—bursting with documents and binder clips. I glanced up at the clock on the wall, calculating how much time I had to clear away the mess, drive home, dispose of the file and drive back again before the tellers began to arrive.

Plenty of time, as it turned out. More than enough. So much, in fact, that it seemed a shame not to take at least one little peek inside this apparently lethal collection of papers. Because what had my mother always said? "Curiosity killed the cat." But what had my father always answered? "And satisfaction brought her back."

My peaceful existence had been gutted like a trout, thanks to my boss's extracurricular activities, and the nosy nature of a certain Fed. If I had to face down an angry Greek gangster like the rotten cherry on the sundae of the worst few days of my life, I'd damn sure know the reason why.

I sat back on the floor and opened the file.

"Holy shit, Regina. Are you fucking kidding me?"

And somewhere between six-fifty-one and six-fifty-two on that Monday morning in May, as I sat in the branch manager's office, surrounded by the debris from the sacrificed drawer, I had a small epiphany.

Okay, it was a pretty Goddamn large epiphany.

My life of quiet desperation was over.

*　*　*

Thirty minutes later, I found Donnelly unloading flats of strawberries at the back of the Pick 'N' Save. He looked disturbingly attractive in his bright white t-shirt and red apron and leather gloves.

"Aren't you cold? It's like forty degrees out here."

He walked away from the dolly to meet me at my car. "What do you want?"

"Good morning to you, too." I handed him one of the two tall cardboard containers of coffee I'd purchased inside the store. "I guessed you like your coffee black, two sugars. Was I right?"

He shrugged. "I thought you didn't drink coffee."

"I lied."

He took the container from me, but didn't drink. "What do you want?" he asked again.

"Man, you're not much of a morning person, are—"

"Cut the crap, MJ." He squeezed the container, and a few drops of

SIN STREET

liquid squirted up and out of the tiny hole in the lid to splash on his thumb. "Fuck. Goddammit."

I reached out to take the coffee from him and he backed up as if I'd pulled a knife. I lifted both my hands in a gesture of surrender and leaned against the door of my car. "Hey," I said. Just that. No more.

His eyes were shot through with red and underlined with dark crescents. He looked like he'd missed a shave or two. I wondered if maybe I wasn't the only one not getting much sleep. He bent and set the coffee on the pavement. When he straightened, his mouth was set in a hard line.

"I'm sorry," he said.

I sighed. "I didn't come here for—"

"It doesn't matter. I need to say it."

"Okay. You said it." I checked my watch. "Listen, the reason I'm here? We need to talk about…your thing." I looked at him, and his gaze sharpened. He nodded. "But I have to get to work," I said. "Can I meet you later tonight?"

"Where? What time?"

I thought about it. Neutral ground would be best, and the closer to the bank, the better. "How about here?" The Pick 'N' Save closed at six on Mondays. "Say…eight o'clock?"

He squinted at me. "Here? Are you sure?"

"Yes. I'll come around back. I have something to show you." For some reason, that sounded a lot less dirty in my head.

He still looked skeptical. "I don't think—"

I reached out and put a hand on his arm. This time, he didn't flinch. "Drew, as incredibly stupid as this sounds, you're going to have to trust me."

He looked at me, flat and expressionless. Then he nodded. "Thanks for the coffee." He bent to grab the container. "Just for the record? It's cream, no sugar."

I laughed and got into my car.

* * *

The meeting with Avramis went just as I'd hoped.

"Yes, sir, I absolutely understand how disappointed you are, and I'm really very—"

"Sorry. So you said." Avramis tugged at his cuffs—a move I was sure was calculated to draw attention to his huge, diamond-and-platinum cufflinks. "I don't care about 'sorry,' Miss—what did you say your name was?"

"Peters. MaryJane Peters. And I completely understand your annoyance, sir. I can't imagine how inconvenient it must be to—"

"No, you cannot." Behind him, in the private conference room where we were seated, Georgie stood immovable as a redwood, his hands clasped behind his back. "And you say Miss James will be unavailable for the rest of the week?"

"Yes, sir. A family emergency. But if there's any way I could assist you—"

"No. Impossible." Avramis's face looked pinched and pissed-off, but his tone was resigned. He made a dismissive gesture and moved as if to stand.

"Are you sure?" I changed the tone of my voice, making it low and almost seductive. I flashed my eyes up at Georgie, then back to Avramis. "I think perhaps I could be of more help than you realize, sir."

Avramis froze halfway out of his seat. "What do you mean?"

I inclined my head and tapped the tip of my pen against the table. "Let's just say Ms. James isn't the only one with access to the…assets…you seek."

Avramis turned his head and looked at Georgie. The younger man shrugged and it was like watching the start of a landslide. Avramis looked at me, his eyes narrow and hard. "I do not play games, Miss Peters. As your Miss James will find out soon enough."

"I'm not playing any kind of game, sir. I'm making an offer."

Georgie shifted his stance behind his uncle's chair, letting his hands fall to his sides. Instantly, my eyes were drawn to his left thumb. Or, more specifically, the thick, white bandage on his left thumb.

Avramis was talking again. "I'm not in the habit of accepting offers, Miss Peters—I'm in the habit of making them." His meaning was clear. It was the difference between bribery and blackmail, and he preferred the latter.

"I apologize, Mr. Avramis, if I've offended you. I certainly—"

He held up a hand to cut me off. "However, since you so obviously have a desire to please…" He leered at me, letting his gaze wonder over the front of the silk shirt I prayed wasn't quite as sheer as it had been when I'd put it on that morning. "What are you proposing?"

I forced a smile. "I prefer not to discuss such delicate matters during business hours." I glanced around the room, taking in every corner of

the ceiling, hoping to make him feel apprehensive. "You never know who might be listening."
Ten minutes later, we had a meeting place and time.

* * *

Donnelly was squatting on the edge of the raised loading dock when I pulled around behind the Pick 'N' Save. He'd lost the red apron and exchanged his white t-shirt for a black one. Other than that, he looked pretty much the same. The sun was down and blue shadows lay over the ground—a setting made to order for a *film noir* rendezvous.

"You're early," I said, beating him to it this time.

He didn't take the bait. "Why are we here?"

A salty breeze picked up over the asphalt, lifting my skirt and blowing my hair into my eyes. I glanced around the lot, feeling more exposed than I liked. "Can we go inside? I have something you'll want to see." My bag felt heavier on my shoulder with every passing second.

He jumped down from the dock, all manly grace. I looked away because this was business. He pulled a set of keys out of his pocket and let us both into the back of the store. Darker there, and my eyes weren't adjusting to the change with anything like speed.

"Careful. It's a mess back here." He wrapped his fingers around my arm, just above my elbow, and steered me down what appeared to be a tunnel. "Somebody paid off the fire marshal." His tone was quiet and flat. As my vision sharpened, I could see the tunnel was, in fact, an aisle created by hundreds of pallets stacked side-by-side and fifteen feet into the air.

We reached an alcove that contained a couple of desks, a water-cooler and a rack of red aprons. Donnelly stretched across one of the desks and flicked on a goose-necked lamp. Then he dragged an ancient steel chair forward, letting its feet shriek across the concrete. "Have a seat."

"No, thanks." I checked my watch. One hour 'til my next meeting—not a lot of time. I reached into my bag and pulled out the file-folder, marked "Avramis" in large, dark letters. "Right before she skipped town, Regina told me to burn this."

He took the folder from me, his forehead crinkled in a question, and leaned on the edge of the desk. I stood in silence, shifting my weight from one foot to the other while he leafed through the documents. The minutes dripped by, slippery and slow, like oil out of an almost-empty jar.

Finally, he looked up. "Just so we're on the same page..."

"Yeah," I said. "Money laundering."

He blinked at me. "She's been feeding him records of the financial transactions of all the local businesses?"

"Apparently," I said. "With special emphasis on cash deposits and withdrawals. So Avramis knows which businesses—"

"Have enough cash flow to cover the occasional influx of money from his activities," Donnelly finished. "And if he spreads it around—"

"Among six or eight different businesses in town? Hell, he's already part-owner of three." I shook my head. "Pretty slick."

Donnelly went back to leafing through the documents. I checked my watch. "There's something else you should know."

"Yeah?" He didn't look up.

"I'm meeting Avramis at the bank in thirty minutes. He thinks I'm offering the same deal as Regina, although I'm not even sure what that was. I know he threatened her because there's a note—"

The folder made a loud, flat sound as it hit the desk. "What the fuck do you think you're doing?" Donnelly stood and took me by the arm.

I could tell from the tension in his hand he was about a half-second from doing the terrier-with-a-squeak-toy routine again.

"I think I'm helping you with your investigation. Setting up your—what d'you call it? Collar?"

He growled. I mean...actually growled. Pretty stimulating, under other circumstances. Not bad under these circumstances, except for the whole he-looked-like-he-wanted-to-kill-me thing.

"What makes you think I need your help?" His jaw was clenched so hard it hurt to look at it. "What makes you think...anything? Ever?" He punctuated that last word with a hard shake and let me go. Then he planted his ass on the edge of the desk again and crossed his arms over his chest.

I rubbed my arm. "You said this case was kicking your ass."

"That doesn't mean—"

"And Avramis is serious business. A real bad guy."

"Right. Which is why—"

I reached out and poked him in the bicep. "Which is why you wanted my help."

We stood there, breathing at each other.

"You're crazy if you think I'm letting you do this." He put his hand on the folder.

I coughed, only because it was more polite than laughing in his face. "Those are copies. But thanks for your high opinion of my intelligence." I pivoted on my heel and started to move.

His hand flashed out and grabbed my wrist. "No."

I turned my head partway, not quite looking at him. "Yeah, Drew. I'll do this alone if I have to."

"How?"

"I have a little tape recorder thingy in my bag—"

"Which he'll search, first thing. And then you're screwed."

I shrugged. "Maybe. But you'll never know, will you?"

"I could hold you here. Keep you until it's too late."

I turned so my whole body faced his, reached into my bag and pulled out the bloodstained note. It had been in the back of the folder, paper-clipped to the last document. I held it by my fingertips, not wanting to touch it. I set it on the desk, in the pool of light from the lamp.

"You do that, and I'll have to leave town, right behind Regina," I said. "And you promised you weren't here to ruin my life. Remember?"

He stared at the note for a few seconds. Without looking at me, he said, "You don't play fair." His voice caught on a jagged note. When he turned his head to look at me, his pupils looked like they were bleeding—pools of black spilling wide into troubled gray. I moved closer without knowing why...except that, for a moment, the balance of power between us tipped. I found my left hand brushing against the inside of his right thigh, where it was hiked onto the desk. My nails scratched against the denim as I traced the seam of his jeans down and away.

He made a raw sound in the back of his throat and pressed his lips into the place where my neck met my shoulder. I heard him mutter something that sounded like...

"Did you just call me...Kryptonite?" I pulled away from him, trying to get a better look at his face. "Glad to see you don't suffer from a lack of ego to go along with that lack of conscience."

His smile in response was neither cold nor wry, but downright wicked. The air temperature around us spiked, sharp and quick as the flare of a match head. He ran his hands up and down my arms, and when he spoke, his voice was sandpaper and satin. "How much time do we have?"

I checked my watch. "Twenty minutes."

"Plenty." He slid my jacket off my shoulders and tossed it on the chair. I felts his fingers playing along the hem of my skirt, just above my knees. "Pantyhose?"

"I didn't know there'd be a need for easy access."

"Lose them." He gave me a gentle shove and reached into his back pocket for his wallet.

"This is a bad idea. We don't have—"

He pulled out a condom and dropped the wallet on the desk. "No, it's not, and yes, we do. Lose the hose."

So much for that tipped balance of power. I kicked off my heels, stripped off the offending garment, balled it up and stuck it into my bag. "Satisfied?"

He grabbed me by the waist and set me on the edge of the desk, like a wayward crate of tangerines. Then he kissed me, all slow and steady and heated, like we had all the time in the world. While he did that, I went to work on his buckle and button and zipper.

He broke the kiss. "Rushing me. Again."

"Next time—"

"Next time?"

"Yeah," I said. "Next time. No rush. Promise." I slid my hand inside his jeans and boxers, and he was ready. Hot and hard, and when I touched him, I felt the tension in his body coil in on itself, tight and barely controlled. He fumbled for a second with the condom, and I took it from him. While I opened the wrapper and set it aside, he nuzzled my neck, murmuring things I'm sure were utterly filthy.

Then he lifted his head and cleared his throat. "This thing with Avramis—you're not trying to prove something to me, are you?"

My fingers froze in the act of rolling the latex down the length of him. "Wow. Score another one for the ego that ate Port Jonah."

CHAPTER 9

I shrugged his hands off my shoulders and slid off the desk, stumbling over my shoes as I stepped away from him. "This may come as a shock, Agent Donnelly, but not everything is about you."

"I didn't mean—"

I shoved at him. "You keep saying that." My voice rose, making a shrill echo. "Do you even know what you mean?"

I think he hated me, in that fraction of a second. I know I wasn't his biggest fan. But when he reached for me again, I didn't fight him. I let him spin me around and push me between his body and the desk. I let him lift my skirt, and when I felt his hand on the back of my neck, I let him shove me down so my cheek was pressed against the folder marked with Avramis's name.

His hands felt hot as they nudged my legs apart, and hotter still on my hips as they held me in place. He didn't pause, and he didn't give warning. There was just the feel of him, heavy and slick against the back of my thigh, and then he was pushing and sliding and almost-too-much.

He didn't wait this time—didn't stop to give me time to catch my breath or ask if everything was good from my point of view. And that was fine because we were in a hurry, right? And he was angry, and I was angry, and angry sex could be…could be very…

My brain gave up searching for the right word to describe it as my hands did this scrabbling thing across the top of the desk, in a quest for something to hold onto. Without breaking stride, Donnelly let go of my right hip and braced his palm against my upper back, stilling me.

"You don't need to be moving now," he said. Only with a broken, raspy quality that made me want to chew on something. "What you need to do...is to lie there," he said, "and let me do...this."

And I was okay with that. Really, really okay. Even when he thrust too hard, banging the tops of my thighs against the edge of the desk in a way I knew would leave a bruise. Even when he dug his fingernails into my hip like he wanted to draw blood. *All good, baby.* I just rocked back harder and smiled when I heard him grunt.

Every third stroke was driving me up on my toes, with a deep bump and drag that set up a buzz in my head, in my blood, in every fiber of every muscle. The hand in the middle of my back began to migrate, sliding over my neck, pulling at my hair. It found my face, and his thumb slipped into my mouth. I sucked on it and bit down on the pad. His hips stuttered, thrusting up sharply, and he let fly with a curse or two.

I could tell he was close, but I needed...something. Because fucking a Fed over a desk in a deserted stockroom ten minutes before meeting a gangster just wasn't enough stimulation for me apparently. Donnelly seemed to get it. He straightened, pulling his hand from my face. Then he ran his still-damp thumb down the cleft of my ass, light and slow, then back up again—harder, pressing...harder. Something dark bloomed behind my squeezed-shut eyes, and someone sobbed, and it was me, breaking under him. I ground myself into the edge of the desk as he slammed me home, talking more of his filth that sounded like love-poems. And then we were done.

He pulled me back to sit in his lap on the chair. His open zipper was scratchy against my hip, and I didn't care.

"We need to move," I said, after a minute.

"Avramis will wait." He took a deep breath and let it out. I pulled my head off his shoulder and looked at him. His hair was over his forehead in a tangle, sweaty and thick, and his eyes were a hazy, unfocused glaze. One of his hands kept drawing tight circles against my back, and I swear I could hear the thud of his heart against the wall of his chest.

"You okay?" I asked.

He laughed, a huff of hot air on my face. "I should be asking you."

"Nah. I'm good."

"You sure? I...uh...think I lost it there. For a minute." He coughed, nervous, and looked away.

I bit the inside of my cheek to keep from smiling. "Ya think?"
He laughed again, real this time. "We'd better move."

* * *

We discussed our strategy on the way to the bank. Like all good plans, it was simple, straightforward and involved my getting out of the way fast and letting the professional do his job. We arrived three minutes late, but Avramis and company were nowhere to be seen. So we sat in the employees' parking lot and made conversation...mostly about the weather and how funny it was that Avramis—a supposed criminal mastermind—refused to trust digital information or computers.

Donnelly shrugged. "His loss. It's a lot harder to wipe fingerprints off a folder than a disk." He sighed and shifted, trying to get comfortable on the floor of the car. Even with the passenger-side seat pushed all the way back, it was a nearly impossible fit. "Can I ask a question without you flipping out?"

"Sure," I said and gripped the steering wheel a little tighter.

"If you're not trying to prove something to me with this Avramis thing, then what's it about?"

It was a reasonable question. I tried to ignore my rising panic long enough to frame an answer. "You remember how I said I'd been such an upright citizen for the past three years?"

He nodded, his expression lost in the shadows.

"Well, it occurred to me that it's not enough."

"But—"

"Listen. I did a bad, wrong thing. And maybe it wasn't for such a horrible reason—maybe I was scared for my dad, and maybe that helps a little. But it was still a wrong thing, and I knew it then, and I know it now." I set my jaw and stared at an approaching set of headlights. They passed the bank and kept going. "Now I can do a right thing, and even the score."

I heard him heave a sigh. "You know what? That's really..."

"What?" I asked. "What is it?"

"Stupid." That's what he said—the word he used. But that's not what I heard. Because his tone of voice turned "stupid" into something else.

Under other circumstances, I might've asked him what he meant, but I couldn't afford to get into it at the moment. I decided turnabout was fair play.

"So…what did you do to pull this assignment, Agent Donnelly?"

He shifted again, and I heard his head thump against the dash. "Damn it."

"Come on, spill it," I said. "The *Readers' Digest* version would be good."

I could feel him looking at me through the close air in the car. Finally, he said, "I was on a case last year, working undercover as a substitute teacher in Kentucky. Anti-government survivalists holed up in a small town in the hills."

"Go on," I said, though something in the flatness of his delivery told me he really didn't want to.

"There was a kid, seventeen years old—a nephew of one of the cell leaders. I got close to him and got him to feed me information about the group."

"Uh-oh." My stomach did a slow roll as I realized where this was going.

"Yeah. The kid—his name was Bobby—set me up to meet his uncle and a few dozen of his uncle's close, personal associates on what was supposed to be a weapons deal." I heard Donnelly swallow and wished I'd brought along a bottle or two of water. "The meeting went bad, and Bobby got caught in the crossfire. End of story."

I felt my hand pressed against my mouth and wondered when I'd put it there. "Was he…did he…?"

"Die? Yeah."

I didn't know what to say to that, other than "That's not going to happen this time." And could I really make that promise?

Headlights swung over the windshield of the car, blinding me. I froze for an instant, my breath dead in my chest.

"Showtime." Donnelly reached out and squeezed my thigh, his hand hot and hard. It was enough to get me moving. I opened the door, swung my legs out and stood.

Avramis met me on the sidewalk. Georgie stood in his usual position, just behind his uncle's left shoulder. I looked up and down the deserted street, at the closed-for-the-night shops for a block on either side of the bank, and shivered. Not a soul around to hear if things went bad.

"Good evening, Miss Peters," Avramis said, his tone pleasant. "I trust you came prepared to do business?"

I nodded. The wind blew stiff and damp, making me glad I'd taken the time to pull on my hose again. "We need to go in through the back of the bank—so no one sees. You understand?" I included both of the men in my gaze.

Avramis indicated with a sweep of his arm that I was to lead the way. It took every bit of my self-control not to glance into my car as we passed it. I unlocked the back door of the bank, disengaged the alarm and headed down the long, dim hallway, around the corner and up the stairs, with the two men behind me. I counted the seconds in my head, keeping my footsteps slow and measured, giving Donnelly plenty of time to get out of the car and follow through the door I'd only pretended to lock behind us.

I flicked on the overheads in the windowless conference room and allowed the men to enter before me. I left the door open so light spilled into the carpeted corridor. Then I reached into the bag for the file.

Avramis held up a hand. "Please, Miss Peters. A formality, but a necessary one—you understand."

I stood still as Georgie removed the bag from my shoulder and set it on the table between us. Then he ran his hands under my jacket and over my skirt. I stared straight ahead at the opposite wall, grinding my teeth and breathing hard through my nose. He lifted my skirt and slid two fingers between my thighs, searching for God-knows-what. I made a noise, high and tight, in the back of my throat, and looked at him. He didn't meet my eyes, though I noticed his face had gone a dark red. When he seemed satisfied I was concealing neither a weapon nor a wire, he grabbed the bag and pawed through it, coming up only with my wallet, phone and the file.

Avramis hummed with satisfaction, his fingers steepled in front of his face. "I'm very pleased, Miss Peters." He gestured toward a chair. "Sit down. We will discuss terms."

I perched on the edge of the folding chair, wincing only slightly. Behind me, in the hall, there was the smallest breath of sound. The hair on the back of my neck prickled.

"I offered your Miss James one-half of one percent of each transaction handled through your institution," Avramis said. He leaned forward on the table, placing his palms flat on the surface.

Georgie stood at attention in his customary place. His face had gone back to its normal pasty tone, but he still wasn't meeting my gaze.

Avramis continued, "In addition, I offered her my personal guarantee of safety for as long as we continued to do business together."

One-half of one percent...and he wouldn't whack her? *What a generous guy.* "That seems very reasonable," I said. "But may I ask a question?"

Avramis smiled wide and spread his hands as if to say he had no secrets. "Of course."

I looked him straight in the eye. "What did you have on Regina in the first place?"

He stared at me for a second or two. Then he laughed, deep and loud and long. "You're direct. I like that."

I didn't believe him.

He shrugged. "Let us just say your Miss James was not always as careful in her personal life as she was in her professional life."

Oh, Regina, what did you do, and who did you do it with? And how did this piece of shit find out about it?

"I see." I clasped my hands on the table in front of me and cleared my throat. "And do you have anything on me?"

Avramis tilted his head, considering me. "Not yet, kukla. Not yet." He pushed his chair back and stood, reaching for the folder.

I stood as well, and stepped to one side. *So far, so good.* I made a move to usher my guests out of the conference room and into the hall, where Donnelly would be waiting, concealed just inside the doorway of the break-room a few feet to the right. It was important that Avramis and his nephew go first, and that I duck back into the conference room and lock the door behind me once Donnelly identified himself and drew his weapon. Very important. Donnelly had made me repeat that part no less than three times in the car on the way over.

"You have to stay out of the middle of it, MaryJane. Do not get between me and the bad guys, okay?"

I reached out and flicked off the overheads, leaving us in the dim, orangey glow provided by the emergency lights tucked up in the corners of the hallway ceiling. "After you," I said, and held the door.

Avramis began to move, but Georgie hesitated, blocking the way. I glanced up and found him staring at me, his mouth working as if he meant to speak.

"Is there a problem?" Maybe my voice came out a little sharper than I intended.

Georgie's face flushed red again, and his lips went thin and tight. He stepped away from the door and stuck his arm out into the hall. "Ladies first," he said. His voice was high-pitched—almost squeaky.

My mind flashed on Mike Tyson. Rape accusations. Chewed off

ears. I tried not to shudder visibly. "No, go ahead. Please."

"You must forgive my nephew," Avramis said. He'd come around the table on the other side, effectively blocking my escape in that direction. "He means well, but his manners lack polish."

"That's...that's fine. No need to apologize." The slightest movement of a shadow in the hallway caught at my peripheral vision. I cleared my throat. "Well, gentlemen..." My voice trailed off. They looked at me expectantly.

I was so screwed.

CHAPTER 10

I tried to think through the terrified babble threatening to take over my brain.

There was no doubt in my mind Georgie was packing a weapon somewhere on his massive frame. It wouldn't surprise me to discover Avramis was as well. I already knew Donnelly had a .45 tucked in the back of his jeans, under the denim jacket he'd pulled out of his locker back at the Pick 'N' Save.

If I stepped into that hallway, I'd be the lone defenseless loser standing among three lethally armed combatants. And I'd put Donnelly at a distinct disadvantage, too. Because I'd begun to suspect he kind of liked me, and didn't want to see me get hurt, you know? Which is a dangerous thing for a cop when he's facing down the bad guys.

Shit.

I did the only thing that made sense in the moment. I stepped out into the shadowy hall, just like Avramis and George were waiting for me to do. But instead of turning right, in the direction from which we'd come—in the direction that would take us to where Donnelly was waiting—I turned left, toward the front of the bank. I was counting on Georgie being just a little slow on the uptake...and, God bless the boy, he didn't let me down.

Three feet, five feet, ten feet deeper into the darkness...

"Miss Peters? Where are we going?" Avramis sounded no more than slightly curious.

I turned completely around and—walking backwards now—grinned

SIN STREET

in what I hoped was a breezy, careless way. "I have something I think you'd like to see, Mr. Avramis. Something...special." I winked at him and glanced up at Georgie, who only just then was waking up to the change in plans. Beyond his bulk, I caught of flash of movement.

Donnelly. Catching up to us.

Avramis chuckled. For an instant, as we passed beneath one of the emergency lights, his teeth gleamed, and I thought of a shark. "What is this thing you have to show us, Miss Peters?" he asked.

"I'm hoping you'll think it's exciting enough to sweeten your offer. Say...a full percent of each transaction?" I tilted my head and picked up the pace, practically skipping backwards—a serious trick in two-inch heels. In the back of my throat, the taste of adrenaline and stark fear combined to nearly gag me.

Avramis laughed again. "Your ambition surprises me, Miss Peters."

We reached the lobby of the bank and stopped. To my right stood the main counter. Beyond it was my desk and Regina's office, which I'd locked that afternoon. To my left, the vault. Behind me, the front doors. Facing me were Georgie, Avramis—and Donnelly, maybe ten feet back, with his gun drawn and his badge in his other hand.

I took one step further into the center of the lobby and said, "It's not my ambition that should surprise you, Mr. Avramis."

You know how people who've been involved in a car wreck or some other bad experience talk about how everything happens in slow motion? Yeah. Like that.

Donnelly's voice was clear and precise as he said, "Federal Agent. Get down on the floor and put your hands behind your heads."

They didn't, of course. They turned and pulled their own guns, backing towards me fast. Donnelly ducked into the hall again and then into that last doorway—the janitor's closet, as it turned out. I heard bullets hitting wood and drywall as I dove sideways for the alcove at the end of the main counter, where folks could pause to fill out a deposit slip or endorse a check. I pulled my legs in, trying to make myself small. But there wasn't enough room, even with my arms wrapped around my head to block out the sound of someone's scream as a bullet hit home.

I opened my eyes in time to see Georgie fall, grabbing at the edge of the counter as he went down. The front of his coat was covered in a dark, spreading stain. He landed three feet from me, gasping like a goldfish in a quarter-inch of tap-water.

"Help me...you gotta...help..." His voice—still that high-pitched, little-boy-lost drone—made my teeth hurt. Instinctively, I leaned out and reached for him, wanting to pull him out of the way of more harm.

"MaryJane!"

I looked up and saw Donnelly crouched at the opposite end of the counter. He held his gun out with both hands, scanning back and forth across the width of the lobby. Avramis was nowhere in sight. Other than his nephew's gasping and gurgling, everything was quiet.

"Please, lady," Georgie mewled at me. "Please..."

"It'll be okay," I said, praying it was true because, even in the dark, he looked like shit. "We're going to get you some help. Just hang on." I leaned out of the alcove again, meaning to put my hand on his shoulder.

You know how those same people who talk about bad stuff happening in slow motion also say you never hear the bullet that hits you? I don't know who those people are, but they're two-for-two.

I looked down, and there was a hole on the inside of my right thigh, about four inches above my knee. I couldn't feel it—yet—but I could see it, and it was the ugliest thing I'd ever looked at. I stared at it a second longer, and then I got distracted by the gunfire.

Only when I made the mistake of trying to pull the leg back into the alcove did it wake up and start to scream. I'm not too proud to say I screamed right along with it. Everything went a little fuzzy for a while after that, but without the luxury of a vodka-on-ice to mellow me out when Donnelly showed up and started pawing at me.

"Where are you hit? Oh, fuck." He sounded seriously pissed off.

"Check on Georgie. He's hurt worse." Yes, I actually said that, but only because I was going into shock. Don't start drawing up the petition for sainthood or anything.

"Georgie's dead. So is Avramis." Donnelly took off his jacket tucked it around me. "I think the artery is nicked. I'm going to call nine-one-one and find something to use as a tourniquet. Try not to move." He was gone again.

I glanced down at my lap and...shit. It was a lot of blood. I turned my head and looked straight into Georgie's very dead face. Tears backed up behind my eyes. Poor kid. Never had a chance.

Donnelly was at my side again, with something long and dark in his hand. Avramis's tie. The irony was almost sweet.

"This is going to hurt like hell," he said. "Go ahead and yell if you have to."

I did. And I did some more. And some more after that, for good measure. Donnelly clamped his arm around me and held on while I got myself under control. Finally, when I had enough of a grip on the pain to push words through my chattering teeth, I said, "Are they coming?"

"Dispatcher said ten minutes."

I nodded. "You think...?" I didn't want to finish the sentence.

"You'll be fine." He cleared his throat. "I think you'll be fine."

"You're a crappy liar, you know that, Donnelly?" I tried to lift my head off his shoulder, but a wave of dizziness forced it back.

"Convinced you I was a grocery store clerk, didn't I?" His voice was soft and ragged in my ear, like an old, worn blanket.

"Assistant manager," I said and coughed. The jolt traveled down my body to my leg, making me steel myself against the pain. "Listen, will you do me a favor?"

"Name it."

I chewed at my lip and thought about how to phrase what I wanted. "If I don't...if..."

"You will. They're coming, they'll be here any minute."

"Yeah, but if I don't." I reached up and found his hand, where it rested on my arm. "Please?"

"What? I'll do anything, just say it."

"Make sure...make sure the stone says 'Eva,' okay? Not 'MaryJane'—'Eva.'"

He snorted, his breath moving my hair against my face. "Christ, that's morbid."

"Yeah, well, I'm that kind of girl." I looked up at the ceiling, so far away and getting farther all the time. "You asked me one question I never answered."

"Yeah? What's that?"

"Why I bothered to change my name when I wasn't convicted of anything."

He pressed a kiss to my temple. "It doesn't matter now."

"Sure it does," I said and licked my lips. "I couldn't look at Eva Pietras in the mirror anymore—couldn't stand the sound of the name, couldn't look at it written on a piece of paper. By the end of the trial, I didn't want to know that person, much less *be* her."

"And now?"

I shrugged, and instantly wished I hadn't. The world faded away in a wash of red agony. When it came back, he was rubbing my arms and murmuring in my ear, warm and low. Making a supreme effort, I said, "And now...like I asked, make sure the stone has the right name. My mother may fight you, but don't back down. Her breath is worse than her bite."

He laughed outright at that. "You're a piece of work, you know that?"

"That's what my dad always said." I blinked a few times in an attempt to clear my head. "I'm trying to remember if...yeah. There's one more."

"One more what?"

"One more lie. Remember how I said Meat Loaf's *Bat Out Of Hell* was vaguely familiar?"

"Yeah?" His voice sounded as far away as the ceiling, even though he was less than an inch from my ear.

"Well, it's not. Vaguely familiar, I mean. It's...I can...quote the lyrics..."

"MaryJane?"

"Call me Eva. Please." Now my voice was sounding pretty remote, too. That couldn't be a good thing. "What's your favorite song on that album? I like..."Paradise By The Dashboard Light"...myself." Getting hard to talk now. Maybe I'd just be quiet for a while.

"Stay with me, Eva. They're coming. I swear they're coming."

And sure enough, I could hear sirens in the distance. Over top of them, Donnelly began to sing to me, if you can believe it. I'd never heard "Paradise By The Dashboard Light" as a lullaby, but he pulled it off—crooning in a broken, off-key baritone and stopping to kiss my ear every few seconds. I didn't have the heart—or the energy—to tell him he screwed up the chorus.

He had to leave me to get my keys from my bag and let the EMTs in the front door. I don't remember a lot after that, except a serious jolt of pain when they lifted me onto the gurney, and Donnelly's voice telling them to "Be a little careful, damn it."

I opened my eyes when we hit the cool air outside, and he was bending over me.

"I'll meet you at the hospital." His eyes...oh, his poor eyes, swimming in all those troubled waters.

"Hey," I said, "cut it out. Superman doesn't cry. Neither does Bogie. Get a grip." Yeah, the morphine was kicking in.

He smiled and opened his mouth to say something, but a hand came down on his shoulder, and McDane's face appeared out of nowhere.

"Son, I think we have something to talk about, don't you?" The chief didn't sound happy. The hand on Donnelly's shoulder held steady, and the gurney to which I was strapped started to move. Up and into the ambulance I went. The doors slammed shut behind me, the engine roared, the siren shrieked and I was out of there.

I didn't see Donnelly again for three days.

CHAPTER 11

"...and these are from Mike Holton," Kristy said, pointing to the huge floral arrangement she'd set on the side table near the window. "You know—the bank president?"

"She knows who Mike Holton is, Kristy." That was Gail, matter-of-fact as ever. "He says your job is waiting for you whenever you're ready to come back."

I smiled and looked past them to where Tonia was standing in the doorway. "Come on in here, Tonia. It's okay to bring Jeffrey. I'm not contagious."

She stepped into the hospital room, her two-year-old clinging to her leg. "Oh, I know. I just don't want him jostling your leg or anything. Jeffrey, don't touch that. It's not a toy."

Kristy took a seat in the chair next to the bed and eyed the tubes sticking out of my arm, and the dressings that immobilized my right leg from below my knee all the way up under my hospital johnny. "So...how long do you think you'll be out of commission?"

I shifted against the pillows, searching for a more comfortable position. "Doc says six weeks to two months, but I can't see myself hanging around the house that long."

Gail gave me a hard look. "You're not going back to that house of yours alone, are you?"

I shrugged. "I'll get a home health aide to help out for the first couple of weeks, and then with regular physical therapy—"

"But, MJ, you need somebody to take care of you." Kristy's eyes had filled with tears. "You can't be by yourself. That's...that's just wrong."

I forced myself to smile at her, even as the throbbing in my leg made me grind my teeth together. Twenty minutes more 'til the nurse was due with my pain pills. "Don't worry about it, Kristy. I'll work something out."

They stayed another ten minutes, promising to return the next day. By the end, I was twisting the sheet in both hands every time Jeffrey bumped the mattress.

I let my head fall back against my pillow and closed my eyes. Maybe by the time they returned, I'd have worked up the guts to ask if they'd seen Donnelly around town. *Then again, maybe not.* I wondered what would happen when the docs finally weaned me off the narcotics, and I was forced to face Donnelly's absence with a clear mind. Would I cry? Throw things? Reach for something eighty-proof and never come up for air again?

What were my alternatives? Sliding back into that life of quiet, anonymous desperation was the slow road to suicide. Mike Holton was a nice man—willing to hold my job and all, after I'd got his bank shot up—but I sensed my days as assistant manager were over. It seemed a pretty sure bet my days in Port Jonah were numbered, as well. Too many memories. I'd never be able to shop at the Pick 'N' Save again. Never be able to drive past Washington Court Place without wincing. Never be able to eat at Crawford's...hell, I wasn't entirely sure I'd be able to sleep in my own bed.

And all after less than a week's acquaintance. If this was true love...? It sucked ass.

The nurse bustled in, carrying two pills in a tiny paper cup. I tried not to snatch at them. Tried not to gulp down the water, but to sip sedately. I smiled at her, and she smiled back like she knew a budding addict when she saw one. I closed my eyes again. The scent of the flowers wafted up over my head to mingle with the aroma of leftover lemon-lime Jello™ on the tray at the foot of the bed. I drifted, listening to the hum of activity in the nurses' station just beyond the door, waiting for the buzz to kick in...waiting...

"Open your eyes, Eva."

I started at the sound of his voice—terse and a little cold. The movement sent a shock of pain from my leg screaming up my spine, making me grimace. I opened my eyes and glared at him. "You're late."

His face wore that flat, even expression I hated. "I was detained. A little trouble working out the logistics between local and federal law enforcement." He'd traded his denim jacket—which, if I recalled, had gotten splashed liberally with my blood—for one in black leather, which he wore over the ever-present t-shirt and jeans.

"I see. And you forgot how to use a phone?"

He shrugged. "I didn't know...I mean, I wasn't sure—"

"Which room I was in?" I pulled myself up straighter in the bed, ignoring the way it made my leg feel as if someone were stabbing it with a white-hot skewer. "That's what they have hospital operators for. Pay them an hourly wage and everything." I knew I sounded bitchy. Ask me if I cared.

"I didn't know if you wanted to hear from me," he said with just the slightest, most infinitesimal trace of...was it uncertainty? Fear of rejection?

Nah. Had to be the drugs kicking in. I sighed and let my head fall back again. "You're an idiot."

He didn't seem to have an answer for that. He moved closer to the bed, leaning over me, looking at my face.

"What?" I said, feeling self-conscious. I'd taken my first shower that morning, if you could call it that. But at least my hair was clean.

"Your eyes. I'm just..." He cleared his throat.

"Oh." I resisted the urge to close them again. The way he was staring was far too intense. "Like I said—just plain, old brown." I smiled then, feeling the first wave of giddiness that came with a dose of really good prescription narcotics.

He straightened and reached into his jacket pocket. "I brought you—"

Someone coughed from the doorway and we both turned to look. Tonia—minus the irrepressible Jeffrey—and looking both scared-to-death and determined at the same time.

"Sorry to interrupt. I can come back," she said, and began to ease her way out of the room.

"No, Tonia, don't be silly. Come on in—it's a party!" My voice was way too loud. Or maybe not. Hard to tell from where I was floating on the ceiling. Should've eaten more gelatin before I popped those pills.

Donnelly was crossing the room, holding out his hand. "I'm Agent Donnelly," he said.

"No, no," I piped up. "It's Special Agent Donnelly. With all the specialness."

He turned his head and glowered at me with long-suffering eyes. "And In Charge," I added. "He's very proud of that."

Tonia looked befuddled. But still determined, somehow. Something in the set of her jaw... "Really, MJ, I can come back."

"Really, Tonia, you should stay and tell me what's up," I said. Because even in my stoned state, I could see the woman had something on her mind.

She came forward to stand at the other side of the bed. I glanced at Donnelly, wondering if he would take this as his cue to leave. He planted his feet, crossed his arms over his chest and looked at me. I had my answer.

"Um...I just wanted to say that I agree with Kristy. You shouldn't go home alone." Tonia's voice was faint. She stared down at the sheet that covered my legs, occasionally stealing peeks at my face. "It's not right—nobody should be by themselves when they're hurt. But especially after what you did. To...to help the town, I mean. To get the bad guys." Her voice grew stronger on the last few words, and she lifted her eyes to meet mine.

Wow. I'd been right about her—still waters really do run deep. "Thank you, Tonia. I really appreciate what you're saying, but—"

"So that's why I want you to come home with me." She held up a hand to keep me from interrupting. "I know it sounds crazy with as many kids as I have, but we've got a big old house, and tons of room, and I just know we could take good care of you. Will you...will you think about it?"

I couldn't speak. Could barely see her for the tears in my eyes. I covered my face with my hands and just sat there, unable to do much of anything.

"Oh, gosh," Tonia said, sounding appalled. "I didn't mean to—"

"It's okay. She'll be fine." I heard Donnelly move to the other side of the bed. "You're a real good friend, Tonia, and MaryJane thanks you for the offer, but she's not going to be alone. I'm going to take care of her."

Tonia's surprised squeak was enough to make me drop my hands. I looked from her to Donnelly and back again, still unable to utter a word. I watched as he gently ushered Tonia out of the room, promising I'd be up for another visit tomorrow, thanking her again for her concern. My last glimpse was of her beaming face as she waved to me over his shoulder.

Then he turned and closed the door.

"These are some really fine drugs."

"What was that?" He was standing over me again, sort of half-smiling.

"Nothing." I wiped my eyes with my fingers. "Except...did you just say...? I mean, I thought I heard you say—"

"If you'll give me the key to your house, I'll move some of my stuff in tonight. Buy some groceries, maybe get the place tidied up." He tilted his head, considering me. "Your doctor says you've got another day or two until you're released and then you'll be on crutches for at least a month. We'll need to set up a regular schedule of physical therapy appointments."

"Hey, hey—slow down. My doctor talked to you? You're not a family member." I tried to inject a little outrage into my voice, but mostly I think I sounded confused.

He laughed at me, the bastard. "You'd be amazed what the flash of a federal badge can accomplish."

I blinked at him. "Talk about abuse of power. That's just wrong."

"I know. Told you—no conscience." He leaned in closer and breathed on me. "You should probably start getting used to it."

I shook my head. "What about your job? How can you just—"

"I'm taking an extended leave of absence, effective Monday."

Something about the way he said it made me wonder... "That your idea, agent? Or are you in trouble again?"

There was a pause. He turned his face to the window. "Let's just say it was a mutual decision." When he turned to look at me, his brow was smooth and untroubled. "But understand, Eva—if I was leaving town, you'd be going too. No way would I leave you here on your own."

"And you're so sure I'd go with you?"

He nodded. Just like that. As if there were no question in his mind. Arrogant son of a bitch. The fact he was right didn't change anything.

The giddy buzz was wearing down into waves of sleepiness, but I still had questions—too many to leave for another day. I forced my eyes open and tried like hell not to slur. "So what're you gonna do with yourself if you're not a big, cool FBI agent anymore, huh? Sit around my house and watch *Oprah?*"

He snorted. "If I don't go back..." He shrugged, and I understood. He wasn't going back, no "if" about it. He cleared his throat and said, "I've spent some time with your Chief McDane over the past couple of days. We came to a meeting of the minds, after he finished tearing me a new one. He says he'll have an opening in the department in about three months."

I could feel my eyebrows wobbling up to meet my hairline. "You're kidding. Tell me you're kidding."

Donnelly laughed. "Close your eyes, Eva. Get some rest."

It was tempting. "Wait...that's the 'how' of it. But what's the 'why'?"

His turn to blink. "Huh?"

I grunted in frustration. "Why're you doing this? Why...why staying in Port Jonah, becoming a small-town cop? Why staying with me?" I sort of knew, of course. Stoned, not stupid. Wanted to hear Special Agent In Charge Of Smug say the damned words.

He didn't because he was a bastard. He just said, "Now who's the idiot?" Then he leaned down and kissed me. As declarations of love went, it didn't suck ass or anything else.

When he pulled away and stood, I grinned up at him. "Cop," I said, and stuck out my tongue.

"Felon," he said, and ran his finger down the side of my face.

After that, I went away for a while. When I woke, night had fallen and the room was dim. I turned my head and saw Donnelly dozing next to my bed, his feet in clean white socks propped on the very edge of the mattress, his head wedged at an odd angle between the wall and the back of the chair. His fingers rested lightly across the back of my left wrist, where it lay on top of the sheet.

I shifted a bit, and felt something slide into my lap. I looked down and there, on the sheet, was a CD case wrapped in a white ribbon, tied in a bow. I stared at it for a second before picking it up, not sure if it was real or part of a very nice, narcotics-induced dream.

Before I'd even loosened the ribbon, I recognized the album cover—hard to miss that distinctive *Bat Out Of Hell* artwork. I glanced over at Donnelly and found him watching me.

"Drew, you shouldn't have."

He smiled in the dark. "I got carried away. Happens sometimes."

We looked at each other for a minute. Then I said, "You're still here."

"Yeah." His voice was quiet. "You should get used to that, too."

I nodded. "I think I can manage."

As it turned out, we both managed just fine.

SIN STREET

DIRTY SHAME

SIN STREET

SIN STREET

CHAPTER 1

You're nobody until somebody sues you for sexual harassment.

Those were the words printed on the oversized coffee mug that sat on the center of the huge, art deco-style desk. From where she stood in the doorway of the office, Joey could read them clearly. The owner of the mug and desk—Carl Beidermeyer, high-powered manager to the stars—sat with his back to her, talking into his shiny, little phone.

"What can I tell you, Frank? The guy will not listen to me, and now his shrink is telling him he has to go back home and work out his issues." Beidermeyer made an unpleasant huffing noise. "Hey, if it were me? I'd hole up in that motherfucking mansion of his with the hottest piece of tail I could find, and let her work out my issues."

There was silence as he listened to whomever was at the other end of the line. Then, "Yeah, you're right. That's what got him into trouble in the first place. I tell ya, Frank, if I didn't like his money so much—" Beidermeyer swiveled in his high-backed leather chair and, catching sight of Joey in the doorway, cut himself off. He put his hand over the receiver and barked, "Can I help you?"

Joey flinched. "I'm here about a job. I got a call yesterday from this office about a personal assistant position?" When he looked at her blankly, she took a deep, steadying breath and said, "My name is Joey Fiorello."

Beidermeyer frowned...or tried to. The muscles in the tanned forehead beneath the expensively cut, graying hair rippled a bit as his brow made an aborted effort to drop itself over his bloodshot eyes.

SIN STREET

"Joey?"

"Short for Josephine. Look, if this is a bad time—"

"Come in and sit down." He muttered something into the phone, turned it off and set it next to the mug. "Why didn't the receptionist ask you to wait?" he said as he shuffled through a stack of papers, clearly searching for something.

"There's no one at the desk outside." Joey shifted her weight in the doorway, but made no move to step into the office. "Mr. Beidermeyer, I think I've made a mistake coming here. I'm going to go." She waited for some acknowledgment from the man.

After a moment, he looked up at her and smiled—bright and flashy and utterly false. Much like the lights of Los Angeles rising out of the summer dusk in the window behind him.

"No, no, don't be silly. I'm just looking for your résumé. I know I had it...ah, here it is." He looked up again and waved her into the room. "Sit down, Ms. Fiorello. Let's talk."

Lead weights—that's what her legs felt like. Lead weights with extra, bonus lead weights strapped to her ankles. She didn't want to sit down, didn't want to talk to this odious man. This insincere combo of self-tanner and Botox and smug.

Then you'd better get used to livin' on the street, babe, said the voice in her head—the one that sounded just like her older sister's tough, streetwise Brooklyn accent. Also smug, but not quite so insincere. And practical. Always so damn practical.

Steeling herself, she stepped forward into the office and lowered herself onto the very edge of the big leather chair Beidermeyer had indicated. She perched there, her hands clenched into fists in her lap.

Okay then. She would talk to this man, who represented everything she hated about the entertainment industry. She would ask him to hire her so she could make this month's rent. But she didn't have to like it.

"I must admit when I had my assistant call you, I thought you were a..." Beidermeyer coughed into his closed fist and shot her another grin. "Well, a guy. A man. You know, with the name."

"It's a common mistake." She tried to return his smile and felt her face twist into a grimace. "Can we please talk about the job?"

"Well, that's the trouble." He leaned across the desk, hands clasped in front of him in a way that implied he was about to tell her a secret. "See, Ms. Fiorello—can I call you Joey? See, Joey, I'm looking for a personal assistant for one of my clients."

"And there's a problem with my being female?"

"Well, yes and no." Beidermeyer's gaze left her face to migrate lower and crawl all over the front of her white tee shirt. "This client of mine...he sort of has special needs."

"What kind of needs?" This was getting weird. If he thought, for even a split second, that her definition of "personal assistant" including anything kinky... She found herself staring at the slogan emblazoned on the mug.

Beidermeyer coughed again. "My client's last assistant was female, and he got into a bit of trouble with that. Maybe you've read about it?"

This was his way of finding out whether she knew who he was talking about without coming right out and telling her his client's name. *Cagey bastard.* And of course, she did know. Everybody knew.

"Dare Daniels? Is that your client?"

Beidermeyer nodded, watching her closely. Making her feel as if he was seeing her—really seeing her—for the first time. Typical Hollywood, never looking beyond the surface unless he absolutely had to. She knew his kind. She despised his kind.

"I'm familiar with Mr. Daniels's recent...uh..." What was a good word for it? Recent misfortune? Reputation-ruining mistake?

Royal fuck-up?

"Then you can see why I feel the need to vet any new candidates for the position very carefully."

"Of course." She could see why Beidermeyer thought a man was the better choice for the job, too. Although rumor had it Dare Daniels screwed anything that held still long enough to be penetrated, so maybe that wasn't such a sure thing. "I understand completely, Mr. Beidermeyer. Maybe next time, right?" She rose from the chair and stuck out her hand, willing herself to withstand a simple handshake from this...snake.

"Let's not be hasty." He eyed her up and down, and she wished again she'd had time to change her clothes before arriving for the interview. But her class had ended late, and she'd figured it was better to be unprofessionally underdressed than unprofessionally tardy. A personal assistant wasn't a glamour position, but it did require punctuality.

Beidermeyer was still checking her out, now with an odd, ruminative expression on his orange-tinted face. A bolt of defensiveness shot through her, and she lifted her chin. "Look, either I'm right for the job or I'm not."

"I think you might do," he said. "Turn around."

SIN STREET

That was the last straw. *If this supercilious bastard thinks he can just—*

Criminy, Josephine, it's not like the goomba asked you to crawl under the desk and blow him. Turn the hell around, why don'tcha?

Joey shut her eyes and did a quick spin.

"Yes, I think you'll be fine."

She opened her eyes and stared at Beidermeyer, who was pulling a sheaf of papers out of a drawer. "I'll have my assistant draw up the contract," he said, "but in the meantime, you should probably head over to Dare's house and introduce yourself. Tomorrow morning, say about eleven? I'll set it up."

"Wait. What? I thought—"

"I think he'll be perfectly safe working with you."

"Safe?" She knew she sounded like an idiot, but this was beyond confusing.

"From temptation." Beidermeyer squinted at her. "You're not his type at all. He goes for...well, women who look like my new receptionist, for example."

"I haven't met your receptionist."

Beidermeyer scowled, obviously bored with the conversation and ready to move on to whatever thrilling task came next on his To-Do list. "Annette is tall and blonde and very slender. As was Dare's last assistant, and the last three women he dated."

"Ah." Now she got it. Tall and blonde and very slender—the antithesis of her, in other words. Dare Daniels—known around town as an old-fashioned "ladies' man"—would have no possible use for someone as short and dark and generously endowed as herself.

Beidermeyer, plainly oblivious to the insulting nature of his last comment, had switched into "all-business" mode. "Dare is planning a trip back to his hometown over the show's hiatus." He paused. "I assume you're familiar with his work?"

"You mean his work on television? The cop show?" She didn't mean to sound contemptuous. Really she didn't.

"It's called *Vegas Knight*."

"Yes, I'm familiar with it." She perched again on the seat of the chair. "Where is Mr. Daniels's hometown?"

Beidermeyer frowned. "Oklahoma? Kansas? Some place out there." He made a vague gesture toward the window. "You can be ready to travel in two days?"

She nodded. "Is there anything else I should know?"

He sat back in his chair and considered her. "Can you be discreet?"

"Would you hire me if I said no?"

He smiled a thin smile. It looked almost genuine. "Dare Daniels is the next breakout movie star. He's going straight to the top of his profession, but only if he can manage to control some of his more...shall we say...problematic appetites."

What's the proper response to a statement like that? She settled for nodding again.

"If you can help him in this regard, you'll be compensated. Handsomely. Do you understand?"

"I think so."

"I need you to know for sure, Ms. Fiorello."

"It's Joey." She rose from the chair and stuck out her hand. "You can count on me to do my best, Carl."

"That's Mr. Beidermeyer." He took no notice of the offered handshake. Instead, he looked hard into her eyes, as if trying to read her soul. "I'm trusting you, Joey. Don't you even think about letting me down."

She tried to ignore the threat hidden within his words.

* * *

The drive to Daniels's house in Studio City, just over the ridge from Beverly Hills, took longer than Joey expected. Her little blue Honda chugged upward, out of the morning's haze of smog and into the brilliant sunshine, hugging the boulders of Mulholland Drive. The winding road and the steep drop beyond the cliff's edge made her progress slow and careful. She hated the feeling of rising so far above the rest of the world, to where even the air was expensive.

When she finally reached her destination, the relatively small size of the house surprised her. For an ostentatious example of nouveau riche arrogance, it looked almost...tasteful. All mellow brick and neatly kept perennial gardens, and nary a tennis court, putting green or guest house in sight. She hit the button on the security box at the gate and waited to identify herself.

After a long pause, a voice crackled through the box. "Yes?" Female and heavily accented. Russian, it sounded like, though it was hard to be sure.

"Joey Fiorello to see Mr. Daniels. I have an appointment."

There was a long, loud buzz, and the gate swung open. She

maneuvered her car down the short drive and pulled into the turnaround directly before the house. The front door opened before she made it up the steps.

"Miss Fiorello?" The middle-aged woman in the apron and bright white tennis shoes smiled at her. "I am Oksana. It is good you are come. Mr. Daniels is in need of your help."

Yes, definitely Russian.

Joey shook the woman's outstretched hand. "I'm not hired yet. I mean, I haven't even met him."

"Still, is good. You are..." She paused and frowned, as if searching for a word. "...necessary? Yes. I think this is true."

But she didn't want to be "necessary." She just wanted a job. "Necessary" sounded like a full-time commitment, and she just wanted—

"This way." Oksana led her through the shadowy foyer to the bottom of a wide, curved staircase. From somewhere above, Joey could hear music. "Go right up. First door on right."

Joey knew she looked as doubtful as she felt, but Oksana gave her another brilliant smile and a pat on the shoulder, and bustled away. The trek up the blue-carpeted stairs seemed as along as the drive up Mulholland. As she approached the landing, the music grew recognizable.

"'Freebird?' Is he kidding?" She tried not to roll her eyes, but it was tough. Talk about a walking, talking cliché, despite his classy house. Then she was standing in front of the door Oksana had indicated and lifting her hand to knock.

And knock...and knock some more. The music was loud enough to vibrate the door's wooden panels. Daniels plainly couldn't hear her, and damn but "Freebird" went on forever, didn't it?

"Mr. Daniels?" she called and pounded with the side of her fist. Still nothing. "Fuck this," she said and turned the cut-glass knob. The door swung open before her, and she was treated to a blast of sound.

"Mr. Daniels!" He was nowhere in sight. But there, not far from the rumpled bed—between the doors that led to the balcony and the door that must've led to the bathroom—stood a wall covered from floor to ceiling with stereo equipment. She stalked over to it and began searching for the volume control or the "off" button. Anything to extinguish the noise that was threatening to pop her eardrums and stain the carpet with her blood.

By the time she found the switch, a good twenty seconds later, she'd lost her temper. It was unreasonable of her, and she knew it—this was his house and his bedroom, and he could play his music at any damn volume he wanted. And where was the crazy, inconsiderate bastard anyway?

She glanced around the room 'til her gaze landed again on the bed. "Oh, shit."

One bare foot hung over the edge of the mattress—the only part of him exposed. How she'd missed it the first time around, she couldn't guess. It wasn't a small foot.

Maybe she could slip out unnoticed. Wait downstairs for him to wake and shower and dress. Or not wait...just make a run for it, back to the Honda and out through the gate and down the windy, twisting road—

From somewhere in the back of her brain, her sister interrupted Joey's headlong plunge into panic. *And then what? A little late-morning Dumpster-diving? Or maybe you'd like to try peddling your sweet ass out on the Strip for lunch money?*

"Shut up, Gina. Just shut up."

"Huh?" The grunt came from beneath the mound of pillows near the headboard. What looked like a mass of wrinkled linen on the bed began to shift, first revealing the ankle and calf attached to the exposed foot, then a muscled thigh covered in soft-looking, light brown hair and then—

Okay, she was not looking there. A well-toned ass was a well-toned ass, but they were a dime a dozen in L. A. And it wasn't like the ass in question hadn't been featured on billboards all over town. Just...you know...covered. With fabric. And totally not nude.

She moved her gaze toward the head of the bed, waiting for his face to emerge from beneath the pillows—although she already knew what that looked like, too. Thanks again to billboards and TV spots for *Vegas Knight,* Dare Daniels's lash-fringed green eyes, cleft chin and lush lips were hardly unfamiliar.

"Oksana? That you?" His muffled question made her flinch.

"Uh, no, Mr. Daniels, it's me." She started toward the door, talking as she went. "Joey Fiorello. I'm here to see you about the personal assistant job? Oksana told me to come up, and I didn't realize you were still in bed. I can leave and come back...or leave and never come back..." She could hear herself babbling way too fast to be understood, but couldn't seem to stem the tide. "I'm so sorry to have disturbed you, I'll just—"

"Who the hell are you?"

His slurred question caught her with her hand on the doorknob. She paused, but didn't turn, listening to the rustle of sheets and the squeak of the mattress as he flipped over onto his back.

"Uh...Joey Fiorello? We had an appointment?" Damn it, why did everything she say come out like a question? She sounded like a thirteen-year-old girl asking permission to exist. She squared her shoulders and pivoted on her heel to face him.

And fell back a step to lean against the closed door. Because the sheer beauty of the man as he sat up in his bed and squinted at her, sheets pooling just below his sculpted torso and streaky-blonde hair sticking up in spikes around his face, nearly knocked her down.

Guh. I mean...wow, Joey. He's, like...

"Yeah," she whispered. "Amazing."

Because when her dead sister Gina was right, she was right. And there was no point in arguing about it.

SIN STREET

CHAPTER 2

There was a woman in his bedroom. At least...he saw a woman. Right there, leaning against the door, staring at him with big, brown eyes. But he was pretty hung over. Maybe she wasn't really there. Maybe this was another bad trip, like the time some dickhead dropped half a tab of acid in his beer, and he woke up thinking there were three girls in bed with him. *Three dead girls, all blonde and bone-thin, with bruises around their necks just like—*

Yeah, that had been a bad scene all around. He shook his head hard, like maybe he could shake that memory out.

This one—the woman in the room with him now—didn't remind him of that time. She wasn't naked for starters, and she was a lot shorter and darker and curvier, from what he could see under the sort of baggy, bluish dress-thing she was wearing. Plus, she seemed fairly lively.

Damn, but he was still pretty drunk. He glanced at the clock. Eleven-fifteen. Too early to be dealing with some crazy fan-girl who'd managed to get past both the front gate and Oksana.

"Who are you?" he repeated, shaping the words carefully. His tongue tasted like something three-days-dead.

"Joey Fiorello," she said, enunciating just as precisely. Like she was talking to a little kid. Or someone not altogether bright. "We had an appointment. Mr. Beidermeyer said—"

"Carl?" *Okay, wait. Something...yes. An appointment to interview...who? For what?*

The woman—who was more like a girl, tiny as she was and no makeup either from what he could see—crossed her arms over her chest. Or under her boobs, really—*and hey, nice rack.*

She said, "Carl Beidermeyer sent me to interview for the personal assistant position." She cleared her throat, and when he glanced up at her face this time, he saw she was frowning.

"Interview. Right." He made a move to slide out from under the sheet, but...no. *Naked. Not a good plan.* "I need to...uh..." He waved his hand in the general direction of his lap, meaning to indicate the dire need for clothing at this juncture. But maybe she took it the wrong way, because her eyes stretched so wide he thought they might pop out of her face. *And oh...bad thought.* Bad, seriously bad thought because it made his stomach lurch, and Jesus God...how could he still be so wasted?

"I'll wait downstairs." She pulled open the door and pretty much threw herself into the hall, slamming the door behind her in a way that made the pain behind his eyes jump up and sing. He sat there, staring, for another thirty seconds, at the space where she'd been standing. His eyelids grew heavy, and he let his head fall back against the padded headboard. He'd get up in a minute. Maybe five.

Then the door banged open again and someone was yelling, "Get out of bed, you lazy good-for-nothing!" Before he could react beyond groaning, the sheet was yanked from his body, and he looked up to see Oksana standing over him, a mug of coffee in her hand and fire in her eye. "What do you think? You're some kind of rude boy to leave that poor girl waiting so long."

"Sorry, sorry," he mumbled and swung his legs over the side of the mattress.

Oksana didn't even flinch at the sight of him in all his glory. She just kept scolding. "You think you're some Mr. Big Shot? To keep nice, hardworking people waiting while you sleep the day away?"

He clutched his head. "Said I was sorry, Oksana. Please stop."

In a kinder voice, she said, "Don't tell me. Tell the girl who needs a job so bad she waits two hours for you."

Two hours? Fuck.

She set the coffee on the bedside table and turned away. Before she closed the door, she looked at him again and said, "Why you do this to yourself, eh? Make yourself so sick?"

"Good question, Oksana. You figure it out, you let me know."

She shook her head at him and shut the door.

SIN STREET

The coffee and a twenty-minute shower went a long way toward making him feel human. As he stood before the bathroom mirror, struggling with his contacts, he thought about the girl downstairs. So young—just out of high school, by the looks of her. Too young to be working for him, and what was Beidermeyer thinking anyway? He'd told his manager very clearly, right after the tabloids broke with Sheila's little exposé of their affair, that he didn't want another personal assistant. Particularly a female one. So Beidermeyer sends him some chick who looked like she's just been cast as the Virgin Mary in her Sunday school's production of the Nativity. *What the hell?*

The contact lens went sailing off his finger and landed somewhere on the surface of the counter. "Screw this." He opened the topmost drawer of the vanity, grabbed his glasses and stomped out of the bathroom and down the stairs.

The marble floor of the foyer felt cold under his bare feet as he stood outside the living room door, contemplating his entrance line. "Sorry to keep you waiting?" *Lame.* Likewise for, "Thanks for sticking around so long." The girl had a lot riding on the job, or she would've bailed ninety minutes ago. And, while he recalled with bitter clarity that feeling of desperation, he wished she had bailed. Because telling her he couldn't hire her after making her wait was gonna suck. Big. Huge.

He took a deep breath and pushed open the door. As he walked into the room, he started to say, "Look, I'm sorry, I really am, but Carl shouldn't have—"

And stopped because the girl wasn't there. Or...wait. Yes she was, but he was looking in the wrong place. He'd expected her to be standing in front of the fireplace, or maybe near the windows that looked out over the pool. Or maybe she'd be sitting on the extra-long sofa—Pacific-blue suede to contrast with the pale moss green of the walls, or so the decorator had said—that stood against the far wall.

He hadn't expected to find her curled in the black leather easy chair just to the right of the door. And he really hadn't expected her to be asleep. Soundly asleep. And looking like she'd been that way for a while.

But the irony? It made him smile. For the first time in three days, he smiled. And then he laughed, and she jumped, sitting straight up in the chair with a noise that was halfway between a squeak and a scream.

"Take it easy," he said and laid a hand on her shoulder. He squinted at her and resettled his glasses on the bridge of his nose. Now that his vision was once again in the vicinity of 20/20, he could see she wasn't as young as she'd first appeared. But her face was pale and a little drawn. "Are you...I mean..." He cleared his throat. "It's past lunchtime. Want a sandwich? Oksana makes a mean turkey on rye."

"Rye?" Her cheeks were flushed pink, and the short, black curls around her face were mussed.

"Uh, yeah. Rye." He let his hand drop away from her shoulder. "Like—bread?"

She rubbed at her eye with a closed fist, reminding him of a sleepy four-year-old. A four-year-old with a pair of red, tender-looking lips that looked like they'd taste really...

No. Nuh-uh. Down, boy. This was how he got in trouble last time. And the time before that. And reason number four-hundred-and-seventy-three he couldn't hire her as his personal assistant. What was Beidermeyer smoking when he sent this girl here?

And what was wrong with him—Dare Daniels, whose mama had been choir-mistress at Breverton Baptist Church from the age of sixteen 'til the day she died—that he couldn't control his fucking libido for ten minutes at a time? He shoved his hands in his pockets and wheeled away from the girl, whose name he didn't remember.

After half a minute of staring out at the empty blue of the swimming pool he'd never used, he turned to look at her. She'd done something to her hair and appeared more alert, sitting there with her hands folded like she was waiting for something. For him? Right. Because in this situation, he called the shots. Something he'd never get used to, not if he lived forever.

He cleared his throat again. "So...about that sandwich—"

"That won't be necessary, Mr. Daniels. If we could talk about—"

"Aren't you hungry? I am."

She bit her lip. Then she went ahead and chewed on it, like maybe it was a better deal than the turkey on rye. Which, from his perspective, it was. He made himself look away.

She said, "I want to talk about the job."

"So do I." *Liar.* The job was the last thing he wanted to talk about. "But let's do it over lunch, okay?"

Her chin came up in a move he recognized as "stubborn" and "prideful." He'd perfected that one by the age of seven. Another good reason she couldn't work for him—they'd likely kill each other when they weren't fucking like weasels. And fuck like weasels they would, he was sure. Because this one was...she was...well. She was somethin' else again, as his daddy might've said. Not his usual type, but look where his usual type had gotten him.

"Mr. Daniels?" She looked like she'd made up her mind about something.

"Call me Dare."

"All right. You can call me Joey. And I'll take you up on that sandwich." Then she smiled, and it was like a punch to his solar plexus. Like sunshine in a Goddamn spray-bottle, misted all around the room. He'd swear the temperature spiked five degrees.

"Well, all right," he said and grinned at her.

She blinked, kind of slow and astonished. He was used to that reaction. He'd been working that particular grin a long time.

She rose from the chair and he ushered her into the foyer, pausing long enough to check out the view as she moved away. That dress she had on was seven kinds of ugly, but it pulled snug in all the right places when she walked.

This had the potential to go very bad, very fast. He sort of wished he knew how to stop it. Or had the strength of character to care.

CHAPTER 3

A sandwich. He wanted her to eat a sandwich.

Gina piped up, sounding irritated. *Oh, for God's sake. You'd think he'd asked you to drop your dress so he could check out your tits. It's a meal...something you haven't had in nearly twenty-four hours, remember? Or maybe you want play the pity card and faint at his feet. That could work, actually—*

"I swear to God, if you don't shut up—"

"Beg pardon?"

She stumbled on her way into the kitchen, and he caught her with a hand on her elbow. She looked around quickly, taking in the state-of-the-art equipment, but no sign of Oksana. "I said, it doesn't look like your housekeeper is here. Maybe I should just—"

"What day is it?"

"Huh?"

"Day of the week. Monday, Tuesday, Wednesday?" He was staring at her intently, like maybe she had a calendar printed on her forehead. The reddish-brown stubble that covered the lower half of his face made his eyes looker even greener behind the glasses. Funny...she'd heard he wore colored contacts. Guess that was one rumor she could put down to jealousy.

"It's Tuesday."

"Damn," he said. "Oksana's market day." When she raised her eyebrows, he shrugged and said, "She doesn't believe in having groceries delivered. Says it's lazy weakness of imperialist slacker-generation." He mimicked the older woman's accent so perfectly, Joey had to stifle a laugh.

"She seems like a great lady."

"The best." He glanced around the kitchen like he'd never seen it before. "I say we head on down to the Klondike for a late lunch."

"The Klondike?" The name was unfamiliar, but it's not like she spent a lot of time eating out. Unless taco stands counted.

"Little place I know on Ventura. Quiet, not too flashy. They pretend not to know me, and I like it that way." He yawned, scratched at a spot behind his left ear, and looked around the kitchen again as if searching for something, his gaze touching on everything but her.

Whoa...classic insecure body language. Did he think she might turn him down? Like maybe this was a date and not an interview?

She opened her mouth to ask him where all of this was going and was interrupted by the buzzing of her cell phone. She flicked it open—caller unknown.

She shot a half-smile in his direction. "Excuse me, please?"

"No problem." But he didn't leave the room. And he was blocking the exit. She sighed and hit the button on the phone. "Hello?"

An oddly mechanical female voice said, "Please hold for Mr. Beidermeyer."

Crap.

"Joey!" Beidermeyer barked. "Where the hell are you? You were supposed to call this office an hour ago to discuss terms."

"I apologize, Mr. Beidermeyer. I was detained."

"Detained? By what?"

"I'm still at Mr. Daniel's residence. We haven't...uh...I mean—"

She glanced at Daniels. He scowled and leaned over the marble-topped island that stretched between them to pluck the phone out of her hand. "Carl? I'm taking her to lunch and then I'll call you." His voice sounded tight. Angry, maybe. She watched as he listened to whatever Carl had to say. Then he handed her the phone. "He wants to talk to you."

She took a deep breath to steady her voice. "Mr. Beidermeyer?"

"Yeah, listen, has anything unusual happened while you've been in Dare's house?" He coughed, and it sounded like a nervous twitch even through her crappy phone. "Anything...weird?"

"Weird?" He probably didn't mean her falling asleep in the living room. She cringed at the memory of wiping drool from her lip and said, "I don't know what you mean."

"Like any strange phone calls, any packages delivered. That kind of thing."

"Not that I know of."

"Okay well, listen," Beidermeyer said, lowering his voice, so she had to strain to hear him. "Dare's been getting some unusual mail lately, care of this office. I'd thought it had stopped, but we got another one today."

She glanced at Daniels again. He'd moved to lean against the mammoth stainless steel refrigerator on the far side of the room and was watching her with hooded eyes. She turned her back on him and whispered into the phone, "You mean like a stalker?"

"Yeah. Maybe." Beidermeyer cleared his throat. "But don't say anything to him about it."

"Shouldn't he be told?"

"No reason to bother him. That's going to be part of your job—protecting him from this sort of thing."

She huffed into the phone. The arrogance of this man and his assumptions made Daniels look like a sweetheart of consideration, two-hour wait be damned. "Mr. Daniels hasn't even interviewed me yet—"

"That's part of your job, too." And now she could tell Beidermeyer was smiling his oily, ingratiating smile. "Convince him. Influence him. Persuade him. Tell him all the ways you'll make his life better. Sell yourself, baby."

Her stomach clenched around nothing. She gripped the edge of the countertop and tried not to spit into the phone. "Mr. Beidermeyer—"

"Gotta fly. Call me when you're ready to talk terms." And he was gone.

She stood staring at her phone for several seconds. Only when she sensed Daniels' movement from his post by the fridge did she take another deep breath and consciously let her shoulders drop from their hunched position.

Daniels came to stand behind her. "What was all that about?"

What should she say? Was the truth out of the question? If anyone knew what a slime Beidermeyer was, it would be his client. "Your manager wants me to sell myself to you." She turned and faced him, feeling her cheeks light up in what she was sure was a lovely shade of magenta. "But I get the feeling you're not buying today. Am I right?"

His eyes narrowed, and a muscle in his jaw ticked. "You don't kiss ass much, do you?"

"Not for a personal assistant's salary." Okay, that made it sound like she'd kiss ass and more for the right price. Not what she'd intended to imply. But he was making her sweat by standing so close. Smelling so good, like soap on tanned skin. Looking so damn...edible. She wasn't accountable for the nonsense she babbled if he insisted on that behavior. Plus, the whole empty stomach thing was becoming more of an issue every second.

He smirked at her comment about the salary, and seemed to be considering her, much like Beidermeyer had considered her the previous day. For some reason, it didn't piss her off nearly as much.

Finally he said, "What exactly are you selling?"

She shrugged. "I'm supposed to tell you all the ways I'll make your life better."

The low, husky pitch of his laughter went buzzing through her, making her tingle. "That'd be quite a trick," he said. "You pull it off, and I'll pay twice the going rate."

"Is that an offer?"

He opened his mouth, and she got the clear impression he meant to answer in the affirmative. But what he said was, "We'll see. For now, all I'm buying is lunch." He made a sweeping gesture in the direction of the doorway and she took the hint, walking out of the kitchen ahead of him, praying he wasn't staring at her ass in the never-did-fit-right peasant dress. Speaking of which...

"Is the Klondike very fancy? I'm not really dressed for—"

"I don't do fancy if I can help it." He smiled at her. The brilliance of it made her heart skip a beat.

You'd better break yourself of that, sister, or you'll put yourself into coronary arrest. Gina's snicker echoed in her head.

"Shut up."

"Huh?"

She stopped in the foyer, just shy of the front door, and turned to look at him. "Not you. Sorry."

A tiny line appeared between his eyebrows, just above the bridge of the glasses. "Right. But you'll let me know if you do want me to shut up, right? Just throw something heavy at my head."

"I...uh..." Okay, he was joking. This would be an appropriate place to laugh, but she couldn't quite...

"Don't sweat it, Joey. I talk to myself, too, sometimes."

Which wasn't nearly as comforting as she was sure he intended it to be.

SIN STREET

* * *

They drove down in his Escalade, which he handled with a sort of smooth assurance she found vaguely annoying. Or arousing. Hard to tell with the hunger-induced lightheadedness going on.

"So," he said without taking his eyes off the road. Eyes that were now covered by what she assumed were prescription-grade, classic Ray-Bans. "What's your story?"

She settled back into the soft leather seat. "I'm twenty-five. I have a degree in English from New York State University at Stony Brook. I can provide references from—"

His snort of laughter cut her off. "This isn't the interview portion of our program," he said. "It's a conversation. Where were you born?"

"Bensonhurst, Brooklyn."

His eyebrows shot up above the sunglasses. "No accent?"

"I did a minor in theatre. Took some vocalization classes to soften my vowels and rediscover my Rs."

He nodded slowly. "You did a good job with it."

"It comes back in moments of high stress." Or when she spent too long listening to her big sister talk shit in her head.

They turned off Mulholland and onto Ventura Boulevard, where traffic was heavier and slower-moving. When they stopped at a light, he said, "What brought you to L. A.?"

Was he playing dumb? She'd just confessed to taking a minor's worth of courses in theatre. "I'm a starving actress. And this sounds more like an interrogation than a conversation."

He breezed right by that to say, "Really? You don't come across like an actress."

"Maybe that's why I'm starving."

They pulled into a parking space, and he cut the engine. "But not today."

He flashed another smile at her. It looked almost genuine, and she couldn't help returning it. Even though she knew she was being played.

Is this how he plays? With the shiny ride and the free food? Sign me up for the major leagues, baby.

Ah, Gina. Always right there with a perfectly-timed, invariably crass remark. And she'd certainly never done a thing about her Bensonhurst vocal stylings, which only served to make her every comment sound like an audition for a bit part in a *Godfather* sequel.

Not all of us are ashamed of our roots, baby girl.

Joey rolled her eyes and moved to open the door of the Escalade.

Daniels beat her to it. He stood on the sidewalk, holding the door, the mid-afternoon glare of the sun striking him just right. Making him look like he was prepped for a photo shoot—the next "People's Sexiest Man Alive," maybe?

When he tilted his head and looked at her over the tops of the shades, she felt her breath catch in her chest. Which might've been the heat, or her hunger, or maybe just a little nervous tension. It had been a stressful day after all, and it wasn't even three o'clock yet.

But when his tongue slipped out to moisten his lower lip? Well...no question about that reaction—one hard, heated, full-body throb like she hadn't felt in a long, long time. Zero to lust in under three seconds. Had to be a new record.

And then?

He smirked, complete with an all-knowing gleam in his eye and lips curled up on one side and...shit. Yeah, she wanted him and that was bad, but what was worse? The bastard knew it.

CHAPTER 4

"Right this way, Mr. Daniels," the hostess said, shooting him a sidelong smile that made Dare cringe. *Damn.* So much for pretending not to know him. Which meant this was likely the last time he'd eat at the Klondike. And that sucked because he really liked their mesquite-grilled T-bones. Almost as good as home.

She led them through the deserted first floor dining room, then up the stairs and through a set of French doors to the balcony that overlooked the patio. Dare glanced back at Joey and found her trailing behind them, staring like she'd never seen the inside of a restaurant before.

"Is this okay?" His voice sounded gruffer than he meant it to.

"Beautiful," she murmured, taking a seat at one of the three empty tables on the balcony. The lunch hour had come and gone, so privacy was a sure thing. The navy-blue awning above their heads cast them in deep shadow. The hostess lit the candle in the center of the table before leaving them with a promise to send a server for their drink orders.

All at once, this began to feel like a bad idea. Or like a date, which was the same thing. Because that's not what he'd intended. Or...maybe it was what certain parts of him intended. The parts that never failed to make him sorry.

"This is very...um...intimate?" Joey said, looking at him across the table with a kind of quirky tilt to her lips.

Yeah, and he needed to stop staring at her mouth. That would be goal number one.

SIN STREET

"It's a good place to conduct an interview. We won't be disturbed." He reached for the ice water the hostess had set before him. "Why does an aspiring actress want to work as a personal assistant?" All right, that was a little abrupt. But he didn't like the way she was looking at him. Or he liked it too much. Hard to say, and damn it, this wasn't a date. It was an interview-slash-consolation prize for her not getting the assistant's job.

Because he couldn't hire her. Not if he wanted to sleep with her, and he was pretty sure he did. Which probably made this a date.

Okay, time to shut down the inner debate and focus on what the girl was saying.

"I'm not getting much work as an actress. None, in fact, and I still have to pay my rent."

He thought about how to respond to that while he switched his shades for his regular glasses. "I'm gonna take a big leap here and guess you're not getting work because you're...uh..." He swallowed, his throat dry despite having drained his water glass. "I mean, because you're not—"

"Five-foot-eight and a hundred and ten pounds?" she said, plainly not even a little bit offended by his ham-fisted try at bluntness. "You don't have to gentle. I know I'm not the typical L. A. ingénue."

He started to deny it, even though it was the truth, and was interrupted by the appearance of their server—a tall, bone-thin redhead with the air and mannerisms of an actress and who pretty much illustrated Joey's point. He ordered a bourbon, straight up.

Joey squinted at him, but said nothing about his choice of beverage. "I'll have iced tea with lemon. And lots of sugar," she said, opening her menu.

The waitress sniffed. Like she disapproved of sweetened tea, but not hard liquor at three in the afternoon on a Tuesday? Fine and dandy, sir, and will that be a double?

Joey didn't look like she'd noticed, except for the way that tiny dimple in her right cheek sort of appeared and disappeared as she stared at the list of lunch entrees.

When the redhead left them, Joey raised her eyes, peering up at him without lifting her head from the menu, and laughed. Tinkly and sweet, it sounded like ice in a tall, cold glass. The kind of laugh he could get used to on a daily basis.

Hire her, or fuck her little brains out? Yeah, this was gonna be harder than he'd thought.

"So that means you're what—a character actress?" Whenever he heard that term, he thought of some old broad with a loud mouth and a cynical air, chain-smoking her way through the role of Mama Rose in a road production of *Gypsy*. Not this chick, who could pass for Natalie Wood's sister. *With bigger tits.* And who in his right mind would complain about that?

Holy fuck, could he be more of a dog?

He knocked his glasses into place from where they'd begun to slide down his nose and sat forward in his chair, determined to listen more and think less, since thinking led to picturing her naked. And that was inappropriate because this wasn't a date. Damn it.

"Yes, a character actress," she was saying, sounding kind of prim about it. "An unsuccessful one. So I'm moving on to other things."

"You mean you're giving up acting?"

She looked amused at the outrage in his voice. "It's a hard life. People give it up every day for something easier."

"Not if they love it." He heard the challenge in his words, but didn't care to cover it. He meant every syllable. You had to love it if you were going to make any sort of life out of it.

"You can love something and still not be any good at it. I don't think I'm cut out for the business. My ego's too fragile."

Their server returned with their drinks. He resisted the urge to toss his back and order another before the redhead could disappear again. It was, in fact, too early in the day to get drunk. He had a choice to make. Better he should do it with a clear head.

They gave their orders—his for that mesquite-grilled T-bone, and Joey's for the pistachio-crusted halibut in butter sauce. This time, the redhead's sneer was harder to ignore. Stuck-up and proud of it apparently.

A flare of anger on Joey's behalf crawled up from his gut and warmed the back of his neck. He made a show of looking the waitress up and down, in her all-black ensemble that made him think of an orange lollipop on a scorched stick. She caught him checking her out and winked at him, making no secret of her willingness to flirt with another woman's companion. Which was his cue to school his features into the perfect mask of bored contempt and tilt his head to study the awning. The redhead made a small huffing sound and pivoted away, nearly running for the stairs.

"That was unnecessary," Joey said.

"I didn't think so."

She sat back in her chair, her brows raised in perfect arches over her wide-set brown eyes. "She can't help it if she's a bony bitch with an attitude problem. You'll be lucky if she doesn't spit in your mashed potatoes."

If he'd been sipping the bourbon, he'd have snorted it up his nose. He ran the back of his hand over his mouth and considered her, watching as she stirred her tea. A personal assistant with a sense of humor. Good company on long location shoots and plane rides. Someone who got along with Oksana—not like Sheila, who'd called his housekeeper "that Commie dyke" and made fun of her accent. *A friend.* If he played his cards right, kept his hands to himself and his dick in his pants...

But really, what were the chances of that?

"Where's the ladies' room?" Joey whispered across the table, as if someone might hear her.

He leaned in close and kept his voice low to match hers. "Down the stairs and to the right." When she stood, he reached out and caught her wrist in his hand. "Watch out for bony bitches with attitude." She smiled and rolled her eyes, and he grinned, feeling triumphant.

While she was gone, he sat and mouthed her name silently, trying it on for size. "Joey, would you please make reservations for tonight?" and "Hey, Joey, could you run lines with me tomorrow?" and "What do you think of this tie, Joey?" And then he imagined her answering—telling him she'd already made the reservations, of course she could help him with his lines, and scolding him for his tacky taste. Then laughing when he made a joke. Being...maybe...his friend.

Good God, what was wrong with him? He knew better than this. Two weeks of working daily with this girl, having her in his space, and he'd screw it all up by screwing her. And then screwing her some more, in as many ways as he could think of and a few he'd look up on the Internet. Maybe even doing her in that bright blue swimming hole out back because he'd never even gone for a dip and wouldn't that be the perfect way to christen it? And that'd be the end of any friendship between them. Sure it would.

He stared into his bourbon, watching it swirl as he rolled the glass between his palms. Frustration tasted bitter and familiar on the back of his tongue. When a light hand descended on his shoulder, he jumped, nearly spilling the liquor.

Joey looked down at him. "You okay?"

"Yeah, sure," he said. He felt his face tighten into a scowl. "Why would anybody with half a brain want to spend her days making appointments for some actor to get his highlights touched up? What's wrong with you anyway?" The echo of his own question to himself jumped past his lips before he had a change to rein it in.

She pulled her hand from his shoulder like it had caught fire. "There's a lot wrong with me actually," she said. She sat down and fixed her gaze on the tablecloth. "Are we going to talk about the job now?"

"Why should I hire you?"

She reached for her tea and took a gulp. Her throat worked as she swallowed. Then she set the glass down and said, "I'm bright, I'm efficient, and I take direction well. I've lived and worked in L. A. for three years, so I'm starting to understand the business."

"The business you don't think you're cut out for." God, he hated how cold he sounded. But he wasn't inclined to soften his questions. He was looking for a reason not to hire her. So he could fuck her instead. If he ever needed confirmation that he was a bona fide piece of shit...

"I may not be cut out to be an actress, but that doesn't mean I can't work in the industry." She still didn't look at him.

He felt his scowl deepen. "As a gopher who makes it her life's work to clean up other people's messes?"

"Is that what I'd be doing if I came to work for you?" She finally lifted her eyes and met his glare head on.

He took a breath and sat back in his chair. "If you're asking that question, I'm guessing you missed last month's tabloids."

"No. Spent a couple hours last night reading them actually. Then I went online and dug up everything I could find about you. Then I rented that slasher pic you did eight years ago—"

"Oh, Jesus—"

"—as well as the first season DVDs of *Vegas Knight*." She stopped to sip her tea. Then she said, "I was pleasantly surprised."

He squinted at her. She'd told him she didn't kiss ass, but come on. That movie was a piece of crap, and the series...well, the sets and the special effects were cool. The writing? His performance of the writing? Not all that impressive.

He would've said as much, but their food arrived. A new server this time—male, late-twenties, with nothing to say for himself but what was absolutely necessary. As he set their plates before them, Dare couldn't help but eye his mashed potatoes with suspicion.

"I'll take another bourbon," he said and turned his attention back to Joey. "So what did you learn about me while you were doing all that research?"

"You really want to know?"

He nodded and dug into his steak.

She pushed her plate back a few inches, folded her hands on the tablecloth in front of her, as if she were preparing to recite a lesson, and said, "You were born Dare Douglas Daniels in Breverton, Kansas, population one-thousand forty-three. Your mother was Merrilee Dare Daniels. Your father was Douglas Daniels. Both also born in Breverton. They died in an accident when you were ten."

Her voice faded a bit on the last sentence. He stopped chewing and looked up from his plate, catching the way her eyes had gone soft and liquid. He nodded and made a "go ahead" gesture with the knife in his right hand. These were just facts. No reason to get all chick-flicky about something that happened twenty years ago.

"You finished growing up on your uncle's farm outside of Breverton. You were set to attend the University of Kansas in Lawrence, but you left town in October of your senior year and came to L. A. instead. You were working as an actor before the month was out." She reached out and toyed with her fork, and he suddenly remembered she was hungry.

"That's enough. Eat your lunch."

"There's more."

"I know the story." He washed down a chunk of steak with a swallow of bourbon, letting the burn steady him enough to look at her again.

She narrowed her eyes. "The tabloid stuff—it's not like I believe it, you know."

"Maybe you should. Some of it's true."

They ate in silence for a solid five minutes before she set her glass on the table with a thunk and said, "Which parts?"

He put his silverware aside, his appetite gone. "Which parts do you think?"

"The stuff I read made you sound like a coked-out drunk with a thing for kinky public sex."

He shrugged. "I haven't done any drugs in"—he paused to think about it—"five years or so." Unless you counted that accidentally ingested half-tab of acid. Which he didn't.

"And the drinking? I can see you like your bourbon." Her mouth pulled down at the corners in a judgmental frown that pissed him off, but didn't make him want to kiss her any less.

"Yeah, I like a drink with lunch. And dinner. And after dinner." He heard the edge in his voice and didn't care. "I need an assistant, not a stand-in for my mother."

She bit her lip and glanced away. "Sorry."

"Are you?"

"Yes," she said. Her gaze wandered over the room. When she looked at him again, he could see resolve in her face. "I want this job. I'd have to be pretty stupid to offend you on purpose. And I'm not stupid."

He nodded. "Okay. Any other questions?"

She hesitated. Then, "Why are you doing *Vegas Knight?* You're clearly better than the material."

"Other folks would beg to differ."

"I think you could do better," she said.

"Good scripts are hard to come by." He cleared his throat. "But I do have something back at the house—"

"Yeah?" Her eyes twinkled at him, all eager enthusiasm. Hard to believe it wasn't an act. But he was trying.

"Yeah. An indie remake of *Cat On A Hot Tin Roof.* The producer said he wants me for the part of Brick."

"God, I love Tennessee Williams. I'd kill to read that script." She bit her lip again, and, even in the dim light, he could see the color rise in her cheeks. "I mean...I guess that was pushy."

"Nah. I'll need a second opinion. It'll be good to have someone to bounce this stuff around with."

There was a long pause. He watched her expression change as his casual comment sunk in. "I've got the job? Is that what you're telling me?"

This was bat-shit crazy and headed fast for disaster—that's what he should be telling her. But outside of how much his dick liked her, he hadn't been able to find a reason to deny her the job. And he needed a good assistant. His life was going to hell a little at a time without someone to tell him where to go and when. What did that say about him? He didn't like to consider.

The whole thing felt like fate. Or, as his mama would've said, divine providence. And who was he to argue with that?

"It's yours if you want it."

All at once she looked skeptical, all squinty eyes and pinched features. "Are you hiring me because you feel sorry for me?"

"Is this the part where you throw your drink in my face and tell me you don't need my pity?"

She pursed her lips. "Only if I were playing the proud, tragic ingénue. And we've already covered that."

God, she's so damn smart. When was the last time he'd met anyone this smart?

"Answer the question, please, Mr. Daniels."

"People who work for me call me 'Dare.'"

"Your housekeeper doesn't."

"I don't know what she calls me when I'm not around."

"You're saying Oksana calls you 'Dare' to your face?" She looked and sounded filled to the brim with doubt, as if he had a reason to lie about something so stupid.

"No," he admitted. "Oksana calls me 'Mr. Big Shot' to my face. Or sometimes 'stupid boy.'"

She laughed, and damn if that didn't make him want to jump right across the table and...

Time to change the subject. "You liked the slasher movie? Really?"

She made the dimple in her cheek appear and vanish again in the blink of an eye. "I wouldn't say I liked it. But it was...entertaining. Especially that scene in the deserted malt shop right before the blonde loses her face in the hot fudge machine."

He groaned and rolled his eyes. "I hate that scene."

"You should. It shocked the hell out of me."

"Yeah? Why?"

"Well, because..." She paused, looking uncertain.

"Spit it out. I promise I won't fire you."

"All right then, you asked for it." The dimple flashed like a warning signal. "For a guy who gets off on public fucking, you'd think you'd be able to pull off a more convincing orgasm in a room full of cameras and people."

CHAPTER 5

Good going, Josephine. Maybe next you can insult the size of his schlong.

Joey flinched, more from the expression on Dare's face than from Gina's rebuke. He blinked at her, his eyes round behind his glasses. She opened her mouth to apologize because even though he'd said he wouldn't fire her—

But he was laughing. Throwing his head back and showing her the long, tanned line of his throat and laughing. She sat there, feeling like an idiot and fighting the twin urges to run away and take a swipe at his Adam's apple with her tongue. How the hell was this going to work? With her wanting to jump on him every other second, and the way he so obviously knew it but chose—out of some old-fashioned notion of chivalry, she imagined—to ignore it.

Earth to Joey. He's talking to you.

"What can I say? I was young. Practically a virgin. I'd do a better job of it now." He made a big show of leering at her, like a cross between Groucho Marx and the big, bad wolf in the old Warner Brothers' cartoons. She tried not to react, but he didn't let up with the eyebrows and wagging tongue 'til she was laughing along with him.

"In all fairness," she said when she'd caught her breath, "it wasn't entirely your fault."

"No?"

"No way. There's gotta be give and take in a scene like that. Seemed like the actress wasn't giving you much to work with. I'm surprised the director let her get away with it."

He studied her for a moment. A breeze made the candle's flame flicker, throwing interesting shadows against his face. *God, so freakishly beautiful.* Botticelli's angels had nothing on this guy. "How would you have done it?"

She choked on a sliver of ice. He waited while she coughed into her napkin. She gave her watering eyes a final dab and said, "Well, for starters, she looked like she was trying to yank your head right off your neck, the way she kept pulling at it. What's sexy about that?"

"Not much, but that's not what I asked you. I asked you—"

"I heard what you asked me." She pressed her lips together in a tight line and looked away. Her answer sat ready on her tongue, but she couldn't bring herself to—

Ah, come on, Josephine. Spit it out. I'm kinda curious myself.

Really, there was nothing like being perpetually chaperoned by an older sister who died without ever learning the basics of tact. No wonder she hadn't been laid in six months.

Dare cleared his throat. "You still with me?"

"Yes. Sorry. I just...don't know how to answer that."

Liar.

"Would it help if I told you the actress—whose name was Larissa Long, by the way—went commando for that scene? She said the flash of panties would ruin her character's street cred."

"Method acting for slutty starlets?"

He nodded. "And a surefire way to get wardrobe to burn the jeans I was wearing for that scene. But you think you could do a better job?" Something about his turn of phrase...or maybe it was the smug quirk of his lips...

"A better job at what, exactly?"

"At getting me to the point where I could fake a believable orgasm."

Son of a bitch. "What are you asking me, Mr. Daniels?" She sounded frosty, but that's how she felt. *Damn him.* He'd almost made her believe he wanted to work with her more than he wanted to fuck her. Because she'd have to be blind, deaf and dumb not to feel the zing of chemistry between them. But she'd really hoped they could get beyond it. She'd wanted this job. A lot more than she did when she climbed out of bed this morning, in fact.

"Hey, you're the one who brought it up." He was backpedaling now, and that just made it worse. "Don't get mad. I didn't mean—"

"Yeah? What did you mean?"

"I sure didn't mean to piss you off. It was a joke."

She eyed him over the candle's dancing flame. "A joke."

He nodded. "Although you surprised me. You don't seem like the type to back down from a challenge."

Bastard. Scum-sucking lowlife. "I'm not, as a matter of fact."

"Coulda fooled me." He looked away, towards the stairs, as if he were anxious for their check to arrive.

Brava, sister. You just screwed yourself out of dessert.

Damn it, Gina. "I've got nothing to prove to you."

He looked at her, his face a perfect blank. Emphasis on the "perfect." "Maybe I'm the one with something to prove. You just insulted my ability to reproduce a universal human experience."

"I said you blew chunks at faking an orgasm."

"Right."

She sighed and dragged a hand through her hair. "So just pull a Meg Ryan, right here and now. If you're so much more experienced now than you were then, it should be a piece of cake."

He shook his head. "I'd need to recreate the moment. For verisimilitude."

"Verisimilitude?" For a guy who hadn't even finished high school, he sure had a hell of a vocabulary. Maybe she'd missed the part in his online biography about his being some kind of genius.

He was still talking. "Of course if you're scared, I totally understand—"

"Scared?" Okay, now she sounded like a parrot repeating random words.

"Yeah, you know, like...chicken?"

She ground her back teeth together, hard.

Which reminds me—make sure you ask him about dental insurance. You haven't had a cleaning in—

"Put a sock in it, Gina."

He smiled, which appeared to be his default expression, yet managed to look mildly confused at the same time. "Who's Gina?"

"Never mind." Joey dropped her napkin on the table and stood.

"Don't go. I was only—"

She moved around the table to stand next to him. "Give me some room to work."

His looked surprised, but pivoted his chair from beneath the table without comment. His eyes never left her face as she stepped closer and then straddled him. Thank God for ill-fitting peasant dresses with skirts three feet wide.

He leaned back in the chair and lifted his hands to either side, as if unsure about his next move and not wanting to cross some invisible boundary by touching the woman who'd just crawled into his lap. Oddly endearing, these flashes of uncertainty. She'd have to watch that. It could get her into trouble.

Yeah. Because mounting him in a public restaurant isn't likely to cause anything like a problem.

"Angelina Fiorello, if you don't shut up and get lost right this second, I swear on our mother's grave—"

Dare's eyes widened. "What the hell?" He turned his head, his gaze scanning the room. "Is this a prank? Are you setting me up? Who're you talking to? Are you wearing a wire?" He sounded panicked.

"It's not a prank." She pitched her voice low in an attempt to soothe him. "There's no one here but us." He looked unconvinced. "Really. I'll explain all about Gina later, I promise."

He eyed her for a long moment. She did what she could to appear innocent, though it was tough, what with wanting to giggle hysterically at the absurdity of it all. Leave it to Gina to make everything harder.

I do what I can, babe.

Finally, he nodded. "You really don't have to go through with this," he said and gestured vaguely at the small space between them. "It's not necessary. I was just—"

"Calling me a coward? Yeah, that was a mistake. We're doing this now, because a Fiorello never backs down from a dare." She smiled as she realized her pun. "Or a challenge, either."

They laughed together, which did interesting things involving pressure and friction and oh, man...had she noted his perfect face? Because that wasn't quite true, as it turned out. Up close she could see how his nose was a little crooked, and his left eye was smaller than his right, and both eyes had crinkles that were known as crows' feet in women, and laugh-lines in men.

And the fact that he wasn't perfect? Made him perfect. If that made any sense at all.

She settled herself more firmly on his thighs. "Where shall we start?"

He looked a little dazed, but he answered quickly enough. "Uh...how about the part where I say 'Shhh...we have to be quiet.'"

She nodded. "Then I say 'To hell with quiet.' And then you kiss me."

That had been her favorite part of the whole movie. The angle from which it was shot let the audience see how Dare used his mouth when he kissed—soft at first, just gentle pressure. Then harder, his lips parting as he leaned into it, sucking at the actress's lower lip before tracing her mouth with the tip of his tongue.

He took off his glasses and tossed them in the direction of the table. She heard them knock against his water glass. "And then I kiss you," he said.

His mouth was just like she'd imagined it. Soft and full, but not mushy. Warm and wet, but not like falling face-first into a busted hot water bottle. Tasting of mesquite and bourbon and something sweeter. She moved closer, going on instinct. Although she really should've been thinking about her moves. She was trying to be an actress here. Trying, in a sense, to audition. But this was no audition any more than their interview had been an interview.

He pulled away a scant inch or two. "Then you grab my hands and put them...uh..."

She reached out and grabbed his wrists. "It's okay. We're just acting, right?"

He said something that might've been "yes" or "right" or just a grunt of agreement. And then she moved his hands to her breasts, which immediately perked up against the touch of his open palms. What was she doing, oh my God, what the fuck was she doing? This was bad. And wrong. And so, so good.

"What's the next line?" Christ, she sounded like Minnie Mouse on speed.

"It's mine," he said. "I think it goes, 'Is this a test to see if I can carry on a conversation and seduce you at the same time'?"

Right. She remembered this part. "Is that what you're doing? Seducing me?"

"You can't tell? Maybe my technique needs work." He tightened one hand on her breast and slid the other to the small of her back, where he rubbed light circles against the cheap cotton and made her breath hitch in her chest with the tenderness of it.

She ran her fingers through his hair, tugging lightly, but not trying to liberate his poor head from his neck, and spoke the next line. "Or maybe I'm seducing you."

There was a pause. He said, "And then we mostly make out for about thirty seconds."

"Right. Got a stopwatch handy?"

He grinned. Then he lifted his hand from her breast, brushed back the curls that covered her ear and whispered, "We can skip that part if you want."

Yep. Chivalrous to the end.

She was losing sight of the goal, which was to get him to...what? Realistically fake an orgasm? If the bulge pressing against her was any indication of progress, things were tripping right along. So wrong, so good, so utterly fucked up—was she really doing this? In public?

"Let me know when you're ready for the next part."

She laughed and was glad to note her voice had lost its squeak. "Ready when you are, captain." This was insane. Even Gina had shut up and retreated, probably out of shock and disgust at the sight of her sister whoring herself for a job. *Except...no.* She already had the job. He'd made that clear.

So why was she doing this exactly? Then he made a path from her ear to her collarbone with his mouth, and she remembered. *Pure, filthy lust.* And by every saint she'd ever prayed to as a Catholic schoolgirl, it was glorious.

He pulled back and licked his lips, his cheeks flushed beneath his tan. "This is the part where Larissa started yanking on my head."

"Yeah. Let's see if I can't improve on that."

She shifted against him and locked her ankles around the legs of the chair. Then she arched backward, reaching for the floor between his feet where she braced herself with the fingertips.

"Wow. Limber."

She laughed. It came out more like a gurgle. "Best damn gymnast Our Lady of Perpetual Sorrow ever saw, my friend." Oh, God, he could see her underwear, couldn't he? Which ones had she worn? The faded pink with the fraying elastic at the crotch? She took a breath and said, "I think this would make a nice shot from an overhead angle, don't you?"

He made a noise. She took it for agreement, then stopped thinking entirely when his hand came down warm and firm on her bare thigh. He cleared his throat. "Is this okay?"

She nodded, then realized he couldn't see her head. "It's fine."

His hand moved, stroking up and down. She closed her eyes and let her body respond. The blood pooling in her head made her vision blur, but it was the way his fingers inched a little higher with each pass that made her heart pound. She heard herself make a noise—something between a moan and a sigh. When he echoed it, she reached for him. He caught her fingers in his and pulled her up with enough force to bring their pelvises into solid contact.

He flinched and shifted under her. "Maybe we should quit."

"Now who's chicken?"

His eyes narrowed. "Bring it, Fiorello."

Wow. Got the pronunciation right on the first try. Impressive. She leaned in to kiss him, letting her arms snake around his neck. He matched the embrace, sliding his hands against her back and holding her as if letting go didn't feature in his plans for the near future.

He brushed his lips over hers, feather light. Then he pressed his tongue inside, delving and licking, and she invited him in like an old friend. His hips started up that slow, primitive roll that ground them together, lighting sparks of pleasure that burst through her, sharp and bright. He set a deliberate pace, like he had a purpose—like she was the one needing remedial help with faking a climax. Not that she'd need to be faking much if he kept up that needy press and slide.

She palmed the blades of his shoulders, raked her nails across his back and felt him groan into her mouth, all thick and sweet, but with a rough bite against the tongue. Like a mouthful of crystallized honey. They could do this forever. Public heavy petting with the danger of discovery always lurking. Giving it that extra edge. Making her want to see how far she could push him—could push herself.

But that wasn't the point. *Wait...what was the point again? Oh yeah.*

Her voice sounded breathy when she said, "You ready to give this a shot? Metaphorically speaking, of course."

He pulled back and looked at her. His lips were glossy, and his pupils were blown wide, the black eating up the green even as she watched. "Huh?"

"You were going to simulate an orgasm for me, remember?"

He blinked. Once. Slow and sort of bewildered. "Right."

"You ready to try?"

Awareness seeped back into his face. He raised a brow and smiled—both wicked and self-effacing at the same time, and how the fuck did he do that? God, what a gift. Beidermeyer was right. Dare Daniels was going to be a star.

"I don't think faking it is going to be the problem. Not to be crude, but—"

"I'm from Brooklyn. What's crude?"

SIN STREET

The wicked element in his expression intensified, at odds with the almost tender way he lifted his hand to touch her face. "I'm about two seconds shy of the real thing. Which could be fun, in a messy sort of way."

A thrill shot through her. Her hands tightened on his shoulders reflexively. She pressed into him, rubbing the crotch of her own more-than-a-little-damp panties against his fabric-covered cock in a slow circle. *Stupid and wrong to do this.* He was her employer, she needed this job, and she was nuts to be letting things get out of hand—to let herself get so out of hand. But he was beautiful and smart and funny, and the way he responded to her made her so damn hot. Made her feel wanton and fuckable. And if that's what dry-humping in a chair could do, what might happen if they got naked? Or horizontal? Or—holy mother of God—both at the same time?

He grunted, then he gasped and then he was holding her hips, keeping her still by sheer force. There would be bruises from his fingertips tomorrow. The thought made her shiver.

"I'm not kidding, Joey. Don't do anything you'll regret. I wouldn't want that."

Regret. The word stopped her cold.

"I'm sorry." She tried to move off him, but he held her tight, and she felt that instinctive roll of his hips. She shivered again, loving the press of him, hard and insistent, against all her most sensitive spots.

"Don't be," he said and nipped at her jaw. Her hands flexed, and she dug her fingertips into his shoulders. He looked at her with heat in his eyes. "You have to tell me what you want here. Are we working together or fucking each other?"

"You're making me choose?" The squeak in her voice was back.

"'Fraid so. I'm a weak man. You'll find that out, one way or the other."

The sound of voices on the stairs made her jump and then bolt from his lap. She turned away and smoothed her skirt down with hands that shook. His chair made a scraping sound as he pivoted his lower body under the table.

"Dessert, Mr. Daniels?" The witchy redhead had returned, accompanied by the dark-haired waiter with the bland face and the sharp eyes. Joey didn't bother to look at any of them. She stepped to the edge of the balcony and listened as Dare settled the bill.

Free lunch. Except nothing in this world was free. This time she'd traded a little of her self-respect. She wanted to be mad at Dare, but it wasn't his fault. He was an unattached, healthy young man who taken what she'd offered. To be fair, he'd been a gentleman. No pressure, no coercion—just too much temptation. And that was hardly his fault.

By the time she turned to face him, she'd settled herself. She found him staring into the guttering candle. When he looked up, his eyes were blank behind the lenses of his glasses. He focused them somewhere over her left shoulder and said, "Well?"

She shrugged. "I need this job. Furthermore, I want this job."

"And you think we can work together like this?"

She didn't bother to pretend she didn't know what he meant. "I can be professional under any circumstances."

He nodded. "Then let's try it. I need you to be at LAX tomorrow at five A.M. for a seven o'clock flight to Wichita with a connection in Denver. We'll rent a car and drive into Breverton. We'll be there for a week. Sound good?"

"Sounds fine. I've never been to Kansas."

"You'll love it. Everybody does." She couldn't tell if that was sarcasm. He'd closed down completely. She reached out and laid a hand on his shoulder. He didn't react, other than the flicker of one eyelid.

"You can trust me, Dare. I won't let you down like…" She'd been about to say "like other people have," but that was too presumptuous, even for her. She cleared her throat. "I won't let you down. As far as I'm concerned, this never happened. We can start fresh."

"Fresh," he said. It didn't sound like a question. "After this?"

"Yes. It was just two actors improvising a scene. And after all, I'm not technically your employee yet. Haven't signed a contract or anything." She was grasping at any rationalization now, desperate to get some response from him.

When he finally looked at her, the disgust and shame she saw in his eyes made her drop her hand from his shoulder and step back. He said, "You can just take off like that for a week? No cats to feed, no boyfriends to soothe?"

"My roommate will take care of the cat."

"And the boyfriend?" The edge in his voice made her chew at her lip. Bad habit. Gina always said she'd ruin the shape of her mouth doing that. She chewed harder.

"You think I'd do what we just did if I had a serious boyfriend?"

"Do what? It never happened. And even if it did, it was just acting."

He looked away again. "That's what you said."

She didn't know how to answer that, so she let it go. A few moments passed in silence. Then he traded his glasses for the shades, got up and walked toward the stairs. She followed. She didn't see where she had much choice.

They drove to Beidermeyer's office in silence. Before she got out of the Escalade, he handed her cash for the cab to the airport. "Your car is fine at my place for the week."

"You're not coming up to the office?"

"No. I never go up there unless I have to. And now that I have you..."

"You don't ever have to." She smiled at him, wishing she could see his eyes behind the dark sunglasses.

As if he'd read her mind, he slid them off his face and turned to look at her. "You never told me about Gina."

Crap. "Umm..."

"Well?"

"It's a long story. Maybe on the plane tomorrow?"

He nodded. "I'm sorry about today, Joey. I promise—" He cut himself off with a huff of what appeared to be frustration. Then he said, "Here's a clue about me. I'm a selfish, spoiled piece of shit who never keeps his word. So if I ever promise you anything—"

"Dare—"

"Don't believe me. Know that I mean it when I say it, but don't ever believe me."

She reached over the console, meaning to touch his hand where it gripped the steering wheel tight enough to turn the knuckles white. "Please—"

"Don't." He slipped the shades back on his face. "Get out of the car, Joey. I'll see you tomorrow."

"Dare—"

"Go."

She went.

CHAPTER 6

Worthless. That's what he was.

His therapist would say he'd let his "id" get the better of his "super-ego" again. His Momma, God rest her, would say he was backsliding and had fallen away from the Lord. But his Daddy? His Daddy—God rest him, too—would just level that cold, dead-even stare, turn around and walk away. Under his breath he'd mutter "worthless." Just loud enough for an eight-year-old boy to hear and understand.

Dare shifted his carry-on bag to his other shoulder and checked his watch. Five-twenty. She wasn't coming. And why would she, after what he'd done? Groping her and making her dry-hump him in public. Going home and jacking off to the memory of mauling her tits through her dress.

Maybe she didn't know for sure what he'd done in privacy of his shower, or about how every time he licked his lips he tasted her mouth, but she could probably guess. Bad enough he'd left no doubt about how much he wanted her. Not like she could miss it, when his dick practically busted his zipper the second she touched him. Worse yet? Now she had solid proof Sheila hadn't lied to those tabloid reporters. Dare Daniels most certainly did have a streak of exhibitionism running deep and wide through his perverted, worthless soul.

"Excuse me, I'm sorry, if I could just—" Joey's voice rose high and sweet over the irritated babble of the crowd standing in line at security some twenty feet away. He turned and saw her struggling through a knot of people, fighting to keep her feet as the huge duffel bag she held like a bundle in one arm threatened to overbalance her. She wore jeans, tennis shoes, and a little pink shirt with a low, round neckline that fit a lot better than yesterday's dress.

"Joey!" He called out before he thought about it, and a few people turned to look. *Damn.* He pulled the bill of his baseball cap low on his forehead and settled his sunglasses firmly in place. Joey looked up and saw him. Her bright smile almost made up for the inevitable murmuring and pointing that suddenly surrounded him. *Five, four, three, two...*

"Are you Dare Daniels? You are, aren't you?" said a woman of about forty dressed in a screaming purple track suit and toting a bulging straw bag. "Can I get your autograph? For my daughter. She just loves you."

And how could he say no? He always wanted to and never did because this was part of the life. You wanted to be a successful actor with a hit TV show? Pay the piper, son.

Then Joey was at his side, pulling a pad and pen from her own bag and handing them to him so he could write "Best Wishes, Dare Daniels" and hand it over to the gushing fan. And look—here were five more lined up right behind the beaming woman. That familiar feeling of panic rose in his throat, threatening to choke him. He hated this part of it. The way they came for him, and never stopped coming. Like they all owned a piece of him and were perfectly within their rights to collect whenever he made the mistake of venturing into public.

"Okay, folks. One at a time and let's back up a few steps, shall we? No fair crowding the man at this early hour, especially when he's a quart low on caffeine." Joey's tone was light and teasing, and when he looked up, he saw how the fans were smiling at her and moving back, leaving him with a little circle of synthetic airport air to breathe. His throat eased.

Between the seventh and eighth autograph, he glanced at her. "Thanks."

She nodded. "No problem. Part of the job, right?"

He opened his mouth to reply and a camera flashed. He ducked and pulled his cap lower. Was it a pic-snapping fan or a professional photog, the kind that hung around LAX waiting for a celebrity to wander through? People called them "paparazzi"—bastardized Italian for "buzzing insects"—but that nickname didn't come close to capturing how vicious and bloodthirsty those assholes could be. More like a pack of starving hyenas, just as likely to turn on each other as

SIN STREET

their prey.

"It's five-forty-five," Joey whispered. "We should get in line."

"Okay." He looked up into the faces of his fans and mustered up his trademarked grin. "Sorry, folks, but if I don't get my butt through security now, I'll miss my flight." When the disappointed muttering rose around them, he slipped off his sunglasses and made a point of making eye-contact with everyone in the small crowd. He even winked at a few of the females because that never failed to satisfy.

Joey hoisted her bag into her arms and began shouldering through the crowd, creating a path for him. Together they dove for the end of the line trailing through security. The guard posted a few yards away nodded at them, then fixed a no-nonsense glare on the few straggling fans who ventured to follow. Dare slid his shades back into place and sighed, the tension draining from his neck and jaw. Joey smiled at him over her shoulder and set her bag at her feet.

He said the first thing that popped into his head. "How did you know I didn't get coffee yet?"

She shrugged. "Lucky guess."

The security chick who checked his boarding pass and ID turned out to be a regular *Vegas Knight* viewer. Still, she insisted he remove his shades and hat so she could make absolutely certain he was who he claimed to be—all the while babbling about how she never, ever missed an episode, and what about that cliffhanger season finale? How was that going to turn out? The line backed up as Dare struggled to extricate himself from the conversation.

By the time they made it onto the plane, he'd earned the ire of every passenger stuck behind them in the line. Someday he was going to buy his own damn jet and learn to fly the fucker, if only to avoid this shit.

"Wow," Joey breathed, after she'd wedged her bag into the overhead compartment and settled into her window seat. "This is nice."

"Never flown first class before?"

"Never." She ran her hand over the leather seat and grinned.

He cleared his throat. "Listen, I want to apologize for yesterday. It never should've happened."

He watched as her face lost some of its glow. Her lips tightened and her brows dropped, and she leaned away from him slightly. Tense. Guarded. Uncomfortable. Pretty much exactly what he'd hoped to avoid.

"It's not a problem," she said. "Forget it."

There was a pause that seemed to last an hour before the flight

SIN STREET

attendant—a woman in her mid-fifties with too much lipstick and not enough rouge—showed up, offering pre-flight beverages.

"Can I get a beer?" It was out of his mouth before he had a chance to think about it.

"It's six-thirty in the morning," Joey said.

She sounded surprised and maybe a little unhappy. And she was right, of course. What he really needed was that caffeine they'd talked about earlier. But now that he'd asked for beer, he'd be damned if he'd take it back. He whipped the sunglasses off his face and smiled up at the attendant.

"How about a cup of coffee instead, sir?" she said, looking at Joey instead of him. Like the girl was his keeper or something. Like he needed a keeper because drinking beer at this hour was way over the top. Well, okay then, he was over the top and proud of it, and he wanted a goddamned glass of suds.

He shook his head. "Beer, please. Domestic or imported. I'm not picky." He turned up the wattage on his smile, going for rakishly charming, and was downright disappointed when the attendant returned his grin and said she'd see what she could do. She hadn't even made him compliment the fit of her uniform, or the snappy way she wore her hair. It wasn't any fun when it came too easy.

Funny how he felt better when he turned to look at Joey and caught a glare that could peel paint. *Yeah—nothing too easy about her.* She'd make him work for every last thing she gave him. Now why did that thought make his chest squeeze so tight?

He tucked away his shades and dug his regular glasses out of his bag. Without looking at Joey, he said, "I take it you disapprove."

Her eyes narrowed. "Tell me now—are you a candidate for rehab? It's only fair I should know up front." The edge in her voice was hard to miss. She didn't just disapprove—the girl was furious. There was a story there somewhere. Something having to do with her and alcohol consumption. If he worked it just right, he could probably get the whole thing out of her by the time they landed.

He opened his mouth to answer her question, and somebody stumbled and shoved the flight attendant, who was already making her way down the aisle with his beer. The glass flew from her hand, dousing his blue button-down with amber liquid and landing upside down in his lap.

"Oh, sir, I'm so sorry." The attendant grabbed a towel from the nearby cart and made dabbing motions in his general direction. He righted the glass and handed it back to her, assuring her that everything was fine, no harm done, what were a few spilled suds among total strangers? Joey sat staring at the stain covering the entire crotch and half the left thigh of his jeans, her mouth hanging open and all traces of fury gone from her face. Apparently, her rage could be extinguished by a single bottle of mid-priced German lager. *Good to know.*

Chaos reigned for a full five minutes, complete with another set of cringing apologies from the flight attendant, and his insistence that everything was cool, no big deal. Then it was time for the instructional safety video. He let his head drop against the seat. Nothing like wet, sticky pants for no good reason.

He felt the warm breath of Joey's whisper against his ear before he heard her say, "Serves you right."

His first instinct was to laugh. Because it did serve him right, and if his Momma had been there, she'd have told him the same. But if his Momma had been there, the thought of Joey close enough to kiss wouldn't be making his dick twitch inside his soggy boxer-briefs. He turned his head to face her, and they were nose-to-nose when he said, "What did booze ever do to you anyway?"

The pretty half-smile that'd been curling the corners of her lips dropped away fast. *Damn.* He was batting a thousand this morning. She looked out the window as they taxied down the runway. When she spoke, her voice was so low he had to ask her to repeat herself.

"I said, my sister was killed by a drunk driver."

Ah, crap. And there he went, cracking jokes and ordering bourbon and beer every chance he got. He sighed. "All I ever seem to say to you is 'sorry.'" He sounded like a sulky kid even to his own ears. "But I am. Sorry, I mean."

She glanced at him. "It's okay. You didn't know."

"You, uh...wanna talk about it?" Yeah, that was slick. Because he was such an expert on the healthy handling of grief.

She pivoted her body in the seat to face him. "It was three years ago. I..." She paused and swallowed, and he panicked because what if she cried? What would he do then?

He held up a hand. "You don't have to really," he said and watched her face change again, her eyes narrowing and her mouth twisting as if she'd tasted something sour.

"It's okay," she said. "I'm not going to weep on your shoulder."

"I didn't mean it like that." The hell he didn't. Worthless, remember?

She shrugged. "Last night you asked about Gina, and I was going to tell you. She's my sister. The one that died."

"Gina? The one you keep, uh…"

"Talking to? Yes."

He glanced around, just to make sure no one was listening. The guy sitting across the aisle was asleep, snoring into his complimentary pillow. He turned back to Joey and lowered his voice to a whisper. "You're saying you talk to your dead sister."

She nodded. "Is that a problem?" She bit her lip. Her eyes had widened again, as if she were afraid of his answer.

"No. I mean, it's a little"—he almost said weird—"unusual."

"I know. At first, I thought I was losing my mind. But I got used to it after the first couple of months."

"Got used to what?"

She frowned at him. "Gina. Talking to me. In my head."

He pressed his lips together and hummed. "She talks to you, too? You have, like, conversations?"

"Why would I talk to her if she didn't talk back? That would be nuts." She said it like it was the most obvious, logical thing in the world. And when she put it like that, it was.

"Is she talking to you now?"

Joey shook her head. "She's not around. I think she's a little unhappy about yesterday. The thing in the restaurant?"

Great. He'd pissed off the dead sister. "She was there for that?"

"Some of it. She took off when I got on top of you."

"She doesn't like me." He didn't phrase it as a question. What was to like? He'd debauched the baby sis. Bad karma all around.

Christ on a cracker, this was insane.

"Oh, she likes you a lot. It's me she's probably mad at. She's afraid I'm going to screw up and lose this job."

There was something so wrong and yet so profoundly sweet about the earnest way Joey was talking about this…like she genuinely believed her sister's spirit or whatever was hanging around, worrying about her welfare. It should've made him wonder if she was playing him. Or if she was, in fact, a few catfish short of a coat-rack.

Instead, he wondered why she needed to believe in ghosts in order to feel loved. And that made him want to rub that place in the middle of his chest where hurtful things tended to stick hard and dig in.

"You were close to your sister?" he said, resisting the urge to let his fingers brush her face or her shoulder. Because he was afraid even that simple touch would telegraph how much he wanted kiss her and pull her against him and then maybe fuck her—which was pretty much the only way he knew how to express what he was feeling. And what was he feeling? Did it even have a name? Something besides his usual persistent horniness, or even the more target-specific "lust." Something...warmer, maybe?

"I wasn't very close to her when she was alive," Joey said. "She was fifteen years older, and pretty much out of the house by the time I was walking and talking."

"And you say she died three years ago?"

"Yes. Crossing the street late at night, on her way home from work. A drunk ran the light."

He could see her remembering in the way her eyes got a little distant and wet-looking, and he wanted to take back the question. Or change the subject.

Before he had the chance, she spoke again. "She was working extra shifts to pay for my room and board at college."

"Extra shifts?" So the sister had been a waitress, maybe. Or a—

"Nurse. Emergency room. She was very good at her job."

He nodded because really...what was there to say? If Joey had been somebody else—any other female of the right age and looking all soft and vulnerable like that—he'd have pulled her into his arms for what would start as a comforting hug and end in a lip-lock designed to melt her every defense. But, as it was, he needed to avoid the let-me-soothe-you-by-sticking-my-tongue-down-your-throat strategy and work on seeming empathetic. Or sympathetic. Something other than a horny bastard on the make.

A little line appeared between her eyes, and she said, "We have a problem, don't we?"

"Huh?"

She sighed. "You keep staring at my mouth. At first I thought I had something in my teeth. But I'm guessing that's not it."

So much for his stellar acting skills. "Very perceptive."

She ignored the bitterness in his voice and cut right to the chase. "What are we going to do about it?"

"Nothing. It'll be fine."

"Cut the bullshit, Dare."

Okay, that was just uncalled for. "You know, Joey? You're cute, but you're not irresistible, and I do have some self-control." And that came out a bunch more hostile than he'd intended. Plus, it was a bald-faced lie.

The line between her eyes deepened. "Maybe you do and maybe you don't. But you said so yourself—we can work together or we can fuck each other. Trying to do both would be a mistake."

He nodded. "Been there, done that, got the ass-kicking in the press to prove it. Not interested in a return trip."

She looked at him, one brow quirked over a dewy brown eye. "On the other hand, maybe it's the kind of thing you'll have to get out of your system. Like you said, I'm only cute. Not the kind of woman men make fools of themselves over. It probably wouldn't take more than once."

Talk about twelve kinds of fucked up, and he opened his mouth to tell her so. To tell her she shouldn't undervalue herself like that. To tell her he wouldn't even discuss it, much less participate in something so cheap and empty. But who the hell did he think he was kidding? Lately, his whole life was nothing but a long parade of cheap and empty.

And she was still talking. "We'll do it once and clear the air. That'll fix everything, and we'll be able to work together without the distraction."

She was watching him, a funny look on her face. Tense, sort of. Like she expected him to turn her down—and he should. Turn her down flat. Right thing to do, better angels of his nature and all that shit. He ran the back of his hand over his lips and coughed into a closed fist, stalling for time. "Uh…when did you want to put this plan into effect?"

She looked away, down into her lap, and he could've sworn she was disappointed. But then she said, "No time like the present," and stood up. "Excuse me, please? I need to use the restroom."

He rose, and she squeezed past him, letting her ass come into direct contact with his damp crotch. Okay, that was on purpose—he was pretty damn sure of it. Any lingering doubt dissolved when she looked at him over her shoulder and said, "I bet you need to use the restroom, too, don't you?"

He stammered and sputtered for a second or two. Then he said, "Yes, as a matter of fact, I do."

She slid out into the aisle and made her way to the first class facilities. He watched her go, counting to thirty. Slowly. Then he followed her, ignoring the stares from the other passengers and the way the flight attendant popped out from the galley to observe him knocking on the bathroom door.

Joey opened the door, pulled him into the tiny cubicle, and reached around him to shove the lock into place. "Did anyone notice?"

"Of course not. Why would anyone pay attention to the guy with the beer-stained tent in his pants following the girl into the restroom?"

She glanced down and smiled. "We'll have to do something about that. The tent part, I mean."

"Whoa." He took her wrist in his hand as she reached for his belt. "You said this would be a mistake."

"I also said we needed to clear the air and remove distractions." She twisted her arm from his grasp and reached again for his buckle. He grabbed for her wrist a second time, mostly because things were moving way too fast. But also because she was taking charge. Again. And maybe it was his turn.

"Slow down and let's talk about this a second," he said and instantly wanted to rip his own tongue out. Sex on a crowded plane had always been a serious, top-of-the-list fantasy for him, and here he was working overtime to prevent it. Why, exactly? Because he didn't want her to think she was obligated? Because he wanted to respect her? Because he wanted her to respect him?

The plane hit a pocket of turbulence, throwing them off balance. They fell hard against the door, make a loud, rattling thump. Dare froze with Joey's face mashed into the middle of his chest, waiting for the inevitable.

"Is everything all right in there?" The flight attendant sounded annoyed.

He smothered his laughter in Joey's hair as she answered for both of them. "Yes! We're fine!" She righted herself and glared at him. "Are you going to cooperate?"

"What's in it for me?"

The glare evaporated and she smiled again, the tip of her tongue peeping between her teeth. "A little release of tension." She made the words sound dirty, her lips shaping them so he could almost see each individual letter.

A trace of Brooklyn had crept into her voice. She'd said her accent popped up in moments of high stress. Interesting. Then she stretched up and stuck her tongue in his mouth. She tasted tangy, like cherry SweeTarts™, and he lost his train of thought.

"You smell like a brewery." She whispered it against his lips as her hand found their way to his belt once more.

"I...uh..." Whatever he'd been about to say deteriorated into a grunt when she worked open his fly and slid her fingers home. Then she leaned her forehead against the center of his chest as she slid his jeans and briefs over his hips and pulled his cock out into the cool, dry air. The pilot's voice sounded overhead. "Ladies and gentlemen, we ask that you return to your seats and fasten your seatbelts, as we'll be passing through some rough air on our way to touch down in Denver."

Well, of course. This was God's way of giving him another chance to do the right thing. Couldn't get much clearer without a divine baseball bat to the head. "Joey? We have to go back to our seats."

"Shut up. This is my show now." She dropped to her knees, pressing him back against the door. "Hold still and try to be quiet. I'll make this quick."

She grasped the base of his cock and ran her finger up the length of him, stopping just short of the crown. He hissed between his teeth in reaction, feeling his balls pull up tight and firm. She wasn't kidding about the "quick" part. Then her thumb slurred over the tip, slipping in the shiny moisture collecting in the slit, and he all but whimpered at the too-much-not-enough sensation. Heat pooled at the base of his spine like a storm threatening to erupt out of invisible clouds.

The plane hit another bump in the sky. Her fingers tightened, holding on, and when she stuck her tongue out to lick all around the rim of the crown, he let his head fall back against the door with a thud and closed his eyes. Behind his eyelids, the pervy part of his soul showed home movies of what Joey would look like with his dick between her lips. Not that he expected her to actually—oh, Jesus.

She'd just leaned in and enveloped him in the warm, wet heaven of her mouth when the pilot's voice intruded again. "Ladies and gentlemen, we're beginning our final descent into Denver. Please make sure your luggage is securely stowed, your seatbelts are fastened, and your tray-tables are in the upright and locked position. Flight attendants, prepare the cabin for arrival."

The rap on the door came three seconds later. "Sir? Miss? You'll need to return to your seats immediately."

At the sound of the flight attendant's voice, the private porn showing in his head faded. Speaking of upright and locked, he wasn't looking forward to stuffing this particular boner back into his jeans, but those were the breaks. And yet—maybe not. Because Joey just sucked harder, using her hand to caress the part of his shaft she couldn't fit into her mouth, her teeth scraping lightly against the underside in a way that made his toes curl inside his ridiculously expensive sneakers. He groaned loud and long over the whir of the overhead fan. Because the folks in the first three rows needed that extra clue to solve The Mystery of the Hummer in the First Class John.

Another volley of knocks sounded against the door. *Time to call it quits.* The hard part—pun most definitely intended—was getting his lips to form words while the hot, slippery suction of Joey's mouth combined with the evil flickers of her tongue were driving him right up to the point of no return.

"Sir! Miss! You need to come out of there right now!" The attendant sounded agitated.

"Joey...honey...we have to—"

She pulled off with a wet, slurpy pop and glared up at him. Okay, that was a no if he'd ever seen one. He closed his eyes again, and this time his twisted brain ran a slideshow starring him spurting all over Joey's sweet face. And that was just wrong. But he couldn't help wanting to mark her that way, like some dirty animal. Show the world she was his by virtue of his spunk dripping off her chin.

God, he was sick. And when did he start thinking of her as "his" anyway?

The silky touch of her fingers around the base of his cock migrated lower to cup his balls. Her other hand stroked him hard, in a long, hot slide up, and down, and up again, over the head with a slick twist. And that was all she wrote, son. He was coming like...whoa. Like liquid fire, like lava that obliterates entire villages. Like shooting his spine out the end of his dick, and it went on and on, and all he could see behind his eyes was Joey's face, painted in his come.

It took half his concentration to keep his hips from bucking like a bee-stung mule and the other half to keep from shouting out loud. As it was, the door banged and shook with his shudders, making all sorts of racket. The little part of his brain not fogged over with pleasure cringed.

And then he was sliding down the other side, his breathing deep but not so urgent and his vision clearing. Joey was still on her knees, nuzzling him gently. He lifted his hands and ran his fingers through her hair, snagging on the wild curls. "I...that was—"

The flight attendant returned, and this time she didn't knock. She pounded. "If the two of you don't come out of there right now, I'll have to inform the captain. This is your last warning."

The captain? Wasn't he busy landing the plane?

"Joey?" he said, wanting her to tilt her face up where he could see it. But she turned as she stood and ran the faucet into the sink.

SIN STREET

"Don't forget, you have a photo shoot this afternoon, as soon as we get into Breverton. It's for the local papers—"

"Joey, come on. Talk to me."

"It's a hometown-boy-makes-good kind of thing," She faced him, but she wasn't meeting his eyes, damn it. What had he done wrong? She fiddled with the hem of her shirt, and he saw a spot on the shoulder where the pink fabric was darkened by moisture. Water, he hoped. At least the civilized, non-territorial part of him did. "And then *Esquire* is sending somebody for a spread to go with the interview you gave last week."

"Stop it. Goddammit, Joey—"

A male voice broke in from behind the door. "Sir and madam, this is your captain. I must insist that you vacate the lavatory immediately. If you fail to obey this order, you'll be facing criminal charges when we land in Denver."

So much for landing the plane. Oh, well. There was always the co-pilot.

Joey reached behind him, unlocked the door and slid it open. He barely had time to yank up his jeans and tuck himself away. When he turned, she was gone, and he was facing an irritated-looking man in an airline uniform, an angry flight attendant, and a first class cabin full of interested onlookers.

The trek back to his seat was a mile long. At least.

CHAPTER 7

"Just a little to the right, Dare. Now smile—perfect."

The photographer's voice droned in Joey's ears, one endless direction after another. "Look into the distance...pivot your shoulders...smile for me—no, that's too much...now give me angry...now give me sexy...now give me happy, like you haven't got a care in the world..."

Three hours they'd been standing around in the hot Kansas sun, first for the people from the local papers, now for the team from *Esquire*. Sweat soaked Joey's shirt and ran down her face, washing away what little makeup she had left after the incident in the bathroom on the first plane, the hour-long layover in Denver, the second flight into Wichita and then the drive to the family farm just outside Breverton.

The incident in the bathroom? Why so coy, Josephine? Call it what it was—a blowjob.

"Yes, all right, the blowjob," Joey muttered under her breath. "Big, hairy deal. Not like it was the first one I've ever given."

First one you ever gave to somebody who signs your paychecks. Unless you've been holding out on me...

"Dare doesn't sign my paychecks. Beidermeyer does."

Again with the coy. You know what I mean, jellybean. You went down on your boss, and that ain't kosher.

"Bite me, Gina. I did what I had to do." Before her sister could call bullshit on that big-ass lie, she grabbed a clean hand-towel from the stack sitting on the hood of the rental car and stalked over to Dare.

"You need more water?"

"No, I'm good." He took the towel from her without quite meeting her eyes and blotted his hairline, taking obvious care not to smudge the layer of orange foundation the makeup crew had slathered on him. Like the pro he was, he hadn't complained once about the sun or the way the photographer had made him change clothes four times and finally decided on a wool sweater over a flannel shirt, for God's sake. Were they trying to give the man heatstroke?

"A few more shots, Dare," the photographer called. Her cue to get her ass out of the frame, no doubt. She stepped away, tripping and nearly falling over a cable as she moved backward toward the car.

Dare glanced in her direction and frowned. "Careful."

"Sorry."

He shrugged and leaned against the fence post, raising his face into the light and closing his eyes. The photographer said, "Turn your head to the left and lift your chin more."

The sun made him glow. Even with the awful fake-tan makeup, he looked like the younger brother of a god.

Gina's snort was loud and instantaneous. *Criminy, Josephine, fangirl much?*

Joey gritted her teeth. Leave it to her big sis to zero in on the very thing that'd been bothering her. The last thing she wanted to be was just another star-struck groupie, believing herself in love because an attractive celebrity had shown an interest in her. She wasn't that shallow, was she?

Dare had followed the photographer's instructions, tilting his jaw, making the tendons in his neck cord against the collar of the shirt. Making her want to run her tongue up and down that length of golden skin—just to see if she could get him to make those noises—the ones he'd made just before he came, back in the bathroom. Sort of growly and helpless at the same time. She closed her eyes and let herself picture the way his cock had leaked clear fluid in beads and little dribbles, like it was crying for her. And God, when he did come—the way his teeth had sunk into that lower lip. She thought he'd draw his own blood, he bit so hard. *So fucking beautiful.*

Oh, no, you're not shallow. Not you.

"Gina—"

I know, I know. Shut up and go away, right?

Joey shifted her weight from one foot to the other, acutely aware of how the inseam of her jeans pressed and rubbed in all the right places, just like it had done back in that bathroom. Her skin felt hot and tight, from the inside out, and she wished...she wished...

You wish what? That he'd returned the favor? Because you're not in too deep already or anything.

Her eyes still closed, Joey said through gritted teeth, "I thought you were going away. And what have you got against my having a good time anyway? Jealous? Don't they have sex in heaven?"

That's for me to know and you to find out. And I've got nothing against your good time—so long as you don't get hurt.

She had no answer for that. Not when the past eight hours had been so damn hard. Any thought she'd had of dissipating the tension between her and Dare was gone—now it was worse than before. Yeah, he'd sure quit staring at her mouth like he wanted to devour it, but now he wasn't looking at her at all. He'd backed way off, polite and distant when he spoke to her, which wasn't very often.

All of which made the drive from Wichita to Breverton among the longest two hours of her life to date. Almost bad enough to make her wish he was the J-Lo or Diddy type, complete with driver and traveling entourage. At least surrounded by sycophants, there was bound to be conversation.

She heard the opening bars of "Freebird" and reached for Dare's cell, which sat on the hood, next to the stack of towels. She opened it and glanced at the screen. *Caller Unknown.*

"Joey Fiorello for Dare Daniels, how may I help you?"

Nothing. Silence...except not quite, because just before the line went dead, she heard a sigh. Soft. Almost definitely female.

Probably a wrong number, right?

Thirty seconds later, her own cell buzzed. This time, she recognized the voice of Beidermeyer's assistant—what was her name? Something that started with "A" maybe? Then Beidermeyer was on the line.

"Hey, Joey, how's it hanging?"

"Uh..."

"Right, just a joke. With the name. Joey—like, it's a guy's name, but you're...never mind."

Christ, was he high? She hadn't known him long, but it seemed distinctly out of character for him to babble like that. "Mr. Beidermeyer? Is everything okay?"

"What? Sure, sure. Everything's great." He cleared his throat. "Everything okay on your end? No problem with the flights or the car, right?"

"No, no problems. We're in the middle of the *Esquire* shoot—"

"Fantastic. So, listen—nothing weird, right? No strange calls or packages or people?"

Should she mention the hang-up from a minute ago? She wasn't sure it could be classified as "weird," exactly. A wrong number, almost definitely. "No, nothing unusual. Why? Has there been something else on that end?"

"Well, here's the thing, Joey. A box was found lying on the ground outside the gate at Dare's house. Don't know how long it was there—housekeeper said it could've been there all night, since Dare left before dawn and wouldn't have seen it on his way out."

"What was in the box?"

There was a pause. Long enough to raise the hair on the back of Joey's neck. Then Beidermeyer said, "Nothing all that bad. Just a length of rope."

"Rope?"

"Yeah. Probably some nutty fan with a bondage kink, right?" He laughed, and maybe it was the distance between L. A. and Breverton, but it sounded forced. "So you'll let me know if you run into any problems, yes?"

"Of course."

"Great, great. Tell Dare that Jimmy Candari is going to call to discuss a couple scripts that've come in." He cleared his throat again. It was starting to sound like a nervous tic. "I'm outtie, babe. Take it easy."

Outtie? Babe? Who talked like that in real life? And who was having pieces of rope delivered to Dare's house? *Creepy.* She shivered, despite the heat.

Then Dare was beside her, his voice making her jump. "We're done here." He pulled off the sweater and began unbuttoning the shirt. A member of the wardrobe crew trotted over and took them from him, smiling her thanks as she stared at his naked torso. He returned her grin, rubbed at the back of his neck with a towel, and reached for a bottle of water at the bottom of the cooler that sat on the ground by the car's bumper.

Joey cleared the leftover towels off the hood of the car. "Where to now?"

She watched as his eyes scanned the farm. She mimicked him, looking out at the falling-down barn with its rusted rooster weathervane, and the little clapboard single-story that could've stood in for Dorothy Gale's abode at an Oz convention. Other than themselves and the folks from *Esquire,* the place was deserted. No people, no livestock, and the fields lay fallow. *Sad.*

"Back to the rental house for a shower," Dare said, "and then out for a bite to eat. Sound good?" He looked her square in the face for the first time since they'd deplaned in Denver.

"Sounds wonderful." God, did she really have to be so breathless about it?

Good question. What's up with that? You thinking about going for the gold in the Dry Hump Olympics?

"Shut up, Gina." Joey said it right out loud, without even trying to hide it. Maybe if her pain-in-the-ass big sister knew Dare was aware of her running commentary, she'd settle down some.

He pulled a white T-shirt over his head and squinted at her. "Your sister again? What's she saying?"

Joey felt herself blush. Okay, maybe she should've thought that one through a little better. "Nothing."

He laughed. "You're like the opposite of Pinocchio. When you lie, your nose scrunches up."

Her hand flew to her face. "Crap."

"Don't sweat it. It's cute." He picked his cell up from the hood of the car and put it in his pocket. Then he glanced around, as if to check for observers. He stepped closer, and his voice dropped to a gravelly whisper. "But I guess you know that, right?"

Something sparked between them—the same something that'd been there ever since he walked into his living room and interrupted her nap. He smelled of overheated skin and heavy makeup and sweaty man. And somehow, it was good. Better than good. She wanted to lick him. Again.

"Looks like you could use a shower, too." He reached up and touched a fingertip to a wet curl where it stuck to her cheek. She swallowed audibly. Then he turned away and got into the car. An instant later, he gunned the engine, nearly drowning out Gina's final comment.

That's right, baby girl. Don't you sweat a thing. Go on back to the house you're sharing. Just the two of you. Alone. For a week. No potential for sweatiness there.

She wanted to tell her sister to go hell. But given how her brain was now flashing the filthiest pictures of herself and Dare getting up to no good under the spray of a cool, soothing shower...well. She thought maybe she'd beat Gina to the devil's door.

*   *   *

The patrons at the Bar Angus were a rowdy bunch—as loud and rambunctious as any Saturday night crowd in a Bensonhurst bar and grill. Except this was Wednesday.

Joey sat all alone in a corner booth. Even Gina had apparently abandoned her, and she tried to feel relieved at the loss of her sister's snarky comments as she watched Dare make the rounds—saying hello to old friends, getting his back slapped and his hand shaken, and a few pictures snapped here and there. Everybody and his cousin wanted to buy the hometown hero a drink. Wonderful. By the time he got back to the booth, he'd be—

"Hey there, pretty lady. All alone?"

A cowboy. An honest-to-God, ride 'em and rope 'em and brand 'em cowboy. Hat and bandana and...she had to fight the urge to look down to see if his boots came complete with spurs.

"Cat got your tongue?" He flashed chewing tobacco-stained teeth and eased his long body into the booth. He had to be four inches over six feet tall, and though his middle-aged frame sported a slight paunch, he looked as tough and hardy as anyone in the place.

"Uh—no. I mean, I'm not alone. I'm here with—" She gestured toward Dare, who was making his way back to her, smiling and weaving through the closely-packed tables.

"With him? Mr. Hollywood?"

She nodded as Dare came to stand beside her. She looked up at him and saw his smile fade as he took note of her companion.

"Gorman," he said, but didn't offer his hand. "Good to see you."

The tall man nodded. "Wish I could say the same, Daniels."

Well, that was just rude. She sat up a little straighter on the booth bench and glared. Gorman didn't appear fazed by her displeasure.

"I was just talkin' to your girl here. Was about to ask her how she ended up with a hundred pounds o' shit in a fifty-pound sack like you." His grin widened. "You seen your uncle yet?"

Dare's face had turned to stone, save for a tiny muscle jumping in his jaw. "I guess that's my business and none of yours."

The tall man pulled himself up out of the booth with a lot more speed than he'd sat himself down. "I guess maybe you're right, Daniels. But when you do see him, be sure to give him my best, won't you? That is, if he don't shoot you on sight."

Gorman tipped his hat at her and ambled off in the direction of the men's room. Joey could feel Dare breathing next to her. Could hear it like a windstorm. She reached up and touched his hand, where it rested on the back of the bench. "You okay?"

He shook his head as if to clear it. "Yeah. Sorry about that. Some folks around here don't like me much." He swung into the booth and faced her. "You had enough to eat?"

She looked at the remains of her meal. A half-eaten medium-rare steak sat before her, along with most of an order of fries. Huge, all of it. She hadn't consumed so much at one sitting in months. "Yeah, I'm done. Are you ready to go back?"

The house Beidermeyer had rented for them was a good five miles out of town, not far from the deserted family farm. Nice digs, if a little fussy for Joey's taste. The number of breakable knick-knacks on the various end-tables and side-tables and shelves made her nervous. Not to mention the whole we're-living-in-a-stranger's-home thing. But the nearest motel was fifteen miles out on Route 166 and barely rated a single star. Nowhere near good enough for an up-and-comer like Dare Daniels.

"Nah," he said. "I need more to drink. How 'bout you?"

She shook her head. "No thanks."

"Aw, come on. We've got nowhere to be in the morning." He blinked at her, then widened his eyes. His lips pulled together in a pout so obvious she had to laugh.

"Does that really work on anyone who isn't already drunk?"

He grinned. "You'd be amazed." A waitress stopped at their booth to clear the debris, and he asked for a bottle of Patron, two shot glasses, and all the limes and salt she could spare.

Uh-oh. "I don't drink tequila."

"What do you drink?"

She shrugged. "A little wine on occasion."

"Well then. Tonight's gonna be somethin' new and different, ain't it?" he said, smacking the words flat with a Kansas drawl.

She rolled her eyes, then the waitress returned with the bottle and shot glasses and good God...truly, all the salt and lime wedges in the place. Maybe in the county.

"Hold out your arm."

"Huh?" She went from staring at the amber liquid in the bottle to staring into his green eyes. "Why?"

"You've never done body shots? Seriously?"

"Dare—"

"Come on. Indulge me."

It was on the very tip of her tongue to tell him how she'd prefer to indulge him. Much like the way she'd already indulged him, back on the plane. Instead, she stuck out her arm and suffered him to roll up the sleeve of her shirt to the elbow. Every casual brush of his fingers on her flesh made her breath catch in her chest.

"You ready?"

"Just get on with it." He pressed his thumb against the pulse-point in her wrist and she jerked.

"Why so jumpy?" But the glint in his eye said he knew.

"Are we doing this or not?"

"Oh, we're for sure doin' it." More of that Kansas accent. On him it was sexy. Or maybe she was just losing her ever-loving mind.

He cradled her hand in one of his, and with his other he grabbed a wedge of lime and held it up to her lips. "Bite," he said, "and hold on."

She bit. Then he lifted her wrist to his mouth and licked, his tongue flashing out fast and swiping at her. It felt like he'd struck a match against her skin and held it there, except the burn was sweet. So damn sweet.

He picked up one of the seven shakers the waitress had left and sprinkled salt over the wet stripe on her wrist. Then his mouth was on her again. She closed her eyes and let herself feel how he took the salt, sucking at her skin and scrubbing with his tongue. She looked again in time to see him knock back the shot, and then his breath was on her face as he took the lime from between her teeth.

Their lips touched briefly, and it almost killed her. Honest and truly, she nearly died from want, sitting right there in the booth. She bit down hard on the inside of her cheek. The taste of copper flooded her mouth, but the pain didn't do a thing to dull the sharp pulsing between her legs.

Some fool chose that moment to drop a glass. The shatter made her recall where they were. She glanced around the room. Nobody was looking…but they could be. The whole crowd had front row seats to this little show. Why did that make her rock forward on the bench and squeeze her thighs together? Public sex was Dare's kink, not hers.

"Again?" His voice was husky, and he looked at her with sleepy eyes.

She started to nod, then changed her mind. "I want to try."

He smiled and pushed back his sleeve. She chose a wedge of lime and slipped it between his parted lips, so full and shiny with tequila and lime juice. The air felt thick and hard to breathe as she lifted his wrist to her mouth. She let her tongue linger longer than he had, and enjoyed the little grunt he made around the lime. Then came the salt, and she sucked that up with just as much care. The muscles in his forearm went hard as she worked to get every last grain.

Then the sharp bite of the tequila, and she refused to choke on it, no matter how bad it burned going down. She leaned forward and took the lime from his lips, letting her mouth press into his another moment too long. The lime pulp burst on her tongue, and she wanted more. All of it. Everything he had.

"My turn," he whispered, and she stuck out her arm. But he got up and came around to sit on the bench next to her.

"What—"

"Shh. Tilt your head away." He popped the lime into her mouth and pulled at the neckline of her shirt, exposing her collarbone. When he leaned in to lick, she closed her eyes. God...God, God—this must be how spontaneous human combustion happened.

Salt, the second lick, watching him down the shot...and then the taking of the wedge of fruit that was more of a kiss every time. They were over the line. The line, in fact, was light-years behind them.

"Your turn?" he asked, his eyebrows high over lazy, dilated eyes.

She nodded. But the liquor to which she was so unaccustomed had begun to kick in, and she couldn't seem to get her hands to work right. He did the hard part—settling the lime between his lips and pulling aside his collar. All she had to do was put her mouth on him, and she was getting pretty good at that. He made a soft sound as she swirled her tongue on his neck, and when she bit down on the tendon, she felt his whole body stiffen.

The tequila didn't burn half so badly this time, and she didn't so much take the lime as share it with him. They held it between two sets of teeth, licking at it and each other until finally...finally...he reached up and pulled it away and kissed her. He used both hands to cradle the back of her head, and his mouth moved against hers, wet and hot and firm. She felt the last of her resistance boil away into just so much useless vapor.

An ear-splitting whoop from the other side of the room made them break apart. She looked over his shoulder, scanning the bar for witnesses, but no one seemed to be paying them any attention.

He licked his lips, catching a stray grain of salt in the corner of his mouth. "This morning," he said, slurring the words together. Much drunker than her, apparently. "You remember this morning? On the plane? In the bathroom?"

"Yeah," she said, grinning. Laughing at him. At both of them, making out in a corner booth. In a bar. In Kansas.

"You made me come so hard I saw Jesus."

She snorted. "You shouldn't say that. It's blasphemous."

"Yeah," he said and leaned in close to touch her face. "You're a nice girl, Joey."

"Not really."

"No?"

She thought about telling him all the reasons she wasn't nice, starting with wanting to lay him out flat on the table in front of them and make him see Jesus again. Instead, she said, "Let's get out of here."

He smiled at her. "So much for clearing the air and getting it out of my system, huh?"

"I think the trouble might be with my system this time."

He nodded, his eyes wide and serious. "Think we can fix it?"

"Or die trying."

"Race you to the car."

CHAPTER 8

"You're too drunk to drive. Give me the keys."

Amazing how she could go from soft, pliable sex-kitten to bossy babe in under a minute flat. He could see by the set of her jaw she wasn't kidding about the keys either. He tossed them to her without comment. She was right. He was way too fucked up to drive. That wouldn't have stopped him if he'd been alone, which only made him stupid, irresponsible and selfish. What else was new?

They pulled out of the Bar Angus's parking lot and onto Willow Creek Road without further conversation. She seemed to know the way back to the house. She seemed to know a lot of things—like how best to make him hard enough to pound nails.

He let himself slump in the rental's soft leather seat. "Let's not go back to the house right away."

"Why not?" She shot him a sideways glance. "I thought you wanted...um...I mean, if you changed your mind, that's—"

"Didn't change my mind. Still want it. Just don't want it in that house."

The corner of her mouth quirked. "Scared we might smash a figurine or two?"

"A definite possibility." He slurred the words, his lips and tongue feeling thick and clumsy. *Maybe this was a bad idea after all.* Maybe he was too wasted to perform. Wouldn't that be a kick in the head? Not that he didn't deserve it.

"Okay, where are we going?"

He looked up ahead and saw the turn-off for Mackenzie Park. "Right up here, past that sign. Turn in and keep to the right. You'll see a road leading off into the woods."

She followed his directions. "What is this place?"

"Public land. Kind of a lovers' lane."

The road narrowed, the blacktop giving way to gravel, which in turn gave way to dust. Up ahead, headlights peeked through the trees. Five sets, at least. He could hear a radio with the twang of a steel guitar rising over the purr of the idling engines. And there…that distinctive orange glow. The kids were out in full force tonight.

She made a surprised sound as they turned the last corner and were confronted by a circle of cars and pick-ups situated around bonfire. "It's not even the weekend."

He smiled and shook his head. "Nothing to do in Breverton. No movies, not even a bowling alley. They have to make their own fun."

"They? Not you?" She sounded amused. "You never had any fun as a kid?"

He shrugged. "I had my share." More than his share. Except it hadn't been all that much fun. If only he'd spent more time in Mackenzie Park, and less time in his uncle's hayloft…

She pulled the car around to a spot in the back, near the trees and out of the pool of light cast by the fire, and parked it a good fifty feet from the rest of the vehicles. Then she turned in her seat and looked at him. His mouth watered when he remembered how she'd tasted with lime on her tongue. She said, "Well, you've got me here. Now what do you intend to do with me?"

"That depends. How drunk are you?"

She blinked at him. "I only had the two shots, Dare. I'm not that much of a lightweight."

He leaned over the console to get a better look at her face. "You sure?"

"You want me to get out and walk a straight line? Maybe recite the alphabet backwards?"

"I like the getting out part."

She tilted her head, looking confused. "You want me out of the car?"

"You were thinking we'd be able to get anything done in here?" He gestured, indicating the lack of space in the front seat, and the nearly nonexistent back seat. Why had he insisted on a sports model again?

She looked at her watch. "All right, but you've got twenty minutes.

After that, I turn into a pumpkin."

"Twenty minutes? Oh ye of little faith." He opened the passenger side door, stepped out and rounded the front of the car. She met him there. Something in her expression had gone sly and mischievous, putting in him mind of a half-grown cat. It was clear she wasn't taking any of this seriously.

"What are you frowning about?" she asked him, keeping her voice low. Barely audible, in fact. As if anybody was paying the smallest bit of attention to them. He glanced around, taking in the fogged windows and the few blankets spread in truck beds and on the ground nearer the fire. The folks fogging said windows and those using said blankets were plainly too occupied to notice newcomers to the party.

He turned back to look at her. "You insulted my stamina. This will not go unpunished."

"Ooh, should I be scared?" She moved closer to him. "Besides, what have you got against a quickie?"

"Nothing. But the first time I take you should be—"

"Whoa." She held up her hand and stepped back again. "The first time you take me? Did we wander into a bodice-ripper when I wasn't paying attention?" She stuck out a finger and poked him in the chest. "And besides, who says I'm not going to take you?"

Yeah. Not taking it seriously at all.

He grabbed her hand and yanked her forward, making her stumble and fall against his chest. She had to crane her neck to look up at him. Still smiling, she was looking naughty and knowing, so plainly sure he wouldn't go through with it. Not out here, with all these people around.

"You think I won't do it? Won't throw you up on the hood of this car and fuck you blind?" He slid a hand around the back of her neck and squeezed. Not too hard. Just enough to make his point. "Don't you read the tabloids, Joey? I'm one kinky dude."

Her grin evaporated, and he felt her shiver against him. He had a moment to wonder if he'd gone too far. Then her hands came up and clutched at his shoulders, and she used them for leverage to force herself up on her toes. Her mouth on his throat just below his ear made him go painfully hard. How did she know where to find those places where his nerve endings were extra-close to the surface of his skin? Then the areas of higher function in his brain began to shut down, like lights switching off in a skyscraper from top to bottom. Something to do with re-routed blood flow maybe?

"You have something?" she whispered.

"Huh?" He leaned back and looked at her. "Oh. Right. Yeah, it's—" He reached for his wallet, pulled it out and set it on the fender. The breeze had changed direction, blowing smoke over them, and she rubbed at her eyes. Getting her out of the wind was as good an excuse as any to ease her down onto the hood of the car.

She fought him at first. "Slow down, can't we just..." She turned her head to one side and then the other. Looking for spectators, no doubt.

"Shh. Nobody's watching." He ran one hand through her hair and down the side of her face in a petting motion. It seemed to soothe her. "I'm going to take care of you. This time it's my turn."

He didn't ask if that was okay with her, but she helped him pull her shirt over her head and lifted her hips when he went for the buttons on her jeans. That seemed to imply she was with him. Didn't it? Or didn't it?

"Hey," he said, "open your eyes."

She complied, and he could barely see her face where it lay in a deep shadow. "What?"

"You good with this? We can stop. I don't mean to—"

She sighed, and it was half a moan. "Dare, I swear to God, if you don't hurry up and fuck me..."

All right then. He finished undressing her and she scooted up higher on the hood so she could brace her feet on the bumper. His cock pounded and pulsed behind the fly of his jeans, but he made no move to release it.

Soon. But not yet.

"What's the trouble?" She sounded impatient, and he realized he'd been staring at her. Just taking it all in—her soft, symmetrical curves and the luster of her white skin against the car's dark paint.

"No trouble. Hush up now." He braced himself with one knee on the bumper between her feet and one hand on the hood next to her head and went for her breasts, since they looked as likely a place to start as any. And by "likely" he meant "perfect" in a God-I-finally-get-to-taste-them kind of way.

He divided his attention between one nipple and the other 'til they drew tight enough to withstand the careful use of teeth. She moaned, starting low and building in volume and pitch 'til he reached up and put two fingers against her lips to quiet her. Because kinky was great, but hell—these were just the appetizers. If she was a screamer, they might be in for some trouble later on, when he served the main course.

SIN STREET

But she seemed to like the fingers well enough, if the way she sucked them into her mouth was any indication. Which is why it surprised him when, in the middle of a switch from one nipple to the other, she grabbed his wrist and pulled his hand away from her face.

"I…" she said and sucked in a breath. "You have to…I want—"

He smiled at her through the shadows, knowing he was being a bastard and not caring. "You want me to fish or cut bait? Is that what you're sayin'?" He used his spit-slick fingers to trace a line between her breasts. "You feelin' okay, Miss Fiorello?" he said, laying on the drawl as thick as he knew how. "Dark as it is, I can see you're lookin' mighty flushed."

She whacked him on the shoulder with her open hand. But then she laughed, and he wanted to just…hug her or something. Squeeze her tight 'til she couldn't draw breath and then squeeze her some more. Squeeze her until he could fold her inside of him—make her a part of him. And then she wouldn't ever leave.

Christ Jesus, where the hell did that come from?

"Shame on you, sir," she said, low and whispery. "Didn't your mother ever tell you it's rude to make a lady wait?"

A car door creaked. They froze, eyes locked on each other's faces. Voices rose and fell as a couple passed them on their way further into the woods. All at once, he realized how open and exposed she was—naked and spread out on the hood of a car. All for him, to do with as he pleased. A little surge of dizziness knocked him sideways, and he shook his head to clear the daze.

"I can't say for certain my Momma ever imagined her baby boy in just this situation," he said and leaned over her 'til he could feel her breath, quick and hot, on his face. "But this is my show now. And I want to play."

"There's a time for play"—her hand traveled down his torso until it settled on the bulge at the front of his jeans—"and there's a time for serious business." Her fingernails scratched at the worn, thin denim stretched tight over his aching hard-on. He bit his lip, fighting to keep some shred of control.

"Serious business? You mean like this?" He ran his hand from her ankle to her thigh, pausing to pinch her calf and tickle behind her knee. She grunted in plain frustration and tried to pull him down on top of her. But he had leverage and she had none, and he wasn't about to give up the position of power. He lifted her knees and planted her feet on the hood so her legs spread wide. He pressed the heel of his hand against her shadowed cleft, feeling coarse curls against his palm. She yelped and arched off the surface of the car. He pushed her down, digging his fingers into the soft flesh at her hips.

"Can you keep still?" he asked her, his voice gruffer than he meant.

She made a sigh that sounded like "yes" and held the back of her wrist against her mouth.

He knelt on the grass and used his thumbs to open her. The soft light from the fire made her glisten, so wet for him. She tensed and shuddered hard when he put his mouth on her, and he heard her muffled moan when he pushed his tongue inside, pulsing it in and out like he wanted to do with his cock. Like he would do with his cock, just as soon as he made his point. Which, if he recalled correctly, had something to do with serious business.

Her free hand flailed against his neck and landed on his shoulder. She dug her nails in and held on. His cue to do his worst? Or his best?

He licked upwards, catching her clit and holding it between his teeth. Her hips rose and dropped again, and her thighs closed around his head as if to defend herself. He forced them open and spread her wider with his thumbs. No mercy. He was gonna make her see Jesus, or at least one of the Apostles. It was only fair.

With that goal in mind, he went to work on her, using every trick he'd ever learned and a few he made up on the spot. Swirling and sucking and nibbling and kissing, holding her down and making her take it until her shudders stilled for one long, tense moment, the muscles beneath his fingers gone taut. With a choked cry she broke under him, falling away and then surging against his face, her head and elbows thudding on the hood. She was all his now—he owned her, if only for the moment, and he'd take all she had to give. The thought of it made him groan against her wet flesh. It was all he could do not to hump the damn bumper.

After what seemed like a full minute, she stilled again. He pulled away and wiped his face on his sleeve. Then he looked at her, lying limp and...Jesus, did she faint? Was she even breathing?

He slapped her cheek. Maybe a little harder than necessary.

"Ow!"

He yanked up her up, and she sat there looking dazed, one hand against her face. "Way to wreck a perfectly good swoon. Jackass."

"God, Joey, don't do that to me."

"Oh, I see. You make me come 'til I pass out, and I'm the bad guy." She tipped forward, and he stretched up. They met in the middle with a

SIN STREET

hard kiss that told him they weren't done here. Not by a long shot.

"I'm gonna fuck you now, Josephine."

"Don't call me—"

He wrapped an arm under her and flipped her so she landed with her hands on the hood and her feet on the ground, bent over the car. As if on cue, she arched her back, forcing her ass into the air like some chick in an eighties' hair-band rock video. It shouldn't have been as hot as it was.

"You keep that up, this is gonna be over real quick." He reached for the condom in his wallet with one hand, while undoing his fly with the other. In another second, his jeans and underwear were pooled around his ankles.

"Hurry up."

"Bossy."

"Slowpoke."

And then he was pushing inside her, rocking forward slow and even. Quarter-inch by quarter-inch, and he thought he might just up and expire from it—the hot-wet-tight of it. Of her.

"You all right?" He had to ask...he couldn't see her face, and she wasn't making any noise.

"Yes. Just...just—"

"What?" He reached up and ran a hand down her back, fighting the primal urge to thrust.

"Move," she said. "For God's sake, move."

He grabbed her hips and lunged. Slammed himself home in one hard, fast pump that drove her forward. Followed it up with six or ten or fifteen more. Pounding into her as she braced herself with both hands, her elbows locked. And realized he wasn't gonna last, not at this pace.

"Need to slow down," he said, trying not to pant like a dog. He stretched over her and pressed his mouth to the back of her neck. She nodded, but pushed back against him anyway, like she couldn't help it. He ached with pleasure. His whole body—like she'd infected him with it.

He took a breath and tried to relax. Uncurled his toes, loosened his fingers on her hips. Then he pushed into her again, slower this time. She slid forward, off her feet, and he found himself lying on her, still rocking easy and smooth. Fucking her into the warm metal of the hood.

"Someone's watching," she whispered.

He looked up, craning his neck to see. *Yeah, over there by that sedan. Two people.* Another couple, taking a break from their own good time?

"Let's give 'em somethin' to look at." He threaded his fingers through her hair and tugged 'til she arched her neck and he could reach her mouth. She bit into his lower lip and held on. The thrill made his hips stutter against her. "Shit. I'm gonna..." He grunted, struggling to hold still. "Touch yourself. Make yourself come for me."

CHAPTER 9

Joey's breath caught in her throat. He wanted her to touch herself? Now? Here?

That couple over there would see and know what she was doing. Hell, Dare would know, and that was freaky enough. She'd never done...that...in another person's presence before.

"I can't," she whispered. "It's okay. Just go ahead and finish."

"No. Need to come with you. Want to." His voice sounded hoarse and stressed, like he was barely hanging on. "Don't you want to come? Doesn't this feel good?"

He started again with those same unhurried thrusts, as if they had all the time in the world. So much tougher to think when he did that—when she could feel every slick, thick inch of him pushing and pulling. Relentless, and so slow she could almost count the nerve endings triggered by every slide and grind. Always moving in one direction or the other, never giving her time to breathe, just...oh, God. Yes, it felt good, and yes, she wanted to come again.

Dare moved off her and lifted her hips, giving her just enough room to work her hand down her belly and against her clit. She moaned at first contact. The pads of her fingers were warm from the heated surface of the hood. Her touch was familiar, but not so well-known it didn't send a jolt bursting through her even as Dare pulled out completely and then crashed home again. She choked on another moan and pressed harder on her clit, rubbing it in time with his thrusts. He picked up the pace, lifting her hips higher, changing the angle of entry.

SIN STREET

A slow and deliberate screw became a hard, urgent fuck, and she had to bite her lip to keep from making noises like an animal in heat.

She turned her head and pressed her cheek flat against the hood. Those people were still watching. Looking at her getting fucked. Playing with herself. She could've shut her eyes, but she didn't want to. She was going to come, and Dare was going to join her, and let them all watch.

The rhythm built in surges of heat and pressure. She took her clit between her thumb and forefinger and cradled it there for long seconds. Then she pinched, tight. Almost painful. Too much and just enough, it forced a climax that came all at once, making her seize and clench and shudder. He pounded into her with a power that rocked her body and the car and maybe the whole damn universe. And that was just fine. Let the universe fall apart, so long as he never stopped.

He slammed into her a final time and held himself deep, shaking as he came. He cursed in a low, rough voice. When he whispered her name, it sounded like a plea.

He kept his tight grasp on her hips for maybe half a minute. She could feel his damp breath on her back. Then he let her body settle gently on the hood and pulled away to deal with the clean-up. Or so she assumed, since at some point she'd closed her eyes. When she opened them, the couple who'd been watching was still there. She pushed herself off the car and tried to turn, but found herself clumsy and stiff and a little limp at the same time, if that was possible.

"Dare?"

"What, sugar? You all right?" That drawl again, flat as the Kansas landscape. Just like music to her ears.

"I'm fine. Just a little worn out, I guess." She looked again and the couple was walking toward them, getting closer by the second. And she was still naked, and Dare hadn't zipped up yet, and…shit. "Help me find my clothes quick."

But he'd seen them already. They stopped maybe twenty feet away and when the flashes came, one on top of another, Dare made an angry sound like a bear and went after them. He tucked himself away as he ran, faster than she'd thought anyone could so soon after…well. The couple didn't seem to wise up to his intentions right away, and he caught them as they turned to flee, grabbing both their arms at the elbow. From her vantage point, he looked as if he towered over them.

She dragged on her jeans and shirt and followed, her feet bare in the damp grass. When she reached Dare's side, he hadn't let go of either kid, but he wasn't yelling. This was a good start. She'd figured on a few raised voices at the very least.

The boy held the camera—and a boy he was, make no mistake. Younger than either she or Dare. The girl was younger still and looking scared. Dare was talking to them in a quiet voice.

"Tell me who put you up to this. I promise you won't get in any trouble."

The boy stared at the grass and stammered a few times. The girl was entirely silent.

"Come on now. I know you didn't think this up all on your own. Not good kids like you." Dare's voice rose just a little, as if making it a question. As if maybe these weren't good kids, after all, if they wouldn't tell him what he wanted to know.

"Oh, Mr. Daniels, please don't be mad," the girl said. "We didn't mean anything by it. The lady said…" Her voice trailed off and she bit her lip. In the half-light, she didn't look more than twelve years old, but Joey knew better. Not grown woman, but no little girl either.

"What lady would that be?" Still with the steady, even questions. As if he didn't have them by the arms and couldn't shake the answers loose if he'd wanted.

The boy answered. "She's at the Guardian Inn on out Route 166. She never said her name."

Dare released them, and they stepped back. Joey got the impression they were poised to run. The boy still clutched the camera. She reached for it, plucking it out of his hands before he could react.

"Hey! That's—"

"Hang on." It took her thirty seconds to figure out how to switch it on, find the recently snapped photos, and delete them. Surprisingly, none of the shots had captured the actual event—Dare taking her on the hood of the car. They were all of the aftermath. She was almost disappointed to miss how they'd looked mid-coitus al fresco.

She switched the camera off again and handed it back. "You should be ashamed of yourselves."

The girl hung her head, but the boy looked defiant. "We weren't the ones fuckin' in the middle of a campground."

Joey winced. He had her there. She opened her mouth to defend herself and Dare cut her off.

"Now, is that any way to talk? What would your momma say?" And then the boy was hanging his head as well. "How did you find us? And what did that lady give you in exchange for the pictures?"

The boy said nothing, but the girl was near tears and couldn't seem to answer quick enough. "She told us to wait around town until we saw you, and then keep a...a low profile, she called it. And then to follow you wherever you went until we caught something that would go with the story she's writing about you."

"Story?" For the first time, Dare's voice grew sharp.

The boy chimed in then. "Yeah. Somethin' about when you were our age and why you had to leave Breverton."

Joey felt Dare go still and saw his face twist into something that looked like pain even in the flickering shadows. Then the moment passed, and he was smiling at the two kids as if he'd known them since they were in diapers.

"And what did you say she paid you?"

"A case of Pabst and a night's stay at the Guardian," the girl said, as if she were dying to admit her sins and save her soul.

"Pauline," the boy whined, "you're not supposed to tell."

"Doesn't matter now," said Pauline. "Beer's gone, motel room's used, and she deleted the pictures. Come on, Tommy. Take me home. My dad's gonna shit a brick."

But Dare wouldn't let them go without getting Tommy's and Pauline's full names and addresses—and ages, which turned out to be seventeen and fifteen, respectively—and giving them a promise to send autographed photos of himself as "Trevor Knight," Las Vegas detective of TV fame and fortune. They left smiling.

"You're amazing," Joey said on the way back to the car.

"Huh?" Dare seemed distracted. "No, I'm not. That's the last thing I am, believe me." He slung an arm around her shoulders, and together they bent and searched for her sneakers and socks. The quiet drive back to the rental house seemed anticlimactic. Literally.

Joey unlocked the front door of the house and they stepped into the hall. The only sound was the distant ticking of the grandfather clock in the dining room. She cleared her throat. Where was she going to sleep tonight? Probably better not to make assumptions. She followed him down the hall and up the stairs, and made as if to turn into the room— the one to the left, with the rose-and-thorn wallpaper and the shelves of creepy dolls with long, blonde curls and vacant eyes.

He grabbed her elbow, much as he'd done to that pair of kids. "Where're you goin'?" He sounded half-drunk with exhaustion.

She smiled up at him though the shadows. "I thought maybe you'd want some space."

SIN STREET

He shook his head. "Space I got. All I'll ever need." He leaned down and pressed a kiss on her forehead. "Come to bed, Josephine."

She listened in her head for some snide comment from Gina, but none came. So she did as she was told.

*   *   *

Thursday morning dawned hot and bright on Joey's face, where she lay with Dare curled around her in the king-sized bed in the middle of the master bedroom suite. She tried burying her head under a pillow to avoid coming fully awake, but it was too late. She was up, and up she would stay.

Nothing on the agenda today. Dare could lie around and be lazy, or go visit old haunts, or do whatever pleased him. Maybe work on whatever it was his shrink had sent him here for in the first place. But in the meantime—coffee. And a shower, which she would've taken last night if Dare hadn't insisted they go straight to bed. The second round of lovemaking hadn't rivaled the first for intensity, but there had been something sweet in it still. Something sleepy and close and comforting. The kind of love to take her mind off being photographed in the nude by high school kids in search of lurid pics for some hell-hound tabloid beastie, who probably considered herself a journalist.

The shower refreshed her, and, with that refreshment, came fury. Cold, hard and implacable. She left a pot of coffee brewing for Dare, and a note that said she'd be back in a few hours. Then she borrowed one of his two pairs of Ray-Bans—the non-prescription ones he wore when he used his contact lenses—and slipped them into her bag as protection against the glare of a Kansas summer morning.

The Guardian Inn was easy enough to find. She drove north on 166, passing farm after farm, 'til the building took form like a mirage in the distance of the flat landscape. She pulled into the parking lot at five minutes after eight, went straight into the office and rang the bell.

The elderly man who answered her summons seemed not at all wary. Joey told him she was looking for a woman staying alone. No name, no physical description beyond, "She comes from L. A." The man behind the counter gave her the room number and all but offered a personal escort and a key. Another reason why Dare was staying in a rented house and not this motel.

She rapped on the door of room eight, and it opened almost instantly. The woman standing on the other side was perhaps forty years old, with salt-and-pepper hair cut in a trendy style and wearing designer jeans of the highest fashion. She, unlike the man at the front desk, looked decidedly wary.

"Can I help you?"

Joey stuck out her hand. "Good morning. I understand you're buying information about Dare Daniels?"

The woman ignored Joey's hand, but her gaze sharpened. "You've got something to sell?" She stepped back from the door to let Joey into the room. "I'm Katherine Mollare. I work for a magazine in California." The way she said the state's name sounded as if she thought Joey should be impressed.

The room was stuffy and, despite the no smoking sign displayed on the back of the closed door, smelled of stale tobacco. Joey stepped inside, her arms crossed over her chest in a defensive posture. She stood a foot from the door, as if prepared to bolt at any second, and hoped the woman would buy the innocence and hesitation she was trying so hard to project.

"You've got something to sell?" Mollare repeated.

"Maybe." She made her voice tentative. Unsure. As if she'd never done anything like this before. Which, of course, she hadn't. "I wouldn't want to hurt anybody. I mean, I know it's hard being a famous person, with everybody stalking you all the time—"

Mollare snorted and turned away from her to reach for a pack of cigarettes that sat on the bedside table. "Don't sweat it, missy."

"Why not?"

"Celebrities think they've got it so fucking tough," she said, then paused to light the cigarette. "They make millions, live in mansions, have a staff to wipe their asses, and everybody loves them. In return they have to put up with a little bad press now and again. Cry me a river."

"Is that really how you see it?"

"Of course. That's how it is." Mollare sat on the corner of the bed and took a deep drag of smoke.

Joey took a deep, steadying breath. Time to cut the shit. "Well, let me tell you how I see it, Ms. Mollare. Working actors do make good money, but Mr. Daniels does a weekly TV show, and it doesn't pay as well as you'd assume. Plus the on-location expenses are huge. You think it's cheap to keep a decent apartment in Vegas? Or maybe you think the studio takes care of that. Think again."

Mollare started to argue. Joey held up a hand. "I'm not finished. In return for the money and the fame—assuming they want the fame, and that's debatable in some cases—they're owned by a corporation. If they work on location, like Mr. Daniels, they rarely see their homes or families. They can't go out without causing a riot. And when they're on set, their whole existence is 'hurry up and wait' for hours between takes in which they have to laugh, cry, fight, and die on cue, when they're not lying around naked with a total stranger in front of a crew of more strangers."

Mollare was squinting at her. "Who the hell are you?"

"I'm Dare Daniel's personal assistant, and I've come here to discuss terms."

"Oh, that's rich. He sent his assistant? Too much of a pussy to do the job himself?" The woman stubbed out the cigarette on the bare wood of the bedside table. "Well, let me tell you something, missy. You wouldn't believe the crap I've dug up on your boss. Really good shit. The kind that sells magazines."

"I have no doubt." Joey kept her voice steady. No way could she let this piranha call her bluff. "But I'd like to discuss—"

Mollare bulldozed right over her. "Do you know the story? About him and his uncle's wife? And the daughter? Un-fucking-believable. I'm amazed he had the balls to come back here at all."

His uncle's wife? And daughter? What could possibly... No, she wasn't going down that road. Everything about this woman screamed liar and cheat. She wouldn't dignify her existence on the planet by asking her to elaborate.

"I'm aware there are some people in Breverton who don't like Mr. Daniels's success," Joey said, remembering Gorman back at the Bar Angus. "Personally, I think they're jealous. I wouldn't give much credence to anything they had to say about him."

"Oh, sweetie, you don't know the half of it. The stuff I've got—man, talk about a dirty shame."

"Ms. Mollare, I'm here to ask you what it would take for you to kill whatever story you're working on."

The older woman laughed. Cackled, in fact. "Too late. I was up all night polishing the copy. Sent it to my editor at six this morning. Goddamned dial-up connection took forever."

Christ, this is bad. Joey could feel her heart twist in her chest as she remembered the look on Dare's face the night before when the kids told him who'd hired them.

"I believe Mr. Daniels is willing to pay to kill the story," she said, crossing her fingers behind her back and praying Dare wouldn't kill her instead for offering to bribe a tabloid reporter.

She needn't have bothered to fear for her life. Mollare sneered at her. "I believe Mr. Daniels can kiss my ass." She stood and made a waving motion in the direction of the door. "Get lost. I'm expecting company."

Joey felt a muscle in her temple pick up the beat of her anger. Where did this woman find her arrogance? Ordering her from the room as if she were a child?

A child...

"Let me ask you something, Ms. Mollare. Did you happen to check the IDs of those kids you hired?" She watched with satisfaction as the older woman's bloodshot eyes widened.

"I...what kids? I don't know what you're talking about."

"The kids you hired to snap pictures of Dare while he's in town. Pauline and Tommy? The ones you're expecting. They aren't coming, by the way."

Mollare stood abruptly, making the springs of the bed squeak. "Listen, you little bitch—"

"Answer my question. Do you know how old they are?"

The woman shrugged. "The boy said they were both twenty-one."

"Lady, you've spent too much time in the rarefied atmosphere of L.A. if those kids looked twenty-one to you." She stood and pulled Dare's Ray-Bans from her bag. "The boy is barely seventeen. The girl is fifteen."

"So they're young," Mollare said with an impressive amount of bravado—but her gaze shifted around the room, as if looking for a way out. "So what?"

"So you bought them alcohol and rented them a room for the night. I'm betting that's at least contributing to the delinquency of a minor."

Mollare's face paled, but she said nothing.

"Did you think they'd be loyal after Dare switched on the charm and explained the rotten thing you'd set them up to do?" Joey sighed. "Here's how it's going to go down, Ms. Mollare. You're going to contact your editor and tell him the information you sent is wrong. You made a mistake, and you're very sorry, but if the story goes to press, that wad of toilet paper that calls itself a magazine you work for is going to be in line for a serious financial spanking in civil court. Am I clear?"

"You're crazy. I won't—"

"Have you met Dare Daniels, Ms. Mollare? Shaken his hand? Been up close and personal with that grin of his?"

Mollare shook her head.

"You miscalculated. Dare had those kids eating out of his hand inside of three minutes. You never had a chance."

Mollare dropped onto the bed as if her legs had given out. Two red spots shone bright and ugly on her cheeks. "I can't do it. They'll fire me."

"To use your phrase, that's a dirty shame." Joey slung her bag over her shoulder and moved toward the door. "If I see or hear even one breath of this when we get back to L. A., we'll be back in Breverton in a heartbeat, and we'll contact those kids. We'll give them a lift over to the sheriff's office to make a statement, and the very next thing you know, there'll be a warrant for your arrest." She stopped with her hand on the doorknob.

"Don't doubt me, Ms. Mollare. I will see you before a judge, and I'll make sure *that* story goes to press in L. A. You'll have a hell of a time keeping or getting job. No magazine—however sleazy—wants to hire somebody with a rep for corrupting children to get a story."

Mollare stood and faced her. When she spoke, her voice was choked and thready. "I don't believe you. Daniels is supposed to be such a nice guy. He'd never ruin my career over a story in a magazine. Not in a million years."

"You're right. Dare is a nice guy. He'd never even consider doing anything like that." Joey slid the Ray-Bans into place, and the already dim room washed away in darkness. "That's what he has me for."

She opened the door and stepped out into the sunshine.

Gina, who'd been conspicuously absent for going on eighteen hours, chose this time to pipe up.

Sounds like your boy wonder has a secret. Something you might want to check out, if only for your own peace of mind, huh?

"It's none of my business." She started the car and pulled out of the small parking lot onto the highway.

No? I think—

"I don't care what you think, Gina. It's not your life, is it?" Both her words and her voice were sharper than she'd intended. Her sister was silent for the rest of the drive back into town.

There was a blue pick-up in the driveway of the rental house when Joey pulled in. She got out of the car and checked it out carefully. Kansas plates. What looked like mud, but smelled like manure, in the tire treads. *A local.* She hesitated on the front steps when she heard raised voices from the front room of the house.

"Why'd you come back here, Dare? Why the hell would you do that to me?"

"It's got nothing to do with you. It never did. I told you that—"

"Yeah, you told me. So did she. But I'm the one left here, working my ass off on someone else's land just to keep body and soul together. The least you could do is to stay the hell away and leave me some peace of mind."

Peace of mind...

She couldn't hear Dare's answer. She crossed the porch and let herself in the front door in time to see him turn to look at the older man standing before him and whisper something. His face was contorted with the same pain she'd seen last night.

Whatever he said enraged the older man enough to make him swing. Dare wasn't expecting it. At least, he didn't duck or step back. Just took it, square across the jaw. The force of the blow knocked him against a glass-fronted cabinet that toppled sideways with a smash. Dare fell in the other direction, away from the broken glass. Joey was kneeling at his side a second later, staring up at the other man with murder in her heart.

"What the hell do you think you're doing? Get out!"

The man, whose weathered face unmistakably resembled Dare's in the line of his brow and the shape of his mouth, grimaced. "And just who might you be? His latest little whore?"

Dare grunted, and Joey turned to look down at him. He held his hand against his jaw and tried to struggle to his feet.

"Be still. You might need a doctor."

He pushed her arm away and she fell back on her ass, missing the shattered glass by inches. "Don't need no doctor. Let me up."

The older man—who had to be the infamous uncle—reached down and hauled him to his feet. They stared at one another, their expressions unreadable. Finally, the man said, "I can't make you do nothin'. Never could. But if you ever had a decent human feeling in your body, boy— go. And don't come back." He turned, and Joey was busy looking at how Dare's shoulders sagged, but she could hear the clomp of his uncle's boots as he made his way to the front door.

"Dare?"

He didn't turn for long seconds. When he did, his face was blank. He held out his hand and helped her up off the floor. There was a bruise blooming purple and red on his jaw, but the real pain was in his eyes.

"Where've you been?" His words ran together as if it hurt to move his mouth.

She thought about suggesting a doctor again, but decided an ice pack would be enough for now. She made for the kitchen and he followed.

"Asked you a question," he said.

She opened the freezer, grabbed an ice tray and then a dishtowel from a nearby drawer. "I've been having a chat with our friend out at the Guardian Inn." She didn't look at him, allowing her attention to be consumed by folding the towel around the ice.

"What the hell, Joey?" He sounded more tired and defeated than angry, and she chanced a glance at him.

"I think I got her to kill the story."

He was silent for a moment. Then he asked, "How?"

"Oh, you know. Flashlight in her face, sleep deprivation, a rubber hose when she wouldn't cooperate." She crossed the room and handed him the jerry-rigged ice pack. "The usual."

"Funny girl," he said and pressed it to his jaw. He winced once and cleared his throat. "What did she say?"

"About the story? Very little." No need to get into it now. Not with him looking like he'd lost his best friend. "Listen, I need to do some laundry. The washer and dryer weren't part of our tenant agreement—guess they don't trust the crazy Hollywood people with something as precious as the major appliances. So if you'll point me in the direction of a Laundromat—"

"I'll do better," he mumbled through the ice pack. "I'll come with you."

She shook her head. "You should get some rest. I'll clean up the mess in the living room later."

"No, I'm coming with you." She'd begun to recognize that stubborn tone of voice.

She sighed. "Fine. Just...let's try not to get into any trouble, okay?"

He moved the ice pack and smiled then—the first one she'd seen today, and it was like a splash of cool, sweet water on parched lips, even with the nasty bruise.

"Trouble? Doing laundry? Surely, ma'am, you jest."

SIN STREET

CHAPTER 10

Of course, they weren't in town twenty minutes before Dare came within three feet of a messy, front-page-of-*Variety* death on the sidewalk of Main Street.

They'd parked down the block and walked to the convenience store on the corner to grab more coffee. The village appeared utterly empty in a way that gave Joey a mild case of the willies, but Dare explained that Breverton's economy, such as it was, was agriculture-based—nobody but a few non-farming souls were likely to be around at eleven in the morning on a Thursday when the sun was shining and there was hay to be made. Literally.

He was walking at her side on their way to the Laundromat, with his cardboard cup in one hand and the box of donuts he'd insisted on buying tucked under his arm. The sun continued to burn for all it was worth, and a warm, dry breeze made the skirt she'd chosen to wear swing up above her knees.

She paused to look at a storefront display of children's clothes. The kind of stuff rural kids wore to church, she guessed. A beautiful christening outfit, all white lace and satin, captured her attention as Dare moved on without her. She glanced up into the shop and saw an older woman smiling at her from behind the counter. Joey's cheeks flushed. What business did she have looking at baby clothes? She wouldn't need them for years, if ever.

Right. Like you haven't spent a single second imagining how a little girl would look with Dare's eyes and smile, and your curly mop.

Oh, Gina... But when she was right, she was right, and there was damn little point in pretending any different. Joey turned away from the window to observe Dare's retreating back. Or, more specifically, to observe his ass in those fine-fitting jeans.

You hate it when he leaves, but you sure love to watch him go, huh?

She wanted to laugh, but that would only encourage her sister, so she settled for rolling her eyes. It was then she caught the movement above, near the railing on the second-story porch of the building up ahead. Was that the shadow of a person behind that cement planter? She couldn't quite tell. But then it didn't matter because the planter was tipping just as Dare was passing beneath it, and she had seconds to either shout a warning or fling herself at him in a headlong tackle. She chose to do both, calling his name as she sprinted and hit him with all her weight. They fell in a heap on the sidewalk. Behind them, the planter hit the concrete with a crash that sent shards of cement flying in all directions.

They lay there together for maybe ten seconds. Joey kept her face buried in the crook of her arm, trying to keep from throwing up or crying or maybe both. She could feel Dare moving under her, trying to pulling himself out of her death-grip. Finally, he wedged a hand under her chin and lifted her face.

"Let me guess—you're also the best damn right tackle Our Lady of Perpetual Sorrow ever saw, right?" He kissed the top of her head. "It's okay, baby. A miss is as good as a mile."

She swallowed the lump in her throat and tried to smile. "I'm glad you can be so cavalier about attempted murder."

He looked at her like she was crazy. Well, of course he did. He didn't know about the stalker, did he?

"Murder? Sweetheart, if my uncle wanted to kill me, he'd use a shotgun."

"Not your uncle—" She started to tell him and stopped. He seemed more concerned with checking out the scrape on her elbow than listening anyway.

They righted themselves and stood staring at the shattered planter. Potting soil and crimson azaleas lay around it like grave dirt and splattered blood.

Nice imagery. When did you get so morbid, baby girl?

"It would've killed him," she whispered.

"Nah," Dare answered, effectively silencing Gina for the moment. "I've got a hard head. But it didn't do the donuts much good."

SIN STREET

The box had been crushed beneath their combined weight. He picked it up and opened it. The contents were smashed beyond recognition, but still edible. The scent rising from the box made Joey drool.

So much for morbid.

Joey sighed and retrieved her purse from the sidewalk. "We'll need more coffee." Miraculously, neither of them had managed to get burned or even dampened by the spilled contents of their crushed cups.

"I'll go back in a while. Let's get your laundry going first." He took her arm and led her to the building that housed the Laundromat, then went back to the car for the actual clothes. In the meantime, Gina ripped her a new one.

Are you seriously not going to tell him? Seriously?

"It might've been an accident."

And I might've been canonized Saint Angelina of Bensonhurst if I'd lived six months longer. You have to tell him, Joey.

"But—"

But what? You afraid the cozy little fantasy world you've got going here will end if you let reality intrude?

She had no answer for that. So when Dare came back with the laundry and they entered the building—which was as deserted as the rest of the little town, and thank God for small favors—she put a hand on his arm and said, "Listen, I need to tell you something."

He listened. She went through the whole thing—the weird letters, the box left outside his gate, the unusual call on his cell that might've meant nothing, and how Beidermeyer had made her promise not to say anything. His face remained a blank throughout, except for when she mentioned the rope they'd found inside the box. Then his lips tightened into a hard line.

When she finished, he said, "You should've told me. No matter what Carl said—you should've told me, Joey. I trust you to be straight with me."

Trust. In the present tense. So maybe she hadn't fucked this up completely.

She nodded. "You're right. I'm sorry. I have no excuse."

He was quiet for a minute or two. Then he said, "This what we're gonna do. We're gonna do your laundry. And maybe later, I'll think about driving over to the sheriff's office and filling out a report about the planter incident."

"Sounds like the title of a bad spy thriller."

He smiled, and she could see the place where his jaw had swollen just slightly. "But in the meantime? We're just gonna do laundry. That's all. Okay?"

"Okay." She looked around and took stock of the facilities. Teal Formica counters, a relatively clean linoleum floor. Two lines of washers and dryers. Nothing she hadn't seen a hundred times before. One dryer near the back of the room rumbled as proof that someone had been here recently, and would likely soon return.

She got to work sorting her things. They made two small loads—nothing that would take longer than an hour. When both washers were going full blast, she turned and looked at Dare.

He was picking at the donut debris at the bottom of the box. As she watched, he chose a larger piece of pastry and stuffed it into his mouth, smearing chocolate across his lips. When he caught her staring, he grinned. His tongue flicked out and collected the frosting, and suddenly it was way, way too hot in the room to take a proper breath.

"Want some?" He reached into the box and pulled out another piece of donut, this time decorating his knuckles with pink frosting.

Oh, come on. Twenty minutes ago, you were thanking God for sparing his life. You really think this is the time or place?

She considered Gina's words and found them pretty much on the nose in terms of being reasonable. But at the same time, she found herself moving toward him as if her feet were taking orders from other parts of her body besides her brain. When she reached him, she grabbed his wrist and tugged. He cocked an eyebrow at her, but let her pull his hand to her mouth. When she licked the frosting from his knuckles, dragging the tip of her tongue ever-so-briefly in the valley between his first and second fingers, he groaned.

"Joey," he said, like someone was strangling him, "you're killin' me here."

"Lots of people seem to want you dead today. Maybe I should take a number."

"Hilarious." He put the donut box on a nearby table and slid an arm around her waist without taking his eyes off her mouth.

The kiss was hard and wet and sloppy, and more than a little dirty. When they broke apart, Joey's breath came in short, uneven bursts.

"We shouldn't…in public…"

"You know what?" he said as he walked her backward, all the way across the room to the rumbling dryer in back. "I think you like public. I think you like it even more than I do maybe."

Her face went red and hot, and she bit her lip. "Maybe."

"Maybe?" He pushed her back against the hot dryer. Then he lifted her and plopped her down on top of it. The vibrations shot through her body as he held her hips and pressed her onto the surface. As if on autopilot, she spread her knees and let him step between them.

"Yes, all right?" she said, trying not to pant. "Yes, I like public. Although private is nice too, so don't think—"

"Shh. We're not going to think anymore about anything." He leaned in close and ran his tongue around the outer shell of her ear, making her shiver. "I've had a bad morning, Joey. The worst in a long, long time. And I haven't lost my temper or gone looking for a drink or even complained. Not once. Don't you think that deserves a reward?"

This so was not happening. Airplane bathrooms and lovers' lanes were one thing, but this? No way. That's what her rational mind was saying. Her big, traitorous mouth on the other hand was murmuring, "Reward, yeah, of course…"

"So I get to have you again?" he asked against the skin of her neck. His right hand touched her knee beneath her skirt, then traveled up her thigh, fast and light. Before she could stop it. Before she could tell herself she had to stop it—had to stop him—because this could go no further. What if Mollare had other spies around? What if the owner of the clothes in the dryer beneath her returned?

She opened to mouth to say no. She knew he'd stop if she asked him to. She had nothing to fear on that score.

Which is why it was so surprising when, instead, she said, "Fuck me fast before we get caught. No more trouble, remember?"

This time his groan was louder and longer. "Say it again," he muttered, working his fingers under the elastic of her underwear. "Say it."

The smooth surface of the dryer gave her nothing to grip when he slid his fingers against her and into her, going right for her clit. She squirmed, making the most of the heat and vibration. "Fuck me."

"Yeah. I can do that." Then her underwear was gone—pulled down her legs and tossed away to somewhere handy, she hoped—and Dare was rubbing in light, quick circles that teased more than satisfied. She reached up and curled her hands around the back of his neck, burying her fingertips in the short, soft hair at his nape.

"Dare, please." Begging now because anyone could walk in and she didn't want to have to stop. Not when just the touch of his hand felt so filthy-good.

She opened her eyes and watched him pull a condom out of his wallet, and thought about asking him if he'd put another one in there this morning because he was planning for this—planning on screwing her in a Laundromat, for God's sake. But trying to say all that was too much work. She'd ask him later, if she remembered.

Then he lifted her, letting her slide down, her back tight against the dryer's door. She braced her arms on his shoulders and wrapped her legs around his hips. He cupped her ass in his palms and squeezed and…oh, Christ. He pushed up high and tight within her. The sensation robbed her breath, stole her sight, closed down her ears to everything but the sound of his harsh breathing. Nothing but Dare, inside, around and over her. She gasped for air and inhaled the scent of sex and the soapy bite of laundry detergent.

He rotated his hips in a slow circle, grinding against her. Then he was pumping—long, measured thrusts that brought them together with a slick, shuddery slide against her clit every time, and she knew this wouldn't take long.

He shifted his hand beneath her. She felt the tip of his finger brush her between her cheeks and then press inside. She tried not to stiffen.

"This okay?" His voice was a rumble in his chest.

She hid her face in the side of his neck and nodded. All kinds of new and different adventures on the sexual front this week. But it felt good—even better when he circled the fingertip lightly and pressed a second time. She turned her head and bit his ear, sinking her teeth into the lobe. He reacted with a muttered curse and a full-body shiver.

Tension coiled low and hot, dragging at her, making the muscles in her belly and thighs quake. The edge of pleasure sharpened 'til every stroke was courting pain, but she couldn't seem to let go.

"Dare," she said and it still sounded like begging.

"Right here," he answered, working his hips harder now. Using the warm, solid front of the dryer for leverage, his finger half inside her and pulsing in time with his thrusts. "Come for me. Gotta feel it. Need to. God, please."

His pushed higher and tighter against her, as if wanting to climb right inside, and she broke through in short, electric surges that made her jerk and fried her brain and didn't seem to want to stop. She heard herself making noise—heard how it echoed in the big room. Dare pulled her down hard on himself. She felt the spike of his pleasure. Felt his muscles lock and tremble. He muttered a curse from between clenched jaws. When he relaxed, it was with a shuddery sigh that ended in a kiss to her temple and another just beneath her ear.

She stroked his back and enjoyed the way the dryer's vibrations enhanced the aftershocks. "I can't believe we did this."

He grunted against her neck and let her drop to her feet. She found her underwear and stepped into it while he took care of the clean-up. After a second or two he said, "Believe it. And if anyone asks, you were the one who seduced me. All I did was offer you a piece of donut."

She didn't have the energy or inclination to argue the point.

* * *

Later, in the car on the way back to the house, it all fell to shit. Because of her and her big mouth naturally.

"We should talk about your uncle sometime, don't you think?"

The bright sky had dimmed. A heavy line of clouds was building in the south, and the air felt thick and no longer so dry. Joey was driving, and Dare was lying back in the front seat with his shades on and a little smile of obvious satisfaction on his lips. Which disappeared the moment she spoke.

"Not necessary. Nothing there you need to know."

"Dare, I can't help you if you won't let me—"

"I don't recall asking for your help."

Okay, that was it. She pulled the car over onto the wide shoulder and let it idle. They were less than a quarter-mile from the house. "It's part of my job to help you. The reason you hired me, remember? To make your life easier and better?"

He never turned to look at her or removed the sunglasses. For all she knew, he was barely awake. "That's not why I hired you."

"No? Then why?"

"Because I wanted to fuck you, and I knew it was the only way you'd let me get close enough."

She told herself he didn't mean it. He was trying to piss her off so she'd drop the subject. She knew that—could see it plain as day on his face, with or without the shades. Anger flared in her chest anyway. "Fine. You can sit there and lie to yourself and lie to me, but sooner or later—"

"Sooner or later what?" He finally pushed the glasses to the top of his head and looked at her. "I'm going to break down and tell you? Why would I do that?"

"Because you'll feel better. It's not healthy to keep secrets."

"Well, thank you Dr. Fiorello. Do you charge by the hour or by the cliché?"

What a bastard. But a bastard clearly in serious trouble. She took a deep breath and waited to see if Gina was going to pipe up with some cutting remark, but her sister seemed to be making herself scarce.

"Dare, I'm not trying to be your shrink."

"Good, because I already have one, and he's a pain in my ass."

She continued as if he hadn't spoken. "But your shrink sent you here for a reason. I'm just curious whether it's working—whatever he thought you'd get out of it."

Dare's snort was his only answer.

Okay, time to try a different tack. "You know, anybody'd look at you and think 'sunshine, summertime and apple pie with vanilla ice cream.' But underneath—"

"Underneath, I'm all fucked up. Tell me something I don't know."

"That's not what I meant."

"Doesn't mean it's not true."

"No. Listen." She reached across the console to touch him, but let her hand fall short. "All that external stuff is nice, right? Shiny and nice, but simple. And you're not a simple man."

He grimaced. The tension in his body rolled off him in waves. "Understatement."

"Who needs simple?" She knew she was pushing him, but he needed to be pushed. She was sure of it.

"Jesus, Joey. The American public fucking loves simple, or haven't you seen my Q rating?"

"No. Simple is boring, and that's not you."

When he grabbed her by the upper arms and shook her, she could feel his fingertips bite into her flesh and knew there would be bruises to match the ones on her hips from the night before.

"Don't kid yourself, Joey," he said. "Simple is good. Simple is trustworthy. Everything I've never been."

"Says you."

"You think you know me better than I know myself? Well, try this on for size. When I was seventeen, my Uncle Hank caught me fucking his wife in the hayloft of his barn."

"Oh...Dare." Why was she so shocked? She knew it had to be something like this, didn't she? Gina had known and tried to tell her.

The pupils of his eyes contracted to tiny points. The irises blazed poison green. A streak of color rose across his cheeks and the bridge of his nose as he continued. "He's a good man, my uncle. Took me in when my folks died and raised me—was a better father to me than my own had ever been. And that's how I repaid him."

His fingers loosened on her arms, but he didn't let go. "And you know the best part? He probably would've forgiven me—forgiven us both because he's that kind of guy—but his wife, Colleen? Never gave him that chance. She was so ashamed, she hanged herself the next day. He said it was my fault. Said I killed her...I killed his wife, Joey—"

"No. That's not true. It can't be." Joey swallowed and tried to pull her thoughts together. None of this made any sense. "How old was this woman anyway? And how long did you—were you—"

"Fucking her? Two years. And she was thirty-five, as if that makes any difference at all."

"But it does. That means you were only fifteen when it started, and she was an adult. I'm betting she seduced you, didn't she?"

He dropped his hands from her arms and looked away.

"She did, didn't she? That makes her responsible, Dare, not you. You were just a kid."

He shook his head. "I knew right from wrong. I knew it would kill my uncle, and that's not all." He cleared his throat. "Colleen had a daughter from her first marriage. Little girl called Patti-Anne. She was three years younger than me, and I loved her. I'd always wanted a sister, and she...she was the sweetest thing..." His voice broke. "I killed her mother, Joey. I destroyed everybody's life, for Christ's sake."

"Oh, Dare."

He looked at her then, and whatever he saw in her face made his own expression harden. "You're disgusted, aren't you? You should be. I'm disgusting."

"No, I'm not, and you're not either." She reached for him again, and this time let her hand drop onto his shoulder. "I'm just trying to take it all in."

"Good luck with that. It's been a dozen years or more and I still can't understand how I could be such a worthless piece of shit."

"No, damn it." The hand that rested on his shoulder balled into a fist. "Not worthless. Broken, maybe, because you can't get a grip on the past, but not so broken you can't be fixed."

"And that's what you want? To fix me?"

"Maybe."

His lip curled. She could see him shutting down and pulling away from her. "Yeah, well, maybe I don't want to be fixed. And even if I did, what are you gonna do? Your closest friend is your dead sister. I guess that makes you the poster child for mental health, huh?"

Ouch. She could feel her eyes trying to tear up. "That's not—"

"Fair?" His voice had risen to a near-shout. "Fair doesn't come into the equation, and the sooner you know that, the better. You wanna know when I'm gonna get a grip on my past? I'll tell you—when you get a grip on the fact that your sister Gina is dead."

Oh, God. "Stop it. Shut up."

"Why? Are you the only one who's allowed to deliver the tough love?" His eyes narrowed and he dropped his voice to a growl. "You can't deal with your guilt over how she died, right? Gone. Forever. Because of you. Because if she hadn't been working an extra shift that night—"

"Stop, Dare."

"She's not in your head, Joey. That's your own voice you're hearing, and whatever it's telling you? You should listen. Especially if it's telling you to stay the hell away from me." He brushed her hand off his shoulder and moved to get out of the car.

"Wait." She could barely push the word past the constricted agony in her throat.

He didn't turn. With the passenger-side door open and one foot on the pavement, he said, "What?"

"Take the car. I'll walk the rest of the way to the house."

There was a pause. Then he said, "There's a storm coming. Could be a bad one."

As if some stupid weather could be worse than what she was feeling. "Stay away a couple of hours, okay? I'll be gone by the time you get back."

He met her eyes. They stared at each other for a long moment. He nodded. She turned off the ignition and handed him the keys.

"I'm sorry, Joey. It's better this—"

"Don't you say it. Don't you even think about saying it."

She got out of the car and began walking toward the house. The sun was entirely gone now, but smell of hot asphalt in the humid air made her cough. She heard the rental car's motor turn over and the squeal of the tires as Dare pulled away. It took everything she had not to turn and watch him go.

Score another one for big sis Gina. She'd been right all along. *What a prick.* Good thing she hadn't let him get under her skin, even if the

sex was pretty damn hot.
Pull the other one, little sister, it has bells on. And incidentally? He's the one who's right. And you know it, too.
She was so startled, she stopped in her tracks. "What?" She used the back of her hand to wipe away the tears and snot she'd finally allowed to flow. "What the hell are you talking about?"
Come on, Joey. You know it's true. Don't you think it's time you let go?
The voice—Gina's voice, so familiar with its harsh Bensonhurst accent and cynical tone—seemed distant in her head. As if it was fading.
"No, that's just stupid. You're real. You have to be."
Why? Because you can't survive without me? Or because you think you killed me and you can't deal with the guilt?
"No. He's wrong. He had no right to say that."
I don't think so, baby girl. And you wanna know what else? You've been using me as a buffer between yourself and the cruel world for too long. Maybe it's time to—
"No! Don't leave me, Gina. I need you."
You need something, sweetie, but it ain't me.
"Don't go. Please."
Silence.
She looked around. The horizon had turned a kind of strange, brownish-green color, like an old bruise. She could hear thunder now, a continuous boom and growl in the far distance. Up ahead and around the bend was the house, but she didn't think she could take another step. What she really wanted to do was fall down in a heap and let the coming rain wash her away. She lifted her face and let the first fat, warm drops fall into her eyes.
The sound of an approaching car made her turn. "Dare?"
No, not Dare. And she was pathetic, but that was beside the point. The car was same general size and shape as Dare's rented coupe, but the wrong make and color. Still, when it slowed to a stop next to her, she peered inside with faint hope. The blonde in the driver's seat opened the window and leaned across the seat to look out. It took Joey a few seconds to recognize her outside of her natural habitat.
"Hello, Joey. I'm—"
"Carl Beidermeyer's receptionist, right?"
"Yes, I'm Annette." She smiled, her already large gray eyes widening. "Why don't you get into the car? I have a message from Mr.

Beidermeyer."

"Okay, that was weird. "Why didn't he just call?"

The blonde shrugged. "Who knows? I do as I'm told."

Go with Annette, or stand on the road and wait to get drenched by a rain that wouldn't wash away anything after all. Joey walked to the car and got in. "What's this about?"

"Why don't we discuss it when we get to the house?"

Which seemed entirely reasonable. At least it would give her time to pull herself together. She dug in her purse for a tissue as they made the short trip up the road. By the time they got there, the rain was falling thicker, and flashes of white-hot brightness lit the darkening sky. Annette pulled into the carport.

"You have keys to the house?"

Joey nodded. Together, they bolted for the front porch just as the clouds dropped a deluge on the yard. Mixed with the rain were small hailstones. It fell so hard she could no longer see the trees across the road. And Dare was somewhere out there, driving in this mess.

"Don't worry about him. He was raised in this weather, remember?"

Joey looked at Annette, startled. But the blonde just gave her a serene smile, plucked the keys from Joey's hand and unlocked the front door.

Something wasn't right here. Something...nagging at the back of Joey's brain. Gina could've told her what was up. Gina didn't miss much, but Gina was gone, thanks to Dare. Maybe she'd never be back. The thought of that made Joey's stomach curl into a twisty knot. She followed Annette into the front hall of the big house and kicked off her sandals.

"What's this about?" she asked again.

Annette turned from surveying the wide staircase that curved upward from the center of the foyer. Her face was a bland, pretty blank, a lot like the faces of the dolls in Joey's room on the second floor. And just as creepy.

Okay, where did that come from? It was hardly fair, given the woman had traveled all the way to Kansas to deliver a message—not exactly a pleasure trip.

Annette smiled. "Mr. Beidermeyer sent me here to check up on you and Dare. He was worried when he didn't hear anything more from you last night."

Last night? Was Joey supposed to call him last night? The past two days ran together in her mind, a hot, sticky muddle. "Okay, but that still doesn't explain—"

The other woman spoke over her as if she wasn't even in the room. "I'm afraid I'll have to give him a bad report. I saw you two at the Laundromat, you know. Right out in public. You're not supposed to do that with the client. Mr. Beidermeyer will be very unhappy."

Shit. Well, what had she expected? And anyway, she didn't work for Dare or Biedermeyer anymore. She could've used the professional reference, but really, what could she say in her own defense? The wild monkey sex Annette had apparently witnessed was a rehearsal? The equivalent of a table read-through of that new indie script Dare was considering—*Hot, Sudsy Bang-Bang.* She was so screwed. As Beidermeyer's assistant, Annette could...she could...

Hey. Wait a minute. Annette wasn't the assistant, she was the receptionist. The brand new receptionist, as a matter of fact. Since when did receptionists fly halfway across the country to make personal visits to clients? No, something was seriously wrong here.

The wind had begun to pick up outside, moaning around the windows and tossing debris. Somewhere in the distance, a siren kicked up.

"You hear that?" Annette asked. "Tornado warning. I think we're in for some weather." Her accent—the carefully cultivated tones of someone who'd worked extensively with a vocal coach—flattened out into almost a parody of Dare's Kansas drawl. Lightning crashed nearby, filling the room with hot light and making Joey jump. Annette never even blinked. Joey looked at her and suddenly understood.

She pulled out her cell and flicked it open, but before she could punch the speed dial, Annette moved in. She knocked the phone from her hand and grabbed her wrist in a grasp that surprised her with its strength. In her other hand, she held a knife.

"I don't think so, Joey."

CHAPTER 11

Dare made it almost all the way back to town before he had to pull over and lean out of the car to throw up the coffee and donuts in one long, painful spew. Then he sat there and thought about what a total waste of skin he'd always been—all his life. Taking up space and air better used by someone who didn't go around metaphorically kicking three-legged puppies and juggling newborn kittens.

Criminy, are you always like this? With the self-pity? Because you're making me kind of sick over here, and there's been enough of that for one afternoon.

Who... He looked up and squinted through the windshield at the falling rain. Okay, the change in air pressure from the storm was playing tricks on his ears or something. Because the voice had sounded like...no. That was nuts.

Yeah. Nuts. You'd know all about that, wouldn't you, boy wonder?

"What?" He looked in the back seat. Empty, save for the T-shirt he'd used last night to wipe away the damp traces of—

Don't even go there. Bad enough I had to sit through it with my eyes closed and my hands over my ears. You're kinda kinky, huh? With the whole "sex in public" thing. Who knew Joey would go for it, too? Shocked the hell outta me. Speaking of Joey...

The wind picked up and hailstones began to drop from the sky, peppering the windshield and roof, loud enough to drown out the voice in his head. The female voice with the Brooklyn accent.

"Gina?" he whispered, half-afraid she'd hear and answer.

Good guess. Not half as dumb as you are pretty.

"What...uh...what do you..." This was insane. He was talking to Joey's dead sister, who was answering him inside his brain. Clearly, the stress of being in Breverton was getting to him.

What do I want? I want you not to break my baby sister's heart. Because against her better judgment, she's falling in love with you. Which makes you one lucky guy, and you should try not to fuck that up for yourself, capisce?

He cleared his throat. "You're not real. Go away."

Silence. Or, at least, a cessation of conversation. The wind continued to rock the car, and now the crashes of thunder and lightning sounded closer. Then...

You know, it doesn't matter if you believe in me or not. It only matters if you listen. So check this out, cutie. Joey is special. You're not gonna find another girl like her—someone who understands your crazy life and still manages to keep her feet on the ground and love you for what you are, and not your fame and fortune. But I think you know that already, don't you?

He wasn't going to listen. Whether it was really some dead chick from Brooklyn invading his thoughts or just his own guilty conscience poking him—he wasn't going to listen to a word of it. Because it didn't matter whether Joey was special or the only girl for him. He did already know that. The trouble was, he didn't deserve her and he'd only hurt her in the end.

"No," he said, because the voice—all right, Gina—seemed to be waiting for an answer. "You of all people should understand. It's better this way."

Better she should suffer now than later, you mean? Yeah, I thought so, too. But now I'm not so sure. I think she was right—you're just broken and need fixing. And if anyone can do it, Joey can.

He opened his mouth to tell her where she could stick her ideas about fixing him, and the warning siren went off. *Shit. Crap. Motherfucking sonofabitch.* He hated tornadoes. The bane of his childhood, that damn siren and the sound of his father's voice yelling for everyone to get into the cellar. "Hurry the hell up, boy. Don't you know it wants to eat you alive?"

He looked around wildly, trying to spot it. There—on the southwestern horizon, coming in fast. Not a big one, but growing and headed right up the highway in his direction.

What the hell is that?

SIN STREET

Gina sounded a lot less sure of herself all of a sudden. He smirked as he threw the car into gear and peeled into a U-turn in the center of the road. "You're in Kansas, home of Dorothy Gale. And that would be an F2 twister, which we're gonna do our damnedest to outrun."

We? Yeah, maybe not, cutie.

He felt his face crease into a full-blown grin. "Chicken?"

In Bensonhurst, we call it smart. Just remember what I said, Daniels, and try not to fuck up. I'll be watching.

And she was gone. He felt her blink out like a warm light gone suddenly dark inside his head. For a moment, he felt sorry, then he felt stupid for feeling sorry...and then he felt like maybe he should pay attention to getting the hell out of there. He glanced into the rearview mirror and caught a glimpse of a swirling, dark column moving up the road behind him. Chasing him. Straight back to the rental house, where Joey was waiting, totally alone.

"Not today, you cocksucker. You're not getting us today."

He dropped his foot heavy on the gas and the car took off, jumping from sixty to eighty. Debris had begun to fly and bounce across the road, and he dodged it, wrenching the wheel from right to left.

Two miles to go.

One mile, and he was outrunning it. He'd have time to get into the house, find Joey and drag her to the cellar.

A half a mile, then a quarter. He blew past the place where they'd had their last conversation. He winced, remembering what he'd said to her. The lie he'd told. How he'd only hired her to get the chance to fuck her.

Not true. Never true, not from the beginning. He'd tell her that, while they were down in the dark, riding out the storm.

There was a car in the driveway he didn't recognize, but whatever. He ran for the front porch, getting soaked by the rain and doing his best to miss the flying branches. As he fumbled the keys, trying to separate the one to the car from the one to the house, he looked through the window in the front door. He could see Joey standing in the foyer with a blonde woman, who appeared to be holding Joey's wrist and in her other hand—

What the fuck?

Both women turned when he opened the door, stepped into the house and slammed it behind him.

"What's going on here? Who the hell are you?" He knew he was shouting, but he wasn't sure if they could hear him. The coming tornado had taken on the roar of an inbound train. They had seconds to get to shelter. The chick with the knife lifted her face just as the overhead lights flickered and went out and he saw...

No. Couldn't be. Not—

"You don't recognize me, Dare? I guess I shouldn't be surprised."

Her voice—that soft, precise tone was different, but he could still hear the childlike sweetness underneath. "Patti-Anne? What are you—"

The crash of a tree falling on the roof made them all look up. Joey, who'd been silent up to that point, took the opportunity to wrench her wrist out of Patti-Anne's grasp and step away, leaving the blonde standing between them with her knife still clutched in her hand.

"That's fine," Patti-Anne said. "That's just fine." She backed away in the direction of the kitchen. The kitchen—the only entrance into the basement. "It was a really good plan, Dare. You would have been proud of me, thinking it up all by myself. At first, I figured Mr. Beidermeyer would call you, and you'd come to the office. You'd read the notes, and see me, and you'd know. You'd understand."

"Patti, what're you talking about?" he said, taking a step toward her. "We have to get downstairs."

"She's the stalker, Dare. The one who's been sending the threatening messages—"

"Shut up, Joey." Patti-Anne's wide, blank gaze shot back and forth between them. "Make her be quiet, Dare. She doesn't know. Those messages weren't threatening. They were verses from scripture about redemption."

"Oh, sweetie, are you kidding me?" Joey's face was pale, but her voice was steady, as if she wasn't at all freaked by the life-threatening weather or the crazy with the butcher knife. "In Hollywood? That's about as threatening as you can get."

"Shut up," Patti-Anne screeched. She turned her attention back to Dare. "I knew you'd understand if you read them, but Mr. Beidermeyer wouldn't let you read them. He's a very bad man, Dare. You shouldn't associate with such people."

"Patti, please. We need to—"

"Then, after I saw you in the Laundromat today, I decided you both needed a good lesson. Because really, Dare, what were you thinking? What would your Momma say if she knew?" Now her voice had gone flat as the Kansas countryside, in the drawl he remembered from thirteen years ago. The last time he saw her, the day after her mother's funeral. The day her real father came from Wichita to take her away.

SIN STREET

The day before he left Breverton for what he'd thought was forever.

Another crash as a second tree fell, this time against the living room windows. The sound of splintering wood and shattering glass made him flinch. "Patti, we need to get downstairs. Come on, we can talk about it in the cellar."

"No. We can't do that, Dare. Because now I know—I know how it has to be." She waved the knife in Joey's direction. Joey stepped back again and was brought up short by the wall. Dare moved forward, but Patti-Anne said, "Don't you do it, Dare. I'll cut her into little pieces. I swear I will."

"Patti, this is stupid." He tried to make his voice soothing. "You don't need to do this. Let's just go downstairs and when the storm's over, we can talk about—"

"Talk about what? About how you betrayed my love for you by having filthy relations with my mother? Or about how you've been living a life of worldly lusts for the past dozen years." She rolled her eyes. "I know all about you, Dare. You've fallen away, and it's my job to bring you back. But first, you need to make a sacrifice."

She gestured again toward Joey. "She'll make a good one. I was going to hang her from the balustrade, right up there on the second floor. So you could find her, just like I found my mother hanging in the barn. But I couldn't figure out how to get her up there, so..." She shrugged and smiled at him, and... Oh my God, when had she lost her mind? How had he not known his long-lost little sister had turned into a homicidal maniac?

But then it didn't matter because the tornado was on them and around them, and the house...the second floor...it was lifting off and raining down on their heads at the same time.

"Get down!" He lunged for Joey, grabbing her around the waist and dragging her against him as he made for the space beneath the staircase. If the stairs fell, they'd be crushed. But if by the grace of God they held, they'd likely be okay. It was the best he could do in the three seconds he had left to save her.

"No!" Patti-Anne shrieked and slashed at him with the knife as he and Joey dove past her. He felt the blade slice into his arm and then they were huddled on the floor in the shadow of the staircase, and Dare prayed as he'd never prayed in his life.

It was over fast—much faster than he'd thought possible. The howling and the crashing came and went, and ten seconds later it moved on to tear up the road on its way north. He stayed curled over

Joey's body, covering as much of her as he could, for a good minute beyond the point where he thought it was safe, just to be sure.

"Dare?" Joey's voice was muffled from beneath him. "Are you all right?"

He pulled himself off her, lifted her into a sitting position, and went about the business of checking her over. No cuts or scrapes or bruises he could see. "Did you hit your head?"

"No," she said, "but you're bleeding."

He looked at his bicep, where Patti's knife had slashed him. "It's not deep."

Together, they peered out into the foyer. The staircase had held, but the windows were gone and the floor was littered with debris. He turned to look at Joey and caught her gazing up through the massive holes in the roof.

"The sky. It's so blue. How can that be?" Tears coursed down her cheeks.

He pulled her against him again and let her cry it out. As much as he despised tornadoes, this wasn't his first, and he could afford to be the strong one. After a minute, she pushed herself away from him and wiped her eyes.

"I need something to drink," she said. She stood and picked her way carefully in the direction of the kitchen.

Patti-Anne lay unconscious beneath the small table by the front door, her knife still clutched in her hand. Dare could see a bump on her forehead and blood on her face, but her breathing was deep and even. He pulled out his cell and dialed 911. The operator told him the twister had missed Breverton, but had whipped through a trailer park just outside town. It might be a little bit before they could get an ambulance out that way, and they should hang tight.

He found Joey in the almost completely undamaged kitchen, pouring them each a little sweet ice tea with hands he could see tremble from other side of the room. Her face had gone paper-white, and he could see where sweat had dampened the front of her shirt. He took the cold glass from her hand and set it on the counter.

"Is she okay?" Joey asked, her voice subdued.

He nodded. "I took the knife and cut the cord from the drapes to tie her feet together, just in case she wakes up and...well, you know." He cleared his throat. "Listen, this might be the wrong time and place for this, but—"

"But what, Dare? I think we've said everything that needs to be said."

He shook his head. "Not hardly. I said a bunch of shit that didn't need to be said. That wasn't true. And I want to take it back, if you'll let me."

She looked tense and stressed out and thoroughly miserable, standing there by the refrigerator. And why shouldn't she? He'd put her through hell, then his past had literally jumped out and tried to kill her. Not to mention the whole tornado thing. He wouldn't have blamed her if she'd thrown that glass of tea smack at his head.

But she sighed and said, "I'm listening."

He walked over to stand in front of her. When he took the glass from her hand and set it on the counter, she looked up at him with tears in her eyes. He smiled, taking care not to flash the phony grin. He wanted everything to be real between them from now on—or as real as it could be while living the Hollywood life.

The faint sound of sirens rose in the distance. The ambulance, on its way. The cops, too, probably. And reporters from the papers would follow, because hometown-hero-gets-caught-in-twister couldn't help but be a story.

She said, "You know, this is going to make the west coast papers. No way we can avoid it."

He shrugged.

"TV STAR SAVES PERSONAL ASSISTANT FROM KILLER TORNADO, VOWS ETERNAL DEVOTION. I like it."

"Eternal devotion?" She pressed a still-quivering hand to her face and wiped away the moisture that dotted her upper lip. "Is that a proposal?"

He let his smile get a little wider. "Do you want it to be?"

"Dare, we've only known each other three days. One step at a time." She leaned back against the refrigerator, clearly rocked to her roots by the events of the past hour. He should ease up, back off, give her some room to breathe.

But now he was grinning and he couldn't help it. "That doesn't sound like a refusal."

She shook her head. "We have a lot to work out. Seriously. A lot."

"Right. Like whether we'll live in my house or buy one further up in the hills, and if you want to have the wedding in Brooklyn, and how many kids you want—"

"Dare." There was an edge of warning in her voice beneath the shell-shocked weariness.

The sirens were close now—just up the road. He leaned down and planted a kiss full on her mouth. "I'm pretty sure I love you, Joey. I know it's not fair to ask you to wait until I get my shit together, but…I'm askin'."

She reached up and ran cool, damp fingers over the sore spot on his jaw, where his uncle had punched him. Jesus, it seemed like weeks ago instead of just this morning.

"Try not to be such a jackass, okay? You know I'll wait."

Relief made his shoulders slump. He moved to kiss her again, but a moan from the foyer—barely audible over the howl of the sirens as the emergency vehicles pulled into the driveway—made them both freeze.

Joey squeezed his arm. "Go to her. She's a nut job, but she needs you right now."

Before he turned away, he looked at her, his smile fading. "I won't fuck this up, Joey. That's a promise." From somewhere in the back of his head came Gina's voice.

Atta boy.

CHAPTER 12

Joey heard the front door slam. The prolonged silence that followed—no footsteps bounding up the stairs in her direction, no call of her name or muffled conversation with Oksana, who no doubt met him in the foyer to take charge of the dirty laundry in his overnight bag—made her wonder if she should go down and speak to Dare. Or should she give him his space? Hard to know the right thing to do in a situation like this. How many times did a guy testify at his sister's commitment hearing after all? There wasn't a greeting card made for this.

Okay, stepsister...whatever. She knew Dare well enough to know it didn't matter. He considered Patti-Anne his sibling, even if the woman herself had always seen him as something else. Which wasn't his fault either. Joey imagined he'd been as easy to fall in love with at thirteen as he was at nearly thirty.

"Joey?"

She smiled and opened the bedroom door. "Up here."

He kissed her quickly when she met him at the top of the stairs. "Missed you." His eyes were bloodshot and underlined with shadows.

"Everything go okay?"

He nodded and looked past her into the bedroom. "The place she's going—it's nice. Lots of trees and grass. You hardly notice the bars on the windows." The bitter undertone in his voice made Joey wince.

"Well, you look like shit, if it's any consolation."

He laughed, and it was the best sound Joey'd heard since the last time he'd done it, burrowed deep beneath the covers before dawn the previous morning.

"How bad was the press?" There was no question the reporters and paparazzi had descended like vultures on the Cowley County courthouse steps.

He shrugged. "About like you'd expect."

"Did she...um...say anything? To you, I mean?"

"No. I guess it was all in the letter."

Joey shuddered. The letter—the one Patti-Anne had sent from her cell in the county jail, before the lawyer Dare hired for her got her moved to a hospital. Rambling and incoherent, it left no doubt she was more than a little disturbed. Apparently, she'd been harboring fantasies of marrying Dare from pretty much the first time she laid eyes on him, at age ten. The shock of discovering his relationship with her mother, combined with the trauma of her mother's suicide, did something to her mind. It was all in the letter—if you read between the lines. The lines that swore eternal devotion and bloody vengeance on the same page.

Joey took Dare's arm and tugged him in the direction of the bedroom. "Come on. You look like you could use a nap."

Twenty minutes later, he'd removed his contacts and most of his clothing, and was stretched out on his back with one arm flung up over his face. The late afternoon sunshine shone through the trees in the back yard, laying dappled patterns over his bare chest. Joey sat in a chair by the window and pretended to read a script.

"Stop staring at me. Can't sleep when you do that."

Damn. Busted. "Sorry. You're just so pretty, I can't help myself."

He groaned and turned over onto his stomach. "Make yourself useful, woman."

She grinned and set aside the script. Then she crawled onto the bed and straddled his hips, thankful she'd worn a pair of shorts with some give in the fabric. "I don't recall back rubs being part of my duties as detailed in the contract I signed, Mr. Daniels."

"Oversight. I'll call Beidermeyer tomorrow and have him make an addendum." His voice was raw with exhaustion. She dug her fingers into the muscles just beneath his shoulder blades, and he groaned again. "You're good at that."

"That's not all I'm good at. Turn over and let me show you."

"You don't have to show me. I remember."

Not the response she was hoping for. And okay, he was tired and wrung out emotionally, but she was willing to do all the work. A tiny

SIN STREET

worm of insecurity burrowed its way into her gut.

"Why'd you stop?" Dare lifted his head from the pillow and looked at her over his shoulder. "Something wrong?"

"No. I mean, yes." She swung herself off him and sat on the edge of the bed. "Are you getting bored with this?"

"Bored with what?"

She gestured between them. "This. Us. Because if you are, all you have to do is say—"

"Joey, why would you think that?"

She shrugged. "We haven't exactly burned up the sheets in the past week or so. I was thinking...maybe regular sex in a bed isn't kinky enough for you?"

He looked at her like she'd lost her mind. Which is probably why he said, "You've lost your mind."

"You're a kinky guy. You said so, yourself."

"You make me sound like a pervert." He sat up and pulled the sheet to his waist. "And you also make it sound like all the kink is on my side of the equation. I seem to recall—"

"Never mind. I take it back. We don't need to talk about that."

He must've seen how her cheeks flushed at the memory—at all the memories. Not just what they'd done, but how she'd responded. He leaned closer to her, 'til she could feel his breath on her cheek. "We don't need to talk about what? About how much it turned you on when I grabbed you and fucked you on the hood of the car? Or maybe you want to forget the airplane bathroom or—"

"Shh," she said. "I don't want to forget any of it."

"Why are we whispering?"

"You started it."

His laughter huffed against her neck. "Oh, no, you definitely started this. Question is, how're you gonna finish it, missy?" His drawl was as flat as a Kansas horizon.

"Well, let's see. We could do it on the floor by the door and pretend Oksana is peeking through the keyhole."

He made a face. "Are you trying to make me impotent for life?"

She leaned back and looked at him, trying to gauge his mood. Yeah, he was smiling, and the devil sparked in those poison-green eyes, but his weariness showed in the pallor beneath his tan.

"You know what I think?" She stood and pulled him upright. The sheet fell away from his body, revealing his erection inside his boxer-briefs. Not bored yet, apparently.

"No, tell me," he said and rested his hands on her shoulders.

"I think after what you've been through in the past twenty-four hours, you deserve a reward."

"Like in the Laundromat?"

"Very much like in the Laundromat, but this time I do all the work."

His eyebrows shot in the direction of his hairline, but he went willingly when she led him from the bed to the chair and asked him to sit.

"Close your eyes," she said. "Pretend we're back at the Klondike. You feel that sun on your face? That's because we're on the balcony again. The bitchy redhead just took our order, and she'll be back in a few minutes to check on us."

She shucked her shirt, shorts and underwear and straddled him again. The chair was wide and deep—the perfect size for her to squeeze her knees on either side of his hips.

She didn't take it slow. He opened his eyes once in surprise when she burrowed her hand into the front of his shorts and released his cock to the air.

"Hey, what—"

"What do you think, genius?" She wasn't playing games this time. No need for foreplay—she'd been hot since he stretched out on the bed, and all the talk of what they'd done back in Breverton had only made her hotter. She wanted to make him come until he was mindless and blind with it. Then he'd sleep, and when he woke, he'd feel better. Her mission for the next ten minutes, and maybe for life.

"Remember," she whispered. "We have to hurry. The waitress will be back any minute."

She levered herself upward, positioned his cock and sank down on him, an easy slide all the way. She felt full and swollen, as if she could burst apart around him. Dare thrust up sharply, as if he couldn't help himself. And that was just fine.

He made noise halfway between a gasp and a groan. Hoarse and almost angry, it sounded. "Feel so good around me. Don't stop."

She lifted and dropped on him, moving faster and forcing him deep. The chair creaked under them, and she wondered if they'd end up on the floor after all. Dare's head fell back, revealing the long, tanned line of his throat, and she wanted to bite it just at that spot where it met his jaw.

His hands clutched at her hips and then her back, as if he didn't know what to do with himself. Each slide of his cock inside her sent raw pulses of pleasure shooting outward. Her palms burned, and the soles of her feet. All she needed was just a little…more…

He sat forward, took one of her nipples between his teeth and bit. At the same time, his palm pressed against the small of her back, pushing her down against him as he arched up. She came, and it stretched out long and taut, like a hot wire connected from a spot deep inside her to every muscle in her body. He followed, his eyes rolling back in his head and his mouth falling open to release her breast.

After, with sweat cooling on their skin, he said, "Marry me."

She didn't know how to answer. All the marriage talk had fallen by the wayside over the past six weeks, forsaken for dealing with Patti-Anne's homicidal psychosis and battling for privacy from the press. Joey hadn't brought it up because…well, because. Dare had said what he'd said in a moment of high drama, and you just shouldn't take stuff a person says after a near-death experience seriously. It's not fair.

Of course, Gina would've had some snarky comment to make about that. But Gina wasn't around anymore. Sometimes, Joey was almost convinced Dare had been right. That Gina's voice had never existed in her head, and that it was all some weird coping mechanism her psyche had invented.

"Joey? Did you hear me?"

"Yes."

"I said, marry me. Now. This week."

"It'll take longer than that to get the license—"

"Nope. I checked it out. We just need to make an appointment with the county clerk. No blood test, no waiting period. We could do it tomorrow if we wanted." He reached up and brushed back a sweat-sticky curl from her forehead. "Of course, I'll have to see what I can do about scraping up the forty-five bucks. That could be tough."

"Funny guy. We're talking about the rest of our lives, and you're making jokes."

"Can I take that as a yes?"

She bit her lip. She wanted—oh, how she wanted—to say she'd marry him. But it would cost them to make that move, and she wasn't talking about the forty-five dollar license fee.

"The press will rip you to shreds. After the…thing…with your last assistant, and right on the heels of this latest disaster?" She reached out and smoothed the line that had begun to appear between his eyes. "We don't have to get married to be together, you know. I'm not going anywhere. Not until you want me to."

"I'll never want you to."

"You say that now, but—"

His eyes narrowed, and he moved to kiss her. She braced herself. But instead of the expected assault on her mouth, what she got was more like a whispered prayer against her lips, soft as a breath, sweet as a plea. Something inside her twisted in a painful kind of joy.

He released her and said, "Contrary to appearances, I'm not fucking around here. Either we're strong enough to do this, or we're not. And I think we are. I think we've got divine providence on our side."

"Divine providence?"

"Something my Momma used to talk about. She was a big believer in stuff like that."

Joey stared at him. As the seconds ticked by, she thought about surviving the tornado and Patti-Anne's murder attempts. She thought about the tabloid reporter, Mollare, and Dare's uncle, and the kids with the camera at the park. The angry flight attendant, and the bitchy redheaded waitress. And how Dare had kept her waiting so long that first morning she fell asleep and drooled on his leather chair. All of that happened within seventy-two hours of meeting each other, and they'd still managed to end up together.

"Divine providence, huh?"

"Yup."

She shrugged and shook her head. "Like a kid from Brooklyn stands a chance in hell against something like that."

His smile beat the sunshine for warmth and brightness. He grabbed her around the waist and lifted her as he stood. They landed together on the bed.

An hour or so later, when they finally ran out of ways to celebrate their engagement, she lifted her head off his chest to look at him, and said, "You can't fool me. I know the real reason you want to get married."

"Oh, yeah?"

"Of course. I happen to know for a fact that it's virtually impossible for a wife to successfully sue her husband for sexual harassment in the state of California." She batted her eyes at him. "You big kinky perv, you."

They laughed a long time, 'til sleep overtook them as they lay curled together, the sunset filling the room with amber light.

* * *

SIN STREET

Somewhere far away and yet very nearby indeed, Gina looked down and smiled.

'Bout freakin' time.

Then she wandered off to discover if anyone in Heaven knew how to make a decent cannoli.

SELAH MARCH

A wife and mother, Selah resides in the northeastern United States. She holds a B.A. in English Literature, and is published in short fiction and nonfiction in local and regional magazines and newspapers. She enjoys solitude, long walks after nightfall, and the bracing rigors of a six-month-long winter.

For more information on Selah, visit her web site:

http://www.SelahMarch.com

AMBER QUILL PRESS, LLC
THE GOLD STANDARD IN PUBLISHING

QUALITY BOOKS
IN BOTH PRINT AND ELECTRONIC FORMATS

ACTION/ADVENTURE	SUSPENSE/THRILLER
SCIENCE FICTION	PARANORMAL
MAINSTREAM	MYSTERY
FANTASY	EROTICA
ROMANCE	HORROR
HISTORICAL	WESTERN
YOUNG ADULT	NON-FICTION

AMBER QUILL PRESS, LLC
http://www.amberquill.com

Made in the USA